WITHDRAWN

A Piece of Normal

Sandi Kahn Shelton

A Piece of Normal

A Novel

Shaye Areheart Books
NEW YORK

Published in the United States by Shaye Areheart Books, an imprint of the Crown
Publishing Group, a division of Random House, Inc., New York.
www.crownpublishing.com

Shaye Areheart Books and colophon are trademarks of
Random House, Inc.

Library of Congress Cataloging-in-Publication Data
Shelton, Sandi Kahn.
   A piece of normal : a novel / Sandi Kahn Shelton.—1st ed.
   1. Advice columnists—Fiction.   2. Divorced women—Fiction.
   3. Sisters—Fiction.   4. Connecticut—Fiction.   5. Domestic fiction.
   I. Title.
   PS3619.H4535P54 2006
   813'.6—dc22   2005030609

ISBN-13: 978-1-4000-9731-9
ISBN-10: 1-4000-9731-2

Printed in the United States of America

Design by Lynne Amft

10 9 8 7 6 5 4 3 2 1

First Edition

To Nan
1956–1995

Acknowledgments

So many people have given me their support and encouragement while I was writing this book. I owe a huge debt of gratitude to my editor, Sally Kim, who has been unfailingly kind and patient as I felt my way along in telling this story, and who understood right from the beginning what I was hoping to say, and then helped me say it. And an equal measure of thanks to my agent, Nancy Yost, who keeps me going and makes me laugh whenever I need it, which is often. Shaye Areheart and her staff have been wonderful above and beyond what I had any reason to expect.

Friends have given me advice, anecdotes, chocolate bars, homemade dinners, and, stunningly, the keys to their empty condominium so that I could have peace and quiet to hear where this story was leading me. I'll be forever grateful to: Karen and Terry Bergantino, Alice Mattison, Leslie Connor, Nancy Hall, Mary Caruso, Diane Cyr, Mary Rose Meade, Kim Caldwell Steffen, Deborah Hare, Jane Tamarkin, Nancy Barndollar, Carol Dannhauser, Sandy Connolly, Margie Gottwalt, Beth Levine, Nicole Wise, Kate Flanagan, and Kay Kudlinski. Judy Haggarty and the staff at the Guilford Free Public Library not only gave me a comfortable place to work (unfortunately next to the irresistible magazine section, where I could often be found loitering) but they even let me bring iced tea into the library, and didn't kick me out when my cell phone rang.

And lastly, I have to thank my family, who have given me love and happiness in abundance: Ben and Amy and Charlie Kahn, Allie and Mike Meade, Stephanie Shelton, Barry and Pat Shelton, Helen Myers, Joan Graham, and Alice and Jennifer Smith. And of course, my greatest thank-you goes to Jim, the one who makes everything possible.

A Piece of Normal

Prologue

*T*he letters come to me by the box load, carried upstairs to my office by Carl the Mailroom Guy, who drops them off and says cheerfully each time, "Well, here's some *more* trouble for you to solve."

He says this every single day as though it was a new thought, and every single day I laugh, and then as soon as Carl leaves the room, I sit down on the floor with the box and start pulling out the letters, one by one, unfolding them and breathing in their scent: the smell of paper and trucks and mailrooms and, yes, trouble. It's like meditation for me—almost *religion*—that moment of unfolding a letter to get at its secret core.

That's it, really: this job is like being the head priestess in the Church of the Advice Column. Services held every morning at the newspaper offices of *The Edge,* circulation 25,000, in New Haven, Connecticut.

My best friend, Maggie, says, "Don't you ever get overwhelmed that people think 'Dear Lily' can solve their problems for them? Don't you just look at that pile and want to go screaming down the hall?"

I tried to explain it to her once. "You want to know what it's like when those letters come in? It's like being given a big platter of warm chocolate chip cookies—no, make that a big platter of assorted cookies—some plain old oatmeal raisin, some with nuts and coconut, some way too dry and floury, and others sticky with molasses or so tart you wish they'd added more sugar. But they're all warm and filled with different tastes and textures that I can sink my teeth into."

Maggie gave that comment the look it deserved. She could see I was hungry at the time. She said she didn't think Ann Landers had ever thought of the letters as something good to eat, and I said, "Well, maybe she did at first. Maybe the first letter she ever got was like a big fluffy sugar cookie, and she was hooked."

I have my favorites, of course. Letters, not cookies. I'm partial to the handwritten ones that come on lined notebook paper or pink scented stationery, that spell out "Dear Lily" with a little bubble or heart over the *i*. Women who write these letters tend to pour out their hearts onto the page, giving all the juicy details, like how jittery a man's voice sounds when he's giving his third lame excuse about working late or how they noticed a certain *look* pass between him and his secretary, a look that told them everything they needed to know.

I'm also fond of the energy that drives a person to type a single-spaced, four-page complaint, clinically documenting examples of a lover's insensitivity as though this were a legal matter—and then the way the letter's tone will suddenly shift and the writer will ask, sadly, wistfully, "So do you think I should stay or must I go?"

I'm even happy to decipher coffee-stained, hastily scrawled notes on scratch pads, complete with arrows and words crawling up the sides of the page. One of the best letters I ever got was written on a cocktail napkin and consisted of one plaintive question: "Do you have to marry someone if you said yes but now you've changed your mind?" I could just see that woman sitting in a bar somewhere with her fiancé, and maybe he's pinching the waitress's ass or making racist jokes with the bartender, and suddenly she just knows he's all wrong for her. I wrote back one word: *No.*

People are in such agony most of the time: that's what my year as an advice columnist has taught me. You see human beings outside in the park, or in line at the grocery store, or having their hair done, and unless they are right then weeping or climbing out the window and onto the ledge of a skyscraper, you don't immediately know this about them, how much they are suffering. People know how to put a good face on things most of the time. We're good at that, as a species.

I'm guilty of that, too. Maybe that's why I love this job so much. Here I am, thirty-four, divorced, and the mother of a little boy I adore, and yet, as Maggie once said to me, it is quite possible that I am clinically unable to move forward in my life. She points out that my life as a mom has taken over my life as a woman. But sitting there in the Church of the Advice Column, seeing people's stories written out before me like a little movie I'm watching, I feel clear and generous and braver than I actually am. I get goose bumps thinking how I can help them fix things up to be just right, just tweak the plot a little this way or that, and set life on its proper course. Maybe I'll be able to fix myself if I can fix other people. That's what I'm hoping for, deep down.

You know what people really need? Somebody who will listen hard and then find a way to tell them, "It's not all your fault. It's going to work out fine. Don't give up."

Oh, yes, and hot baths, cinnamon toast, and kisses. I strongly believe in the restorative power of kisses.

1

$\mathcal{S}$peaking of kisses, I know this may sound weird, but in the past month, I have set up three first dates for Teddy, my ex-husband. I'm not sure he's had any kisses—restorative or otherwise—from any of the three women, but at least on tonight's date, he called to say the woman actually liked what he calls his First Date Outfit, the purple shirt with the orange hummingbirds. If you ask me, the hummingbird shirt is a test he unconsciously gives women, and frankly, it's often lethal. If he detects even the slightest wince when a woman first sees it (and he has a finely tuned wince detector, believe me), he won't ever call her again. Of course this latest woman loved it: he was dating the receptionist from my work, Kendall, and if there's anything she would respect, it's a man who can confidently pull off wearing *anything* purple. She likes unconventional types.

That's the good news. The bad news, I suppose, is that it's only ten minutes until nine and he's already back at my house, drinking wine and getting ready for the post-date analysis.

Until Teddy arrived a few minutes ago, I'm afraid I had been conducting a dangerous experiment in the upstairs bathroom, totally unlike anything I've ever done in my life: giving myself blond highlights with one of those do-it-yourself kits. I had just finished putting white goop on the last strand of hair at the very back of my head, craning my neck around so I could see it in the mirror, when I heard the back doorbell ring and then heard Teddy calling, "Lily? Lil, you decent?"

I ran to the top of the stairs and stage-whispered, "*No*, I'm not decent—don't come up." I didn't want to yell for fear of waking up our four-year-old son, Simon, who actually can sleep through anything, including possibly a helicopter landing on the roof—but you never know. I'd just spent an hour singing songs and reading him stories to help him fall asleep, and I wanted to make sure he would stay asleep. Sometimes, you know, just the whiff of intensity in a parent's voice can bring a kid to full alert status, if he suspects that all the fun is happening without him.

"Well, get decent and come on down here," Teddy called up way too loudly. "I've brought us some wine."

I gave my reflection one last desperate, prayers-to-the-universe look—I looked kind of bizarre, really, with all those white stripes all over my brown curls, like somebody in a community theater production playing a ninety-year-old woman—and then, because I didn't want Teddy to know what I'd been doing since he'd immediately see how desperate I am to change my life, I put a towel over the whole mess and went down to hear about his date with Kendall.

It's one of those unseasonably warm nights in early June, so he and I go sit out in the rocking chairs on my back porch, which looks out over a little inlet on Long Island Sound, in Branford, Connecticut. Everybody in the six houses along our little bay colony—unofficially called Scallop Bay because of its shape—seems to be outside tonight, as though they're all here to usher in the first warm nights of late spring. You can see their silhouettes against the lit-up windows, hear their bug zappers and the strains of music from their stereos, make out the jumpy flames of their candles. The air tonight smells like a combination of dead fish and low tide, a smell that Teddy hates (he thinks the Environmental Protection Agency should be out here every day, measuring our air currents and possibly bringing in buses to evacuate us away from this odor)—but to me it's just the backdrop smell of ordinary beach life. That's probably because I've lived here in this converted beach cottage, a hulking blue duplex that backs up to the Sound, for most of my life—lived here, in fact, even before I was born. I tell people that I was once an egg and a sperm cell here, my essence riding around in my mother and father, and one day, perhaps due to my subliminal urging, they hooked up so that I could get started. This smell, this air, even these splinters on the porch: this is all probably encoded somewhere in my DNA.

"So why in the world are you back here so soon?" I ask Teddy. I accept the glass of merlot he's holding out to me and try surreptitiously to straighten the towel wrapped around my head. My scalp is itching something fierce. What do they make hair color out of, anyway—ground-up fire ants? "This hardly even qualifies as a full date, you know," I say. "I think legally you're still in the first half, and we may have to send you back in."

"Lily," he says, giving me his deadpan look and tuning up his whine. "I'm not going back in. Your friend Kendall is out of her mind, as I'm *sure* you knew. You planned this date for your own sadistic amusement, didn't you?"

This is exactly what he said about the last two dates: Jillian, my hairdresser, and Norma, who works the drive-through at my bank. Both of them are sweet and attractive and actively looking for a nice man, but with both of them, I was accused of sadistic intentions. Jillian, Teddy said, announced at the outset of the date that she had PMS and also that she'd once had Botox injections, two things he didn't want to hear about; and Norma's crime—I forget Norma's exact crime, but I think she told him she never liked Meryl Streep movies. And—well, neither of them raved about the First Date Outfit.

"Oh, Teddy, for God's sake. All your really good people these days are out of their minds in one way or another," I say. "Come on. You've got to get a grip."

"I know, I know. It's me, isn't it?" he says mournfully. "I'm really not meant for getting along with the other humans." This is one of his favorite topics—Teddy Kingsley, adrift in the world of crazy people, the sole voice of reason howling alone in the wind. He's a New Age psychotherapist, and he spends his days with well-meaning though often eccentric people who optimistically ask for Reiki and Rolfing and aromatherapy and crystals, which he doles out with doses of calm, measured gloom. I've actually heard him say to clients, "Well, this may not work as well as you hope . . ."—which cracks me up every time. He thinks positive thinking and affirmations are a waste of human energy. True happiness, he says, comes from lowered expectations.

"Listen, you big galoot, the time of everybody being fully sane has long passed," I tell him cheerfully. "Forget that. The modern-day quest is just to find people whose insanities fit together nicely with our own. Now tell me what happened with Kendall so you can get back and continue your date. She's probably waiting for you in a parking lot somewhere. Believe me, Jillian and Norma may have been mistakes, and I'm sorry for that, but I think Kendall is your woman."

He laughs, a raspy sound, like two dry husks rubbing together.

"Come on. You said when you called from the restaurant that she loved the shirt," I say. "So what happened then?" Teddy is possibly the only man in the world who would make a cell phone call to his ex-wife while his date is in the ladies' room, just to give a mid-date progress report, only to hang up quickly when the date returned. I could hear Kendall's bright, curious, uncomplicated voice saying, "Oh! Who are you talking to?" and him mumbling, "Omigodshe'sbackbye" before a great deal of muffled-sounding fumbling, and then the cell phone (with me in it) seemed to land inside his pocket, from where I heard clanking of dishes and silverware and the faraway sound of Teddy's raspy laugh.

He stretches out his long legs and leans back in the rocker. He's handsome, really, or would be if he didn't look so worried all the time. He's tall and kind of bony-skinny, with curly, longish dark hair and big vulnerable brown eyes, but he has the naked, startled look of somebody who never learned how to hide his feelings so that the rest of us can't poke at them. He's the type of man people tend to instinctively speak softly to, perhaps because they don't want to be responsible for getting him further alarmed than he already seems. And right now he's a man with a long story to unpack, and he doesn't care how long it takes to tell it. This is because he has no hair-care products ticking like a time bomb on his head.

May I just stop right here and tell you the two things about hair coloring that are beginning to occur to me? One is that I, who am usually so careful about everything—I even go downstairs twice each night just to make sure I've locked the front door—got so distracted by Teddy's arrival that I didn't check the time when I finished applying this stuff, and so I have no idea when it needs to be rinsed off. That's the first thing, and it seems very, very bad. The second thing is, it might not have been the best idea to just smush my hair up underneath a towel after I'd painstakingly made such long, careful streaks. A third thought pops up then, too, which is that maybe nothing dreadful has happened yet, and I could run in the house right now and rinse the whole thing out immediately, and we could just forget this ordeal, and I could keep my boring long chestnut brown hair that I've had since I was a child. What was I *thinking,* anyway, doing this to my hair? It was obviously a moment of insanity.

I take another sip of wine to calm myself down. *I am in need of a change. This is a change.* Teddy is saying, "She hates me. She hopes she'll never see me again. Right now she's calling all her friends to tell them how terrible things went. I know her type. She's one of those women who probably calls her friends 'girlfriend,' as though that's their title. And she's saying, 'Girlfriend, this guy was such a *bore.* He'd never even been to Cancún or on a singles cruise. He didn't even appreciate my *espa*-somethings.'" He looks at me. "What are those shoes people wear, that look like they were made from a bunch of old wine corks and a lot of too-long shoelaces?"

"Espadrilles," I say.

9

"Right. Whatever. She must have gone on about them for ten hours. At least. The whole first half of the date. I thought I would go into a coma hearing about those shoes. Oh, and Lily, by the way, just so you know, she lives way out in the middle of the woods, like where a wicked witch would draw children to with bread crumbs—there aren't even any streetlights or sidewalks—and the house is filled with hundreds of thousands of cats, all of which she's *named*. And she talks to them like they're people. 'Sadie, get off the couch, so Teddy can sit in all your filth and cat hair.' 'Bubby, go do that in the litter box when we have guests.' It was unbelievable. And all these cats are just sitting there looking at me, telepathically communicating, 'You take your pants off here, bud, and we're shredding those private parts you've been taking such good care of all these years. Don't even *think* you're leaving with your manhood intact.'"

"But she liked your shirt," I point out.

"Yeah, probably because it had birds on it, and she was thinking of it as food for her feral cats. That's all that was." He sighs. "Then, after she's lectured me about her shoes and she's introduced me to all the hostile cats, we finally get to the restaurant, and the waiter comes over to take our order, and she can't just order something off the menu. Oh, no. She has to ask him approximately four million questions about the food—how they make it, what it has in it, where it used to live before it came to the restaurant, who it hung around with and what its name was when it was still a cow. *You* know. Then she made the chef—the *chef,* a busy man who should be back in the kitchen making sure that botulism isn't being introduced into the food sources—the actual *chef,* Lily, had to come out into the dining room, to our table, just so he could reassure her that the mango salsa didn't have any cilantro, and that the swordfish had never, for one minute, been inside a freezer, and that the asparagus hadn't come from South America, because as anyone would know who *cared,* workers are mistreated in South America."

I look at him, trying not to laugh.

"God, you know how I hate having authority figures come to my table," he says, whining, in full Lovable Curmudgeon mode now. He sniffs. "Jeez, it smells particularly awful here tonight. Do you think it's possible that the Sound has turned somehow into a toxic waste site and that the government doesn't want us to know?"

"It's just nature."

He looks at me for a long time. "Say, why do you have a towel on your head? You always wash your hair in the shower in the morning, and then you blow it dry on the medium-heat setting after you put on your white terry cloth bathrobe and that rose-scented after-bath splash that you pay an arm and a leg for even though Wal-Mart probably has the same stuff for half the price. Why the change?" He narrows his eyes. "Uh-oh. What have I interrupted? Is there a guy here, ha-ha-ha, waiting for you to come back upstairs?"

"Ha-ha-ha," I say. We both know there have been no guys. I am the only celibate thirty-four-year-old I know. Maggie says I'm *pathologically* celibate. The truth is I don't have time for a new man. I have Teddy hanging around all the time. When would I see someone else? That's when Maggie points out that nowhere in my divorce agreement did it specify that I was responsible for lining up a new partner for Teddy before I could find one for myself. "But I just want him to be happy," I tell her. "Think of him as my project. When I get him settled, then my project will be settling *me*."

"Um, I don't think that's how the world works," Maggie told me, but who is she to talk? She's married to her boyfriend from fourth grade, the only guy she ever loved (violins, please), and—well, he's turning out to be what we in the advice business would call a Problem Husband.

"So, why the change?" Teddy asks again. Like any good therapist, he doesn't let go of a question until he's gotten an answer. Never mind that I'm not his client and this isn't therapy. The sad truth is that, even though he thinks of himself as my very good friend and thinks that we can talk about *anything*, I do not want to tell him

I'm highlighting my hair. There's something about my going in for some personal enhancement, as it is my inalienable right as an American to do, that would set off all the alarms in his brain, I think. He'd want to know *why*, he'd start digging around in my fragile little psyche and ask all those leading questions, trying to draw me out. And I'd end up having to admit something to him that I'm barely getting around to admitting to myself: I think about sex all the damn time. Okay? And somehow—in a connection I'd prefer not to have to explore with him—blond sun streaks in my hair seemed to go right along with all that thinking.

"I put some conditioner on my hair," I say without looking at him. "My hair is drying out from the sun."

Because, really, Teddy, I want to look good. I want to turn men's heads. I want to light up somebody for just once, to have somebody attracted to me—scores of men attracted to me. And why shouldn't I?

The truth is that I get Dear Lily letters from people all the time—women in their thirties and forties, in particular—who say they've missed out on their good years, that their chances of finding love now are worse than their chances of getting killed by a terrorist. I frankly never paid much attention to that desperation until recently. I don't think that's the way the world works, and I thought it was unseemly for a woman to go about her life fixated on her chances of finding love. Love just happens, I would have said. But now—well, now I realize that the thudding in my heart when I wake up in the middle of the night just might be loneliness.

TEDDY AND I have been happily divorced for two years now, long enough to have forgiven each other for most of the various emotional crimes committed during the marriage. I know, I know. People will tell you that there is no such thing as a happy divorce—that if you can be good friends, then you could have made the marriage work—but they're wrong about that. He and I should be the poster children for how a nice legal split-up can help preserve a perfectly dysfunctional relationship. Besides, we were awful, simply awful as a married couple. I have never been one who likes to fight, but with him I noticed that we could argue as passionately over sex and money as we could over the outcome of the O. J. Simpson trial, what the acronym RSVP really means, and whether we should teach Simon to call adults Mr. and Mrs., or just let him use people's first names. And aside from the fact that he disagreed with me on nearly everything, *including* Coke versus Pepsi, breast versus bottle, winter versus summer, and mountains versus beach, he also was always depressed and low-energy. I'd knock myself out trying to cheer him up, and when that failed, I couldn't help it—I'd get mad at him for not being happy.

His gloom seemed like such a personal affront, a stubborn refusal to enjoy life, and it even seemed like a dangerous way to bring up a baby. You shouldn't let people new to the planet know how difficult life is, I told him, at least not right away. So I'd withdraw, and he'd sulk and complain that if I really loved him for who he was, then I'd accept the fact that he was sad, hostile, and prone to making long lists of complaints. "I *love* complaining, *okay*?" he once yelled at me. "Will you let me be my goddamn self and let me just loathe everything without trying to make it all right for me?"

That had been a real eye-opener, believe me. My God, he *wanted* to be this way. And I was married to him. Forever.

But, in fact, he was the one who called it quits. One day we were fighting about, oh, paper towels, I believe it was—whether it was best to spend a little more and buy the ones that were truly absorbent (my position) or whether you got more value from giant paper towel rolls that were the approximate thickness of toilet tissue (his position, coming directly from his lifelong policy of frugality in all its forms). I didn't think of this as one of our red-letter fights; it was just the routine annoyance of married life. But then that night, after we got into bed, he turned and looked at me and said in his Eeyore voice, "You know, Lily, this isn't working. I can't do it anymore."

"You can't do what anymore?" I said. I honestly thought he meant he couldn't tolerate my buying the good paper towels, wasting our money that way. I was about to say something smart-alecky when I saw the look on his face. He reached over and touched my cheek.

I almost started hyperventilating. But Teddy kept talking to me in his low, mournful, Teddy voice. It was his fault, not mine, he said. He'd thought, he'd *hoped* that marriage to me was going to be some kind of magic pill that would make him less anxious, less depressed, that it would save him from all his fears and craziness. It was him, all him. I was like some gorgeous butterfly in his life—that's what he said; I'd been this miracle that had touched down for him, but even I couldn't make him be somebody he wasn't meant to be. And it was too much pressure for him. He couldn't take the stress of it, of trying to be the right kind of husband and father all the time.

"You. Are. *Killing*. Me," he said slowly, "with all your plans and your optimism."

"Don't leave," I said. "I can want less. And Simon needs you, even if you are crabby." But even as I was saying it, there was a part of me that knew that breaking up was the right thing. Hell, I couldn't want less. I was already half-starving. Maybe it was all the psychotherapy I'd had, but even in the throes of the packing and arranging and telling friends, filing papers, and contacting attorneys, I knew I was being let out of a cage whose bars I would have had to break someday, just to get free. Simon and I could be happier alone. What a rude awakening that was.

But then, a few months after the divorce came through, Teddy invited me out for coffee and declared that we couldn't lose each other simply because the state didn't mandate that we sleep together anymore, and I realized with surprise that I'd healed enough not to be so angry at him all the time. I didn't want him back, but I did miss him, and it was heartbreaking how Simon searched for him every morning when he woke up, saying, "Where's Daddy? Dad-deee, come out, Daddy!" So that day, when Teddy sang a little chorus of "They Can't Take That Away from Me"—"The way you wear your hat / The way you sip your tea"—right there in the coffee shop, my eyes filled up with tears, and I agreed that he and Simon and I could hang out together.

After that, before I even realized what was happening and what it would all mean, he moved into a garage apartment right down the street from me. Thankfully, the other half of my duplex was by then rented out, or otherwise I'm sure he would have made the case that he should move in there, and then I'd have him sleeping right on the other side of my bedroom wall for the rest of my life. How horrible would that have been? What would have been the point of going to all the trouble of divorcing him?

Since then—well, it's sort of evolved that he comes over nearly every night. He officially comes to see Simon, of course. The two of us read him stories and sing him songs and put him to bed, and then, because we're lonely and neither of us has been able to come up with anything resembling a new life, Teddy hangs around. It's okay. We talk and analyze everything that either of us has thought or heard about during the day, telling each other most of our secrets.

But then—and this may be the best part—he goes home to his own bed.

2

A breeze rustles through the beach plums, and the water laps against the pilings of the dock down where the lawn gradually gives way to a sandy beach. It really is a beautiful night, filled up with the promise of the summer to come: little sparks of fireflies out by the beach roses, the twinkle of lights from all the other houses along our little bay colony, even the last wispy clouds of the day floating out above the sea, catching the moonlight.

Oh, God, God, *God,* how I wish I hadn't put this bleach in my hair. Why in the world did I ever think this was a good idea? It is so unlike me to fall for a kit like this. I never do this sort of thing. I'm a careful person; I like to know how things are going to turn out. If someone wrote me a Dear Lily letter about her search for personal transformation through peroxide, I would tell her, "No! No! Stop! Do *not* go the do-it-yourself hair color route. Meditate. Do yoga. Learn to make a baked Alaska, or take up clog dancing—but do not think that changing your hair color will change your life."

I get jolted out of my teeth-gnashing by Teddy, who is now going on, in a voice you'd swear came right out of Woody Allen's mouth, "Well, I think I just have to face the fact that I'm meant to be single, that's all. And it's not *such* a horrible existence, if you don't count the fact that by the time I ever get a chance to have sex again, I won't remember how it is you do it and my prostate gland will be shriveled up to the size of a grain of sand . . ."

Despite my own personal agony, I very nicely point out to him that if he didn't go psycho over the names women call their house cats, then perhaps someday he *could* have sex again. He laughs gloomily, and just then—as if on cue, perhaps summoned unconsciously by the mention of sex—Sloane, who lives in the other half of my house in exchange for doing handyman chores, shows up with a giggling woman on his arm. I have to tell you about Sloane. He's the son of one of my mother's oldest friends from her days in the Art League, and he's one of those twenty-something types you see everywhere these days—he plays guitar in a band, broods, does odd jobs, does more brooding, paints houses to make a living, and through sheer excessive unshaven handsomeness, he always looks as though he's on the verge of doing something dangerous and masculine. You could just see him riding a motorcycle into the house, for instance, if the thought occurred to him. Frankly, he makes me just the slightest bit hyperventilational, even though—well, I wouldn't do anything about it. I won't even admit to wanting to, except to Maggie. I know what's inappropriate for me to do, after all. And Sloane is squarely in that category of being interesting but off-limits.

Still, I do enjoy watching him walk across the lawn toward me, the woman next to him tripping in the soft grass in her platform high heels, and Sloane trying to hold her up. They look like they were made for each other, although I would swear he came home with a different woman just last night. He may be just a tiny bit slutty, I think, especially lately, now that his band is playing the clubs. As he comes up on the porch, he stops nuzzling the woman and says, in a hyperserious voice, like a child suddenly coming upon the tribal elders, "Oh, hello, Lily, Teddy. How are you tonight?"

"Great, just great," says Teddy stiffly. "How's the band?"

He says, "The band is deee-licious!" like it's a private joke, and the woman starts laughing so hard she has to be propped up. Obviously she's a bit drunk. Sloane laughs, too, and he and the woman make their way through his back door. It slams behind them. Then

17

he pokes his head back out and says, "Sorry, Lily—and by the way, sorry about taking today off, but I promise I'm going to get to those gutters tomorrow," and he closes the door more softly.

"The soul of good manners, that's our Sloaney," says Teddy. He sighs. "Now just one more time, could you explain to me why you have to have the world's most hunky guy living in the other half of your house?"

"Hmm, maybe it's because he's willing to climb ladders and he knows how to fix the furnace."

"Come on. You know I'd do those things if I had to."

"Teddy, get real. You freaked out the day you had to go up higher than the fifth rung on the ladder. And besides that, remember that time when you got up in the middle of the night and turned off the main switch because you thought the furnace was going to blow up?"

"It was making a funny noise."

"That funny noise is called a motor. And anyway, Sloane lives there because his mother wants him to, and she was a friend of my mother's."

"Well." He sniffs. "I just think if your father had had any idea what kind of situations were going to breed in that apartment—and I do mean *breed*—he would have transformed this cottage from a duplex into just one house, and that would have been best for everybody."

Teddy doesn't really know. That *wouldn't* have been best. My mother would have hated it. Throughout my childhood, that other half of the house served as her private studio, the place she went to be away from the family so she could paint her watercolors in peace. That's how she stayed sane, my father told me. *Leave her alone while she's working; she goes a little crazy if you bother her.* My little sister, Dana, and I spent our childhoods knowing we were forbidden to interrupt her—unless we saw smoke billowing out of the windows, she always said. She used to say, in the dry, exaggerated Southern accent she used when she was being funny, "Y'all can interrupt me right after you call the fire depahtment. Anything else goin' on, ah don't want to know about so don't even think about comin' lookin' for me."

It got to be a game we played. What if there was a nuclear attack? What if I broke my leg? What if homicidal maniacs came looking for young girls to torture and they carried us off? What if . . . ? What if . . . ? Could we interrupt you *then?* The answer was always, "Nope, nope, nope. Only for the fire depahtment."

WELL. The fire department never did have to come, and despite that, my mother and father are both gone now, killed twelve years ago in an automobile accident. They were fifty years old, still good-looking, in glowing health, and coming home from one of her art shows when an oil truck driven by a man with three DUIs and a suspended license skidded across the median divider on I-95 and plowed into their car. There they were, less than an hour away from home, and except for being suddenly dead, everything was going just right for them. My mother, just the day before, had won several awards for her experimental impressionist watercolors of nudes, and she and my father, a partner in a New Haven law firm, had recently celebrated their twenty-fifth wedding anniversary. I think they were even happy, certainly happier than most. But then—well, then they were just gone. Smashed up to nothing and then burned to death in an oil fire.

I can't let my mind stay on the details of that crash for more than a few seconds before I get that deadness in the pit of my stomach. It's as though that was the moment, more than anything else, that divided my life into its two parts. Lily, before and after.

Naturally, all this thinking about my parents conjures up their ghosts, who come wafting up from their resting places under the porch, settling in and around us like some foggy coldness in the breeze. I don't necessarily believe in ghosts, but if I did, this porch is where my parents would choose to haunt. This is the spot where I always picture them. They gave hundreds of dinner parties out here over the years. They were the golden couple of our little beach colony. Avery and Isabel Brown, always hosting everything from elegant, effortless affairs to wild theme parties and barbecues—each known for its good food, music, dancing, great conversation, and— okay, some out-of-control wildness. Tonight, perhaps lulled by the subsequent years of quiet, I look around and find it hard to believe that this porch was once the center of life here. But it was. Oh, yes, it was.

Teddy always accuses me of glorifying those old days, but he wasn't there, so he doesn't know those days deserve to be glorified. He doesn't know how the crystal gleamed in the candlelight on the porch, or how my mother's brightly colored Fiestaware looked on the white tablecloths, or how perfectly her flower arrangements— roses and peonies and coreopsis—stood just *so* in their sparkling vases. Her baskets of red geraniums and white petunias, window boxes riotous with color. And the music! Frank Sinatra and Miles Davis blaring across the lawn. Billie Holiday lamenting. Harry James's trumpet providing the sound track of our lives, smooth and rich as the macaroni and cheese my mother made, the banana pudding, the collard greens, the always-present pound cake with its drizzle of lemon glaze. Old-fashioned music, old-fashioned Southern food, as if it were the 1950s instead of the 1970s. My parents leading the dancing, shimmying, holding each other, rubbing noses, and laughing.

Nothing has ever replaced for me the spirit of those parties, with my mother floating around in her gauzy, almost see-through dresses or her toreador pants, and all the colony grown-ups (we kids called them the "growns") dancing under the paper Japanese lanterns, smoking, flirting, and drinking brightly colored cocktails.

We, the Scallop Bay children, or as one father called us, the Scallopini—there were nine of us, including Dana and me—played hide-and-seek in the beach plums and all along the shore, or spied on our parents from the lawn, giggling over their conversations and imitating the way they danced. The growns seemed to us like brightly colored, unpredictable beasts, I remember, acting so ridiculous with all their teasing and hugging and fake laughing. The games they played always seemed so mysteriously heavy, supposedly all in wonderful fun but always with a crackle of tension to them. Looking back, I suppose all that slow dancing, all that nuzzling meant that they were carrying things just a tad too far with one another, going right up to the line that flirting would take them—and then sometimes falling over it and having to spend weeks patching up the problems they'd made.

The Scallopini were allowed to roam far into the night. We were a grubby band of urchins, playing games like flashlight tag and dodgeball, and a game Dana loved—piggy tag, in which the older kids would carry the younger ones on their backs and joust back and forth. Most nights, when it got late and no one had called us in, we'd all fall asleep on the beach or in somebody's family room, watching late movies or, when we got older, doing some experimental making out. I had my first druggy kisses with those colony kids— Tim Franzoni knew how to french before anyone else, and taught us all one summer. We'd lie on the scratchy plaid couches in his family's den with the lights off, kissing for hours: Tim and me; Jane Wiznowski and Jonathan Arterton; Bethanne Franzoni and David Wiznowski; Maggie with Mark Travers, who lived in town but whose parents would occasionally let him hang out with the Scallopini.

It seems unbelievable to me now that our parents really left us on our own for so much of the time, that they were so unconcerned about what we might be up to. They didn't see "parenting" as the all-consuming big deal it is today, certainly. I think they regarded us · as the mostly uninteresting by-products of their sex lives. And they probably just figured we'd somehow make it through to adulthood without their help or interference.

And—well, I guess we did, more or less. Most of the nine of us grew up okay and now are busy with all the life complications that happen to people: raising children, making mortgage payments, working too hard, spending too much, arguing with spouses, glorifying the old days. Maggie and I are the only ones of the Scallopini living here full-time, but the others come from away to visit the beach in the tiny slivers of vacation they carve out when they can—or when they can no longer avoid coming. I wave to them across the beach— they and their spouses and kids piling out of SUVs and arguing over beach toys and property rights and how long you have to wait after eating before you can go swimming.

None of the remaining growns are as close to one another as they used to be. You'd think they'd be nostalgic for those old days, too, but if they are, I never hear it in their voices—which are scratchy now with complaints and disappointment about the fact that they are old and everything hurts them and the price of medication is too high and it's hotter than it used to be and people don't try anymore and people who wait on you in stores are rude and the language on television is horrible and you take your life in your hands going onto the highway.

If you ask me, I think they simply miss the way they used to play on my parents' porch. I think the world has changed for us all, and, at least for us here in the colony, we all got older and not better.

ACROSS THE BAY, I hear a woman's sudden tinkling laugh, and if I squint, I can make out the silhouettes of old Leon Caswell and his new young wife, Krystal, sitting on their porch. Leon and Krystal are the exceptions to the generalized crotchetiness of the colony. In fact, they are currently the scandal of polite colony society because they broke all the rules and got married only three months after Leon's first wife, Mavis, died of cancer. Leon and Mavis were always my parents' favorite couple to hang out with. Leon was married to

Mavis for approximately 150,000 years, and he loved her and took good care of her. Then she got sick, and he hired a live-in nurse to come and help him. And damned if that wasn't Krystal, and damned if he didn't fall in love with her. So what that he's in his mid-seventies and she's twenty-seven? He's one of those cute old guys you see sometimes—always telling jokes, always dancing, always twinkling.

After my father died, Leon taught me to play the ukulele because he said my father always loved that, and he came over to kill Horrible Bugs whenever one was loose in the house, and he showed me how to change the oil in my car and how to put in the storm windows, and then, when he was old, he convinced me that hiring a handyman was a good thing and not a sign of moral laxity. He also told me things would someday start to feel a little bit better and that I mustn't put my whole life on hold just because my parents had died—and we've been good buddies in a father-daughter way ever since.

I love it that he got married again, and that Krystal said, "Damn them all," and wore a long white gown and a veil and flowers in her hair, and that she had scads of bridesmaids, as well as two ring bearers and two flower girls, and that she had her father give her away to Leon, who was about two decades older than her father. And I love it that I got to be Leon's "best woman" and stand up at the altar beside him, smiling as Krystal came down the aisle to be married to him. At the reception, when it was time to make the toast, I said in a voice filled with tears, "To the man who saved my life when I was only five years old and nearly drowned in Long Island Sound, and who has saved me countless times since my own father died, including killing spiders and teaching me to waltz at my own wedding— may you and your beautiful Krystal find every happiness, and, please, Leon, bring back the parties on the porch. Unite us again."

Sadly, though, of all the colony people, only my mother's best friend, Gracie, was there to hear my toast. The rest were boycotting the wedding, on account of they loved Mavis so much.

I HAVE TO GO rinse my hair. I absolutely have to see what is happening underneath this towel. Not one more second can pass. . . .

I stand up as Teddy says, "So what did you and Simon do tonight?"

"Well, we played outside until it got dark, and then Simon caught a firefly in his little screened bug jar," I say quickly, taking baby steps toward the door. What I want to do is break out into a run, of course, but then Teddy would guess something was up. I have to pretend to be nonchalant about this.

"Wait, where are you going?" he says. "Stop and tell me. He caught an actual insect?" As though I'd said he'd bagged an elephant or something.

"Yeah. He did. A real honest-to-god insect."

"My son, the hunter."

"It was a proud moment, believe me."

"Hmmm. So maybe there's hope for the Kingsley lineage after all. He'll avoid his old man's fate of being an intellectual wuss, and he'll get to date cheerleaders and play football," he says. Then, "So what happened to this trophy firefly? Was there some tragedy involved I need to know about?"

"No. Not so far. He named it Lily and put it to bed on his pillow next to him, in Boo Bear's place. Wait. I have to go inside for a minute."

Teddy looks at me as if he hasn't heard. He's still dealing with the staggering fact of Simon's catching a firefly. As I said, Teddy didn't grow up here with the beach roses. He doesn't know that fireflies practically come and beg you for a chance to get into your jar. "Wow," he says. "This is very Oedipal of him. Naming it after his mom. Perfect. Right on schedule."

The phone rings. Great. I can go in and pretend to be answering it, and then quickly dash upstairs and wash out my hair, put the towel back on, and finish whatever strain of conversation we're going to next: Oedipus, Teddy's dismal dating life, intellectual wusshood. Whatever.

But no. He jumps up. "Okay, here we go," he says. "You *know* that's Kendall calling you with the date report. Come on. Let's go listen to the answering machine and get *her* take on things. Then you'll see how hopeless it all is. Let's go hear what rotten things she has to say about me."

I've never seen his eyes so glittery. "Are you crazy? We're not going to do that. That's so junior high. Besides, Teddy," I say. "Listen, that conditioner I put on my hair . . ."

He doesn't hear me. "So what if it's junior high? I'm all about junior high. And think how much time it could save me," he says. "It'd be great if I already knew what she thought so I wouldn't have to worry if maybe I should call her again because it turns out that she *thought* I was the love of her life or something, only she couldn't communicate it due to an emotional disorder that I'll be able to diagnose and cure, and it turns out she really is willing to get rid of all the cats, she's just keeping them for her elderly grandmother, but she's about to give them all back . . ."

"Teddy. Come back to earth." The phone rings for the fourth time and stops. I know that upstairs, next to my bed, the answering machine has picked it up. I don't care. Teddy's face looks stricken, as though he suspects that Kendall was his last chance, or that there was more horrible stuff that happened on the date, stuff he doesn't even want to admit to me. He is so pathetic, my Teddy, so . . . so scared of letting people in. Of having a life. Of embracing anything different. What I wish I could say to him is—and maybe this is just from thinking about my father and Leon and all the growns—*Where is your manhood? And when exactly did you guys turn into such cowards?* Back when Leon Caswell and my father were waltzing women around the porch and pouring them bright purple drinks and pretending to swoon over their perfume, *they* wouldn't have been thrown by a woman who had a lot of cats and wore interesting shoes and wanted to make sure her food was the way she wanted it. They would have dismissed all that external stuff and gotten right down to the main thing: Would she be fun? Would she tell funny stories and make everybody laugh? Would she go to bed with them?

Maybe men were just braver then. Nothing threw them. You wouldn't find them hovering around an answering machine waiting to hear if a woman had dissed them. Even if they'd had answering machines.

"Teddy," I say, "listen to me. Kendall is just a little bit wacky, not even seriously bad wacky. Couldn't you have tolerated a teeny tiny little bit of a shoe obsession and a few conversations with cats? Can't you make room even for *that*?"

"I didn't even get to the worst part," he says mournfully. "She was a former beauty queen."

We look at each other for a long time. Then I start laughing, hard.

"Stop it," he says, but he's laughing, too, and trying not to. "You don't understand. Girls like her, they eat guys like me for breakfast and then spit us out of their car windows on their way to their photo shoots. They string us along and make us think we're fabulous, but really they're just after us for our sexual prowess and nothing else. They don't want to be seen with us. That's why they're always doing stuff like calling the chef out from the kitchen, just to prove their power over mankind."

I might be laughing too hard to breathe. I start choking on the wine, and Teddy leans over to beat me on the back, and his hand catches on the towel and it falls to the ground, almost in slow motion, and then he says, "Oh my God, Lily. Oh my God. Something really weird and terrible has happened to your hair."

3

$\mathcal{A}$s if this isn't awful enough, something really bad happens next.

I have to tell him what I've done, and then he goes into Therapy Mode. You haven't seen psychotherapy in action until you've seen Teddy shifting into gear, like a police officer taking off after a bank robber, or Superman about to leap a tall building. You'd swear he was a triage nurse at the scene of a natural disaster, the way he suddenly drops back into a calm, studied slow motion. He walks me inside, puts his arm around my shoulders as though I am a mental patient who just may totally freak out now, leans into me, and asks me all kinds of questions in a soothing, concerned voice—the kinds of questions you might ask someone you suspect is slipping into shock.

"Lily," he says, both heavily and singsongy at the same time, "do you remember when you felt the first impulse to put orange stripes in your hair? What were you thinking when you decided to buy this kit and use it? Let's go back to that moment. What was going on for you then?"

I shake him off and rinse the stuff out at the kitchen sink, feeling irritated and embarrassed. I just want him to leave. But he stands by, too close really, leaning against the counter and shaking his head mournfully. Every now and then he lets out a big sigh, and says something like "But, Lily, *why*? This isn't like you," as though I've been caught shooting heroin instead of putting a little Miss Clairol onto my hair.

"It's going to be all *right*," I say through the running water. This is in spite of all evidence to the contrary. The glimpse of it that I saw in the mirror as I ran upstairs to get the shampoo packet from the kit could *not* have looked worse: not only had the color come out a bright, iridescent, sick orange, but it was not even in tame, ordinary streaks running through my curls in an orderly way. Instead, because I had smushed it up underneath the towel, it now looks like the work of a Modernist painter, perhaps Jackson Pollock himself, who used my head as a canvas while he threw orange paint at it.

Teddy is shaking his head. "I can't believe it," he keeps saying. "Why would you do such a thing to your beautiful hair?"

"Teddy, please. *I don't know.*"

"Were you not aware that you had one of the world's best hair colors?" he says. "And may I emphasize the word *had*? This is so *sad*."

I say nothing, which may be a mistake, because by the time I've turned off the faucet and squeezed all the extra water out of my hair, Teddy has evidently diagnosed me as someone who is screwed up beyond belief and who, in her loneliness, is desperately crying out for help via hair color. And then he has apparently completed some necessary calculations of his own personal situation, perhaps as it relates to his third unhappy date in one month, and—well, voilà! Within seconds, he has come to the conclusion that, despite all previous evidence to the contrary, perhaps we are meant to be together after all.

When I get my hair piled into the towel and open my eyes, he is staring at me. Using the icky pet name he used to call me when we were first married, he says, "Look at us, pookie. We are two out-of-control misfits, aren't we? But you know something? We don't *have* to try to make it in the outside world. We weren't meant for getting along with other people. Let's just face facts and cling to what we've got right here."

At first I can't imagine what he's talking about. Face *what* facts, and cling to *what* that we have right here? And . . . *pookie*? Have I accomplished nothing with this man in the years we've been apart?

"We've been divorced two years, and neither one of us has made it work with anyone else," he says. "You know what that means. We can't."

"Oh, no, no. Wait just a minute. You're talking about getting back *together*? As a couple?"

"That's the beauty part," he says. "We won't be like other couples. You know, I'd keep my apartment so I'd have a place to go and chill out whenever I was feeling . . . you know . . . like I get . . . but basically we'd forget all this other stuff, the dating and the . . . the *striving*. I just want to stop striving."

"Teddy, come on. Don't make me remind you of all our world-class arguments. Please don't put us both through this. You know we don't work as a couple."

"It might not have been so awful," he says.

"If what? If RSVP didn't stand for '*répondez s'il vous plaît*,' not 'respond *something* very properly'? If you could bring yourself to admit that O.J. is guilty, guilty, guilty? Do you not remember the screaming fights and the daily agony we went through? Nothing of that remains in your head?"

He is unflappable. "Who cares about that? That stuff isn't important, and you know it. Look at our lives. We're together nearly every day. And now that I think of it, why are you always setting me up with women who obviously are not my type, huh? So you don't have to worry about my ever really, really leaving you and being happy with somebody else." I must have a strange expression on my face, because he pauses, watching me, and then he says, "Yeah. Sound familiar? Even if it's unconscious, Lily, that *is* what's going on. Maybe you're trying subconsciously to prove to me that you're really the only one I can bear to be with."

"But I'm *not* the only one you can bear to be with," I say. "We haven't yet found the only one you can bear to be with. You yourself know that you can't stand being married to me. You and I were hideous together. We're both far happier apart, and the only reason we spend every day together now is because we have Simon, and because we can get away from each other whenever we want. You know that."

His eyes darken. "That's not the reason. Lily, I know we don't *love* each other the conventional way people are supposed to. We're not good at all that stuff because we're not conventional types. But the bottom line is this: I'm comfortable with you. You're comfortable with me. Our pathologies match up in some weird way."

Oh, it gets worse. He runs through a bunch of arguments, following me around the house while I look for combs and brushes, hats I can possibly wear, bags I can put over my head, a stun gun—anything to keep from standing still and facing him. My hands are trembling. Every time I happen to pass a mirror or catch my reflection in a window, I nearly stop breathing again.

But he's going on. He's made a list of his reasons, in record time, and he fires them off at me: We're getting older now. And who needs drama and romance, anyway? We're too settled in our ways for other people to ever penetrate to the real us. We *know* each other. We'd know what we were up against this time. No surprises. Neither of us can stand anyone else anyway. Then he heads back to the misfit theme.

I am shaking my head, because I am not a misfit—a curmudgeon perhaps, a person who's made mistakes, but I'm not yet ready to throw in the towel on romance and drama. He says, "Come on, Lily. Admit defeat. Let's just give up on all that stuff. You know where I'm coming from, and I know where you're coming from, and that's enough. Give it up. Surrender to the inevitable. This is *enough out of life.*"

"It's not enough," I say quietly. "I wish it were enough. I wished it were enough back before we split up. But it's not."

"Look at what you've done to yourself," he says. His whine is getting higher and higher pitched now. He motions up to my head. "You've obviously got some fixation that you're addressing, trying to make yourself look *attractive* for somebody, for some man to notice you. And you don't have to go to all that work. Stay with me, and you can get fat, dye your hair Bozo orange for all I care. We'll get fat and orange together. I mean, look at this gut on me." He pulls up the hummingbird shirt and points to two-tenths of an inch of excess flesh. "Who else is going to put up with us besides each other? You've got orange hair, and I've got a gut. So what?"

"There's more to life," I say. "And I am not going to have orange hair by this time tomorrow, believe me." I hate how he's looking at me. He suddenly stops and says very quietly, "Wow. Two rejections in one night. This has got to be a record for Teddy Kingsley."

"Oh, I am not rejecting you, Teddy Kingsley," I say, in as no-nonsense a voice as a person with orange hair can pull off. "And anyway, I am in the middle of an absolutely horrific drama right here, on my head, and now you're just trying to take my mind off it by bringing up all this other crap. So even though you've called me a misfit—which I am *not*—I am going to overlook it because I see that you're really just trying to help." I press a smile onto my face, a meant-to-be-comforting, consolation-prize smile. "And, now that I think of it, it sounds to me like *you* were the one who rejected Kendall, not the other way around. I think you have had no rejections tonight, actually. You're zero for two in the rejection department."

"Two rejections. One night," he says again, and now he's back to being Eeyore on barbiturates. "Come upstairs and let's listen to the answering machine. I'll prove it to you. When you hear what she has to say about our date, you'll see."

There's nothing to do but to go up, which is not a great idea, really, because the answering machine is right next to my bed,

31

which used to be *our* bed, and before that, was my parents' bed. It still has the wedding ring quilt that my Aunt Juniebeth made for my mother. It's a bit awkward standing there just then, in the dark room, with Simon's loud, stuffed-up breathing coming from across the hallway, the scenes of former conjugality running through both our heads. I turn on the lamp quickly and look down at the blinking light on the answering machine. I am praying that Kendall didn't say anything horrible that is going to make Teddy stay even one second longer. I need him out of here so I can start my official freak-out about my hair—and possibly my life situation and my loneliness— which I can just feel coming up inside me, ready to be let loose. Also, Teddy is scaring me with this neediness, this willingness to settle for nothing at all, this complete amnesia about what it was like when we were married to each other.

What if he's right? What if there *is* nothing better than this?

I reach over and press the button. The tape whirs and clicks, runs through its little menu of responsibilities. And then, instead of Kendall's rather breathy voice, there's the voice of a guy. A man with a ten-gallon hat of a Southern accent. He drawls onto the tape, "So, Dana. Haven't heard from you in a long time. Call me when you git in, will ya, baby?"

4

*L*et me put this in a little perspective. My sister, Dana, has been gone for ten years now. Guys don't call for her anymore. By now, it's known around here that I'm the last person she would tell her whereabouts to. Some people even know that she's told the attorney who mails our monthly trust fund checks that I am not to be told where he sends hers.

Her last words to me were "Bite me." This was probably shorthand for "Thank you, my dear older sister, for leaving your fabulous life in California and coming home to take care of me after our parents died, so that I could stay here and not have to go live with our mother's relatives in South Carolina. But now, in spite of your warnings and abundant love for me, I really do have to leave and go find my own way, which may involve fucking half the guys in North America."

"Bite me," though, was how it came out. She was eighteen, and she yelled it as she walked across the yard and got into her boyfriend's beat-up old school bus, with its broken windows and its black puffy letters that said MORBID GULLETS on the side. She was wearing all black, head to toe, with a dog's studded collar around her neck. Lovely, just lovely. She'd dyed her naturally blond hair shoe-polish black and shaved off most of her eyebrows and redrawn them into two arches too high on her forehead. She looked not only pale but perpetually surprised.

Still, it's funny, isn't it, how when someone changes her style so quickly there's a part of her that for you never changes from the way she used to be. Back then, looking into her face—even distorted as it was with tarlike eyeliner—I could still see traces of the snub-nosed, wide-eyed, rosy little girl she'd been. She was—is—six years younger than I, and she was always following me around everywhere when she was little, trying to pretend she was my age and that my friends were her friends; always getting into my bed at night, poking me with her elbows and knees and asking me a zillion questions about why Momma was so weird all the time, and why didn't Momma's best friend, Gracie, have any children, and why didn't Daddy stay home more. She stole my makeup and my earrings and listened in on my phone conversations and then wanted everything she'd overheard explained to her satisfaction later. She was my sidekick, my own personal fan club, and the reigning queen of the tattletale society.

When she was twelve and I was eighteen, she cried and begged me not to go all the way to California for college. I had to go. And after I left, she made me cassette tapes of all the sad, missing-you music she could find and wrote me long letters begging me to come back because everything "just wasn't the same." For a while, at least. Until she stopped writing, and didn't seem to want to have anything to do with me. When I'd come home for visits, she seemed too pre-occupied to talk to me, and when she did say anything, it was to brag about stuff she had done with Momma and the new clothes Momma was buying her all the time.

Standing there in the driveway that day, stunned, watching her leave, I doubted that she even remembered she had once adored me. Her boyfriend helped her into the bus and turned and shrugged in my general direction. He was a blond, skinny, dissolute-looking guy named Thor, manager of the Morbid Gullets, a heavy-metal rock band. The thing was, I liked Thor. He talked to me. He enjoyed my cooking. He had a tattoo of a skull on his forearm and was never seen without at least two razor blades dangling from his ear lobes, which I found an interesting choice for a fashion accessory. I often wondered how he and Dana kissed without either of them losing parts of their chins. I thought that it was brave of them to try.

And now she was going to be touring the country with this band and sleeping with Thor in the bus. So that was that. I stood there watching them roar away, the bus smoking and lurching down the street, and of all the things I should have been thinking, the one thing that was uppermost in my mind was: Jesus, is she more likely to die in a bus accident or bleed to death from razor cuts while she sleeps? And this: Do I have it in me to get in my car, chase this bus, cry and beg and plead for her to come back, the way *she* did for me when I left for college? Would she recognize the gesture and soften toward me?

It's when you ask yourself that question and come up with the realization that you don't have the energy even to try it, that you realize you've failed. Really, really failed.

YEAH, I've got to admit now that I was terrible as a surrogate parent. I tried. I really did. But I was twenty-two and Dana sixteen when our parents died, and although I *thought* I was all grown up, I seriously didn't know the first thing about how to mother anybody.

When the crash happened, I was still living in Isla Vista, the student community outside the University of California at Santa Barbara, even though I had graduated a few months before. I'd intended to remain a Left Coaster, waitressing at the Bluebird Café, and continuing my affair with Joel, the English professor guy, and just waiting to see what was going to happen to me. Would it be book contracts? Grad school? Organizing the community theater productions that Joel and I had become part of? I hadn't the slightest idea, and didn't waste much time thinking about it. But the day I got the call—"your parents' car was hit by a truck, and they're in intensive care," followed by the more hysterical call from Dana: "Lily, they're *dead*! Momma and Daddy are *dead*!"—I put everything I cared about into a suitcase, told Joel I was leaving, put everything I *didn't* care about on the curb (including my diaphragm and all of Joel's letters to me, both of which seemed suddenly childish and inconsequential), and flew home.

Dana and I were both devastated into zombiehood. I felt as though a blowtorch had come through my life and that everything extraneous had been blasted away. We looked like those big-eyed children in Margaret Keane posters, clinging to each other through the funeral and its foggy aftermath. There was all the deciding-about-the-future that had to be done. Everything seemed up for discussion. Keep the cottage? Sell the car? Divide up the trust fund? Life was suddenly a blur of decisions—of muted, polite, and helpful conversations with my father's accountants, financial gurus, and planners, all ushering in this new era in which I was seen as the Resident Grown-up. Even Gracie, my mother's oldest, dearest friend and our neighbor, was gone, off on a two-year poetry fellowship, teaching in Italy. She telephoned sometimes, wild with grief herself, but she was not there.

It was just me: grow up or give up.

And then came the relatives. Our parents, Avery Brown and Isabel Spencer Brown, had been from old-money families in South Carolina. They'd moved to Connecticut when Daddy had gotten into Yale Law School, and had always planned to go back down South once he got his degree. But then, just before he graduated, even after they bought their plane tickets to return home, he cut loose from everybody's expectations and fell in love with the shoreline area around New Haven. Somehow he managed to talk my mother into buying this shabby little beach cottage and staying in Connecticut for good. Two days after she told him yes, so the family legend goes, he bought himself a rowboat and lobster pots and was learning how to do clambakes on the beach. And soon after that, contractors showed up, put an upper story and a sleeping porch on the house, and expanded the back porch so that it could hold a picnic table *and* a dance floor. My mother planted beach roses and a vegetable garden and started to paint in earnest.

Their Southern relatives had been apoplectic. They'd always felt that Avery was book smart but not very life smart, and now he'd obviously lost his mind and had overcome Isabel's better judgment and forced them both into Yankeehood. *Nothing* was worse than being a Yankee, my grandmother wrote to my mother. "All the ancestors are just spinning in their graves, darling. *Please* come back home so that PawPaw and Meemaw can rest in peace. We can't hold our heads up at church anymore, honey. Folks *talk.* Your children are going to grow up and marry Yankees, you know, and next thing you know there'll be Yankees in the *family tree . . .*"

As kids, whenever we'd be hauled down to South Carolina to be shown off, my mother would work with us on softening our Connecticut accents. "Drop the *g*'s when you talk," she urged us. "And remember to use 'y'all' as much as possible, instead of 'you guys.'"

Now that my parents were dead, these same relatives wanted us to come back home and reclaim our Southern heritage. There was a whole slew of cousins and aunts and uncles at the funeral, with names like Juniebeth and W.P. and Mary Shirley, all of whom looked as though they'd been sent there by Central Casting. The world could be set right on its axis after all, apparently. As Aunt Mary Shirley explained to me, "We look aftuh our own, darlin', and your momma and daddy woulda wanted y'all to be with *family* at a tahm lack this."

I stood up to them and said no, thank you. I knew that staying in Connecticut was the right thing. We were connected to a community, after all. Dana was still in the eleventh grade, and shouldn't be expected to go to school among strangers in the South, should she? Not at a *tahm lack this.* Besides, we had good credit at the grocery store, a trust fund, a paid-for beach cottage, and best of all, we had tons of friends, both our own and our parents'. We had Scallop Bay colony. And Maggie Mahoney, who'd been my best friend back when we were little, was living back at home now, nursing her mother through cancer, and she was delighted that we'd resumed our friendship. We would be fine, I told everybody who asked. Just as soon as we stop crying, you'll see how well things will go.

Dana, who seemed to me a lot younger than sixteen—no longer bold and brave, like she'd been as a kid, but now sort of soft and tentative in everything she did—might not have been so sure that we knew what we were doing. "We're *orphans!*" she kept wailing to me during the week of the funeral. "What do we know about taking care of ourselves? What will we do?"

She thought maybe we should get an expert in to help us. "And who would that be?" I said to her. "You really want to leave here and go live with Aunt Juniebeth? You want *Mary Shirley* over there to be telling you when bedtime is? Believe me, we can do this." Then I held her and told her that I *knew* what was to become of us: we'd be sad for a very long time, but we were strong, and gradually we'd assume the reins of our lives and go on. We're like oak trees, I said. We've lost a few branches, and we're bowed down, but we'll be standing upright and reaching skyward in no time, you'll see.

What I imagined was that we'd grow close, the way we'd been when she was little, before I went off to college. In my head I guess I harbored the notion that it would be a "you and me against the world" situation, and that we'd become the heroines of our own lives, bonded to each other for life. People would say, "Those Brown girls are so brave and capable. Look how they've kept up that lovely house, and how you always see them smiling."

The only thing I hadn't figured on was the grief.

I guess I thought that when people you love die, that the first day is the hardest ever, but after that, things slowly get better. I thought it was like a scab healing—that the crusty part would take control of the bloody mess underneath and you wouldn't see the work being done, but then eventually it would start to itch and then someday it would fall off completely—and voilà! Healed!

Nobody ever told me all the interesting ways grief has of

knocking you upside the head, as my mother would have said, and then flinging you against the wall, stomping on you, and then—in case you're not convinced you're beaten—dividing you from everybody and everything you ever trusted or loved. *That's* grief. The emotional state I was imagining—well, that was just sadness, hardly even a pale ghost of the real thing.

Dana and I settled into our life of pain. My theory was that we'd heal faster if we kept on doing all the regular, normal things, such as attending high school (her) or going to work as a secretary at the veterinarian's office where Maggie worked (me), which was the best use I could think of for the English/theater degree I'd just gotten. Whenever anyone asked how my degree was helping me, I explained that I spoke English to the dogs and cats there.

We kept busy. The colony people, of course, insisted on keeping an eye on us. Leon Caswell, my father's best friend, kept the place in repair and mowed the lawn. His wife, Mavis, and the other women brought over casseroles, which we accepted politely and then let mold in the refrigerator. People called, wanting to be assigned tasks. I brightly told them that we were just *fine*. Really. No, *really*.

It was very educational, actually. I paid attention to the surfaces of things, as though if we just kept the outsides okay, our insides would follow. I learned what a three-prong outlet was for and how to pay the bills on time. I fixed the toilet so it wouldn't run. I did laundry on Mondays, vacuumed on Tuesdays, dusted on Wednesdays. I learned how to make casseroles and pound cakes like my mother had made them, how to wash my sweaters by hand, how to wear my hair so it wouldn't hang in my eyes. And I made sure we kept busy. I insisted that Dana keep her grades up, eat three square meals a day, and not drive her car into ditches on purpose. For good measure, I said we should try to make our beds each day, keep our teeth brushed, not have pizza delivery more than twice a week, and tell people we were doing okay when they asked.

Dana had a different view. It wasn't anything she could articulate, but her plan seemed to involve us eating all the Drake's cakes we could get. On her way to the store to buy these, it was almost required that she have some sort of minor automobile issue: either a fender-bender, a breakdown, or a drive-off-the-road incident. And when we were sick of Drake's cakes—or when the cashier, a friend of our mother's, took us aside and said she felt that Drake's cakes really *didn't* meet the daily nutritional guidelines set by the government—Dana was more than happy to switch to canned pink frosting, which she said protocol required we eat directly out of the can, with our fingers.

God, I wish I had gone for that. I see now—twelve years later—that she was right. How I wish I hadn't been so intent on appearances, on scrubbing the sink each night before I could fall asleep, a habit I still have and can't break.

Hell, we *should* have lain in the bed with the pizza boxes and Chinese takeout containers and empty frosting cans piling up around us, watching old movies and crying until we had no more liquid left in us. We should have wailed, screamed, laughed like hyenas, jumped on the mattresses, maybe bought a convertible with the trust fund money and sped down I-95 with the top down and the radio up as loud as it would go. How I wish I hadn't ever said, "We need to stop wallowing in this and get on with our lives." But at the time, with the whole world wobbling all around me, I tiptoed through the house, not disturbing my mother's elegant little touches that were everywhere, pretending that life could just take up where it had left off. I straightened the paisley scarf that my mother had draped *just so* over the piano, dusted behind the silver picture frames, scrubbed the Italian tile floor with a toothbrush, waved off all attempts by the neighbors to help us with cooking or cleaning.

"We're doing great," I wrote in our Christmas cards that first year. (Christmas cards! Somebody should have taken me aside and smacked me.) "Dana's in school and has a ton of friends, and I am learning how to manage a household of two. Why, I've stocked up the freezer with healthy things, and I've learned to put in the storm windows before winter comes. We're doing just great."

After we'd been living this way for six months—with me claiming things were okay and Dana trying to convince me they weren't—she started *really* acting out. Her eyes were dark and smoky-looking by then, almost opaque, like the hurt in them might be permanent. She stopped doing her homework, started wearing clothes that were so tight they looked as though they'd been painted on her skin, and, worse, one day she announced that she and Momma always had a sloe gin fizz every day in the late afternoon, and that she was now going to continue with that little tradition. Only, because of all she'd been through, she'd have two, she said: one for her and one for Momma's memory. I looked at her in surprise. She didn't seem soft anymore. She'd grown a hard shell around her.

Then guys started to appear at the house—and not just your gangly, everyday adolescents who have acne and look panicked when an adult talks to them; *oh no,* these were your higher-octane specimens of young manhood, the kind with muscle shirts and gold chains and slicked-back hair. I'd come home, exhausted from wrestling the town's dogs and cats into getting their shots, to find Dana and some guy drunk and entwined on the couch, not bothering to pause in their athletic, sweaty efforts or even to cover up when I came in.

Huge batches of teenagers suddenly converged on our house. I'd find them sprawled across the furniture, jumping off the dock, crushing beer cans with their bare hands, peeing in the rosebushes, and even, on a few notable occasions, having sex on our beds.

Maggie thought I should go with the flow.

"Go with the flow? *Go with the flow?*" I said. "Do you even *know* how scary this is for me? They're these big, hulking, sexual beings. They're, like, oozing hormones when they walk across the room! The air is thick with testosterone."

She laughed. "For God's sake, Lily, listen to yourself. Find

Sto

---

yourself somebody *you* can have sex with. You need it, in the worst possible way."

So I tried, for a while—like, maybe two days or so—to be the cool, understanding older sister. Let's all sit down and talk, I said to them. It's great that you're here hanging out, but would you just mind *not* having sex, you know, in my bed? And how would it be if people made the effort to use the nice downstairs bathroom for urination purposes instead of, say, the *yard*?

That didn't go over so well. One girl told me I was so *cute*. Like a parent but young, she said. "You should just try to loosen up a little bit, and you could be really cool," she said.

So then I grabbed the next available arrow in the surrogate parent arsenal: shameless pleading. Whenever I was alone with Dana, I begged. Please, please stop. Please, I can't take this. Please, I love you. Please respect yourself. And if you can't respect me or respect yourself, please, please respect *Momma's* house.

Please.

By then, though, she was so preoccupied with romantic intrigue, it was like a full-time job for her. I took to screaming. To grounding her. To making rules and regulations and posting them on the refrigerator. Laying down the law. Setting curfews. Leaving notes that said, "Dana, you may not go out again until you've put away the laundry and emptied the dishwasher. I would like it if guys stopped throwing their crushed beer cans over the fence. And please, do not let people pee on the shrubbery anymore. It kills the roses."

She carefully ripped up all my notes and left them in a neat little pile on the floor. So I'd stop talking to her for days, and then, when that didn't work, I'd take to shrieking. One night I flew into her room and threw two guys out of her bed—okay, so all they were doing was sleeping, but *still*—and sent them home.

Oh, but there was more to come. Lots more. Perhaps to mark the one-year anniversary of our parents' deaths, she suddenly dropped the guys on the football team and took up with the misfit crowd. Now, instead of the house reeking of Old Spice and testosterone, it smelled of dirty hair and patchouli oil and pot. Guys with nose rings and mohawks, dressed in layers of black clothing and wearing the prong collars that you see mostly on snarling rottweilers, came and went. Some, like the troubled and sad Rufus, were nice and could carry on insightful conversations about the way you felt when you woke up at four in the morning and wanted to kill yourself. He and I bonded over that. We both thought that antidepressants were for other people, and we both much preferred lying awake and imagining that the end of the world had truly come, and seeing if we could think of any reason to be sad about that. He thought alcohol and oral sex might be reasons to go on. I didn't want to tell him that my raison d'être lay in the beauty of a stainless-steel sink, scrubbed so it was almost like a mirror.

By the time the second anniversary of our parents' deaths came along, Dana had already moved through the five stages of grief, though not the ones Elisabeth Kübler-Ross had had in mind. Dana's phases were: slut, Goth, doper, biker chick, and groupie. At different times, her wardrobe ranged from little wisps of see-through fabric that left nothing to the imagination, to heavy black robes with hoods and barbed-wire chains.

She was now the official head groupie of the Morbid Gullets, she told me proudly, and the best thing in the world had just happened for her: they had promised her she could be the "tambourine girl" and actually stand with them on the stage. She got to dress scary, too, with a ton of black eyeliner and white lipstick, and all the barbed wire and prong collars she could wear. Oh, and now that she was part of the band, she needed to help with the expenses on the road—so did I think she could have part of her trust fund settlement in a lump sum before she headed out?

I just stared at her. A tambourine girl in a punk band—standing there with her dull eyes, eyes that held just as much pain as they had on day one, eyes that stubbornly held onto all their anger and grief and blamed me for everything. I was suddenly so mad I wanted to throw something at her. Instead I said, as nicely as possible, "I will fight that with every ounce of energy I still have left, after what you've put me through."

Bite me, she said. And left.

I just wished I could have bitten myself.

5

*B*ut there it was: she was gone. That was it.

I hate to tell you what I did next, which was almost nothing. I got up that first morning as if things could just go on like normal, dressed for work, and headed down the stairs—but then I turned around, took my clothes off again, folded them neatly, and quietly got back into bed. I said to myself that maybe I needed just a little bit more sleep. That was all: just a tiny bit more sleep. And maybe a little comforting social glass of wine would be just the thing to relax me. So what if it was still morning and there was no one there to be social with? I had a taste for it. So I went downstairs and poured myself one, and then carefully, lovingly brought it back to the bedroom.

When I woke up at two in the afternoon, I didn't feel all that rested, and there were five messages blinking very *redly* on the answering machine. Instead of being Dana telling me she was so very sorry, they were just people wondering why I wasn't where I was supposed to be. I had nothing to tell them, no possible explanation, so I erased the messages right away. Maybe just another glass of wine, and then I could go to work, I thought. I went downstairs and poured a glassful and sipped it right at the counter while I stared out the window at the way the sun sparkled on the water. And then I poured another one to take with me outside. I could go in to work later—after I had rested a little more. Nothing much was going on there anyhow. One day wasn't going to make any difference. They didn't really even need me, I told myself. *No one* needed me anywhere, was the truth of it.

I went outside and sat in the sand on the beach, staring out at the calm blue water. I was so tired I could barely move my limbs. I actually had to think hard about how you went about lifting your arms.

There was an orange raft on our dock, and my father's blue rowboat, badly in need of paint, lying upside down on the dun-colored sand. I looked at these objects for hours, trying to make sense of them. Later, I may have dug a little hole in the wet sand. That's how it started, the digging thing. The digging *problem,* as Maggie still likes to refer to it. What can I say about it? I dug holes—large ones and small ones. Lots and lots of holes.

Days started to pass, to speed up, as though the calendar were flipping off pages faster than I could live the days. I just sat on the beach, with my bucket and shovel, and dug. The job went away, but I didn't care. I knew I had money coming in from the trust fund. I couldn't have said where the checks were piling up—on the dining room floor perhaps? I couldn't remember why I had ever worked at the vet's office in the first place. Didn't I have a degree in English? What *did* that have to do with animals? No, really. The speaking-English-to-the-dogs answer was wearing a little thin by then. The desire to shop, to go out with friends, to have people over—all those things went away, too. Life seemed pared down in good and necessary ways. Things felt crisp, their outlines drawn in heavy, dark lines rather than the blurry way they had been. I didn't drink wine anymore, couldn't be bothered to go buy it. Out there in the hot sun, digging away, I felt chastened, bleached out, somehow absolved from my inadequacies. It was as if the blowtorch that had paid me a visit two years earlier had returned, blowing off even more of the excess, leaving me with the bare, clean bones of my life. Each day, I dug some more holes, and then they'd fill up with water, and by the next day, there would be hardly anything left of them—just an indent where the holes had been. That seemed a metaphor for my life, too. Everything I'd accomplished just getting erased, barely leaving a trace.

My heart was filled with missing everybody I'd lost. One day, I had such a fit of generalized missing that I almost called my former lover, Joel, the professor back in Santa Barbara. But what was the use? His wife would probably answer the phone, and I'd be stuck talking to her. "Oh, Lily!" she'd probably say. "You left so suddenly—and Barstow misses you so much." Barstow was their three-year-old son, whom I used to babysit. There had been so many crazy days when I'd leave Joel's office at the college after we had made love and then performed the requisite, guilt-induced postcoital breakup, and then, still dizzy from the emotional roller coaster of him, still with the *smell* of him wafting off me, I'd invariably run into his wife. Maybe she was subliminally summoned by his pheromones. But there she'd be, at the health food store where I had stopped to buy an orange, or pushing a stroller along the street on the road to the beach, and she'd see me and say brightly, "Oh, Lily! I'm so glad I ran into you. Can you babysit tonight? Joel and I need to rekindle the old spark, you know!" She always said that, with a big smile, one woman to another—rekindle the old spark. I wanted to grab this clueless, ditzy woman with her skinny body and say, "I can't help you with that, you idiot! I'm sleeping with him, too!" Instead, I'd say yes and go and babysit the kid, and then when he'd gone to sleep, I'd sit by his bed and tell him I was his real mother, that the woman he called Mom was just a pale imposter. I love you and I love your father, I'd whisper when he was asleep. *Tell him in the morning that you want a new mommy, and you want it to be Lily.*

THE INEVITABLE day came when I got around to thinking about my mother. I had straggled out to the beach and had lain there in the summer heat, sensing it wasn't a good digging day. It was hot, a

47

day good only for lying down. My hair was tangled, my skin sun-burned. I arranged myself on an old towel so that the hot sand wouldn't burn my legs, and I tried to remember how long it had been since I'd bothered to change my nightshirt. Three days? Four?

I closed my eyes. And suddenly all I could think about was how my mother would have been horrified by me. My eyes smarted when I remembered how hard I had tried to please her. What a waste of time *that* had been! She was all about looking and smelling good. She never would have gone even one waking hour without mascara and lipstick and perfume, or without something pretty to wear. She was unashamedly her own most important artistic project. "It's all about presentation," she'd explained to me once as though she were passing along a great truth. "*Presentation* is all we've got for making people know who we are inside. It's all about the surface."

I was her biggest disappointment.

It wasn't that I didn't try for good presentation. My surfaces just couldn't measure up. I was thin and serious as a child, more like my father than like her. My inadequacies, although she attacked them with great energy at first, turned out to be unfixable: I sucked my thumb. I wanted to ride my bike instead of take ballet. My hair was a dull brown while hers caught the sun's brilliance and shone. Worse, while she could cook anything, I dropped things in the kitchen; and while she could create a painting in one afternoon, my attempted watercolors looked like pieces of paper that had been splattered with food coloring and then sprayed with a hose. Instead of being good at all the things she did so effortlessly, I liked sitting on the beach and reading, or going out with my father to tend to the lobster pots. I didn't mind picking up the spiny old lobsters, wrestling them out of the traps, a skill my mother thought wasn't worth even talking about. And the time I managed to swim all the way out to one of the Thimble Islands, she wouldn't even come to the shore to see me wave.

But, really—I want to get this right, because otherwise it just sounds like I'm bitter, and I'm not, I'm really not—she was something special. She sailed through life, sure of each move. She knew how the kitchen towels should be hung and what color they should be for each season, which ornaments should be arranged and exactly *where* on the silver-and-white Christmas tree, how my hair should be parted, what shoes went with which outfits. *Everybody* consulted her: her friends, her artist colleagues, even strangers in public—"Do you think this looks right?" "Does this hat go with my hair color?" "Do you think I should wear red lipstick or go with the coral?" She ran the Art League and the Garden Club and any other blah-blah-blah club that people might want to call themselves part of. People listened to her. She was, as Maggie once described her, still Prom Queen in her own head.

Lying there in the sand, I had a sudden moment of clarity I hadn't ever experienced before. She had not loved me.

The truth of this baked into my bones as I lay there in the heat. *She had not loved me.* I was the one project of hers that hadn't turned out the way she'd hoped, the one person who reflected back to her some imperfection of her life. Even Dana had done better. They were soul mates, my mother told me once, when Dana was a teenager. It was the year they were dressing alike and whispering and giggling together the whole time I was home from college, the year when I'd come into a room where they were, and they'd stop talking and put on blank faces.

She had not loved me. I would like to say that the knowledge of this hammered into me like a body blow or that I felt a stab of sadness when I realized it. But that wasn't it at all. It felt like a truth that I'd always known somewhere.

And here was another thing: my father, whom *I* adored, adored her. He was *smitten* with her. Moony over her, even. He was tall and thin like me, serious, awkward, and composed of all brown-gray tones—while she was all colors. He and I were house sparrows, and she was a peacock. They complemented each other, I guess you could say, which is maybe another way of saying they were mismatched. She was the artist; he was the lawyer—kind of an Atticus Finch type, who cared about social causes and always had fascinating cases to talk about. My mother always made fun of him; she called him the Only Lawyer Who Cares, like that was a silly thing to be. She would be touching him when she said this, straightening his tie or picking imaginary lint off his coat, and the look on her face would be closed to him, while he looked at her with such intensity, searching each time for a sign that she meant it with affection— which I really think she did not. I must have watched this scene a million times and I never knew until now how it pierced my heart.

When I was in high school, he and I would sit up late together, as though we were the guardians of the night. He'd go upstairs with her for a while at around ten, after she'd come home from her clubs or from visiting with Gracie, and he'd settle her in. Then he'd come down, his tread heavy on the stairs, and he'd spread out all his legal pads around him on the kitchen island. I'd be in the armchair by the kitchen fireplace, doing my homework or reading. We were the family insomniacs, I suppose. We liked to work at night. We talked sometimes, drank cups of decaf coffee, went over his cases and my homework, agreed with each other about politics, ate slabs of the pound cakes Momma always had sitting around, licking the glaze off our fingers.

Sometimes, when he'd speak of her, something would happen in his throat, some sheen would come across his eyes, as though she were an unearthly presence he'd managed to persuade to come down and live with him on the planet, and he was still marveling at his good fortune. His job was to make her life comfortable so that she could simply be who she was meant to be.

He and I never spoke of it, but I understood somehow that we, he and I, took care of everyone else. That was who we were: the caretakers. We were the strong, capable ones. We lived in the real world, and Dana and Momma—well, we loved them, but they maybe needed a little help sometimes. They swooned and fell, they drank too much, they wept. We picked them up, we loved them until they were right again—and we got our strength just from the trust they had in us to keep on keeping on.

But now all of them were gone. That's what I had to get used to. I wished I could call out to my father, ask him what I was supposed to do *now,* now that there was nobody to take care of. "Avery Brown," I said up to the sky, "you didn't tell me that *everybody* was going to go off and leave me here. What is all this about? What the hell do I do next?"

I went back to digging holes and waiting for Dana to come back. I was going to be ready this time, to do things right for her, try to be her soul mate and best friend, to replace my mother for her. That was what I needed to do. No wonder I hadn't been any good at surrogate parenting. My sister had lost her best friend. I had forgotten that part.

Maggie tried to get me to let her come live in my spare room and look after me, but I said no. And Leon, bless him, used to come over and tell me stories about my parents, and talk to me about weather patterns. He'd been a meteorologist before he retired. He liked clouds and big thunderstorms.

It was Leon who sorted the mail, deposited my checks, and paid the electric bill before the power could get turned off. Mavis brought over blueberry pies and bagels with cream cheese and left them out on the counter, the way you might do for a feral animal.

Finally, one day, Gracie, my mother's radical lesbian-feminist best friend, arrived home from Florence, where she'd been on a fellowship for the whole two terrible years, teaching poetry to Italian undergrads. She'd missed my parents' deaths, missed my flailing around trying to raise Dana, missed the whole disintegration of everything. And now she was back. She came out to the beach, and I told her right up front that I wasn't up for talking about anything, and that the kindest thing she could do would be just to leave me alone, because as anyone could see, I was toxic and poison and good only for digging holes in the sand. She said matter-of-factly, "You've just been through too much, that's all. You're exhausted. We'll fix you up."

"I'm *fine*," I said.

One day she came out of her house next door and eased herself down next to me on the sand. Out of the corner of my eye, I saw that she was wearing sparkly artist-type clothing like my mother had worn. I thought of her then as a carbon copy of my mother, sort of useless and self-centered, not really helpful. She just sat there silently and watched me digging. It turned out she'd brought a book of poetry with her, and after a while she read me a poem by Thomas Hardy.

It was a long poem, about sadness over a death. I couldn't make myself pay attention to it. Poetry isn't my thing. Her voice was gruff while she read, but then when she got near the end, she got all choked up. I looked up at her and watched her read the end.

"'I seem but a dead man held on end, To sink down soon . . . O you could not know, That such swift fleeting, No soul foreseeing— not even I—would undo me so!'"

In the heavy silence after she finished, a chorus of cicadas started buzzing.

"I miss her, too," she said when she had finished. "But life doesn't have to stop."

I sat in the hot noon sun and listened in the roar of the afternoon. Later she said, "I've got to say, I like what you've done with the place," gesturing at the dozens of deep holes I had going. I don't remember when she went away that day, but that night, I noticed that she had left the poetry book on the kitchen table for me, along with a lobster roll from Lenny and Joe's Fish Tale restaurant, which I gobbled up in about two and a half bites. I had forgotten about lobsters and lobster rolls, how buttery they tasted, how they melted in your mouth.

The next day she came over with plant food and fed my mother's roses. Later, she talked me into going out in my father's boat near dusk, and we paddled around the bay. She leaned across the boat and told me that she was so very sorry she hadn't come home when my parents died. Her short gray hair lifted in the breeze, and her green eyes were kind and serious. I couldn't look away. She said it was the grief that had made her stay in Italy; she couldn't bear the loss. "I should have been here with you, though," she said. "Your grief was what I should have helped with. This is where I needed to be. You needed me, and I'm sorry."

That's when I first got an inkling that Gracie and I might belong to each other, in the way that people who have nobody else grope their way toward creating a family.

A week later, I picked up the phone and made an appointment to see a grief counselor. If I was going to have a family, I wanted to get better.

THE COUNSELOR was helpful, and she loved my grief so much that it became part of who we were together. She said I'd had something of a little nervous breakdown, or at least that's what they called it in the old days. Now I don't know what they call it: an emotional collapse, maybe, a chemical imbalance, a spiritual crisis.

In our little show—the counseling show the two of us were privately putting on—I was Lily, fucked up and grieving, and she was Marianna, who was healing me. Only I noticed that every time I started to feel better, Marianna said we maybe weren't truly facing *everything* that needed to be faced. Perhaps we should wade in once again and drag out some other dead, lost thing to grieve over.

As she got to know me better, she would sometimes indulge

herself in making fun of a guy who had a practice in the same building, a New Agey sort named Teddy Kingsley, who used crystals and did energy work and drove an old, beat-up VW Bug. This was wicked of her, she said, to ridicule another therapist—but surely no one could take his methods seriously. "Really," she said, and something about the mean look in her eye reminded me of my mother and drilled a hole right through the center of me, "who could believe in any of that stuff that involves rocks and things that smell funny? You'd come out crazier than when you went in."

So on the day I told her that I didn't want to drag out any more griefs, and she said I was once again in denial of its power over me, I stopped in Teddy's office to make an appointment with him. He was soft-spoken and disheveled, and I liked him immediately—the kind look in his eyes, the way his curly hair had a life of its own, how the long lines around his mouth seemed to have been carved out by emotions he'd honestly felt.

He was about to write down the time on a little card, but he kept writing down dates and times and then scratching them out, and then writing in new dates that were closer to the present. And then, suddenly, he looked up at me with such a naked, flustered look on his face that it almost stopped my heart, and he said, "But if I see you professionally, then I can't see you socially, so would you mind if we did that instead?" I said no, and he tore up the card right in front of me.

We were married a year later. By then, I had Gracie for a substitute mother and now I was going to have a husband, too.

6

$\mathcal{S}$imon comes padding into my bed-
room early the next morning, carefully carrying in his pudgy little
hands the little screened jar containing his firefly. He climbs up on
the bed, and I make room for him under the covers, and for a while,
the three of us—two humans and one insect, in an example of in-
terspecies accord—snuggle under the blankets. Then he whispers,
"Why is your hair like that?"

"What is it like?" I say.

"I don't know," he says. "It has orange spots in it."

"I had a run-in with a bottle of hair coloring," I tell him.
"Don't worry. It'll get fixed up later today."

"I like it," he says. He reaches over with a plump finger and
touches it gently. "I think you look like a firefly."

"Great. That was exactly the look I was going for." I tackle him
in a bear hug and roll him back and forth, and when I stop, he
wiggles down close to me. And fidgets.

"What if we all had fireflies in our hair all the time and we
couldn't sleep at night because our room kept flashing off and on
and off and on?" he says. This is the first what-if question of the
day, and I know from experience we can get up to one hundred by
breakfast.

I say, "Did Lily the firefly keep flashing all night in your room?"

"Yeah," he says. "That's how fireflies talk."

Then he remembers his very favorite activity when he's in my
room, which is making a quick burrow to the bottom of the bed,

churning up the covers as he goes and making motorboat-in-distress noise. I have to hang on to the sheet for dear life or it will be caught in his vortex. Then, from the bottom of the bed, he says in his automatic robot voice, "Now. I. Am. Going. To. Be. A. Radio. Man. And. Talk. To. You. Are. You. Ready?"

"Ready, Radio Man."

"Okay. Lily Brown. Question. Why. Isn't. Daddy. Your. Husband. Anymore?"

"Well, Mr. Radio Man," I say, "we got a divorce. That's why."

"Lily Brown. Why. Did. You. Get. A. Bevorce?"

"Because, Mr. Radio Man, we made a mistake when we got married in the first place. We thought we could stick it out for fifty or sixty years, but, alas, we could not. Let's go get some pancakes, shall we?"

"Why?"

"Why, what?"

"Why, alas, you could not?" He pokes his head out, speaking now in his regular voice.

I just look at him. Um . . . how to explain it? Innocence, grief, unrealistic plans for the future, the O.J. verdict, the RSVP thing? Maybe the fact that Teddy is always expecting the very worst and needs daily—no, minute-by-minute—pep talks? Maybe because he isn't at all like the men I am normally attracted to? Maybe because he isn't like my father?

"It's hard to explain. Sometimes mommies and daddies just can't stay loving each other even when they wish they could."

Simon sits cross-legged on the bed and looks at me from underneath his long bangs. He has the most delectable chubby cheeks, and brown hair that reminds me of milk chocolate with butterscotch swirled in. "Maybe," he says nonchalantly, "if you don't want to marry Daddy again, you and I could maybe get married sometime. If you want to."

I smile at him. "Thank you. That's a very nice offer, but they

56

don't let mothers and sons get married. Causes problems with the genetic codes, I think."

He laughs and scrambles to his feet and starts jumping on the bed. He's wearing his red railroad pajamas, and his hair flies up in the air with each jump. He's grinning from ear to ear. "Come on! Jump with me!"

So I do. I put Lily the firefly carefully on the floor, and then I get up on the bed, too, and take both of Simon's hands, and we jump as high as we can—up and down, up and down, until we are nearly breathless.

SIMON AND I always go to the diner for banana pancakes on Saturday mornings, so once we've discussed our marriage options and jumped on the bed to the point of exhaustion, we get ourselves dressed and walk into town. Even though it's a warm, humid morning, I'm wearing my dad's old watch cap because, frankly, when I looked at my hair in the mirror this morning, I nearly passed out from the shock of what I'd done. I actually got a little queasy standing there—queasy enough that I called Jillian, my hairdresser, and confessed everything. She was not all that sympathetic, I've got to say. Wanted to know if I'd lost my mind buying a home kit instead of going to her, a Certified Professional, to have her put highlights in my hair—and then she told me she couldn't help me fix it; she's heading off on a two-week vacation and she's all booked, even when she gets back. She ended the conversation with "So you'll have a month or two of looking kind of punkish. It'll give you a chance to express your wild side."

It's possible she's still mad at me for setting her up with Teddy.

After I talked to her, I called five other hair salons—but it's Saturday, as one woman acidly reminded me. Nobody has an extra two hours in their schedule to fix a hair disaster. And in fact, no one has any time all week, when it comes right down to it.

"You know what this means? You are forcing me to go and buy yet another kit," I said to her, but she'd already hung up. I continued on with the dial tone: "When I have to go around looking like a complete freak, it's going to be because of people like you. I hope you can live with yourself."

Naturally, Simon and I run into everybody we know at the diner—Joe Wiznowski is grouchily out running errands, which he has to do all by himself since his wife, Paulette, died last summer; Anginetta Franzoni is on her way to the post office; Leon and Krystal are lollygagging and grinning over strawberry waffles with piles of whipped cream—and they all say I'm insane to be wearing a winter cap on such a warm morning. I tell them my hair has been sent out for repair and I didn't want to sunburn my scalp by going around bald-headed, and they all laugh and say, "Oh, *you!*" and "Simon, your mom is such a riot, isn't she?" Then Simon and I finish eating and go to the drugstore, and after I study all the possibilities in the hair-care aisle, I buy another hair-painting kit just like the first one. Perhaps, with one more try, I really can even out the blobs and make them into nice delicate highlights. Hair coloring, I think, might be just another one of those things in life—like motherhood and marriage—that you have to practice until you get it right.

I LOVE Saturday. For me, it's house-cleaning day, which I have to confess I'm a little addicted to. I know, I know. This smacks of the 1950s and Donna Reed running around in heels and a ruffly little apron, pushing a carpet sweeper and smiling. Believe me, I'm the last person who ever thought this would happen to me. But it's while I'm getting out all my special cleaning products—the beeswax furniture polish, the fragrant sandalwood oil, the nonstreak glass cleaner, the ostrich-feather duster, and my apron with all the pockets—that I feel most connected to this house, and to myself. There's something therapeutic about shining and polishing everything, especially when there's no one around to point out that you've missed a spot, or that perhaps this isn't a worthwhile use of time, that it's something losers do, people who have no life.

Today, with Simon gone to his friend Christopher's house for a playdate, I put on Bonnie Raitt full-blast and dance around the rooms, waving my feather duster in the air and singing at the top of my lungs. I shimmy past the windows, dusting the sills. I love getting at all the little crevices and grooves in the old wood. Outside, I see that the Sound is calm and flat, a silver coin against a sky almost deep purple with wispy fluffs of clouds. A breeze stirs my mother's old lace curtains. I watch the dust motes float down through a sunbeam, and, just as I did when I was a child, I try to catch them with my hands before they land.

I love this house. It was once just a drafty turn-of-the-century summer cottage, with beamed ceilings, wainscoting, and plank floors, until my parents winterized it and tried to make it civilized. They may have made their mark on it, but nothing they did ever changed its damp, salty character. I know every board, every knothole in the floors, and all the places where the glass in the upstairs window gets so wavery that the outdoors looks like an optical illusion.

There are, of course, at least a million things wrong with the house: the stairs creak and groan under our footsteps, the closet under the stairs has a family of mice I can't seem to get rid of, and the porch railing needs painting from blistering in the sun. The bookshelves in the living room are starting to sag. One year I had to put in all new storm windows because the old windows were leaking and ruining the siding. And three years ago, I replaced the roof when my bed kept getting wet. The trees need trimming, and an evil woodpecker has drilled a hole in the side of the house.

But it's all mine. My favorite room is the kitchen, which is large now and light, with Italian tile floors, a central island, a stone fireplace, a large picture window that looks out over the Sound and the garden, and a sliding door leading out onto the porch. Big copper pots hang on hooks from the ceiling beams, and the sideboard is filled with my mother's colorful Fiestaware and mixing bowls. The round oak table is the same one I used to sit at in my highchair, and when Dana was born, she sat there, too, and then Simon. I had my first kiss in the mudroom off the kitchen, and I both conceived and then went into labor with Simon in the upstairs bedroom.

There are three bedrooms upstairs—the master bedroom overlooking the back of the house and the Sound, and two smaller bedrooms. Simon sleeps in the room that Dana had, and my old bedroom is now the place where I've put my mother's paintings—the secondary ones, the ones that aren't displayed on the walls—and her old, cracked watercolor sets and canvases. The closet, I think, even has some of hers and Daddy's clothes, things I've never been able to bring myself to part with.

I'm upstairs dusting the carved mahogany pineapples on the bedposts of my parents' old bed when I look over and see that the answering machine light is blinking twice. The first message is from Teddy, who whines that he wants me to let him know immediately if Kendall calls. I laugh and shake my head.

But I stop laughing when I hear the second message. It's from that Southern guy again, the one who left a message for Dana last night. In a teasing, lazy voice, he says, "Hey, chick, this is Randy. I need to talk to you. Call." Then he clears his throat, like he's waiting for her to pick up the phone, and then he says, in a voice that sounds much more ominous, "Oh, Daaaaana? Ever heard of a little thang called grand theft auto? I'd hate to have to lay that on you, sweetheart. You better call me. I'm waaaaiting . . ."

7

$\mathcal{A}$s soon as I'm finished cleaning the house, I get out the new hair-coloring kit and stare for a very long time at the beautiful, sun-streaked blonde on the front of the box, a woman who probably did not use a do-it-yourself product to get that look—or if she did, it's clear that she didn't get interrupted by her ex-husband and have to wrap a towel around her head. I take ten very deep, cleansing breaths for courage, and then, when that doesn't make me feel better, I do a few rounds of calisthenics, some abdominal crunches, and some muscle flexes for strength. Then back to cleansing breaths. I will flood my body with oxygen . . .

The phone rings, startling me. I just know it's going to be *that guy*. I snatch up the receiver and shout, "Who *is* this?"

There's a silence, then Maggie says in a low voice, "Um. It's me. Is this a bad time?"

"Oh, thank goodness it's you," I say. I tell her about the weird phone calls for Dana and then how I've dyed parts of my hair the color of Cheez Doodles, and how that led Teddy to think we should get back together. To each of these alarming developments, she says, "*What?* Are you kidding me?" And then I say, "Listen, just get off the phone and come over and help me put some more streaks in my hair because right now I look like some kind of freak, and I can no longer go outside among the other humans."

She can hardly keep herself from laughing. "Did you lose your mind or something? What made you do that?"

"I have no idea. But now I need you to come help me."

"I can't. First of all, I've got to work this afternoon, and second of all, if you think I could succeed in getting your hair to be the right color, you really do need a shrink. God, this is so not like you. And why did you want highlights? You've got great hair."

"You are not helping," I say.

"Why don't you just go see Jillian?"

"She's on vacation. And anyway, I bought another kit. It won't be hard to get rid of the orange."

"Listen. I'm sorry. I think you should go get Gracie to fix you up. She's your surrogate mom, and I think this is in her job description."

"I thought it was in the best friend job description."

"No. Surrogate moms do hair color. Best friends are certified for manicures and hangover remedies and man troubles and a bunch of other stuff. Gracie will make your hair look perfect."

I sigh.

"Okay," she says, "I've got to make this quick because I'm on my way to work—but I've got a Dear Lily question for you. And be honest. You know how Mark used to say he wanted us to have kids, and lately he's been kinda backing off from that?"

"Yeah." We've had about a hundred conversations about this lately. They've been married for five years, and now, just when Maggie really wants to have a baby, suddenly Mark—who really is turning into a Problem Husband—is making her use two different kinds of birth control. He even makes her *show* him that she's taking her pill and putting in her diaphragm. It's kind of creepy, actually.

"Well," she says, "I was thinking I'd, you know, *fake* the birth control, you know, like poke a hole in the diaphragm and see what happens. You know? Because I think he'd be happy once he actually *had* the kid. He's just weirded out about it in advance. And I could say it was an accident. You think that's wrong?"

"You're joking, right?"

"How else am I going to get a kid, Lily? And I swear, he's going to love being a dad once it happens."

"Here's how you get a kid with him: you go to couples therapy. You talk it through."

"But you know how he is. He's just going to keep putting it off until I'm too old to have kids, and then that's going to be that. And then he'll be as sorry as I am that it didn't work out. We'll live our old age regretting that we don't have any grandchildren to love us."

"Oh, I get it. You're tricking him so you can save him from all that regret later."

She laughs a little. "Hey, yeah. It's a humanitarian gesture on my part."

"Oh, Mags, I feel so bad for you, but, sweetie, you don't want a baby under those conditions. Mark would be furious, and he'd have a right to be."

She's silent for a moment, and then she says, "I've gotta go," in a thick voice. "I just got to the office."

"Okay," I say. "Listen . . . I'm sorry. I really am. He's being a jerk, but you should talk about it with him again."

But she's hung up the phone.

GRACIE IS fearless and brave in every way, and when I show up at her door with my heavy heart, my orange hair, and my highlighting kit, she pulls me inside and says all kinds of no-nonsense, comforting, motherly things, including that she's seen worse—hell, she's *done* worse—and she thinks she can fix my hair right up. "And if we need it, there's always Plan B," she says.

"What is Plan B in this particular case?" I ask her. "Professional help?"

"Actually, I was thinking more like shaving your head and becoming a Hare Krishna and hanging out at the airport, soliciting money. Or did they outlaw that?" She studies me for a moment. "But now that you mention it, why *are* we amateurs trying to fix this? Why don't you just go somewhere and pay the money to have it look perfect?"

"Because no one can do it for at least a week, and because we are strong, capable women who can correct our own mistakes without experts," I say. "And corporate America would not sell us a kit that was designed to make us look this hideous."

"Okay," she says. "I'm in."

I laugh. Gracie is close to seventy years old, and she always dresses in caftans and vests and cool things with embroidery on them, all left over from her counterculture days, when she described herself as an angry, visionary lesbian-feminist. Her short gray hair stands up in what she calls "exciting little spikes," which I know she forms with something called hair wax.

Whenever I come over here, I'm always struck by the amazing fact that she and my mother were best friends for so many years—my mother, who was so cool and elegant and such a neat freak, a woman of gleaming surfaces, and Gracie, who could not be more opposite. She is a professor of poetry, and she prefers a life filled with papers and books stacked in haphazard piles around her house. Even her kitchen, where we settle down for tea served in smudgy mugs, has floor-to-ceiling bookcases crammed with pamphlets and hardbound first editions and paperbacks and CDs. Her stovetop burners are covered with a microwave (a nod to the need to sometimes have hot food), the *Oxford English Dictionary,* and a CD player, which is right now playing Bach's *Goldberg Variations.*

Gracie moves a stack of books off a kitchen chair and plugs in her little teapot, which comes to life, hissing and spitting. "First, some green tea," she says. "When you're fighting with your hair, you need plenty of antioxidants." She grins at me and says, "But I think this is actually a fight with your personality, am I right?"

I blink. Of course she's right. "Please," I say. "Don't start telling me how I had the perfect hair color and now I've ruined it."

"Okay. It was hideous before and now it's practically wonderful."

"Well." I trace a circle in toast crumbs on her table. "I made mistakes. For one thing, Teddy came over to my house while I was doing this kit, and I didn't want to have a whole conversation with him about why I was doing it, so I just wrapped a towel around my head and then left the stuff on too long. What I *wanted* was nice exciting blond highlights."

"Oh, they're exciting, all right," she says. "But we can fix them. I think. Now did you *want* them in these interesting circles, or should we go for long streaks? What do you think?"

"I think I'd be happy if I just looked somewhat normal."

"Okay. Normal look coming up."

We mix up the bleach stuff in the kit's little white plastic tray, and I show her how she's supposed to paint it on my curls in nice thick streaks. We drink our tea and I find myself telling her about Teddy's date with Kendall and how it was so awful that he suggested we get back together again, and then about the phone call for Dana and how it makes me feel so uneasy. For the first time since last night, I feel how tense I am. It's a tension that even cleaning the house didn't take care of.

For a moment she's concentrating on getting the white gel placed just right on my hair and then she says in a thoughtful voice—I call it her poet's voice—"You know, sweets, sometimes when people do something like throw orange dye at their own hair, they're really making a statement about other things in their life. Tell me the truth. You're feeling old, aren't you?"

"Yeah." I look over at her. She looks about a hundred herself, with her crazy stick-up hair and the gridwork of lines and wrinkles on her sun-weathered face. I find myself idly wondering if she feels she missed out on a lot of life because she never had a real partner.

As long as I can remember, she's lived alone, and although I imagine she's had lovers and admirers—how could she not?—there's never been anybody she felt close enough to to make a life with here in the colony. She's had her poetry, of course, and conferences and a little circle of friends and colleagues—but I can't imagine her getting, well, *laid*. Funny how we talk about lots of things, but never about her love life. I think it's because she's from a different generation. *And* she's my surrogate mom. Who wants to talk to a mom about her sex life?

"I suppose," she's saying, "that a person can just go so long in the same old rut. . . ." And I think, surprised, that she has read my mind and is now going to tell me about some lover she's met. But then I realize she's talking about me—and my hair.

"And you've been in this rut for a pretty long time now," she says. "Taking care of everybody else, not really having any action for yourself."

I laugh a little. "I don't think I'd know what to do with action," I tell her. "I just want to take care of Simon and do my column and keep the house. My life is really the way I like it right now."

"Well, possibly, but I think your hair is telling a different story."

"A cry for help?" I say and smile at her. "Listen, to paraphrase Freud, sometimes a box of hair color is just a box of hair color. It doesn't mean anything else, except that last night I was in the drugstore buying baby shampoo for Simon, and then I got seduced by all the highlighting kits. That's all this is."

She has a way of looking at me as though she sees right through to what I'm not saying. "So. No guy on the horizon?"

"A guy! Are you kidding? I'm always hanging around with Teddy. He's over at my house six evenings out of seven these days. There wouldn't be room for a guy on the couch with us."

She laughs. "Ah, our poor little Teddy," she says. "And poor little Lily, who feels somehow that she's got to take care of him and find dates for him. Just tell me one thing: Where did you get this overdeveloped sense of responsibility you seem to have? Why don't you tell Teddy to get his butt on home, and then you find yourself some nice man and have a little fun? Come on. You're only thirty-four!"

She pauses. "I know it sounds like a stupid cliché, but your life isn't going to stay on hold forever, you know."

"My life isn't on hold. I'm living my life."

"I think, if I may offer some advice—and I know that I can, since you're sitting here with goop on your hair and can't run away—that you need to force yourself to move just a tiny bit forward. I know you feel guilty as hell about divorcing Teddy"—I start to protest, but she holds up her hand and goes on—"and before that, you felt guilty as hell about Dana running away, and before that you probably felt guilty as hell about . . . who knows what—the fact that the sun comes up in the East and not the West—but I think you've paid off whatever guilt debt you thought you owed, and it's time you got on with things. Simon's nearly five, Teddy's truly capable of living his own life without your help, and Dana is long gone. So it's your turn. Live a little. Take a lover. Believe me, you have the choice of deciding if you want to stay in fear of change your whole life, or . . ."

"But do you think Dana's okay? I mean, that phone call . . ."

She leans down close to my face. "Do not," she says, "worry about Dana, because I can guarantee that wherever she is, she's not worried about you. People like Dana always end up on their feet. They make their own opportunities. For God's sake, Lily, give yourself a break."

LATER, she rinses the dye out and, afterward, we stand in front of the mirror together while I towel-dry my hair, both of us smiling like happy idiots, waiting, expecting everything to be so perfect because we're incurably optimistic and that's the way this should turn out.

Then, when I see the results, I almost can't breathe. The parts that were orange have now turned a breathtaking, rancid yellow, and there seem to be new orange streaks here and there among the brown and tarnished gold. We stand there together, staring in silent dismay.

After a long moment, Gracie says, "Hmm. It may be time to get the shaver out and then go to the airport. I'll play the tambourine there with you, if you want."

8

$\mathcal{I}$'m a wreck when I get home, all restless and edgy and dislocated. Numb, really. "It's ridiculous to get this way over hair color," I said to Gracie—but she said, "We both know it's not just hair color." Just the same, though, she twittered around, went through her desk drawer, her closet, and her bedside table, and came up with some Indian print scarves for me to wrap around my head.

"You'll look so cool in these," she said. I stood there, looking at her numbly. "A whole new personality! Who knows what kind of change you'll attract if you put these on?"

Right. Like *I* could get away with the flamboyant look she can wear. I'd look like a little girl playing dress-up. But I was too tired to explain that fact to her—that she and I are different. She is brave, and I am so tired and fearful. I took the scarves so that I wouldn't hurt her feelings, just in case she felt awful about making my hair now a tricolored disaster instead of just a bicolored calamity.

"Listen," she said, "I've got to leave now because I'm going to meet some people in New Haven for dinner. Why don't you come with me? You'd love these women."

"No, no. I'm fine."

Before I left, she hugged me and said she was so sorry for me and my hair, and that those kits ought to have warning labels on them; if a professor of poetry and an advice columnist couldn't make them work, what hope did the rest of humanity have? Obviously they weren't fit for regular people to use.

"So what *will* you do tonight, if you won't come with me?" she said, running around and gathering up her bag and her keys to go out.

"Simon and I are going to have our usual wonderful Saturday night together catching fireflies," I told her.

She frowned at me.

"We like catching fireflies. How long since you caught a firefly? It's so much fun."

But then, while I'm walking back home along the street, my cell phone rings, and it's Teddy, saying that Simon is going to stay over at his friend Christopher's for supper. They're having hamburgers and hot dogs, and the boys are having such a good time Christopher's mother would love it if he stayed. "I'm out anyway, so I'll bring him home later," Teddy says.

So. A free evening. Maybe it's a sign. What I *should* do, I think, is go over and knock on Sloane's door, and when he answers, just push him up against the wall and start kissing him. That would be dramatic, wouldn't it? *That* would bring about a little change, huh?

But I won't.

Well, I might.

No. I won't.

Let it be noted for the record, though, that I thought of it. That Dear Lily, stuck in a rut, maddened by stubborn orange and yellow spots in her hair and carrying three Indian print scarves she has no intention of ever wearing, at least entertained the possibility of having great, hard-driving sex, and then operatic romantic complications, with a young stud.

The house, when I get inside, has that lovely early-twilight hush, with the yellow light streaming through the kitchen window, lighting up the island, slanting across the tile floor, and illuminating the blue vase of roses that I picked yesterday. From the front hall, you can see all the way down to the Sound, see the dazzle of light on the deep blue water, see a little piece of the lawn and the beach plums, as well as a wide swatch of blue sky with wispy white clouds.

I go to the kitchen and just stand there, looking out at the flat blue water. I don't know what I'm looking for—boats, maybe. A life, perhaps. Something on the horizon. Anything. Then, out of the corner of my eye, I sense something moving, and I turn my head slightly toward the sliding glass door.

I scream as loudly as I ever have in my life.

My sister is standing outside on the porch, her face pressed against the glass, grinning in at me like a psychopathic maniac.

9

*T*his is awful, but my first inclination is to open the glass door and start pummeling her. But that's just the screaming hysteric inside me talking. I hate getting startled this way—always have. And actually, as soon as my throat recovers somewhat from being turned inside out and my heart manages to return to a normal rhythm, I am quite overcome at the sight of her, at the knowledge that she's really, really here. Except for the thing about wanting to knock her unconscious, I might even be sort of glad to see her.

I unlock and open the sliding door, and she comes in laughing and grips me in one of those iron-clad death hugs that leave you paralyzed for a bit, and for a moment I close my eyes tightly and think, *This is Dana. Dana is hugging me.* But I am still limp from fright. I am capable only of the most rudimentary imitation of a hug.

"You scared the daylights out of me," I say.

"Well, what do you think you did to *me?* I thought some monster was sneaking up behind me, the way you let loose," she says, still laughing. I can't help but notice that she's got a Southern accent—a little bit synthetic, like something that came from the factory rather than straight out of anyone's childhood. She doesn't look at all like she looked before; the Goth accessories are gone, and her hair is now back to its original dark blond and she's wearing it up in one of those careless, artless wads that look like a geyser has sprouted at the top of her head. But it's her, all right. It's just that she's twenty-eight now—not eighteen anymore. People change.

"Whew," she says, looking around. "I didn't think you'd evah get home." She's got on a flimsy pink knit shirt, white capris, and flip-flops. She's wearing pale pink lipstick and—I don't know why I notice these things, but I do—her fingernails and toenails are polished a bright lime green, but they're all chipped and her fingernails are bitten down, almost to the quick. She's all tanned now, dried out, and—well, she's still rail-thin, like she was when she was a teenager. When she hugged me, in fact, it was a lot like holding onto a baby bird, those little shoulder blades sharp like wing bones. Her eyes are glittery bright as she takes everything in.

"So look at us!" she shrieks and flings her arms wide. She doesn't seem to notice that I haven't moved one inch, that I seem to be rooted to the spot next to the door. "Gawd*damn, girl! We're together again!* I'm here! Can you be*lieve* it?"

I nod. But everything seems all wrong somehow, like something she pictured herself saying as she was waiting out there on the porch before she knew I'd go catatonic at the sight of her.

I try to remember that my reaction is probably important to her, so at first I concentrate on looking pleased instead of shell-shocked, and next I strive for some movement of my limbs just to show I'm alive; I walk over to the sink experimentally. She's looking around the house like she's in a museum, which is how it must seem to her, like something from the ancient past.

"Wow! Would you just look at this place! My gawd, I never thought I'd get here again!" she squeals, and then she's walking around the kitchen and picking things up and putting them down again, talking without really saying anything, the way people do when they're way too tense. She says she's been sitting out there on the porch swing for more than an hour now, waiting for me to come home, and that she met the "hunky guy" in the other half of the house, and he gave her an orange to eat and assured her that I still lived here, and then they talked about guitar playing and bands, and how did I get so lucky to have somebody who looks like that living right next door, and then she's on about the weather, and how her feet are swollen from the humidity, and that she hid the truck on another street because it's got these Texas plates—yes, she's been livin' in Texas, don't mess with Texas is so true, never was a sayin' more true than that one—and she wanted me to be surprised but maybe not *that* surprised. She thinks now it's just a good thing I hadn't had a gun when I first saw her, and wow, this place looks just the same. How surprising, really. Didn't I want to change everything around, make it really mine? Didn't I?

This is a question. She stops talking and looks at me, waiting.

"No," I say. "It seemed fine to me the way it was."

"Oh, *really?*" she says. "Really?" She picks up, one by one, the saltshaker, a pot holder, a candlestick, and looks at them as though they were relics, saying to each one, "Wow. Wow." And then, "Oh, wow, *this!*" over the plate my mother used to put her pound cakes on. "You can't imagine what a rush this is for me, to see all this again. It's like it all stayed right in the same place this whole time, you and the saltshaker . . . you know? . . . I feel like the earth has just stood still here or something. I don't know how else to explain it."

"Yeah, the saltshaker and I just stayed right here."

She grimaces.

I try to browbeat myself into being nicer, but I can't. I still feel wobbly inside, from being startled by her, and angry. Ten years—*ten years* and she's standing here talking about how I'm using the same saltshaker. It's almost surreal.

"So." She turns to me with a bright, high-wattage smile and comes and flops down into the armchair, swinging her legs over the arms. "Tell me about you. Hey! You've got a kid now. A boy, right? I'm tryin' to think of how old he'd be."

A memory comes back to me now, of writing to her after Simon was born. I had gone into our attorney's office armed with a fairly substantial case of postpartum emotional overload, which made me reckless and sure of myself, and I'd insisted, hysterically, that the attorney include a note from me when he sent Dana her next check. He agreed, out of a pity that was just awful to behold. I remember I was filled with moisture everywhere—breasts, eyes, nose, privates, everything was leaking—and I sat down damply, with Simon strapped to my chest, and wrote to Dana that she was now an aunt. "His name is Simon," I wrote in an unsteady hand. I missed her so much at that moment that I would have struck out, walking, across the United States to find her. What I really wanted was to shake this bespectacled, bald little man until I could make him tell me where she was, just where he was going to send the check. Instead, I sat there, kept writing, "He looks like you. Please, please come and meet him. And please, please always know that I miss you and love you."

It wasn't until six months later that I got a response. Even then, it wasn't addressed to me, just to Simon's initial, which she'd scrawled on a postcard: "S.—Congrats on getting born. Make your mama take better care of you than she usually takes of things. P.S. Look around at the houseplants, and you'll know what I mean."

Remembering that little slice of hatred that the postman handed me that day sends me reeling back into thinking how hard all this has been.

"He's four," I say.

"And his name is . . . uh, Sam?"

"Simon."

"*Simon.* Duh. I'm really strikin' out. And—well, the guy next door, he said you weren't married but you might as well be. Your ex is hangin' over here all the time, he said."

"Oh, really?" I say.

"That's what he said. He said the ex can't keep away from you, that you're like nectar to the bees for him."

"No, he didn't say that."

"Well. He didn't, it's true, but he was thinking it. I could tell." She smooths down her shirt, which has ridden up a little on her midriff, and looks at me dead on. There's a long silence, and her expression changes. "So. You're still real pissed off with me, aren't you?"

I don't want to be pissed off—God, I don't want to be pissed off. I want to be able to go over and hug her for real this time, and welcome her home, and show her where she can put her suitcase (assuming she has a suitcase), and open up my whole life to her. I close my eyes a little bit and ask something inside me to work up even just a little piece of that emotion—just a start, I say. I promise I'll work on it, too, if just the first little inkling could come my way. I can't, right just then, speak.

"God almighty, you're *freaking* pissed," she says. Then, when I don't answer right away, she jumps up from her chair. "Well," she says. "It's been real nice seeing you. I'll get out of your way now."

THE FACT IS, oddly enough I like her a little better after she says that. It's like she's finally acknowledged that things just aren't going to be so fakely sweet and nice, that there's *stuff.* I realize as she's walking fast through the front hall, headed for the front door, that I don't want her to leave. Of course, I also don't want to say so, either. All I can think to do is just trail behind her, trying to keep up with her while making it look as though I'm just nonchalantly walking toward the front door myself, strolling there, really, while I try to think what to say next.

I think how weird this would be if she just got back into her truck—wherever she's stashed it—and headed back to Texas. What a weird chapter in the story of Lily and Dana that would be. I think of telling the colony people, "Yep, Dana was here for ten minutes and then she left again." And then how long before I'd ever see her again?

"Wait," I say finally, out of breath from fear.

She keeps walking.

"Look, I just got startled . . ."

She doesn't turn around, and I beam fury and rage and frustration into the back of her head. And then, at last, at long last comes the feeling I have hoped for: of wanting to get it right this time around. I try to send that into her instead. And, what do you know, she stops at the front door and turns to me.

We stand there facing each other. She has the same freckles I remember from when she was a kid, and her chin is still pointy and her eyes have that kind of dazed look that I remember from when she was so little and was mine to protect.

I reach over tentatively, let my arm float noncommittally in the air as though it *might* be coming over to touch her but also might just possibly be thinking of scratching my back instead, and she reaches over, too. We hug each other, awkwardly. She's about three inches taller than I am, and my nose bumps into her chin.

I say, into her shoulder, so low I don't think she can hear me: "Are you planning to stay? Are you back here for good?"

She laughs into the top of my head and says, "Lily? What the hell were you thinking with this hair?"

WHAT CAN I SAY? Everything is weird, just at first. She wants to—*needs to*—go through the whole house, touching every object, as though there's a power in them that she must come into contact with. She also can't get over the fact that I've changed so little of it. "The *couches*?" she says. "You didn't even change the couches?"

"Why would I change the couches?"

"Anyone would change the couches," she says. "This has been your house for *ten years.* You would want to make your mark on it, I would think. Make it yours. This is still very much Momma's house, you know."

I shrug. "I must have missed that lesson in life," I tell her. "The lesson I got instead was, if the couches aren't torn up and no cats have peed on them, why not just keep 'em?"

"But you haven't changed *anything*," she points out. "Except, apparently, your hair. But, really, the pictures on the wall are the same pictures. What have you been doing for the past decade?" She turns and looks at me. She is really asking me this.

I don't have an answer. What *have* I been doing? I got married. I had a baby. Got a divorce. I learned how often you need to water the rosebushes and what kind of fertilizer they like. And which Horrible Bugs you can live with and which ones need an exterminator. And when the taxes on this place are due. And how nice the floors look when you use beeswax on them.

"Do you work?" she says with just a touch of concern in her voice, like an occupational therapist might say it. *Do you have any interests, dear?*

"Of course I do."

"What do you do?"

"Actually, I write an advice column for the newspaper."

At that, she laughs so hard I think she's going to fall off the couch. I just sit and stare at her. When she can speak again, she says, "That is so perfect, sooo perfect! You get to tell people what to do? Talk about typecasting! Wow. How'd you ever get *that* gig?"

I tell her it's a little start-up paper and that it's not really that big a deal. I'm no Ann Landers, after all. "And what do *you* do?" I say.

"Oh, I'm just fucked up. It's pretty much a full-time job for me," she says happily.

LATER, at her request, we sit on the porch swing, and while I study her, she hand-selects little episodes from her life that she would like me to know. It's like she's carefully picking pieces of celery and onion out of a bowl of tuna fish salad, that's how obvious it is that I'm getting the edited version of her life. But I can't tell yet if the little bits she's handing me are the ones designed to show me that

78

deep down she's a competent human being, or if they're meant to make me feel she's just as dangerous, exciting, and madcap as she ever was, while I am stiff and boring and one-note. She tells me that most recently she lived in Texas, and was supposed to be getting married, *is* probably still supposed to get married, to a guy named Randy, when she just upped and split and drove back home.

"Oh, well, congratulations," I say, only barely listening. Suddenly I'm so tired and foggy I would like to just stretch out on the wooden floor and fall asleep.

"For what?"

"Didn't you just say you're getting married?"

She stares at me. "I said I *upped and split* on the guy. That means I'm not marryin' him."

"Maybe you're thinking it over. There's a long tradition of people taking long drives while they think over marriage proposals."

"Oh, really? And then what happens? Do they go through with it after the drive?"

"Depends on whether Hollywood is writing it or not."

"Oh. Well, I don't know who's writing it. I told you: I'm fucked up." She laughs, and I know that, for her, this means being fucked up is fun.

A couple of things suddenly come together in my head. "Oh my God," I say. "Did you say the guy is named Randy? He's been calling you here for the last few days. I think he wants his truck back."

She yawns and stretches out one of her long, tan legs, flexes her toes, frowns at the green nail polish, which deserves a frown, and says, "Well, he's not gettin' it, and he knows it. And if he thinks he is, he's stupider than I thought."

"Well," I say. "He wants you to call him."

"*I'm* not callin' the fucker. He doesn't have the sense to come in out of the rain, and he cheated on me with his dog trainer, and I don't think you can get any more of a cliché than that. He can kiss my behind if he can catch it, which I very much doubt he can." She sits back and drums her fingers on the back of the swing restlessly. "Jaysus, he's got some nerve. Callin' here."

I look at her. The sprouts of her hair are catching the last golden rays of the sunlight, and the little curls on her neck lie damply against her delicate white skin. I trace the back of the wooden swing with my index finger. "Dana," I say in a low voice, "why did you leave here? Back when you did?"

She looks at me in surprise. One of her very thin, almost pencil-thin eyebrows arches up. "Gawd, Lily, who remembers now? I just had to, is all. You remember how I was then. I was fucked up beyond belief. But let me tell you about Randy and what he did to me. You're just not gonna believe what I've been through!" And without missing a beat, she launches into a story of how she lived with him in a little old tract house in the suburbs with his sister, Dreena Sue, and *her* husband, a guy named Willems. When she says Willems's name, she stops and looks me in the eye and says, "Remember that name, honey, because this is the guy I really love. He's my soul mate." Then she says that although she's waited for him through lots of ups and downs, and they are always *there for each other,* it has become very clear that he's really not going to leave this Dreena Sue, and there is no point in Dana's waiting for him any longer—not that she wants him to get divorced, you understand, since she doesn't believe in breaking up families . . .

"So then why were you planning on marrying Randy?" I say, although I know the answer is going to make me feel even more tired, and it does.

She grins at me. "Ah, the advice columnist goes to work, right? That's you. Well, I'll tell you. Willems is this older guy, much more mature, and he has this theory that when you love someone, it's not the actual person you love—it's just that you've entered the force field of love, and so you're drawn to whoever is vibrating at that same frequency as you. So, it could be anybody! You see? And so he thinks that if I make Dreena Sue happy by marryin' her brother, then I could stay there and help her take care of her and Willems's little baby, and we'd all be together."

"Willems and Dreena Sue have a new baby?"

"Yeah."

My head is beginning to hurt. "Wait. So why would you *want* to stay there forever if it meant marrying a guy you didn't love, and if the guy you *do* love has a new baby with somebody else?"

"*Well,* you nut, because I wanted to be near Willems, and it was worth it because of the whole force field thing," she says, as though this should be obvious to anyone, and she gets that old familiar look on her face, the one that means I can't be expected to understand such undying, complex emotions. Each point has to be driven home into my head, and I'm already tired of having to nod so expressively just so she won't keep hammering at me.

"But start at the beginning," I say with some effort. "Tell me where you went right after you left here ten years ago."

"Oh, it's all such a long story," she says. "I think I might have to be drunk to tell it." She beams me over a sly smile and jumps up. "Say, do we have any Southern Comfort?"

"I don't think so. I don't even know what it is."

"Oh, it's the best thing ever, dahlin'. It's like a peach liqueur they make from bourbon. Best-tastin' thing in the whole world, I swear. I'm a little hooked on it, in a totally good way, of course." She stands up and does a few stretches and some side bends, touches her toes, and then unfolds herself until she's upright. Then she stares at me. It's apparently my turn to talk.

"Well," I say, "I'm sorry I don't have any of it. I've got some red wine, though. Merlot. Maybe a couple of beers in the fridge. Some Cokes."

"That's okay. I'll get some out of my truck. I just thought I'd save myself the trip if you had it in here," she says. "I really, really want you to try it. You're just not going to believe how good it tastes—and then, how you get so *calm* and *collected*"—here she imitates a glider, soaring through the air—"*and* if you have the sense to stop there, everything's just fine as it could ever be in the whole world, but if you keep on goin', you just get wasted, wasted, wasted. Sometimes I find I want to feel one way, and sometimes the other. I think a homecoming day calls for the other, frankly." And she laughs and grabs both my hands and pulls me to my feet. "Can you *believe* we're together again? Can you fucking believe it? I'm *here*!"

"Actually," I say, "I can't believe it. I feel like I'm in a dream or something."

"Let's get drinking!"

"Well, this isn't such a good time for me to start drinking. Teddy will be bringing Simon home from his friend's house, and to tell you the truth, I haven't had any dinner yet. I was about to start cooking when you came."

"Wow! Cooking dinner and everything," she says and pats me on the butt. "Aren't you just the homey little domesticated one!"

10

$\mathcal{I}$ expect that the fact that she couldn't remember Simon's name or his age means she won't have much interest in him, but I'm wrong about that. As soon as he gets home, she goes off like a set of Fourth of July fireworks. She's in the bathroom when Teddy's car drives up, so as soon as I hear the slamming of the car doors, I go outside and say, "Guess what! My sister is here. Simon, your Aunt Dana has come!"

Teddy raises his eyebrows at me and says, "Here? She's here?"

I nod at him, smiling steadily, and just then Dana swoops past me out of the door and goes right for Simon, as though he's a baby bird and she's a chicken hawk. Normally he doesn't go for this type of thing. He's a dignified child who prefers that strangers go through the proper stages—shaking hands first, telling him their name, perhaps inquiring about a specific interest of his—and then he will decide if he wants to pursue a more personal relationship. But he seems stunned into compliance by this auntie of his, who picks him up and starts twirling him in circles, saying nonsense things over and over. "This is Simon Pieman! Simon Pieman! And I'm Auntie Dana! Auntie Shanty Danty!"

Teddy and I have nothing to do but stand back and watch.

He points to his watch, meaning *When did she come?* And I hold up two fingers: *Two hours ago.* He motions: *Everything okay?* And I shrug: *Yeah. I guess so.*

"Tomorrow," she says to Simon, "you know what? I'm going to give you a big pack of gum. Because I've been readin' up on what aunties are supposed to act like, and they're s'posed to bring gum to their nephews, is what I found out! Did you know that? You probably already knew that, didn't you? You read the *Aunt and Nephew Code Book* long ago, I bet."

Then, after smothering him with hundreds of kisses, which she claims were sent special delivery to her just to give to him and to him only—it's corny but he laughs—she puts him aside and turns her attention to Teddy, palavering over him as though he's the real, current brother-in-law she was always dying to meet, hugging him and laughing about how it's just too damn bad she didn't get here in time for the actual marriage to still be intact. But these days . . . well, things don't last like they used to.

"Lily put up with me for two years, and then she couldn't take it anymore," he says in as Eeyore-ish a voice as you're going to hear outside of a *Winnie the Pooh* video. And she throws back her head and laughs and says, "Funny, she could put up with me for only two years, too. Maybe that's her cosmic limit with people."

Funny how they gloss over the part about how both of them were the ones who left *me*.

AFTER ALL the introductions and hugging, we go inside and I get out Momma's old daisy-covered tin recipe box, with all the index cards in Momma's handwriting—foods Dana used to adore. Cooking seems safe, I think. It'll give me something to concentrate on, something to do with my hands, which are so fluttery that they need to be put to work. Dana is all over the place, a jittery bundle of nerves. It's as though she's got to make her mark on everything, reclaim her territory. She does the human equivalent of peeing on the furniture: bouncing around the rooms, pulling stuff off the shelves, talking way too loud, playing records she used to remember, then taking them off the stereo and putting on new ones, hauling out the photo albums of us when we were little, calling to me to look at each thing she's rediscovering. She puts on Frank Sinatra as loud as possible, and takes one of Momma's seascapes off the wall, marches it over to Teddy, and says in an authoritative voice, "Look! Would you just *look* at the way my momma did clouds! You know anybody who does clouds like that?" She waits, staring at him, her eyes intense. "*Nobody* does clouds like that—nobody!"

Teddy laughs in confusion. Some screw in my head tightens another half turn, but I smile at her and wave recipe cards in her direction to get her attention. "Dana? Dana? Dana! Would you like mac and cheese, or meat loaf, or fried chicken?" I say. I have to yell to be heard over Frank Sinatra singing "The Lady Is a Tramp." Finally I go over and turn the sound down and look at her. "Listen, sweetie, I want to make you a coming-home feast! Just tell me what you want, and I'll make it."

But she's suddenly intent on dancing around the room with her eyes closed, crooning along with Sinatra, banging on her hip with an imaginary tambourine, and coming perilously close to knocking over lamps. We all watch her. You can't help it. Her energy takes up the whole space. I decide on the dinner myself—mac and cheese from scratch, the most comforting of the comfort foods. It used to be her favorite.

When the song's over, Dana's eyes fly open and she gets all excited again and insists that Simon and Teddy *must* go with her to her truck. Men love this truck! It is an excellent cherry red pickup with all kinds of quads and duals and traction stuff, cruise control, blah blah blah, she says. Teddy laughingly admits he hasn't the vaguest notion of what any of that stuff means, and she says, "Really? Because I was just showing off for you. I don't really have any idea what's under the hood of this thing. I just know that Texas men seem to think it's excellent."

Anyway, they're not *really* going out there to admire the engine, she tells him, winking. She wants to get the Southern Comfort and have the three of us drink some. You know, to really celebrate.

"Because *this* is my homecoming day! I didn't think I'd ever be here, but here I am. Yee-*hawwww*, honey!" And she spins Simon around in yet another circle.

We're all dazed somehow, as if she's cast a spell on us. I'm stunned to realize that my cheeks hurt, and only then do I see that they ache from smiling. I didn't even know I was smiling. It's more like a rigor mortis clench, actually. I grate up the heaps of sharp cheddar cheese, and whip up the cream and the flour and the eggs. It's then, looking down into this old blue bowl of my mother's, hearing the whirring of the mixer, that I have a moment of clarity, see that I'm simply showing off, trying way too hard to please her.

Look, dear prodigal sister, look over here! I have, for your pleasure and enjoyment, my ex-husband and my charming, precocious, friendly child. And here is the macaroni and cheese I can make at a moment's notice, just for you. And yes, here is the house itself, the house of your childhood, all clean and ready for you to step into again, out of life's turmoil. Music and familiarity and laughter and redemption. All for you.

All for you.

By the time they come back from the truck, I've put the macaroni in the oven to bake and am cutting up vegetables for a salad. Teddy pours the Southern Comfort—"May I?" he says gallantly—and then he puts on music and stands around smiling and looking debonair with his drink in his hand, like Hugh Hefner without the smoking jacket.

Simon, shy but sensing that this is going to be an important person in his life—a *relative*, after all, which we are short of—starts dragging out all his toys one by one for Dana to admire. He tries to get her attention with each one. She stops and pulls him into a dance with her while Grace Slick belts out a song about some pills making you larger and some pills making you small. Then she sinks down on the rug and really looks closely at the mechanism on Simon's toy backhoe, as though she's never seen anything more interesting.

"Look at this adorable boy!" she cries, and I suddenly love her for noticing him and seeing that he needs her to love the backhoe as much as he does, and a few minutes later I also love the way she just casually takes Teddy's arm and the three of them sway together, Dana and Teddy serenading me while I'm cooking, and Simon watching them with smiling, amazed eyes.

IT DOESN'T TAKE long for word to get out somehow that she's back. First, Maggie calls and wants the whole lowdown. Dana gets on the phone and squeals to her for a while: "I'm back! I'm back!" Then, after that, Leon stops by to bring back a jar of nails he'd borrowed, and is overwhelmed to see her. He has to keep dabbing his eyes while he gives her lots of fatherly hugs. He tells her about Mavis dying and that he's met a wonderful new woman who agreed, against her better judgment—and against everybody's better judgment *for* her—to marry him. He says the only thing that makes him happier than that is to think of Dana and me here together again, as sisters. "Your father would have wanted this," he says with watery eyes, and hugs us both.

I resolve again to stop minding Dana's quirks and to be nicer to her.

After they leave, Dana says, "So does that horrible Gracie still live here?"

"Gracie? Why do you think she's horrible?"

She rolls her eyes. "Well, don't you?"

"No. I like her. She's wonderful to us. She'd be here now, I'm sure, but she went out to dinner with a friend."

"Oh, really? Wow. I thought for sure she would have moved on to Provincetown or Northampton or someplace where she could have found some cute little chicks. . . ."

"No," I say. "She stayed." I can't remember if Dana had a problem with the fact that Gracie was gay, or if she didn't like it that she was Momma's best friend, or just what it is she could be objecting to. And before I can even think more about it, the oven timer goes off, and I get busy putting food on the tray, lining up the drinks, giving the salad a final toss. Finally we take our plates to the picnic table on the porch. It's dark, so I light some candles.

Dana takes a deep breath and flings her arms out wide, ready to make another pronouncement. "The smells of home!" she says. "You know, Willems has a theory that smell can actually reactivate all those centers of your brain, and you actually change the chemistry and can go back and see where your personality came from. He says you've reentered the force field that made you who you are, and that is a sacred place to be."

Teddy laughs indulgently and puts a huge helping of macaroni on his plate. "And just who is Willems?" he says.

"Oh, now, you haven't heard about Willems?" I say. "Willems is the love of Dana's life, past, present, and future, and he's big on theories about force fields."

Dana makes a face at me, and Teddy smiles at her and says, "Oh, is that so? How nice to have your future of love all sewn up!"

"It would be *very* nice," she says, and laughs. "Too bad he's married." She takes a drink of Southern Comfort and looks around at us. "But, then again, if he wasn't—hell, then I'd have to actually do somethin' about him, like get my act together, you know."

"Well," says Teddy. "You don't seem that far from getting your act together, if you ask me."

I look up just in time to see something, just a little *zzzt,* pass between them.

HERE'S SOMETHING WEIRD. She doesn't eat. I've compulsively gulped down about three huge helpings of mac and cheese when I notice that Dana has just pushed hers around her plate for a while, ingesting only a micron or two, and now has taken out a cig-arette. This irritates me, after all the work I did making the stuff for her. And now she's fouling the air with smoke? I don't think so. So I clear my throat and tell her that we don't really let people smoke on the porch or in the house. I tilt my head toward Simon to indicate that he might be the reason for this. He's digging into his mac and cheese.

"Can't smoke? What do you *mean*, I can't smoke?" she says and laughs. "Ohhhh, yeah, I forgot. I'm in *Connecticut* now, not the good ole South. In Texas, everybody still smokes. They're very civilized there when it comes to lettin' people have a good time."

"Well," I say tightly, "if you recall, I never did let you smoke in the house."

"Still—the porch *is* outside, and there is a breeze. I don't see what the big deal is with smoking here."

"The smoke goes inside," I say. "The porch is near the doors and windows."

Teddy shoots me the aren't-you-being-a-little-unreasonable look. I frown at him.

"Well," says Dana with a bitter little laugh, "then I guess I'll just have to go down on the beach to smoke. *That's* okay, isn't it? Doesn't interfere with the gills of the fish or anything?" She stands up.

"I think cigarette smoke could only be an improvement on the horrible, unhealthy smell that's already down there," Teddy says.

She laughs and looks at him. "So, big guy, you want to come down to the beach and keep me company while I perform a death-defying unhealthy act?"

"That's it?" I say. "You're not going to eat the macaroni and cheese I made?"

"Oh." She looks down at her plate, as if she's surprised all that food is still there. "You know what? I should have said something before. I don't really like to eat."

"You don't like to eat," I say flatly.

Simon gets out of his chair and sits on the floor to play with his toys.

"No," Dana says. "It's not my thing, really. I mean, this looks delicious, and I know this is really good stuff that you made and all that, but eating—well, lately, it mostly makes me feel sick. God knows what's wrong with me, but, hey, it keeps me thin not eating, so I say, why not just go with it?"

"Maybe you should get that checked out," I say, gathering up the plates.

She makes no move to help, just looks over at Teddy and smiles. "You comin', Teddy?"

He says he is, and shrugs at me apologetically. I wave him off. *Fine. Go.* "You might want to kiss Simon goodnight, because I'm putting him to bed while you're gone," I tell him, at which point Simon looks up from playing with his dinosaurs on the porch floor and starts protesting that he wants Auntie Dana to read him his stories and put him to sleep.

"Nope," I say cheerfully. "You've got me tonight."

"No! No! Auntie Dana! Auntie Dana can put me to bed tonight!" he yells. This really is one of the drawbacks nobody ever tells you about having children, the way they will turn on you in a heartbeat. I try to beam my most pointed I-Am-the-Mother expression in his direction, but he is having none of it. He goes over and hangs onto Dana's leg. She laughs and tells him that she would just *love* to put him to bed, but right now she has a blinding headache and she needs a cigarette almost worse than she's ever needed one in her whole life. "When you grow up, you'll understand," she says, and then sees my face and amends her remark to "Well, maybe you won't ever understand the need for cigarettes, but you'll no doubt need *something* very badly. And so I promise to put you to bed tomorrow night and we'll look at all your toys, I promise. It'll be fun."

Simon and I watch as she and Teddy head down to the beach.

She's saying, "Now have you always been Teddy or are you really a secret Theodore? Or an Edward? I'm just Dana. Dana Isabella, which I never thought went together. You know?"

Teddy is going to come back in a psychotic trance from all this talking she does, I think.

I look over at Simon. "Well, what do you think?" I ask him. "You like having an auntie, huh?"

"I think tomorrow she's going to give me gum," he says.

"Do you want gum?"

"I'm ready," he says grimly.

11

After I read the stories and sing the songs and get Simon tucked in, I go across the hall to the spare bedroom where Dana will sleep, and put clean sheets on the bed and straighten the desk. The room is not messy, exactly, just very tiny and cozy, with a sloped ceiling. It's the official guest room, although I can't remember the last time anybody slept here. While it waits for visitors, it serves as a kind of miscellaneous room, a borrowed room that belongs only to the past, a room filled with boxes of Christmas ornaments and old photo albums, stacks of art books, old bills, books, and things I never want to think about: my mother's unfinished artwork, invoices for home repairs, tax records, all that stuff I've had to force the adult in me to take care of. Now I put these things in the closet and close the lace window curtains. If Dana is staying—well, then I suppose we'll need to fix this up more.

If she's staying. My heart does a little series of calisthenics, a slow rollover. I can't begin to think of how that's going to be, if she's staying.

I can hear Teddy talking downstairs, and then there's the sound of an unfamiliar CD twanging on the stereo, the refrigerator door opening, and then the sliding glass door slamming shut. They've obviously come back from smoking, refreshed their drinks, and now they've gone back out onto the porch.

While I still have an ounce of privacy, I go to my room and call up Maggie.

"Wow. The *sister* returns," she says. "Who woulda thunk? How's it going, anyway?"

"It's good . . . I think."

"So. Where is she right this minute?"

"She's out on the porch with Teddy. I just put Simon to bed."

"Oh, good. You can gossip about her. How does she seem?"

"She's . . . okay. She's different, that's for sure. Not Goth anymore, but . . . well, actually she's still a little scary in a mostly annoying kind of way. Loud. Talks all the time but says nothing. I've already wanted to hit her five different times."

"Well, duh!" Maggie laughs. "She was *always* scary in an annoying kind of way, and you *always* wanted to hit her. The important thing is, how long is she staying?"

"That's the worst part. She hasn't said."

"Why don't you just come out and ask her?"

"I think I'm scared to know the answer."

"Yeah. I don't blame you. Sheesh." She's silent for a moment. "This is big."

"I know."

"Well, do you know why she came home? I mean, now?"

"She broke off an engagement, took the guy's truck, apparently, and came here."

"Oh, how nice. She's a fugitive car thief."

"Well, *Mags,* he cheated on her with his dog trainer. What else you gonna do but steal his truck and go? I mean, really."

"Obviously."

"Also, she's in love with a guy named Willems."

"Is he the guy who cheated?"

"No, apparently he's married to the *sister* of the guy who cheated. It's all unbelievably complex. We mere mortals aren't expected to truly get it."

"Don't worry. She won't stay long. She'll be bored here in no time."

"Yeah, but she doesn't do exits well, as I recall. We could be in for a wild ride." We're quiet for a moment, then I say as lightly as I can manage, "So, did you poke holes in your diaphragm yet?"

"No," she says and sighs. "There seems to be a new development. He now has decided that—get this—he doesn't want to have sex anymore."

"Ever?"

"Well, not for a while, he said. He came home today from a meeting with some clients—because, even though it's Saturday, he has to put in as much overtime as possible—and I got naked and waved the French tickler in front of him, and you know what he said? He said sex makes him too tired, and he can't function when he's not sharp."

"Did you remind him it's Saturday, and he doesn't need to function?"

"I tried to. He said he stays tired for days after sex."

There's a silence, during which I take the opportunity to cut off the circulation in my index finger by jamming it in the coils of the phone cord and wrapping the cord tight. Just yesterday at work I got a letter from a woman who found out her husband was cheating on her, and the first sign of it was that he didn't want to have sex anymore. When I can't stand it anymore, I say, "Maggie, I don't want to say this, but . . ."

"I know what you're going to say," she says.

"Do you ever, you know, call him on those nights when he's working late?"

She clears her throat. "What you're supposed to *do*—I read this somewhere—when you suspect your husband of *that,* you know, is get all the cell phone bills and the credit card receipts. Calling him when he works doesn't tell you anything. Even if he's at a hotel . . . what's that going to prove? You won't know. Not really."

"True."

"So I'm circling in on doing that," she says. "Maybe. When I get up my nerve."

"Yeah."

There's a silence, and then she says brightly, "Or maybe he's just got some weird neurological problem and sex makes him really, really tired."

"Well, sure," I say. "Let's go with that for tonight."

WHEN I GO out to the porch, Dana and Teddy are both curled up like commas at opposite ends of the swing, and talking in low voices. Thank God she seems to have come down from whatever antic, go-for-broke mood she was in. When I open the sliding door, he's leaning toward her, smiling.

She looks up at me and says, "Oh, honey? Could I have another glass of Southern Comfort while you're in there?"

"Sure," I say, although I'm not technically still in there.

"Me, too," says Teddy. "What the hell? It's Saturday night."

I go in and get both of them another glassful, and then go out and seat myself down across from them, in one of the rockers. I am just the slightest bit tense now that I've had a little while away from her. Also, the conversation with Maggie has not exactly improved my good feelings about the world in general. "So," I say in the friendliest possible voice, "what have you been talking about while I was gone?"

"Oh, I don't know—a little of everything, weren't we?" Dana says, undoing her hair from its scrunchy and shaking it out. Her hair falls to her shoulders in crimped little waves, wrinkled from being tied up. Her blond highlights catch the candlelight. I find myself wondering why fate gives some people nice, natural-looking streaks while other—perhaps even more deserving—people just get globs. Life is so unfair.

"I think," she says, "if you want to know the truth, that I was horrifyin' Teddy with the stories about growin' up here—how we all just walked into each other's houses and wore each other's clothes and slept in whatever bed we wanted to. He says we had no *boundaries*"—here she laughs and sort of pokes him with her toe—"but we didn't know nothin' 'bout no boundaries back then. We thought that was just the way the world was. Remember that? In fact, I *still* think that's the way the world should be. You know? I almost never think of my clothes as strictly my own. They kind of belong to anybody who can fit in 'em, is the way I see it. And I get everybody else's. That's just the way I am. He thinks I'm wacko, I'm sure."

Teddy, curmudgeonly, crabby old Teddy, who can't even buy anything from consignment shops because of the possible alien cooties that could get on him, laughs. "No, no, I think it'd be wonderful if life was that simple," he says. "I don't happen to think it's like that here these days, though. Not with all these old people. Hard to imagine Anginetta Franzoni wandering over and getting into a pair of your jeans, hey, Lily?"

I try to think of something clever to say but, really, I'm not in the mood for clever talk about the past. I was hoping we could move on to new business. I take a deep breath. "So, Dana," I say, smiling. "Wow! Everything's been so hectic tonight, with dinner and Simon and all, and then I'm afraid I hurt your feelings with that smoking thing, and I'm so sorry, but I really can't stand the smell of smoke anymore, just can't take it. But I've got to say, you look wonderful! Did I tell you that before?"

She's smiling at me warily. Anyone can tell this is the big windup for something. Teddy coughs a little. I finally just say it, "So, exactly what's up with you? Are you staying? Are you going to move back in? What's going on?"

The two of them look at each other. Dana starts laughing, and Teddy makes a little "ahem" sound, as if he's her spokesman for handling these matters. But she waves him off and says, "No, no, Teddy. Lily is somebody who likes to have things spelled out and organized, and I respect that." She looks at me and gathers her thoughts. "Well, sweetie, you know how I told you how I broke up with Randy when he cheated with the dog trainer? I left home mad, and then just on an impulse I decided that, hell, I'd keep on going and come to Connecticut just to see what was left of this place. I didn't really think you'd even still be here, to tell you the truth—I figured you'd gone back to California, or moved to Italy to buy a winery, or, let's see, that you were running a sweet potato farm in Oahu or somethin'." She laughs. "But now that I'm here— I don't know. I guess I don't ask those kinds of questions of myself. I just do what I do. I know that's a bad way to be, but it's the only way I can think of."

Then Teddy says, as if he needs to explain Dana to me, "She needs a rest. This woman has done a *lot* of running. Wait until you hear the stories."

"Well," I say. "It's good you came back." Something sticks in my throat as I'm saying it, though. It's hitting me that she's come back not because she missed me—or even missed being *here,* in this house—but because she woke up one day and had a fight with her boyfriend and so decided to take a nice, long drive. To Connecticut. How, I want to ask her, how had she ever cut herself off so completely? The real question, I realize, is not why did she come back, but how did she ever stay away? How cold does a person have to be simply to walk away and not come back for ten years?

I stare out into the darkness, trying to remember to breathe, trying to remember how breathing cures powerlessness. The truth is, she has all the cards. If she gets mad tomorrow, she'll get in the truck and go. If she sees something she wants here, she'll stay. And somehow that seems to mean that I have to make room for her in my little life, and put up with all her high energy and her smoking and whatever music she wants to play. I have to share this house with her—after all, it was left to both of us. And do I even have a say in the matter?

When I look back, she's watching me. "I did miss you," she says, as if she's read my thoughts. "And then it had been so long that

I didn't know if you'd even let me come back again. You know?"
She laughs. "But now I think the question *really* is: Can you put up
with me without wantin' to kill me?"

Before I can answer, Teddy jumps in and says, "See there? You
two are *sisters.* Look at you. You're family, and you'll work it out.
Lily has pined for you, Dana. She's looked for you for years, and
sometimes back when we were married, I'd wake up in the middle
of the night, and she'd be there lying awake with tears rolling down
her face, and she'd say she was thinking about where you were."

"Hey, who appointed you the spokesman here?" I say to him.
"Dana and I are perfectly capable of doing our own talking."

Dana slaps her knee and says, "You know, I just gotta tell you
this. Y'all are just the cutest couple together. I mean, I know this
sounds crazy because you're not even technically together anymore,
but it's just hard to imagine y'all bein' any more married than you
are right now. You talk just like an old married couple."

"Oh, you should have seen us when we *were* married. God!"
says Teddy. "We were hideously ill matched. In fact, I would be the
first to recommend divorce as a cure for a lot of marriages. We're
much more civilized as a divorced couple than we were as a married
one. Aren't we, Lily?"

"Well, that's how *I* see it," I tell him. *Hideously ill matched?* Is this
really the man who just last night was claiming that we need to re-
unite because no one else could ever put up with us? I feel a flicker
of annoyance, like heartburn rising up in my chest. He has to get
out of here. But before I can stand up and announce that it's time
for bed, Dana says brightly, "You know what I was just thinkin'
about—what I really, really, *really* want more than anything?"

We look at her.

"A party!" She beams. "You remember those wonderful parties
that Momma and Daddy used to have here on the porch? Let's do
another one of those—invite the whole colony and the Scallopini,

and string up those little lanterns, and play the Frank Sinatra music! Can we?"

"I guess so," I say. Funny how I'd been thinking of those parties just last night as I sat here lamenting Teddy's personality defects.

"It could be me saying 'I'm baaack!' to the whole colony," she says.

"*Are* you back?" I say. "Are you really back?"

She looks at me. "If you think it's okay for me to stay . . ."

Teddy laughs and puts his arm around her. "Well, Dana, *damn,* woman, if you ask me, I think this is your *home.*"

"Oh, Teddy," she says, "that is *sooo* sweet."

12

After I get Teddy packed off—which does take some doing—I go into the kitchen and put away the bottle of Southern Comfort. I rinse the dishes and load them into the dishwasher, scrub the kitchen sink, and fix (again) the time on the kitchen clock, because it insists on gaining five minutes each day. Then I turn out all the lights downstairs and we make our way up the stairs, after Dana grabs a beer out of the fridge.

"Want one, Lily?"

"Uh, no thanks," I tell her.

"So, Teddy's pretty great," she says brightly, from behind me on the stairs. This go-to-bed beer is making me just the tiniest bit nervous. It doesn't feel absolutely clear that she's intending to go to sleep anytime tonight.

"Yeah, he is. He's terrific," I say.

"He's like—I don't know—an old uptight guy, but then you see he has a great sense of humor. Very dry," she says. "Like when he was trying to speak for both of us. I know he was annoying you, but I can just see you two being married to each other."

"Yeah, I suppose," I say.

"And Simon . . . he's just the sweetest thing . . . and you know, you have such a great life here. It just makes me so . . ." She stops in the hallway, carefully puts her beer bottle on the floor, places both her hands over her face, and starts weeping—loud, copious, theatrically accurate weeps, as if she'll never stop. I freeze in my tracks. At first I think she must be faking, but then I get this awful feeling, as if my bones have turned to water. What if she's here because she's sick? That's why she's so thin and why she doesn't eat. She's obviously dying and has just been waiting for the right time to tell me. Maybe she didn't want to say so while Teddy was here.

I wrap my arms around her and lead her into my room, so that we don't wake up Simon. I say, "Are you okay? Just tell me what it is. I'll try to help you, whatever it is." I'm suddenly wide awake and braced for whatever is coming. I try to picture what the next few months will be like: getting to know her again only to lose her, the trips to the hospital, the long slow progress of her mysterious disease, and then—well, then there will be the memorial service. The colony people will consider her the long-lost daughter. We'll all wring our hands. It'll be worse than last year, when Mavis died. Thinking so morbidly ahead like this is a special talent of mine.

Dana sits down on the bed and buries her head in her hands, and for a few moments I hold onto her arm. "Tell me," I say. "Are you . . . ill?"

She looks up at me, wipes her tears, and says through sniffles, "No, of course I'm not ill. Why would you say that?"

"I don't know. I thought that might be why you came back." I let go of her hand. "And you said your stomach . . ."

"Why? Because I don't like to eat?"

"Yeah, I thought . . ."

"No, it's nothing. God, you really do worry too much about everything. I remember that about you now. Always worrying over something. It's just that food disgusts me sometimes. All the chewing and swallowing. And I want to be thin."

"Dana, every woman in the United States wants to be thin, but they still eat."

She rolls her eyes. "Well, I'm *fine*."

"Okay," I say. "But I thought there might be something else going on. That's all. Don't get all huffy on me."

"Don't *you* get all huffy on me. God! Just pretend that I ate that whole plate of macaroni you made, and then you'll feel better." Her eyes drift around the room, taking everything in, and then she stares for a moment at the headboard and pushes down on the mattress. It groans, and she starts laughing. "Oh. Lily. Oh my God. I just realized something. This is Momma and Daddy's old *bed*! It is, isn't it? You *sleep* in Momma and Daddy's old bed! And not just their quilt and frame and stuff—it's their mattress, isn't it?"

"So what?" I say. It's true. I do sleep in my parents' old bed, and, okay, so this mattress does have some serious sloping issues, but I don't care. I fit right in a comfy little groove.

"Oh my God. This, I've got to tell you, is so gross." She's trying to stop herself from laughing so hard. "Lily, think of the cooties you sleep with! The old, ancient dead cooties that must be in this thing, and the lumps and bumps and the stains—ugh!" She runs her hand across the wedding ring quilt that Aunt Juniebeth made, and then looks at her fingers as though they've come into contact with toxic waste, even though this quilt is perfectly clean. "God, I've slept on the floor of buses and in sleeping bags in people's basements, but nothing is weirder than this," she says. She looks at me closely. "What *happened* to you anyway? Don't get mad at me, but you seem stuck in—well, kind of a pitiful way."

"Look," I say, feeling myself flush all over, "I stayed here for *you,* so that if you ever got it in your head to come back, your home would still be here. Because you wouldn't let that damned attorney tell me where you were, I figured if I was ever going to see you again, it'd have to be right here. Did you ever think of that—what that meant when you told him not to give me your address?"

She looks a little taken aback.

"And while we're on the subject, I didn't *used* to be stuck. If you recall, I had moved to California, where I was planning to stay and live my life. But then I came back here for you! Yeah, for you, as you've so conveniently forgotten. Just so, after Momma and Daddy died, you wouldn't have to move away, go get raised by the Juniebeths. So don't you *dare* come in here now and call my life pitiful! You hear me?"

We glare at each other.

"I'm just talking about your *bed*," she says. "Jesus. When did you get such a hair trigger on you?"

"Oh, let me think. Maybe it was when I got to wondering what kind of person doesn't let her sister know where she is for ten years? Huh? Who would do that? Just why did you do that?"

"I didn't want you to come looking for me."

"Oh! You didn't want to be in the same family with me! And yet now—well, you're back, so I'm supposed to just open myself right back up and let you into my life, and be glad about it? We're just going to sit out on the porch, and you'll make friends with Simon and Teddy and get to be a part of the family. And then when something makes you mad again, you'll just get in your stupid stolen truck and tear out of here again. Is that it? Is that the deal you're offering me?"

"Yeah," she says. "Yeah, I guess that's the deal."

"Well, no thanks. I don't want it."

She's quiet, picking at a loose thread on the quilt. Then she looks up at me and says, "But think of this: the deal you're offering *me* is that if I stick around, I get to feel guilty for the rest of my life for leaving here and not ever calling you." She shrugs and wrinkles her nose. "Those are our deals. Might as well get used to it."

"I'm going to bed." I go into the bathroom and turn on the water and start washing my face and brushing my teeth. When I come out, she's still there.

"Well?" she says. She's lying on her stomach on the bed. "*Isn't* that the deal? I mean, the real honest-to-God, not-just-a-fake-nice kind of deal? Face it, Lily. This *is* who we are, and we're not going to change. You're stuck, and I'm a fuckup."

"I put fresh sheets on the futon in the guest room. You'll be pleased to know there are no parental cooties in there. Take your beer and go sleep in there. I'll talk to you tomorrow."

She gets up, and I get in bed and snap off the lamp. "And close my door, please, when you go."

She stands there in the dark for a moment more, illuminated by the hall light, and then she stalks off to the other room. I hear her groan as she stomps around, tossing things off the bed. After a while she's back. A beam of light from the hall slices across my bed. Then she's breathing loudly, standing at the side of the bed.

"What do you want?" I say.

"Lily?" she says in a tiny voice. "Lily, can I get in your bed just for tonight? Please?"

It's just what she used to say when she was little. I remember now: she never could stand to be alone.

I lie there for just a split second, and then I hold up the covers for her. "Okay," I say thickly, just like I used to. "But you know the rules: don't kick me and no peeing in the bed."

13

$\mathcal{T}$he newspaper I work for—called *The Edge*—has its offices in a converted old Victorian house on a busy section of Orange Street in New Haven, a part of town with lots of houses and little mom-and-pop markets, and hardly any place to park. So on Monday morning, I park my car blocks and blocks away, mainly so I can savor this time to be alone—free to walk and think without anybody yammering at me. After a weekend of being with my sister, I'm so happy to be alone that I feel like collaring the other people on the sidewalk and saying, "Look at me! I'm by myself!" But then they'd probably think I'm even weirder than I look—and I do look weird. Yep, even though it's a hot summer day, I'm wearing my dad's old watch cap to hide my hair. God forbid my bright orange and yellow blobs should be visible. Cars might crash. Airplanes flying overhead could lose visual contact with the tower.

Dana has made me *insane.* All the questions, the veiled critical analysis of my life: "So, Lily, tell me about your boyfriends. What? You don't have any? What was the point of getting divorced if you didn't get some new boyfriends?" And then: "Why don't we go to the store and get *another* kit and try something else with your hair? Or better yet, why don't we cut it all off and make you look really cute and punk? Or—I know—let's straighten your hair! In fact, why *do* you dress like that? Oooh, let's go through your clothes and throw out the ones that make you look too old!"

And on and on and on. My weight, my friends, my short marriage and long divorce, even the placement of the furniture, for God's sake—everything is up for discussion.

All I want right now is to get to my cozy little upstairs office, the one that looks out over the sidewalks of New Haven, and sit there with my boxes of letters that Carl will bring in. I want to immerse myself in other people's troubles with my mind and heart clear, and let my own life just simmer on hold for a while.

When I come up the stairs, Jackie Mahon, the editorial assistant, looks up and motions me over. "Gotta tell you, The Rooster wants to see you. And he's in one of his moods."

"Oh, great," I say.

The Rooster is really named Casey McMillen, but the staff calls him The Rooster because of the way he struts around the place like some proud little banty, and also because his hair sticks up in little points. The editor and co-publisher of *The Edge,* he is the most focused, one-track person I know. He will someday be scary, but right now, at twenty-four, he simply looks as though he might be somebody's nerdy twelve-year-old brother who happens to have strong, odd opinions and more power than he knows what to do with.

He and his friend Lance Hamilton, who looks possibly thirteen, started the paper two years ago with money they found in their daddies' couch cushions, I think, just to give the local daily a big scare. They decided they were going to appeal to young people, or what Casey always calls the "underserved youth market." Nobody thought it would work, least of all their fathers, I'm sure. But surprisingly, within a few months they were gobbling up ad revenues, and by the end of the first year they were actually turning something of a profit. They hired a slew of reporters and photographers, including me. My job was to write theater reviews for community theater productions, which I was terrible at, mainly because I couldn't bear to say anything bad, even if the play was awful. I praised everything. Teddy once said that I held the record for using the greatest number of synonyms for the word *good.*

Then one day, about a year ago, standing around in Casey's office, totally bored and overcaffeinated, I happened to pick up the Ann Landers column—now that she was dead, Casey and Lance were rerunning old columns—and started riffing about how lame it was that Ann Landers was so obsessed with the way people hung their rolls of toilet paper, of all things. Anyone can make fun of an old Ann Landers column and sound cool. This was not my best stuff, you understand. But The Rooster was dumbfounded at such insights. His jaw went slack. His eyes were like bright saucers.

I said, "If we're trying to go for the underserved youth market, I think we have to consider that no one under thirty has ever once cared about how to change the toilet paper roll"—and somehow, by the end of the hour, Ann Landers reruns were out and I was the new advice columnist. Yeah, me—former ringleader of the Scallopini, den mother to all of Dana's misfit friends, and survivor of a breakdown, therapy, and even marriage to a therapist. I was now going to have a new incarnation as an advice columnist. Casey was practically jumping up and down like the twelve-year-old he really is deep inside.

"You've got to be edgy and tough and opinionated," he said. "This will be a no-holds-barred, I'll-tell-you-what-your-friends-wouldn't-dare-tell-you kind of column. You gotta be sarcastic. I want irony." I said, "Yeah, yeah," and thought that in a moment he might start barking and running in circles around his desk.

In the press release he sent out later that day, I was described as a young woman who had known marriage, divorce, motherhood, and "personal tragedy," and who was uniquely qualified to write about people's life experiences, their romantic dilemmas, even their parenting concerns. Plus, he said, I was mature. (We, the staff, got a good laugh over that one, since anyone compared to Casey is mature.)

Within a couple of weeks, my desk in the newsroom was piled high with letters from people wanting help; after a month, I got my own little upstairs office just to contain all the mail that was coming in; and now, a year or so into it, The Rooster has put an advertisement for my "Dear Lily" column on buses all over the city. With my picture. (I have dull brown hair in the photo, curled into little corkscrews, and the expression on my face is that of somebody striving to look tougher, edgier, and more opinionated than she really is.)

Now Jackie is staring at me and popping her gum. "So what's with the winter hat? Did you get to fooling around and shave your head or something?"

I shift my purse to the other shoulder. "Hair disaster. Not shaved yet, but I'm considering that next. What does The Rooster have in mind? Any clue?"

"Oh, it's just one of those restless moods. He was over in Sports earlier, telling them they have to cover Little League as though it's the majors. A kid's picture on the cover every day. I think a couple of the sports writers are sending out their résumés for new jobs as we speak. If you want my humble opinion," she says, "I'd say, don't argue with him. I think he has the male version of PMS."

"Just what I'm in the mood for," I tell her.

Then, when I get to my desk and check my e-mail, there's even more bad news. There's a message from Kendall, saying, "*Teddy???* That was your best idea of who to fix me up with??? We are so going to lunch today!"

I type back, "Expecting a Rooster Attack soon. Can't promise lunch until I see what's left of me." In all the excitement over Dana's coming, I'd actually almost forgotten about Kendall's date with Teddy. But of course we haven't had the postmortem from *her* point of view. How many times do I have to relive this date? That's it. I am not sending him out with anyone else. He has to find his own women.

I've just gotten her reply—"NO EXCUSES, BROWN. We're going to lunch even if I have to come up there with a chicken hawk to get Mr. Rooster to leave you alone!!!"—when I look up to see Casey standing in the doorway. I press the delete key as quickly as I can, but I'm still laughing and flustered when I turn to him and say, "HI!" far too brightly. He looks at me quizzically.

"Glad *you're* in a good mood. What's with the hat?" He comes in and hovers around my desk, then plops down in the guest chair and starts picking at a clump of dried mud on his old Birkenstocks and drops it on the floor. He really does act like a twelve-year-old. Then, wouldn't you know, Carl shows up with the fresh, new letters, and Casey takes the box and starts going through them. I hate it that he gets his dirty paws all over them first, idly picking them up, reading a few lines out loud mockingly, and then throwing them back in the box. I want to say, "Stop *contaminating* them!" but I don't.

"So what's up?" I say. "Jackie said you wanted to talk to me."

He puts down the letter he's holding and looks at me through his owly glasses. "Yeaaaah. Not happy. You're losing it, Brown," he says. "Column needs more edge."

I bristle. "It has edge."

"No. I hate to say it, but the column sucks lately," he says. "We agreed this was going to be a hard-hitting, opinionated, *short* answers kind of column—one two three. Bada-bing, bada-boom. In and out. Yes. No. Leave him. Tell her to forget it. Over and out. Entertainment, not psychoanalysis. You're going on too long."

I look at him. "The column," I say, clearing my throat for emphasis, "is about people's problems. That in itself makes it entertaining. People love to read about other people's problems."

"Yeah, but you write like some normal suburban mom from Branford who doesn't have a clue. Get tough with these people. Make it funny."

"Casey—"

"No. Don't argue about this. I mean it." He looks at me for a long moment, and I see in his eyes how he thinks about this paper all the time, that it's his life. He eats, sleeps, and breathes it and wakes up worrying about it in the middle of the night. I actually understand that kind of worry. I can sympathize with him. But then he says, "You know, the trouble is, *you* could use some more edge yourself. *That's* what's going down here. You don't change, Brown. You're the same old, same old."

"Casey," I say, and rip the cap off my head. "Look, just *look* at this hair! Tell me, is this the hair of somebody who doesn't have *edge*? Just look at me! Would a suburban mom from Branford go around with hair that looks this crazy? Well? Is this *edge*? Is it?"

He stares at my hair for a long time, quietly, calmly considering it, and then he shakes his head. "No, no, that's not edge. But the cap," he muses, "now the winter cap in the summertime: that's *approaching* something like edge. Write like you're wearing that cap all summer long. And be sarcastic."

After he leaves, I sit there and stare out the window. What the hell *is* this, Improve Lily Week? Push Lily into a Corner, and Then Stomp on Her Week? I think that if one more person tells me that I need to change, I'm going to scream. I'd just like to know if there is any person in the world—anybody at all—who thinks I might be just right.

AND, IF THINGS aren't bad enough, I have to go to lunch with Kendall.

"It is possible," I tell her as we walk over to Claire's Corner Copia for lunch, "that The Rooster has lost his mind." I try to set the scene for her, tell her about how he just barged in, said he wasn't happy, then made fun of some of the newest letters. Made fun! She doesn't seem to be listening, which is weird because she always agrees with me about The Rooster. We stick together on all things concerning him. "So *then*," I say, "he goes into how I don't have edge, I'm not tough, and I'm just a suburban mom from Branford, and then he leaves me with this warning. He says . . ."

Kendall's walking two steps ahead of me. I stop talking, just to see if she's listening. She *doesn't* slow down and say, "A warning? What did he say?" In fact, she doesn't show any interest at all. Her

eyes are pointed straight ahead and she's walking so fast in her espadrilles that I have to take an extra little step every now and then
just to keep up with her. It occurs to me that she hasn't even asked
me why I'm wearing a hat.

I catch up with her. "Hey, why are you walking so fast?" I say.

She says in a hard voice, "Are you really this clueless? I am so mad
at you right now it's all I can do not to start screaming right here."

I blanch. "Wait. You're that mad? . . . About the Teddy thing?"

"Hell, yes, I'm *that* mad about the Teddy thing. You just go on
and on about this *stupid* little scene with Casey—just another work
thing—and, I'm sorry, but it's clear that you couldn't care less how I
must be feeling after that horrible date you sent me on with him."
She stops walking and faces me. I see that her face is red. Like, she's
really mad. "How could you have set me up with him, Lily? God! I
open up to you completely and tell you how much I wanted to date
a nice guy. I tell you that I want to get married—and your idea of
helping me is *Teddy*? Was that supposed to be some kind of joke?"

"Of course not," I say. "Listen, he's sorry he acted so weird. He
feels really bad about it."

Her eyes widen. "He *told* you? Oh, *great*! So he even talks about
it? Oh, God!"

"No, it's just that . . ."

We go inside Claire's and stand in the order line, along with half
the population of New Haven. Kendall's face is so red that I'm afraid
she might burst into tears. But then she turns to me, and I see that,
no, she's going to go the other way. She's going to be furious instead.

"So he actually has already told you about the date? I can*not* believe this. He doesn't talk to me the whole time, just sits there looking like he wants to die, and then he takes me home at eight-thirty.
And then he goes and tells *you* the whole thing. So tell me. What
exactly did he say about me? What didn't he like?" She glares at me.
"No, never mind. I don't *care* what he said."

"He didn't say anything bad, just that—"

She makes a zipping motion with her lip. "No! I said *don't tell me.* I don't care what that man thinks. He barely even spoke to me. He was like somebody who'd gone into a coma. I had to do all the talking, *all* the work. Tell me this: what were you *thinking,* setting us up? Could there *be* two more opposite people on the planet?"

"I don't know. I-I guess I thought the two of you might hit if off."

"You must think I'm *pretty* desperate and pathetic if you thought I was going to want somebody like that," she says. People are starting to turn and look at her—not that she cares.

"He . . . I don't know what's wrong with him. He's not great with the social skills. He's just . . . well, that's Teddy." I shrug. "I'm sorry. What can I say?"

She says loudly, "You know what it is. You know perfectly well that he's still hung up on *you.* Why do you set him up on dates with other people when obviously it's you he wants to be with? That's what this is, you know. He wants *you.*"

"He's not really hung up on me. He's just out of practice with dating. I'm sorry."

But she can't stop. "You know what he needs? A quarantine sign around him saying DANGER: IN LOVE WITH SOMEONE ELSE."

The guy in line behind us laughs a little uncomfortably. *Oh, please,* I think. *Not an interactive audience for her.* And sure enough, Kendall turns to him and says, "Can you believe this, what I'm trying to tell this woman here? Swear to God, it's all true. She divorces this perfectly nice man, and then she gets all her friends to date him, and then she wonders why it never works out! Like, *duh.* She's becoming a public nuisance with this guy."

"Kendall," I growl.

She says, "You look like an intelligent, sensitive man. Is that not a hostile act? Isn't it? I actually dressed up for this guy, went to the trouble to clean my house, just in case he might want to set foot in it." She pauses, shifts gears, smiles at the man, and then holds out her hand. "I'm sorry. My name is Kendall. And you are?"

The guy shakes her hand and says his name is Alex. I am hoping he'll ask her out right then to make it all up to her, and we can stop talking about Teddy. Just then the order taker behind the counter barks out to Kendall, "What's it gonna be?" and she now has to start mulling over the chalkboard menu for the first time, even though we've been standing in line for nearly ten minutes. Of course she doesn't see that everyone in the line and behind the counter is getting annoyed with her.

Alex and I seem to be left with each other. He says in a low voice, "Wow. Are you all right?" He looks at me closely. He has nice eyes, neon blue, as if they have lights on behind them. "I'll bet you didn't think your ex's date was going to end up being something all of New Haven got to hear about."

"You got that right."

"Wait. Do I know you?" he says. He tilts his head. "You look familiar."

"No, I don't think you do," I say, staring at the floor.

"No, I think I know you. Really."

A bus rumbles past the open door, and he laughs. "Aha! You're Lily," he says softly. "Dear Lily. From *The Edge*. You actually just rolled past on that bus."

"Did I?"

"Without the hat. Would you think I was some fawning psychopath if I told you how much I like your column?"

"Thank you," I say. Maybe he could come and face down The Rooster.

Kendall is asking loudly if the corn for the tostadas is organic or not, and whether the mesclun greens in the salad were grown locally or were imported. And are the avocadoes fresh and really, really ripe without being overripe? Is the lettuce hydroponic?

Alex says in a low voice, "Does your friend have a volume control button, by any chance?"

"No," I say. "I think we're just going to have to muzzle her."

"It might be a challenge, but I think the two of us could take her down," he says, leaning very close so Kendall can't hear him. "And I bet some other people in line would be willing to help out. And possibly your ex-husband, the poor guy."

"Well . . ."

"I didn't mean it like that. He's probably not a poor guy at all. He's a rat. I'm sure that whatever he did to you in the divorce agreement made him deserve your fixing him up with her."

I laugh. Alex not only has very nice eyes but he also has straight sandy-colored hair that flops into his eyes in a very pleasing, schoolboyish kind of way. He's wearing a blue knit shirt, khakis, and boat shoes. Obviously not what you'd call a working man. Probably a Yalie, and probably too young for me—not that I'm in the market, but you never know. Lately I notice these things. "Actually," I say, "it's crazy, isn't it, but I was just trying to be nice."

"Yes, but to which one of them? She looks like she could be a handful." We both listen as Kendall delivers a lecture on genetically engineered corn to the order taker.

"He's kind of a handful, too. I figured it could work."

"Hmm," Alex says. He stands back and smiles at me, as if we are old friends and I won't mind anything he has to say. "So, if you can stand any more personal questions, what exactly did you do to your hair that made that knit cap seem like a good idea? And if you say chemotherapy, I'm going to go kill myself."

I laugh. "No, not chemotherapy. I turned it orange. Part of it orange, and then in trying to correct it, I ended up with yellow gold *and* orange."

"Ooh, what shade of orange? Tangerines, orangutans, or . . .?"

"More your Cheetos family. With spots here and there that

might look like neon gold. Some butter yellow—butter that's been sitting out in the sun."

"Ah. Interesting. Any overripe banana color, too?"

"Oh, yeah. Mostly my bangs are that color."

He laughs. "Yeah, been there, actually. And when I went to correct it, the whole hair got a greenish tint to it."

I look at his hair, which is a very sane color.

He brushes it out of his eyes. "Not recently," he says, seeing me look. "Back in the day. I had a band, so it was required."

I want to ask him if he was by chance a Morbid Gullet, but just then it's my turn to order—after Kendall, the order takers are practically shouting for people in line to make up their minds quickly—so I order pita bread with hummus because I think that will be easy for them to make. By the time I finish placing my order, Kendall has sashayed over to the window and found us a table and is practically jumping up and down waving at me to come over, so I have to go. I turn and smile at Alex and say, "Well, thanks. And have a good day."

"Hey, you too," he says. He leans in close and says in a low voice, "And if you see your ex, tell him people in line today think he deserves a medal for sticking it out with her until eight-thirty. You know?"

When I get to the table, Kendall says in a grumpy voice, "All right. I've decided to forgive you. I'm sorry I'm being a pain."

"It's okay," I say.

"I don't know why I get so mad," she says. "I guess I just had my hopes up too high. But I'm over it."

I clean a little bit of refried beans off the table with the corner of my napkin. "It's okay," I say again. "So . . . how have you been since the horrible date?"

She's launched into a story about her housecats when my cell phone rings, and wouldn't you know, it's Teddy. At first I think I won't pick it up, but what if it's something about Simon? So I try to put my hand around the phone so Kendall won't hear Teddy's voice. But of course he talks so loudly that she can hear perfectly well that he's asking me to meet him somewhere for lunch, and then, when I say I can't come, he tells me he'll pick up something for dinner, if I want. He's willing to barbecue tonight. I get him off the phone as quickly as I can and look up to see Kendall fixing me with her meanest stare.

"Oh, this is just unbelievable," she says. "Un-fucking-believable! And you can sit there with a straight face and tell me he's not still hung up on you?"

I wish I could explain to her that this is just how he is: he attaches. It's not me he wants. Really. Win him over, and you've got him for life. He'll transfer this affection and all his complaints and his noon check-in phone calls to somebody else. He's ready. Convince him that he's lovable, and he'll be barbecuing at your house later tonight.

She stands up, her eyes looking dangerously glittery, something between playful and Mount Vesuvius. She waves across the room. "Oh, Alex! Yoohoo! Alex! Isn't that your name? You're not going to believe this! Come here!"

"Don't," I say.

"No, he should join us anyway." She looks down at me, speaking in a low voice for once but smiling a fake pageant-y smile. Maybe she really was a beauty queen, I think. "I think he likes you. He'd be good for you, I think. Oh, *Alex*! Alex! Yoo-hoo!"

I don't look to see if he's coming over. Instead, I feel myself get up, as though I'm on automatic pilot. I sort of glide to my feet in one fluid motion, sling my purse over my shoulder, and pick up my lunch tray. At first I can't believe I'm doing this—I think maybe I'm going to throw out my trash and then possibly go back and sit down across from her again—but then, well, something takes over and I just . . . don't. I throw out the trash and keep on walking—out the door, away into the warmth of the afternoon.

14

*Y*ou know what's nice about being an advice columnist—even a non-edgy one whose boss is disappointed in her? You get really good at giving yourself little pep talks, as if somehow the letters to others are just practice for the *real* business: keeping yourself in line.

For the next few days, I walk around wondering what I'd advise a person who wrote:

Dear Lily,

My sister, who has moved back in with me after not talking to me for a whole decade and who doesn't say how long she is staying, insists on sleeping in my bed and trying to improve me, when anyone can see that she's the one who needs improving. Also, she's messy and leaves her clothes all over the place and then laughs at me when I get mad about it and says that I am too anal-retentive and should loosen up. Also she talks, talks, talks when I need to go to sleep. Please tell me what to do.

P.S. She is really, really good with my kid, who thinks she possibly hung the moon.

Sometimes I feel myself saying to this mythical letter writer: "Breathe. Take things one at a time and not in large chunks. Try to hold the big picture in your head. If her clothes on the floor bother you, don't get into a fight with her, but talk to her about how it makes you feel and then let it go. Learn to enjoy the bigger moments between you, the fact that you are forging a relationship that had been pronounced dead."

Still, despite everything, I have trouble following my own advice.

After Dana has been there for three days, I come home, for instance, to find her rearranging the furniture in the living room. She's got one of the couches pushed out into the hall and upended. When she sees me standing at the door, all she says is, "Oh, hi. Will you help me lug this outside, and then let's go get some beanbag chairs tomorrow, okay? I think this room needs something casual. It's too formal in here with all these stupid couches."

"I don't like beanbag chairs," I say. "They crackle under people's butts."

She comes over and puts her arms around me and whispers, "No. What you don't like is *change*. The butt-crackling is a whole other issue we won't go into now."

"I liked that couch, as a matter of fact," I say. "Since when do you get to come in here and change everything around to suit yourself?"

"It's my house, too," she says over her shoulder, and heads upstairs. I think she's mad, but in fact, it turns out she's just gone to get a lava lamp that she happened to bring with her from Texas. A lava lamp! She puts it on the table where our mother's favorite philodendron—"Phil"—had sat. The philodendron is sent out to bake on the back porch.

"There," she says, standing back and regarding the place with a satisfied look on her face.

"You know he'll die there," I tell her.

"*He?*" she says, and laughs. "Last time I checked, plants were still considered inanimate."

"Phil was Momma's. I'd think you'd want to help him live just because of that," I say, and she laughs as she goes upstairs. I bring Phil back inside, remove his dead leaves, and put him back in his place in the living room. Then I unplug the lava lamp and put it in the corner of the room, behind a chair. I am sorry, but I cannot tolerate a lava lamp in full view, and I will tell Dana that when she comes downstairs.

But when she comes back, she's dressed up in a white tank top, jeans, and high-heeled sandals. She has her hair down and curly, and her eyes are ringed in mascara. Her bag is slung across her shoulder. This is a surprise. She's mostly seemed happy just to sit on the porch chatting with Teddy and me until far after the time I'm ready for us to go inside to bed. Three days, and obviously we're starting a new chapter.

Before I can think, I say, "Where are you going?"

She rolls her eyes. "Gee, I'm having a déjà vu all over again. Isn't this where we left off ten years ago?"

"Okay. Forget it."

She clicks herself over to the fridge, takes out a liter of Coke, and drinks straight from the bottle. "No, no, I'll tell you so you won't *worry,* you little worry monkey, you. Today I was downtown and I met this guy I used to go out with—Seth Tomlinson. Remember him? He was on the swim team, so he had really big muscles, and he was really good at smashing beer cans into his head?"

"Uh, vaguely."

"See, it blows my mind that you didn't keep up with anybody after I left. I would have thought you'd have been interested in what happened to all those people who hung out here all the time."

"Did *you* keep up with them?"

"Well . . . that was different. I was moving on."

"I moved on, too. Moved on to the point where I didn't have to keep track of the town juvenile delinquents anymore."

She laughs a little. "Yeah, I suppose. Well, anyway, Seth Tomlinson became a cop. And we're going out so he can fill me in on what everybody's doing these days. And maybe help me find a job."

"You're getting a job?"

"Well, duh!" She taps me on the top of the head as she passes by me. "I have to work, don't I? By the way, I saw what you did with my lava lamp, and I just want to say: this fight is *not over*."

As soon as she's gone, I move the couch from the hall back to where it was before. The room looks so much better this way—nice and elegant and *finished*.

"WHAT IN THE world is going on?" says Gracie on the telephone later that evening. "Are these rumors I hear true—Dana's back?"

"Yup. Despite our predictions, I have a sister on the premises," I tell her.

"Wow! And is she a new-and-improved version of herself?"

I laugh. "Well, hard to say. She's not Goth anymore, but she talks all the time, and she doesn't pick up her clothes, and she wonders why I didn't throw out the couches, and she has put a lava lamp in the living room. Oh, and she says the deal between us is that I get to make her feel guilty for leaving, but she gets to criticize me for staying. Which she does nearly nonstop."

"Wow. Isn't family just a wonderful thing?" says Gracie.

"You should come and see her," I say.

"How does your hair look, by the way?"

"Oh, the same. I'm trying to think of what to try next. Meanwhile, I'm buying hats and trying to appear eccentric in public. You really should come and see her."

She still doesn't answer that. "Did you try the Indian scarves?"

"Um . . ."

"You didn't."

"They didn't look right on me. By the way, why don't you come over for dinner tomorrow night? Teddy's here every night cooking yummy stuff on the grill—yummy stuff that Dana eats about two half bites of and then pushes around on her plate—so we could use a real eater."

"You know, I think I have to take a pass on that. Thanks for the invite, but I'd have to put on full armor, I think, to be in the same vicinity as Dana, and I haven't had my armor polished lately."

This feels so weird. Gracie wasn't around, of course, during my two-year ordeal with Dana after our parents died. She was off in Italy on that fellowship, and she didn't come back home until Dana had already flown the coop. She didn't even see the worst of it—the parade of guys and the weird costumes (the dog collars and such), the beer cans on the lawn, the naked teenagers swimming off the beach in our backyard—so I'm not sure just where this animosity between the two of them has come from. I figure it must have started up when I was at college and they were both rivals for my mother's attention. I can just see my mother playing them off against each other, like fifth-grade girls: *You're my best friend today, and she's my best friend tomorrow.* My mother could be so fifth grade.

"Okay," I say to Gracie. "I understand."

"But you," she says before we hang up. "Are you really okay with everything?"

"Sure. She's just a little needy. And, I don't know, it's good to see her and everything, but she's . . ."

Gracie laughs a little. "I know."

"I mean, I love her and I want her to be happy, but she's just got this weird energy about her. She never settles down. And she won't tell me where she's been all this time. I feel like I spend my whole time trying to figure her out. It's exhausting."

"Yep. That's our Dana."

"Um, you don't have room for a lava lamp, by any chance, do you?" I say.

"Please. You've seen this place. I can't even fit another type-writer ribbon in here."

"Gracie, get real. They don't even make typewriter ribbons anymore."

"But if they did, I still couldn't fit one here. And I'm definitely not taking your castoff lava lamp."

MUCH LATER, I'm scrubbing the sink for the night and resetting the kitchen clock and thinking I could get a much-needed head start on sleep before Dana comes home, when I hear the truck door slam, and then there she is, her high heels clicking on the tile floor. "Hi," she says and leans in the doorway, looking tired. "Why oh why did I bother to wear these goddamn shoes? Can you just tell me that? Huh?" She pries off the heels and then, groaning, sinks down into the armchair and rubs her feet. I'm wiping down the counters and watching her out of the corner of my eye. Her hair's all messed up, and her makeup is smudged under her eyes.

"How was your date?"

She scowls, kneading her toes. "It wasn't a date like you're thinking 'date.' He's engaged to a woman disc jockey in New York. This was just a get-reacquainted-with-Branford session."

"Oh. Did you know that when you went?"

"*Yes,* I knew that when I went. Jeez."

"So . . . how was your get-reacquainted-with-Branford session?"

"Fine." She sighs and flings herself backward, letting her head loll back across the arm of the chair. "I guess it's all fine. He told me all about everybody I used to know here. A lot of the Gothies are still here, but they're all pretty mainstream. And that girl, Lainie, who used to hang out here—the one who thought you were so cute— she's a fashion designer in New York. And a guy named Joey fell out of a window at college and is now paralyzed. Couple people got married. You know." She rubs her heel, hard. "But—well, he didn't know the thing about Thor. I had to tell him, and that was hard."

"Thor, your old boyfriend from the Morbid Gullets?" I say. Obviously she doesn't remember that she hasn't told *me* the thing about Thor. "What happened to him? It wasn't a razor blade accident, was it?"

She looks over at me as if I've just said the most insensitive thing possible. "If that's what you want to call it. The cops called it a suicide."

My hairline feels as though a piece of ice has just melted on it. "He committed suicide? Oh, no! Oh, that's terrible. I liked him so much. Were you there . . . I mean, when it happened?"

"I left him, and that's when he did it," she says in a flat, dull voice. "Listen, I've just been talking way too much about it, and I'm kind of talked out. I don't want to think about it anymore."

"Okay. Sure. I understand." I see the butter out on the counter, so I put it in the refrigerator and then stand there at the open refrigerator door, staring at the cold food and thinking about Thor.

After a long silence, she says, "Do you know what I want to do right now?"

I close the door to the fridge. "I'm almost scared to ask."

"I want to go and dig in the sand."

"You're kidding."

"Yeah, will you come with me?" She sits up straight. "Please! And don't say it's too late. I really, really want us to just go sit down on the beach and dig in the sand together."

I look at the clock. "It's nearly midnight, and I have to work tomorrow."

"Come on. *Please*. We never really get to talk."

I hesitate. "For fifteen minutes," I say. "And then I have to get some sleep."

"Fifteen or sixteen," she teases me. "Maybe twenty, at the outside."

THE SAND is shimmering in the moonlight, glowing almost white. We go walking across the cool, wet grass to the beach. There's a slight breeze that lifts my hair, and the air smells deliciously like salt and fog and the wet wood of the dock. I try to shake off the image of Thor.

"God, would you believe a person could miss sand?" Dana is saying. "I *missed* sand. How dorky is that?" She flops down on the beach and starts digging so industriously it's as though she's going to start trucking piles of the stuff back to the house for later. I lower myself down beside her and kick off my shoes, staring at her in amazement; I could have used her skills during my digging months.

I have a knot in my stomach. "When you first left," I say after a while, "I sat on this beach—almost right in this very spot—for days in a row, just digging holes. I couldn't do anything. I didn't even talk to anybody."

"Jesus," she says. "Why'd you do that?"

"I don't know. I think I had a little breakdown or something. At first I think I stayed out here because I was listening for that Morbid Gullets school bus to come back, and bring you home again. But after a while, when I realized that you weren't coming, I still stayed out here."

"Wow," she says. She stares at her fingers, which look now as though they've been rolled in brown sugar.

"Yeah, I couldn't even go to work. Maggie was counting on me to be there but I couldn't do it. Couldn't talk to people." Everything gets a little blurry. "And I couldn't sleep—except for when I'd sleep for days at a time."

At first I'm not sure she's even heard me. She puts her arms down in the sand and rolls them around so that sand sticks to every inch of them, which seems to take all her concentration for a moment. Then she looks over at me and says, "God, would you just look at us, Lily? Look at us! The agony of us! We had so many bad things happen to us. Why does everything have to be so tough all the time?" Her eyes are shining in the dark. "We've got to get over all this stupid childhood stuff, get our minds right again. We made everything harder than it had to be. Why couldn't I have just said, 'Sorry, I'm grown up now. Good-bye,' and then you could have said, 'Fine, see you around,' and then we could have parted friends and maybe even kept in touch? You know? Don't you get it? It's all that bad stuff from childhood, just clinging to us like a bad smell."

I realize then that what I wanted was for her to say, "Oh, I'm so sorry," but I can see she's not going to. I shouldn't have expected that she could do that. It was too much. I look away, feel my eyes stinging with tears.

"Anyway, look at your life," she says softly and leans over and pokes me in the elbow. "You did great. You've got a wonderful life here; you know you do. I mean, your hair is ridiculous, and you somehow never learned how cool lava lamps can be, *and* you sleep in a bed with deceased cooties. But compared to me, you're like the queen of coping. I wish I was like you."

"Oh, you do not. Don't even give me that crap."

"Oh, I do so!" She leaps up and pulls me to my feet. "Hey, you know what we need? A reconnection ritual! Let's see—what can we do?" She looks around, as though materials for reconnection rituals are going to be lying around on the beach. "Okay. I know. Let's go skinny-dipping! Come on. What do you say?" In a second, she's ripped off all her clothes—the jeans and the tank top and her underwear—and thrown them over her shoulder onto the sand, and is standing there, illuminated in the moonlight, grinning at me like a crazy person. "Come on, you! Drop trou!"

Her skinny body, tanned all over, has practically no boobs to speak of, just tiny dark nipples standing up on little tan mounds, and only the merest shadow of pubic hair. The Brown women don't specialize in those attributes.

"The water is going to be freezing."

"Aw, so what? This is a reconnection ritual. A rebirth. You have to suffer to have a rebirth." She sprints down to the water and runs right in, as though it's going to be a hospitable temperature, which I know it is *not*. She doesn't even yell as she goes under, just slips into the water and comes up and shakes her hair.

"Come on! It's not that bad."

I watch her for a moment, and then think, what the hell, and so in slow motion, I step out of my sweatpants and underpants and take off my T-shirt, fold them neatly on the sand, and walk over. She's watching me while she treads water. I can see the bright wet skin of her arms gleaming in the darkness.

"Hey, where did you get those boobs?" she calls. "Holy cow! Did you buy those? They're *melons*!"

I have two of the smaller breasts on the planet today (miniature plums rather than melons), but they did slightly improve—in size, at least, if not in quality—after childbirth and a year of industrious breastfeeding, so at the moment they are possibly three microns larger than hers. "Simon brought them," I say, just a little shyly.

"Wow! Babies are just too good! I've got to get me one of those!"

Once I get to the water, I have to ease myself in. I can't quite believe I'm doing this. The water is unbelievably cold at first, but then I go into a state of numbness and realize that it's still possible to live under these circumstances. My nerve endings give up their screaming after a moment. Lying on my back, naked, feeling the inky black water surrounding me and holding me up, I finally discover the way of just giving up all semblance of fight and letting myself go limp. I stare at the big bowl of stars overhead, the trails of clouds, the fuzzy glow of the moon. After another few moments, I stop shivering completely and just drift there, going along with the ripples, tasting the saltiness at the corner of my mouth. It's just me, the sky, and the cold, salty water.

I think I could go on this way for a long, long time. Who knew that peace was just outside the back door? Why wasn't I doing this every night?

15

*W*e float for a while, listening to the far-away traffic noises way out on Route 1 and, closer in, to the sound of frogs and peepers over in the reeds. Then I realize that what I thought was water lapping quietly against the dock was really sniffling.

"Are you crying?" I say.

She says in a choked-off voice, "Look. He just went crazy, okay? Always harping on this and that, and being really gross on the bus, always stoned and being really negative."

I tread water for a moment. "I assume this is a continuation of our nonconversation about Thor, right?"

"Yes. I just want to tell you this, and then we won't talk about it ever again." She makes snuffling noises. "He was getting to be really moody and bad, and then the bass player, Stony, started liking me, and he told me he liked me lots more than Thor did. God, I feel so guilty saying this. But Stony was so . . . *good* to me, and that just made Thor get worse and worse. He was always getting high, and then he'd be impossible. And so one day the two of them were being real pissy with each other, and then things got out of hand, and as a joke, kind of, they had this huge fight with knives and all. And then they came in the bus, all cut up and stuff, and told me that Stony had won me. They were both laughing, like this was just so funny. He'd *won* me, they said, just like I was a piece of property or something. I thought they were joking, but they said, no, no, it was really true. I was Stony's now. And so . . . then Thor was all drunk and crying, and he said for me to get out, and so I left the bus in the middle of the night and walked into town . . ."

"What state were you in?" I paddle over closer to her. I need to see her face.

"State? Emotional state?"

"No. *United* State."

"Oh. Vermont."

Vermont. I feel a little stab of shock. She was just two states away, two *tiny* states away. I could have driven there in a few hours, could have picked her up and brought her back home. If she'd called. I would have been so glad to come.

She's going on in a flat voice, oblivious to the fact that my heart has just broken again. "I walked into town and went to a little diner that opened at, like, four in the morning, and I was telling this cool guy who owned the place that I needed a way to make some money, and did he know where I could get a job, and then he just says, 'Well, my name is Kristoff, and my wife, Anya, and I have three babies, and we live on a farm growing vegetables, and she's a painter who never can find time to paint, so why don't you just come home with me and you can help her out?' "

"Just like that?"

"Yep. Went there that morning and stayed for a few years, actually. Anya and I baked bread and grew vegetables and wore long skirts and boots and took care of the babies—there were five of them by the time I left. I let my awful black hair grow out, and I became like this organic farm person. People kind of came and went, and we played music at night and had bonfires, and Anya and I did all the cooking. We were real hippies."

"Man, you take risks. I can't believe the risks you take."

"Risks? What was risky about that?"

"No, I mean the whole thing. Risky to just walk off in the middle of the night, and risky to have gone off in the bus in the first place, come to think of it. And then you go home with some man you don't even know, just because he *says* he has a wife and three kids. And you stay for years, just join up with their life. I could never have done that."

She laughs and shakes out her hair. Little droplets go everywhere. "Well, that's me, I guess. Always jumping headfirst into things. That's kind of what I do."

"So when did you meet Willems?" I ask.

"Oh, well, Willems is actually Anya's father—I told you he was older, right?—and he moved in with us for a while. And he and I totally started hanging together and, oh, Lily, then we hooked up and, well, you know how that is—you want to *do it* all the time, and we were keeping it a secret, but then one night Anya found out and she just totally freaked on us. And I had to leave. Bad time. Really, really bad time."

"Did Willems leave with you?"

She looks away. "No. He couldn't. Family pressures," she says. "Everybody's, like, totally scared of Anya. I kinda freaked out and— now don't get all weirded out by this, Lily, but I took a bunch of pills. I wasn't serious, you know. It was—"

"Oh, *Dana.* You tried to kill yourself?"

Her face is luminous in the moonlight. "No. No. I didn't want to die. I just did it to get back at all of them. I know, I *know,* it was really a stupid thing to do—and, well, I had to do a little time in the hospital—"

"Oh, Dana!" I close my eyes.

"No. No. Don't worry about that. It ended up being the best thing in the world because then Willems came to see me and he gave me a plane ticket to *Hawaii.* He'd gotten me a job there, working with this old friend of his, Connie, and she and I were going to do event planning together. He said I'd be great at it, and it could give me a new start. It was so sweet of him!"

"And did you do that?" My head is starting to hurt.

"Oh, yeah. For a few years. Connie was this really cool older lady, and we ran this little company putting on events for big corporations, and we dressed up every night, and I drove her little red convertible and looked all corporate and respectable. I had white-blonde hair and a tan. Lived in a hotel in Waikiki. Made a lot of money. I was hot stuff."

I can't help staring at her. "But—but how did it *feel*? You know, you were so far away from home and everything you'd ever known . . ." *Did you miss me? Didn't you even want to tell me where you were?*

"Oh, I don't remember. Fuck all that." She swirls her arms through the water. "I was just having fun. Connie and I dated guys from all over the world and half the U.S. fleet. It was a gas! By the way, I can still hula, if you ever need a hula dancer."

I'm surprised at how dull her eyes look. Maybe it's just the way the moonlight is hitting them, but she seems so distant from the story she's telling, as though it happened to someone else a very long time ago, and she's simply responsible for recounting it. "So," I say, feeling disconcerted, "where's Connie now? You two still good friends?"

"Oh, Christ, I don't know. Probably still doing the same old thing. I got tired of it after a while, and then I made the teeny tiny little mistake of sleeping with the wrong guy—a client's husband, whoops—and she booted me out." She sighs. "It was like I went from being the best thing since sliced bread to being an untouchable in one ten-minute period. Connie was like: 'Out! Go! Get off the island! I don't want to see you anymore!' Which was just as well, because I was like thoroughly sick of that island. I wanted *land* and *space,* and the ability to stop driving around in circles trying to get somewhere. I was too, too happy to go, believe me."

"But you were such good friends, weren't you? After those years of working together and building the business?"

"Yeah. Well, welcome to the real world. That's what I've learned about people. You do something even slightly out of the ordinary, make some perfectly innocent little mistake, and they just turn on you. Nobody really cares about anybody else out there. That's just the way it is. You know?"

"Well, but, Dana, I don't think that's true. I think maybe she was just angry, but you could have patched things up if you'd wanted to. Did you apologize to her? Or to Anya, either, for that matter?"

"*Apologize?* I should apologize for falling in love?" She starts hitting the surface of the water with the palm of her hand, creating little waves. "Come on. Are you *really* an advice columnist? You tell people that kind of advice? People can't help who they love, Lily. It is out of our control! These guys picked *me*. And anyway, these women did *not* want to hear any of that from me. And the men . . . well, except for Willems helping me out, the men were just scared shitless of the women. That guy in Hawaii—Clem was his name— he just ran to the hills with his tail between his legs, ready to do anything to patch up his marriage. So what that he'd been telling me he was going to leave her? I never did believe him anyway. Who listens to that shit?"

"You got your feelings hurt."

"Hell yes, I was hurt! But then I thought about it, and I realized this was the *best* thing that could have happened to me. Shit ends, you know? You have to make your exit. You think people are your friends, but how's that friendship if you have to be so *perfect* to keep them? I'm sorry, but those are not friends. Not real friends."

I'm shivering so hard I can't move. "So, I'm almost afraid to ask, but where did you go then?"

"Again, *don't* freak. More pills, another hospital, but then I tracked down Willems, who was by then in Texas."

"Still living with Anya and her family?"

"No. Oh, no." She starts talking fast now, with the tone of voice of somebody who's wrapping up the boring ending of a story and just wants to be allowed to get through to the end of it without further questions or interruptions. "He's living with someone new, this little cupcake of a woman named Dreena Sue, about twenty-five years old, and she's just *the sweetest l'il ole thang,* and all she wants is to marry Willems and have his baby. *And* so they do that—I help her talk him into it because she's so good for him—and then I lived with them and helped out with the baby when he was born. By then, I knew all about babies from all of Kristoff and Anya's kids. Things were going good for the four of us, but then soon Dreena Sue's brother—that's Randy—moves in with us because he's between jobs. And he's nice, you know, so then Dreena Sue got it in her head that it would be so *great* and symmetrical, you know, if Randy and I got married, and we could all just be together forever. And so he asked me, and I said yes."

"Wait. You said yes? Did you love him?"

She thinks about it. "Well, I didn't *not* love him, and also, you know, marriage isn't a fatal disease. You can always get out of it if you don't like it. So let me finish. Anyway, Dreena Sue was planning this wedding for us, and it was going to be a lot of fun. She really was getting into it. But then one day I found Randy getting it on with the dog trainer, and I just thought, very calmly, well now I don't have to marry him. And so I left him in the middle of the night while he was sleeping. Left all of them. Didn't even leave a note."

"Wow," I say.

She paddles around in a circle. I get dizzy watching her.

"And so there you have it: the up-to-the-minute story of Dana Brown," she says.

"Dana Brown, looking for a home," I say.

She looks over at me. "Looking for a party is more like it. Say, when are we gonna have that big bash on the porch?"

A FEW NIGHTS LATER, as I'm scrubbing the sink before bed, she says to me, "So . . . when you had Simon, did you feel relieved that you'd never have to be lonely again?"

I think back to Teddy handing me the baby to hold in the delivery room and looking down into Simon's calm navy blue eyes staring up into my own, and feeling almost a piercing sense of belonging between us. He was *mine*. I looked at how tiny and helpless he was, ran my finger along the delicate curve of his ear against the blanket, and felt his rabbity little mouth searching hungrily at my breast, and at that moment I ached with such tenderness that tears ran down my face. But was that feeling relief that I wouldn't be lonely again? I don't think so.

I look up at her waiting for my answer.

"I think," I say slowly, "that what I felt was that I just wanted to get it right with him. And to make sure that he never felt left out and that he always knew he was the most important thing in my life."

"Oh," she says, and seems slightly disappointed. But then she says, "Wow. You're such a great mom! Who else would think like that?" And she flashes me a big, fake smile and wanders over to the counter to take a swig of her Coke.

Wait, I want to say. Do you want to talk to me about how lonely you feel? But I don't say it, and the moment passes.

Later, in the middle of the night, I wake up with a start and can't fall back to sleep. My heart is racing. Dana, sleeping on the pillow next to mine, looks so young and fragile in the faded bathroom light that falls across her face. There's a drop of spittle at the edge of her open lips, and her dark blond hair lies in a tangle across the pillow. Her hands are curled up near her chin, fingernails still wearing their little chips of green nail polish, chips that are smaller every day.

God, I am so scared for her.

It's because of those stories she told—but no, not the stories as much as her creepy, detached tone when she described her life for the past ten years. All those scenarios, those lifetimes—and she told them as though they had nothing really to do with her; she was simply there, a bystander taking up with other people, living their lives alongside them, and never once wanting anything for herself, never taking action except when she was forced into it. Just reacting.

That, I now see in the clarity of three o'clock in the morning, is what has *always* made me ache for her, the way she is like a chameleon, willing to be whatever anyone needs her to be, drifting along to something new when things don't work out.

That's the way she was with Momma, too. I remember one day when she was thirteen. I was home from college, and we were sitting on the porch swing, and I casually asked her, "So who are your best friends these days?" and she said, with a big smile, smoothing down a gypsy skirt with sequins that our mother had picked out for her: "Well, I don't like hanging out with girls my age anymore. They're so boring and stupid. Momma's really my best friend."

Now I can see it. All of those other life scenarios didn't really even touch her. If she described them so dispassionately, it was because she was simply acting out whatever roles anyone asked her to play. No wonder she would be stunned and hurt when, as she puts it, she made "one little mistake" and lost everything.

And even now, even here, in this house that should be a safe haven for her, she's just unthinkingly trying to adapt herself to my life, hanging out with Teddy and me, playing with Simon, flattering me even while she tries to improve me. She'll change little things, like the couches, and she'll bluster about how I've got to make changes—but it's all just her act.

My heart is reeling. I reach over and run my finger along the soft little blond hairs that grow on her arm. She murmurs in her sleep, and for just a moment she opens her eyes and looks at me, unseeing. From her dream, she smiles vaguely and pats me on the arm before she turns over, facing the wall.

I wonder what the "one little mistake" will be that, years from now, she will claim she made with me, the thing that will end our little idyll here. Because the thing that woke me up, I now realize, is the knowledge that we won't go on this way, two sisters in the same house. Something is going to change.

16

"So you're over being mad?"

It's Casey, standing in the doorway of my office a few days later, rooster's crest and all. I feel like asking him if he even owns a mirror or a brush—if, in fact, he's actually ever seen what is riding around on his head—but then I remember that I'm a fine one to talk. With my current hair disaster, I've taken to wearing a straw sunhat with a wide brim and a black ribbon, and to tucking my hair up underneath it. Dana says I look like a bald woman who's hoping against hope that a square dance will break out.

"I'm trying to write edgier replies, if that's what you mean," I say to Casey. "As for my being mad, I frankly have more to think about than whether I'm mad about it."

"Good." He comes in and sits down across from me. "Because I've had another major idea about the column. Instead of calling it 'Dear Lily,' I want to call it 'Eeek!' Three e's and an exclamation point. I think that helps drive the point of it home."

"Oh, Casey . . ."

"Like it?" he says. He draws all the loops of the e's for me in midair and then puts a pantomime exclamation point with a determined dot at the bottom, just in case I can't visualize this.

"Casey," I say carefully. "'Eeek!' is what people say when they see mice in their kitchens. It doesn't have any seriousness to it at all. But, hey, here's a plan! Why don't we just call the column 'Stupid Advice for Stupid People,' and be done with it?"

"Gee, I was looking for something shorter," he says, and laughs.

"Nobody is going to want to write me letters about anything serious. Don't you *see* what you're doing to this column?"

His face darkens. Then he remembers, as usual, that it's his newspaper and he can do what he wants. "Well, I still say it's going to be called 'Eeek!' I'm in love with 'Eeek!'"

And he waltzes out, calling over his shoulder, "It'll grow on you, I promise. Eeek! Eeek! Eeek!"

I call out to him, "You need a life in the worst way."

I TRY TO turn my attention to the piles of letters that Carl has brought me, but they seem pathetic somehow when I consider that they're going to have to run under the title "Eeek!"

Still, there's a letter I'm drawn to, from a guy who signs himself "Disillusioned." He says he's just discovered that an old trusted family friend, a man his parents' age, is gay. "I know I'm wrong to mind," he writes, "but somehow I just look at him differently now. I feel as though he's not the same person he always was. Now that my parents are dead, he expects that we'll still be good friends, even like family members the way we always were, and that he can talk to me about his guy friends, but I find I'm avoiding him. And I hate myself for feeling this way, but I can't help it."

This makes me think of Gracie. I try to remember a time before I knew she was a lesbian. It seems it was just one of those unspoken, long-known facts, the kind of knowledge that children just grow into. Maybe this is Disillusioned's problem: he wasn't really as observant as the family friend just assumed he was, and so he had to be told. And it was in the telling that things got weird.

When I was very little, I thought Gracie belonged completely to my family, that surely she must be Daddy's other wife. It was the only possible explanation. After all, she was always at our house, a permanent fixture, not even a guest anymore: walking in and out as she pleased, doling out Band-Aids when needed, fixing drinks, answering the phone, sitting on the couch at night with my parents, or else heading out with them to restaurants, all dressed up and smelling nice, with my father's arm around her as well as my mother. They were always together, she and my parents. And just like a regular family member, she took sides in arguments, helped with homework, and did her own work at our house, writing poems on the porch in the late afternoon, or typing in my mother's study while my mother painted.

"Why doesn't she have her own family?" I said to my mother once. I must have been about nine.

My mother looked at me. "Not everybody has to have a family," she said. "Sometimes when you have good enough friends, that's better than family. And Gracie has us."

"Do you think she'll ever get married?"

"Oh, I don't know. I rather doubt it," said my mother.

I must have been a teenager when the knowledge fell into place for me, sort of like a missing piece of a puzzle flying in from on high and taking its place with a satisfying click. Gracie didn't have a family, wasn't going to get married, because she loved women. But when did she have sex with women, I wondered. She never had anyone over. Did being gay mean you just didn't get to have any sex at all? I looked closely at the women friends she and my mother shared. All they were interested in was talking and drinking and painting and poetry. How did you have a life in which the people you wanted to have sex with couldn't be seen with you?

I remember asking my mother when I was about sixteen, "Does she . . . have women she loves, do you think?" My mother answered very slowly, "I think her life is very hard. It's not easy being gay in this culture."

I am essentially writing this to Disillusioned: *Don't be judgmental. Your friend is still the same man you've always known. Try to talk to him about your discomfort, let yourself be open to seeing him as he really is, and know that his wish to be authentic with you is an act of trust.*

I'm on sentence three, which by Rooster standards means I should be wrapping up, when the phone rings. It's Dana.

"I'm bored."

"Bored, huh? Why don't you go look for a job?"

"God, you sound just like a mom. Not *our* mom, but a mom nevertheless. I'm surprised you don't just send me to clean my room."

"You don't seem to have a room," I say. "You've taken over mine, and apparently you like it that way."

She laughs. "I know. It's sick, isn't it? Here I complain about you sleeping in that bed for ten years, and what do I do but sleep in it, too?"

"I've wondered about that myself."

"Today I made a couple of changes though." She's chewing something crunchy while she talks. Potato chips, no doubt.

"What changes?"

"I took down all of Momma's paintings. I've gotta tell you something really, really honest, and you can hate me if you want, but it's the truth. I didn't really like the way she painted, did you?"

"I don't know. They were all right. I liked having the artwork hanging on the walls. They kind of belonged there." *They were all that is left.*

"They creeped me out. Let's get other things."

"I don't know . . . what did you do with them?"

"Oh, I took 'em over to Sloane. He said he needs decorations, and besides that, there's a kind of justice to their being there, don't you think? Since that's where she painted them in the first place?"

"I don't know," I say again. "I'll have to look them over again."

There is a long silence, then she says, "I've been thinking about men today."

"Have you now? Sloane has that effect on people."

She laughs. "He's something, all right. So . . . do you, you know, have anyone stashed in the wings now that you're divorced? Anybody you think about?"

"Well," I say, and surprising even myself, I tell her briefly about meeting that guy Alex at Claire's Corner Copia, and how nice he was.

"Oh, and how often do you see him?" she says.

"Well, actually, just that once."

"Once, meaning that day at lunch, or once that you had, like, a one-night stand?"

"No," I say. "It was more like just a five-minute stand."

"Oh." She laughs. "I don't think that counts for much. Say, do you want to have lunch?"

"Okay," I say.

"Let's go to Claire's, and while I'm in New Haven, I can look around and see if there's a job for me. By the way, who's the woman who answers the phone there at the paper? She sounds rude. Maybe I could get her job. Then I could totally take over your life."

"You wouldn't like my life," I say. "It's kind of boring."

"Oh, have no fear, I'd overhaul it first," she says.

"SERIOUSLY," she says to me at Claire's, "I think I should have that receptionist's job at the paper. Do you have any idea how awful she is? Today, when I went in there, she wouldn't even let me go upstairs to see you. She said she'd page you when she wasn't busy anymore. And then she cleaned out her purse."

"That's Kendall, and she hates me." I can barely concentrate on my hummus and pita bread because I'm looking around to see if Alex is there. I don't think he is, but that could change at any second, so I am forced to keep checking the crowd.

"Ooh, sounds interesting. I *love* to hear about stuff like this. Why does she hate you?" Dana, food rebel that she is, is eating a huge piece of carrot cake for lunch and drinking some politically correct brand of soda that comes in an ominous brown bottle. "It's not Pepsi," she told me when she chose it, making a bad face, "but at least it's got *some* sugar in it, which is more than I can say for anything else in here."

"She hates me because I tried to fix her up with Teddy. And some other stuff."

Dana puts her fork down with a clatter. "Get out. You tried to fix up *Teddy*?"

"Sure," I say breezily. "I try to fix up Teddy all the time. Kendall was actually number three."

"And it didn't work?"

"To say the least." My spider sense tells me that two men have come in behind me, and I drop my napkin on purpose so that I can turn around and peek at them while I bend down to get it. Neither is him.

"But why would you *want* to fix him up?" asks Dana when I resurface at the table.

"Why not? He's a friend of mine, and he needs somebody," I tell her. "He's lonely."

"Hmm. Interesting," she says.

"What?"

"That *you* would take it upon yourself to pick your own successor, I guess. That's one thing. And then the other thing is, who are you to say he shouldn't be lonely? Maybe he needs to be lonely for awhile."

"It's bad for the earth if he's lonely," I say. "One less lonely person would maybe change the axis of the planet in some small way and be a good thing for all of civilization."

"You sound like Willems," she says and looks at me with wide eyes.

"I was *joking*."

She licks a piece of cream cheese icing off the edges of her mouth and looks at me. "So. When are we having my party?"

"Very soon. I think first we have to think of who to invite."

"Well, let's see." She gets out a piece of paper and starts writing. "All the colony folks, of course. And Seth Tomlinson, and maybe he can bring his fiancée, if she's not too busy. And Lainie, that woman who now works in New York, I guess. And . . . oh, the receptionist, Kendall. I'll give her lots of double-strength drinks and then take her for a boat ride to see the lobster pots, and then she'll fall overboard, and I'll come back and say there's been a tragic accident, and then later I'll get her job."

"We're so not inviting Kendall, Dana."

"Okay, then let's invite your boss, and we'll give *him* the double-strength drinks, and then I'll go over and sit in his lap and stroke his hair and whisper in his ear and talk him into giving me Kendall's job. That's even better."

"I don't see why you want Kendall's job, even as a joke," I say, but my voice trails off and I can't hear anything she answers because I have just completed my fifth scan of the place and discovered Alex sitting at a corner table, way in the back. And he's with a woman.

I can't tell if he's seen me. Maybe he wouldn't even know me, in my new straw hat. Maybe I should go and say hello to him. But what if the woman is his girlfriend, or his wife?

I feel fifteen again.

"What just happened?" says Dana.

"What?"

"You've left the building."

"Have I? I was just thinking of all the work I have to do today. I've got to get back. We'll do the rest of this later." Alex, I see out of the corner of my eye, has stood up, and he and the woman are ambling toward me. I regress from age fifteen down to five, and look down at the table. This is crazy, being this way. I've met him *once*.

He sees me and smiles. "Oh, hi," he says. "It's Dear Lily. I almost didn't recognize you. You have a new hat."

"Yes," I say. Just *yes*. I can't right then think of another bright remark.

"And—a new lunch partner," he says to me and nods toward Dana. "Nice to see one that isn't screaming at you."

"Yes, this is my sister, Dana. Dana, this is Alex," I say, robotlike.

He says, "This is my boss, blah blah blah." I don't catch her name because my knees have just gone a little weaker. She's his *boss*. The woman with him smiles/grimaces, the expression of somebody who wants to get on with the business of her day, who doesn't see why she has to stop at this particular table.

"So," says Alex. He reaches over and touches the edge of my hat. "A whole new look. Color still, um, not up to speed?"

"It's not the color. She's just hopin' to meet somebody who knows how to do the do-si-do with her," says Dana. I will kick her later for this. She sticks out her hand to the woman. "Hi. I'm Dana Brown. So, if you don't mind me asking, just what kind of work do y'all do? I'm just back in town and I'm looking for a job, so I'm asking everybody what they do and how they like it."

The woman looks at her watch and then at Dana as though she'd rather be mugged and dragged off somewhere than answer such a question, but Alex grins and says they run a radio station—WNUT— and that he's the station manager, and Dolores here is the owner. He takes a business card out of his wallet and hands it to Dana. "Come on down," he says. "I don't know that we have anything now, but we can always put your résumé on file. And you never know."

"You never know," says Dana and smiles broadly at him.

He smiles at me. "So good luck with the hair. Are you ever going to let me see this hair calamity, or do I have to just keep imagining it?"

"Alex—" Dolores starts.

Dana interrupts. "Hey, listen, Lily is throwing me a big party on our porch next weekend, and you should come. We're gonna have volleyball on the beach and lots of good things to eat—you too, Dolores. Both of y'all should come. We're celebrating summer being here, and also I'm sort of moving back here possibly, after being away for years and years, but now—"

Dolores says, "I'm not from the area. In fact, Alex, *the train*."

"Oh," he says. "Right. We should get going."

While I sit there in a catatonic state, Dana pulls a piece of paper from her purse, writes down our address and phone number, and hands the slip of paper to Alex. "The date is next Saturday, at—what, Lily? Five o'clock?"

Had we said next Saturday for sure? Had we said five o'clock?

"So will you come?" says Dana, and Alex looks at me—a *should I?* look.

"Sure," I say and swallow. "Please do."

I YELL AT DANA all the way back to the office. Why does she put people on the spot that way? Why would she start asking people to the party without checking with me first? It looked like I put her up to it. We don't even really know him. And this is going to be so awkward . . .

"Wait." She stops walking. "He *is* the guy you like, isn't he?" she says.

"Well, yes, I like him, but I don't—"

"I *thought* he was the one, by how smooth you were acting. The five-minute-stand guy." She laughs.

"Well, he is, and that's all the more reason why I should be the one to invite him to things when I'm good and ready, not have you step in and muck things up."

"I hardly think I mucked anything up. He looked pleased to be invited."

"We don't even know anything about him."

"You should be happy I did that. It would have taken you five more months to find out anything about him."

"You're impossible."

"No, you're impossible. You're actually happy he's coming, and you know it."

"He didn't even say he's coming."

"Oh, he's coming." And she laughs again.

Then I think of something even worse. "I just hope you're not serious about going to work at his radio station."

She throws back her head and laughs even harder.

I stomp back to my office with her trailing behind me, practically whistling. When we get to the little stoop, I turn to her and say wearily, "Well, I'll see you back at home . . ." but she's gone right past me and is opening the door. I stand there for a moment, looking beseechingly at the people in the street, as though they might have the answer for me. And when I do bring myself to go inside, I see that Dana is leaning over Kendall's desk, holding out her hand to be shaken, and they're both smiling.

I go right past them and up the stairs to my office. Unbelievable.

LATE IN THE DAY, I'm busy finishing up my reply to Disillusioned, just putting the finishing touch on urging him to be understanding and forgiving, when I hear a tap on the door. Kendall is standing there, smiling and looking sheepish. She comes in, plops down in the visitors' chair, and flips back her strawberry blonde hair, beauty pageant contestant style.

"So, Lily. I didn't realize you had a *sister*," she says.

"Yep. I do." I shuffle papers.

"Listen," she says. "God, how can I say this? I've been just terrible to you, and I've been wanting to come and say I'm sorry, but I just didn't know how to do it. I don't blame you for walking out on me that day at Claire's. I mean, I was mad, but when I thought about it, I realized you were right. I was being obnoxious. And I'm sorry."

"Well," I say. "I accept your apology. Thank you."

She stretches out her legs and looks pleased with herself. "So, your sister has invited me to your little party."

I want to say: Did she mention the part about how she's going to row you out on the bay, dump you overboard, and take your job? Instead I say, "Oh, how nice."

She goes on for a moment about the wonderfulness of parties in the summertime, especially parties at somebody's beach house, and then she says, "So, I was sort of wondering . . . do you remember that guy Alex? From Claire's that day? He was talking to us in line?"

"Oh, yeah."

"Well, after you walked out that day—remember I was calling him over to our table? When you left he actually *came,* and he and I sat down and talked for a little while. He is so *nice. And,* well, he's the station manager at WingNut, which I was very surprised by. That's a very good station. I listen to it all the time, do you?"

"No. I listen to Raffi all the time."

She looks taken aback for a moment, then she laughs. "Oh, yeah, Raffi! You have a little boy, that's right. Anyway . . . so I was thinking, well, you know, I think I might try for Alex. And I just wanted you to know that, well, I kind of liked him, and since we sort of discovered him at the same time, I thought I'd tell you and make sure you wouldn't mind, you know, if I . . . well, if I started dating him."

I stare at her. This is so icky. I mumble something to the effect that she certainly doesn't have to check with *me.* What kind of code does she subscribe to, anyway, one in which two women who talk to a guy on the same day have to check with each other before one of them dates the guy? Is this some sort of beauty pageant rule? Then it hits me, what she's really asking, one split second before she asks it: "So would you mind very much if I asked him to come with me to your party?"

"Actually, this is kind of weird, really, but he's already been invited. Dana and I just saw him at Claire's, and Dana invited him. That woman is unstoppable."

I see Kendall's face fall for a split second. Then she recovers and says how good it is that he's already coming. Maybe they can ride in together. "I really would like to go out with him, I think."

Casey passes by my doorway, sticks his head in, and asks about the newest "Eeek!" column. I tell him it's wafting its way through cyberspace to him.

As soon as he goes away, I say to Kendall, "Have you considered dating The Rooster? A little romantic fling could be just the thing to humanize him. I am not even joking; I promise you, the staff would put up a statue in your honor."

She leans forward and says in a loud whisper, "Actually, the person somebody should be dating is our darling publisher, Lance. Did you know his family is like one of the richest families in New England? I read about them in a magazine. They're like the Bill Gates of Massachusetts or something. And his sister—I overhead him telling one of the salespeople—his sister is getting married this summer on Cape Cod to some super-rich guy she's been in love with since she was four years old or something. The whole clan is gathering. It's like two dynasties merging."

"Well, isn't that the nicest thing?" I say, biting back a yawn. "It's so good when rich marries rich."

"I just wish I'd met the love of my life when I was four years old," Kendall says. "Think of the time that would have saved me."

I think of Maggie, who pretty much did that, just five years later is all. "It's not all you think it is," I tell her. "Sometimes people aren't fully formed yet when they're little kids, and you can't see the jerks they're hardwired to turn into, and then you're in for a bit of a shock."

Which reminds me, I haven't talked to Maggie in days. I have to call her and tell her about the party. She'll be amazed we're giving one after all these years. Also, I need to hear how she's doing with Problem Husband, if he's truly sworn off sex with her altogether.

Kendall is smiling at me. "So what you're saying is that maybe it's just as well that I'm meeting Alex now instead of when I was a kid. I can live with that. I just have to make up for lost time."

I watch her as she walks away, flipping her hair over to the side and swaying in a girlish side-to-side way, and I think I really don't like her one bit. I wonder why I ever thought she and Teddy could be a pair. I must have been out of my mind.

17

$\mathcal{L}$ater that week, I get home from work one day to find Dana and Teddy sitting out on the porch having a beer together. Simon is running around the backyard on all fours, barking and growling, with a piece of paper in his mouth. I put my purse down on the island countertop and watch them. Dana calls over to Simon. He leaps up onto the porch, panting like a dog, and she takes the paper from his mouth. She reads the paper, makes her mouth into a perfect little O shape, and smiles at something Teddy is saying. Then she inserts the paper back into Simon's waiting mouth.

Such a perfect little family moment out there: a couple and their puppy. I open the sliding door and step out onto the porch.

"Hi, everybody," I say. Simon comes four-legging himself over to me and gets up on his knees and holds his hands in front of him in the doggie-begging position, pointing to the paper with his paw.

"Ool-skay etter-lay," says Teddy as I reach over and take it. "Perhaps a little anxiety, I think. Regression to og-day ehavior-bay."

Simon is panting, "School retter . . . school retter . . ."

Sure enough, it's just your routine chatty little form letter from the superintendent of schools, inviting us to a kindergarten open house the first week in August, where we can have the opportunity, he says, to meet and get acquainted with Simon's new teacher, Renée Simone.

I look down at Simon's big brown eyes. He's wagging the equivalent of his tail.

"Are you excited?" I ask him, and he nods his head up and down.

Dana says, "Ooh, shall we invite Renée Simone to the party, too?" To my shock, Teddy pretends to grab her around the neck and give her noogies. I can't believe what I'm seeing—Teddy? Giving *noogies*? And since when do they act this way with each other?

"Today I caught Dana walking through the colony knocking on doors and inviting people to this mythical party we're apparently throwing," he says to me, by way of explanation. He's still got her head caught in the vise grip of his arm and is rubbing a circle onto the top of her head while she flails at him. "Now I gotta put some sense into her, one way or another."

"Well," I say. "In her defense, the colony people had to get invited. They *are* the party. Did you invite Gracie?" I ask her.

Teddy lets Dana go. Laughing, she sits upright and rubs her head, looking at him accusingly even while she's still laughing. "Ow, ow, ow, Teddy Kingsley. I'm going to get you for that."

"I said, did you invite Gracie?"

Dana hits Teddy on the arm, a cute, girlish imitation of a slap fight. Simon runs over and gets in between them, hitting them and letting out banshee yells.

"Stop, stop," I say. "All of you, stop it."

"That's right. This is only funny until somebody loses an eye," says Teddy. He pretends to brush himself off.

"Oh, Lily!" Dana jumps up from the porch swing. "Guess what! I almost forgot. I went to the drugstore this afternoon and got lots of stuff for your hair. Tonight, girl, *we* are going to get your hair fixed up all beautiful. I bought all kinds of colors just so you could choose, but Teddy and I took a vote before you got here, and we both decided you should be a blonde."

"A blonde?" I say, and then, "You went out and bought hair dye?"

"Yep. You obviously have to do something. And we think you've got too far in the orange-yellow category to head back. At least that's what we figured, didn't we, Teddy? Plus, you look sort of cute where your hair is yellow. I even called a hair color hotline, and they said blonde would be easy to get to from where you are right now. So tonight, after dinner—what do you say?"

I don't know what to say.

"We can touch up mine, too," she says. "We'll be the Bright Blond Brown sisters."

"The *bad* Bright Blond Brown sisters," says Teddy. "Say *that* three times fast."

"Dana," I say, "did you invite Gracie?"

"For tonight's hair extravaganza? No."

"For the *party*. Did you invite her to the party?"

"Also negatory," she says.

"We are absolutely not having this party without inviting Gracie."

"No, we aren't," agrees Teddy. "Gracie is part of our lives here."

"Okay," Dana says and sighs. "But could somebody else do the inviting? She'd never believe it if I invited her anyway. She'd think it was a mean trick and she'd never come. I doubt she'll come anyway, just knowing I'm here."

I can't believe she's still competing with Gracie for my mother's affection.

"She'll come. Of course she'll come," I say.

WISELY, I have conditions that must be met before I can submit to another nonprofessional hair-coloring experience—without general anesthetic, that is.

One, Teddy is not to be on the premises. Given his negative energy during the last hair fiasco, not to mention his tendency to bring up cancer statistics associated with hair dye, I feel his presence would make it impossible for me to have a good result.

Two, I need Maggie to come over and stand next to Dana while she puts the stuff on my hair. She does not have to actively participate, given that she's a known coward, but I need her there to oversee the proceedings and prevent any sister-induced horrors.

Three, we must have a public reading of the literature that comes with the hair-coloring materials, and if anyone feels the slightest bad vibe there, the merest hint that the product could backfire and isn't meant for the likes of me, we will go no further.

Four, there must not be alcohol. *No drinking* until my hair color is secure.

Five, Simon must go home with Teddy for the night. Anyone can see that this is not a scene that innocent children should witness.

I HAVE NEVER been blond—just my boring brown and, more recently, of course, decorated with spots of gold, orange, and butter-left-out-in-the-sun yellow. But both Dana and Maggie insist I have the right complexion for it; I was somehow cheated of my rightful blond hair, they say. After all, Momma had it, and Dana got it, too. Through some genetic mistake, I inherited my father's dark hair and yet Momma's light skin color. This must be set right.

Rule number four—the alcohol rule—gets broken immediately. We all need to drink because—well, how can you not, when something this huge is taking place? Dana makes us banana daiquiris, and Maggie puts on Hair Bleaching Music, which turns out to be anything by Blondie, and she turns it up full blast. They mix up the bowl of stuff in the kitchen, and Dana recites an incantation she claims she learned from a native woman in Hawaii.

I sit on the kitchen stool as if it were a throne, a towel around my shoulders, while they hover over me like handmaidens. The test strand I make them do turns out a nice mellow golden blonde, just what you'd hope for. So they slather the stuff on the rest of my head. It is a great night, and I have that quivering frisson of excitement that you have sometimes when things are changing and you're being swept along by events like in a dream, but you know somehow that everything is going to turn out all right. The right people have shown up, and it's all going to be fine.

Dana starts in with teasing Maggie about letting me slide into life inertia, as she calls it. "Lily hasn't so much as moved the salt-shaker here in the whole time I've been gone," she says, which is becoming a resounding theme with her.

I roll my eyes. "Don't start with the saltshaker again."

"No, really, Maggie," Dana says. "Wouldn't you have thought she'd want to make this place her own by now? I mean, Momma is *not* coming back to yell at her if she repaints a wall or something. Hasn't it started to scare you how passive she is?"

Maggie laughs and pats me on the shoulder. "Oh, Lily's just a status quo kind of gal," she says.

"Well, *I* think our next project has to be painting these walls," Dana says. "I was thinking an orangey red for the kitchen. That is such a cool color, and think of how great it would look around the fireplace," she says. "It would pick up the colors in the bricks so fantastically."

"I don't know," I say. The kitchen is a cream color now, with wallpaper along the wall near the table, picked out by my mother: little bluebells on a delicate green vine. It's okay-looking paper. I have looked at it for every meal since I was a little girl and have never thought much about it.

"And the living room—I've been thinking that should be a deep blue," Dana says. "It's a fantasy I have—deep blue walls, like the place is an aquarium or something. With green couches and beanbag chairs, lots of pillows and plants . . . can't you just see it?"

Well, I can't, frankly.

I say, "Let's drink more banana daiquiris and leave the walls the color they are."

So we drink and get to laughing hysterically over the silliest things. Maggie makes a batch of nachos with extra cheese and sour cream, because Mark, she says, won't let her eat them at home.

"He won't *let* you eat them?" Dana says.

"He worries that I might get fat, and then I wouldn't be the fabulous trophy wife he needs and counts on me to be," Maggie says, striking a pose, and somehow even this unbelievable piece of news seems hilarious tonight, and so then we all start telling Horrible Sexist Pig stories. Dana marches around the room with her chest thrust out, doing an imitation of Randy showing off his truck, always reaching down every few seconds to touch his privates. "He can't do anything without checking to make sure his precious dick is still where he left it," she says. "God knows it might fall off and start a life of its own, you know?"

Then Maggie, who's been leaning over the nacho tray, eating them fast and furious, jumps up in the air and says, "Ooh! Listen to this. I've got my diaphragm in my purse—and don't say this is gross—but I need you to help me stick an ice pick in it and make a hole!"

I start shaking my head. "Oh, Maggie, no . . ." but Dana pumps her fist in the air and yells, "Bring it on, sister! We'll stick a hole in anything tonight! . . . Uh, why are we doing this to a diaphragm, though? Just tell me that first."

"I want a baby," Maggie tells her, "and Mark is undecided, so I read somewhere that one tiny pinprick can let in, like, enough sperm to create a small North American town."

"She wants to trick him," I explain to Dana. "And now she wants us—"

"Whoa," says my inebriated sister. "That is such a radical idea! Wow. You know, I totally support you, Maggie, because I want a baby, too. You know? Being here and hanging with Simon just makes me want to have somebody who's all mine."

"See? That's *it*," Maggie says. "That's how it starts. Simon had that effect on me, too. Now I'm so obsessed with babies that the other day I found myself sobbing near the nursing pads in the drugstore. Sobbing. I'm not even sure what nursing pads are *for*, but I wanted to buy them and bring them home and set them around the house for good luck."

"But I still think it's not a good idea, tricking Mark," I say. "He won't like it one bit."

Maggie shrugs at Dana and tilts her head toward me. "Lily is the loyal opposition. But I think Mark secretly wants to be a father; he just can't make up his mind."

"Like Willems with Dreena Sue," says Dana excitedly. "Willems didn't want a new baby; he has, like, eight kids from, like, eight different women, but then when the baby came, he was *thrilled.* Guys don't know what they want. I'll help you if you want, Maggie. Go get the thing and I'll get the ice pick."

Right then, though, *thank goodness,* the timer goes off, and we all get busy rinsing my hair. In a matter of five minutes, complete with chanting and prayer and much sloshing of water on the floor, my hair has become a dazzling Jean Harlow blond.

No, seriously. I don't mind telling you that I look fantastic. Fantastic! I look like I was meant for this, like I've always been cool, even in high school. I run up to my room and put on a little bit of pink blusher and some lipstick and mascara—items I usually can't be bothered with—and while I'm there, I pose in front of the mirror, smiling, looking serious, and then I practice looking wicked.

"Alex," I whisper to the mirror, and I'm only slightly drunk. "Come here."

WHEN I COME back downstairs, Dana has decided that the three of us need to go skinny-dipping—something about sealing our Sisterhood of the Hair Dye, she says. I roll my eyes. She's really drunk now, I think.

"Look at us, we're young and cool; we should go outside and live a little! Come on, you won't regret it, I promise!" she says. "It'll be one of those things you tell your grandchildren about." Her eyes are way too bright.

Maggie and I look at each other doubtfully. Dana is already

stripping down, stepping out of her denim shorts and heading out the sliding glass door, looking over her shoulder at us. "Come on!" she hisses. "We did the hair thing, we've danced, we've eaten, we've laughed, we've cried. Now, for God's sake, let's swim."

Maggie shrugs. "You want to?"

"I dunno."

"We might as well. We can't let her go out there by herself. If she drowned, we'd never forgive ourselves."

"I suppose. Okay, let's go. But I don't want to get salt water in my new hair color. I don't think Marilyn Monroe would have dared swim in the Sound with her blond hair. Even Madonna. You never see Madonna in the ocean, do you?"

We go out into the cool night and to the darkness of the beach. I take off my sweatpants, T-shirt, and underwear, fold them up self-consciously, and put them on the sand. Maggie slips out of her gypsy skirt and peasant blouse. Dana's already in the water, splashing around, turning in circles, and then dipping underneath the water and coming up again and again, like a baby seal.

"If we're really going to do this, we should hurry up and do it," I say.

Maggie turns to me and says in a low voice, "I just want to say, before we get in, I asked Mark about, you know, if there's anybody else, like we were wondering, and he was totally reassuring," she says.

"I thought you were going to check the credit card receipts."

"I couldn't. I decided I'd just ask him, it would be better. And it was. He was shocked that I'd thought that—and you know what he said?"

"Come on, you guys!" Dana calls.

"Sssh!" I tell her. "People are sleeping." Then to Maggie: "What?"

She's talking fast. "There's a business conference coming up, in Santa Fe, with people from his company. And, guess what—he wants me to come. Says we've been spending too much time apart. We'll stay in a hotel, he says, and I can shop while he's at the conference, but then the nights, I think, are just ours. I think this is going to be really good."

"Oh, Mags, that's great." I try to make my voice sound completely thrilled, but it comes out hollow. Still, she smiles at me, one of her big toothy grins, and leans over and knocks into me with her shoulder. "So *that* is where we're going to get our baby. A little baby conceived in old Santa Fe."

"Come on in," Dana yells.

"So you're really going to do the diaphragm thing?"

"Did it," she says. "Now don't get all judgmental on me. I know you don't approve, so Dana and I did the deed while you were upstairs."

WE ARE SILENT for a very long time, the three of us floating side by side. Far away, I can hear cars on the main road, but the central sound I hear is a kind of watery silence in my ears, the little ripples easing themselves around me, like comfort. My hair is right at last. So maybe, I think—as if there could be a connection, all good things starting to happen—maybe Mark Travers *isn't* having an affair and isn't such a jerk after all. Maybe he'll come to see that he wants a baby, and Maggie won't have to trick him. And maybe Dana will find what she needs and not be so frantic with need.

"Hey, how's the party planning going?" Maggie says.

I tell her the progress I've made, which is that everyone has now been invited, and I've looked up Momma's old recipes and unearthed her string of Japanese lanterns that were in the attic. Simon has been practicing walking around with a tray of hors d'oeuvres, and the other night Teddy figured out how to hook up the stereo speakers so they could be out on the porch and in the living room at the same time.

"So all the old colony people are coming?"

"Yeah. Maybe it's crazy, but I want it to be just like the old days—like a party Momma would have given," I say. "Just to prove I can do it."

Dana makes a snorting sound. "What's new about that? It seems to me that *everything* around here is just like Momma used to do it. The whole place is nothing more than a fucking shrine to the way Momma did things. That's the whole trouble."

"No, it isn't. You always say things are just the same, but there have been lots of changes."

"Name three."

"Whoa, whoa, whoa," Maggie says. "Come on, you two. It's been such a nice night; you don't want to argue." She paddles her way over toward Dana and says in the kindest possible voice, "Wow, I bet it's hard for you being back here without your mom. I don't think I've ever seen a closer mother and daughter than the two of you were. I used to be so envious of how you could talk to each other."

Dana says in an aggrieved voice, "God, this makes me so angry! My mom and I were *not* close. Why do you guys insist on saying that?"

"Well, maybe because you used to say she was your best friend," I point out. "And—oh, let's see—there was also the fact that the two of you used to dress alike and hang out together all the time and finish each other's sentences."

"Stop it! Just stop it!" she yells. I look at her in surprise at how furious she sounds. She takes a deep breath. I remember that she really has had a lot to drink. "Okay, listen. You want to hear a story about me and Momma? Want to know what she was really like to me? I'll tell you!"

"I don't know. Do I?" I say, and Maggie flashes me a warning look.

"Tell us what it was like," she says to Dana.

"Okay. Try having a mom who comes in while you're doing your homework, bringing you a sloe gin fizz that she's made you, and the two of you sit there drinking together, and ooh, she tells you all her little secrets—and then three days later, she gets mad at you for something and tells your *dad* she caught you drinking, and, whoops, you get grounded." Her voice is quavery, filled with anger. "Or—oh, how's this? You finally get a decently cool boyfriend, and she says, 'I want to meet him,' so you invite him over, and right in front of you, she flirts with him and then she scares him off, telling him that you love him so much that you're going to want to get married right out of high school. Oh, yeah—and try having a mom who gets pissed if you want to go out and see your friends because she says all your friends really like *her* the best."

"Oh, my goodness," Maggie says. I can't think of anything to say.

Dana's voice is getting more and more shrill. "But you want to know the worst? The very worst? She and Gracie were having some adventure, and she wants to tell me about it, and I say, 'I can't. I can't listen to this,' and she just sits back and looks at me with those cold green eyes of hers, and she says, 'Ohhhkaaay. Well, kid, this is who I am, and if you can't handle knowing me, then you and I have nothing to say. Don't come to me trying to talk or asking for my help anymore. Just stay out of my sight.'"

"So what did you do?" I say. I feel sick.

"What do you *think,* Lily? What does any fifteen-year-old do when her mother has cut her off completely? I stayed away from her for a few days, but then, when she really wouldn't talk to me or even look in my direction, I couldn't stand it anymore. I was so scared and shaky and I couldn't sleep, so I went to her and said I was *so* sorry and that I really did want to know her secrets, and please please please forgive me and tell me everything. I really, really do want to know. All your secrets. Tell me, tell me." She laughs bitterly. "How pathetic is *that?* And you want to know the sickest part? I *miss* her. I still miss her. She was *fun.* When she wasn't psychotic, when she wasn't trying to manipulate everybody, she could be wonderful." Her voice breaks. "And I loved that part. I just miss that part so much."

There's a roaring in my ears. I see Momma's face looming before me. I remember how dismissive she could be, how everything had to go her way. But I had no idea she had been so cruel to Dana, her pet. How could I not have known? I shiver. Somehow the night feels that much colder all of a sudden, and when I look up, I see that the clouds have completely covered the moon. But that can't be why it's cold. The moon doesn't give any warmth, so when it disappears, you shouldn't even feel it.

18

*F*ive days before the dinner party, I come home to find a truck in the driveway and two burly guys delivering a brand-new mattress, as well as a sleeper sofa.

"What's going on?" I ask them, and one of them shows me the purchase order, signed by D. Brown. I go inside, feeling weak, and ask Dana if we shouldn't have talked about this, agreed upon it maybe. She just says, "Oh. I thought we did. You agreed with me that the mattress was old, didn't you? Don't tell me you didn't want a new one!" And then she goes off into a twenty-minute blather about price and quality comparisons, and how this is the best mattress money can buy, blah blah blah, and she's paying for it from our trust fund, and we really did have to do it.

Fine. We probably did need a new mattress. And the sleeper sofa will replace the hard futon in the guest room. Maybe then she can move in there, and I can get my room back.

Then the next day, I come home and find the kitchen has been painted a brand-new color—bright Montezuma brick red—a wild, southwestern, wake-you-up-in-the-morning, get-your-heart-rate-going color. Dana's standing on a ladder with drop cloths all around her. I don't know what to think, I tell her.

"Think *positive!*" she says. I stagger over to a chair to sit down. She jumps off the ladder and comes over to me, leaning down and putting her hands on my shoulders and grinning into my face. She does look happy, I think. Maybe this was all it was going to take to make her feel okay. She's getting rid of Momma. "Think how lovely it is that things are finally being put right around here," she says. "We're taking back our house. This is *our* house, Lily."

"Okay," I say.

"Now, doesn't it look nice?" She holds my chin and nods my head up and down and laughs. "Now don't you like it?" And she mechanically nods my head yes again.

Okay, it's nice. If you don't mind your blood pressure going up while you're eating your breakfast. But I don't say that. I have other immediate concerns. For one thing, I have this dinner party to give, and frankly—outside of caring for Simon—I've been thinking of little else.

Left alone in the kitchen, I concentrate on trying to channel my mother's dinner party spirit. I still feel sick from the other night when I think of how cold and unloving she was to us—to Dana even more than to me—but maybe, by giving this party, I can put to rest some of that anger we feel. Or something. I'm mindful, as I look over my mother's recipes and make lists and search for the tablecloths and silver candleholders, that she still has power here. Twelve years dead, and she's still Topic A.

This party, I think to myself, is now not just about reintroducing Dana to the colony, but about reclaiming this house and the porch and, yes, even the party-giving mentality. That's it. And with my new shiny blond hair, I feel reborn as a person who can give dinner parties effortlessly. It's like final exam time at college, when you just beam your whole self toward aceing the test, and everything else falls away.

I make lists with exclamation marks. "Cole slaw! Potato salad! Twice-baked potatoes! Grilled lobsters! Barbecued chicken! Corn on the cob! Clam chowder! Salad with my mother's buttermilk dressing!" *Please.* Nothing is too hard. I even make two loaves of homemade bread and a pound cake with lemon glaze drizzled over it.

WHEN THE DAY finally comes, I find the cut-glass punch bowl and make sangria with lots of orange and lemon slices floating on the surface. Then I drag out the huge grill from the shed and set it up in a corner of the lawn, where Teddy will do the lobsters and clams. I set the tables on the porch with the white tablecloths, leaded crystal, and the wedding-present silver. I hang the Japanese paper lanterns, point the stereo speakers out the living room windows, put out all the old music: Frank Sinatra, Tony Bennett, Miles Davis. Inside, I've polished the bathroom fixtures until they shine, buffed the kitchen floor, fluffed all the pillows, cleaned out the cabinets, put flowers on display, blow-dried my hair, picked out a slinky pink cotton sundress, shown Simon how to walk with a tray of hors d'oeuvres while offering them to the guests, and tried to keep Dana from drinking too much before the guests get here.

And then—well, it's showtime.

SIXTEEN PEOPLE COME. All the colony folks, of course: Leon and Krystal; Bob and Virginia Arterton; Joe Wiznowski, who's alone now that Pauline has died; Anginetta Franzoni and her grown son, Bert, who helped out with my sex education back in the days of yore and who now has gone to seed and is morose and overweight. Also: Maggie with Mark, who reeks of cheating-husband aftershave so much that I have to remind myself that he is officially on the record as *not* cheating; Seth Tomlinson, the gossiping cop, and his fiancée, Teresa, a pale ghost of a girl in a pale pink dress; that former high school Goth queen Lainie, who now has managed to make Goth into her livelihood, marketing chain-link jewelry and black clothing in New York. Sloane ambles over with a woman who's dressed in a red chiffon dress and who looks like she's just come from a Shirelles revival. He tells us with a straight face that her name is Feather. Honest to God.

But I'm getting ahead of myself. Anginetta and the Artertons, Bob and Virginia, are the first to arrive. They come toddling over, the three of them so cute in their white polyester slacks. They're all wearing bright-colored knit shirts, and the two women have on lots of heavy gold jewelry and have sprayed their silvery hair into shimmery bouffants. We exchange hugs and kisses at the door, and I admire their outfits, and they admire my new hair color. Anginetta, holding her white vinyl purse up close to her chest, looks around and says she hasn't been in this place since forever, and how nice that it stayed in the family.

And Virginia says, "Well, that's because Lily is the colony's girl. She's content to stay right here and look after things, God bless her."

"She's always been loyal, that's for sure," says Anginetta, as though I'm not standing right there, "although I've got to say—and don't get me wrong, I don't mean this mean—I think she should leave the blond hair to others. She looked more herself as a brunette—no offense, dear."

"None taken," I say. I ask them all what they'd like to drink, and try to coax them farther inside. Teddy brings them the bourbons and whiskey sours they requested, but, it's the strangest thing—they stand right where they are planted, as though they're rusty and can't remember how it is that one attends a dinner party.

"Come out, come out to the porch!" I sing. "Look! Our Dana is here. It's like old times," I tell them. I put on their old favorite music, and yet *still* they imitate cardboard cutouts of themselves, standing tensely in the front hall and the living room, frowning.

Then things get worse. Leon, who's always been the colony's master of ceremonies and all-around favorite guy, comes waltzing in, grinning and cracking jokes, his arm around Krystal's waist.

Anginetta actually puffs up like a big scary toad and glares at

Leon, and when he leans over to give her a peck on the cheek, she explodes. "So you're hot stuff now, marrying a girl young enough to be your granddaughter, eh?" she says.

Leon answers by taking her white vinyl purse out of her hands and setting her drink on the table, and, while she protests, dancing her around the room, his face next to hers. "Aw, Angie, don't be like that," I hear him say. "My new wife isn't jealous. We can still dance cheek to cheek, you old sweetheart."

"Such a tragedy, what you did to Mavis's memory," she says, trying to keep herself from being waltzed across the floor, but failing. "I couldn't bring myself to honor your wedding. I lit a candle for Mavis on that day."

"Of course," says Leon, still smiling. His hair is slicked back in his party style, and he's wearing a lime green sports coat with a black shirt underneath. "What would Mavis have thought of you, going to my wedding? But I want you to know, Anginetta, I had a talk with Mavis's ghost before I did anything, and that ghost told me—you know what she told me?"

He leans in and whispers something into Anginetta's ear, and she drops his hands, looking at first as though she will laugh, but then she paves that expression over with disgust and goes back and gets her drink.

"Save me a dance for later, Angie," Leon says. "It's been too long since we cut the rug, and my wife doesn't know the old dances like you do."

"Your wife doesn't even know the dances my *kids* know. She's a baby, your wife," says Anginetta, and Leon laughs.

Out of the corner of my eye, I see that Virginia Arterton has Krystal cornered over by the piano, and she's saying, "It just doesn't look good when the *nurse* marries the widower. Don't you see, dear? And it was too soon."

"Hey, I'm a hot ticket!" Leon calls out. "Krystal, honey, they're just mad because they wanted me for their old-lady groups. An eligible bachelor. And one who can dance. And do other things."

Bob Arterton laughs and raises his glass to Leon in salute, then wanders outside with Bert Franzoni in search of a less complicated conversation, I suppose.

"Virginia," I interrupt. "Have you seen Dana? Isn't it wonderful that she's back?"

"I'd given her up for dead," Virginia says. "And I bet you had, too, if you're honest with yourself."

"I know. But she's not. She's here. And she looks beautiful, doesn't she?" Dana comes over. I put my arm around her, and she smiles and leans against me. She's wearing a filmy long skirt and a halter top, with her hair down in curly ringlets around her face.

Virginia scowls. "I'm an old lady and I say what's on my mind," she says. "Beauty on the outside doesn't count. She's a heartbreaker, this one. Broke your mother's heart with all that wild behavior." She looks at Dana hard. "You had no excuse to do what you did. Broke your mother's heart."

"No," says Dana, "you've got it wrong. My mother broke *my* heart with all *her* wild behavior. I didn't do anything wild until after my mother was dead." And she turns and walks away.

"You shouldn't talk of the dead like that," Virginia calls out after her. "Your mother was your mother, and I know what I know. I came here because I just wanted to get a look at you, see how you turned out after all that. Your sister—now *she's* made a life for herself and her boy here."

Dana calls back over her shoulder, "Oh, please."

"Dana, come back," I say. "Virginia, it's good news that Dana is here with us. Come on. Be nice."

"I know what I know," Virginia says and folds her arms.

"Jeez," I say. "Next we'll be challenging each other to duels and throwing each other in the Sound."

That's when I realize that Kendall and Alex have walked in and are standing behind me.

"So soon with throwing each other in the Sound? Are we that late?" Alex says in my ear. And then he stands back and says, "Wow, look at you. You're a blonde underneath that hat! My goodness! And all this time I'd been led to believe you had something weird going on with your hair. You look great!"

Somehow I resist the urge to fall into his arms, and then Kendall, chattering away about nothing at all, leads him away to search for sangria and the beach . . . and a place away from me.

I KEEP HOPING things will improve when Gracie gets there, but she comes late, bringing a tray of deviled eggs, which I now remember was her contribution to all my parents' old parties, too. But she's not any more easygoing than the rest of them. She takes her eggs to the kitchen, reels in astonishment at the new color of the walls, and then fixes herself a rum and Coke and goes out to the porch and sits down on the swing, where no one else is, and watches everything through the sliding doors. Her body language says "Don't mess with me, and I won't mess with you."

I hazard a visit over to her, holding my glass of sangria. "Well, you missed the fireworks," I say.

"Let me guess. Anginetta versus Leon."

"Yeah. And Virginia took on Krystal. I didn't see that one coming. I can't believe how mean they are to him. I thought he was always their favorite. And now they just turn on him." I sink down on the swing next to her.

"Yeah, well, I think they had him penciled in to grow old and crotchety right along with them. Hard to forgive somebody who surprises you like that. He didn't stick to the script. Not at all." Suddenly she puts her glass down on the table a little harder than necessary. I see that it's almost empty already. "You know something?" she says. Her eyes are opaque. "I shouldn't be here. I think I have to go."

I pat her knee. "No! Gracie, no. Please stay."

"I'm just not in the mood for all their shit tonight. I'm sorry. I know you wanted this to be a wonderful revival of neighborliness and all, but things here are different now."

"I need to make it good," I say. "I'm reclaiming parties."

"Sometimes you can't make things the way you want them just by reclaiming them."

Maggie, who has been over by the grill with Teddy and Mark, overpromoting motherhood by showing Mark all of Simon's cute little skills, catches my eye and comes over. "What's going on?" she says.

"I'll see you two later," says Gracie. "I'm afraid I don't have it in me for the colony people tonight."

"Oh, please stay, I'll protect you," says Maggie. And I chime in: "Gracie, *please*. We can't have a colony party without you. Who'll do the limbo?"

"The limbo," she says and shakes her head. "No more limbo. No more *limber*. Just look at these old coots, will you?" she says. She gestures over to the cluster of old people, all of whom are grimacing. "God, they've gotten so narrow-minded and meanspirited and opinionated. Get 'em all together, and all they want to do is to tell you how to run your life and what to think and what you're doing wrong with your life. They don't even *remember* fun."

"We'll remind them," says Maggie. "Let's get 'em drunk."

I lean over and whisper, "Hey, see that guy over there?" I surreptitiously point to Alex, who Kendall is introducing to the Long Island Sound as if he's never seen water before. "I know this is probably crazy to say, and I wouldn't want to announce it to the whole party or anything, but *if* I were to get interested in anyone, that would be the one." I take my last sip of sangria and gaze out at him. I like his sandy-colored hair, the way it just grazes the top of his collar. And even how he's standing, one hip taking on most of the weight. And his khaki shorts and boat shoes.

"Really?" says Gracie.

"So, see? There's a reason to stay," says Maggie. "To see if Lily manages to both give this dinner party *and* get him away from that woman who's got him in her clutches."

"I'll need another drink," says Gracie.

Simon comes over, sucking his thumb, and climbs up in my lap. I stroke his head.

"Look over there—at Leon," I say to Gracie. "He is not letting those women get to him. Look how he's laughing and dancing with that fashion woman who used to go to school with Dana. You know, I think this party is going to work out. There's magic in parties. You know there is." For a moment, I actually feel lighter. Watching Alex has cheered me up.

Gracie looks at me and says, "You poor misguided crazy person," but I notice that she stays.

"If my mother were giving this party, everything would be different," I say. "Somehow she knew how to make everyone act nice, and I just have to figure it out, too."

Gracie and Maggie don't try to argue with me.

THINGS DON'T stay calm, of course. Little eruptions are everywhere. I hear Anginetta saying to Krystal, "Surely there were boys your own age who were appealing . . .", and Virginia chimes in: "Did Leon lead you to believe he had a lot of money, dear?"

And as the evening progresses, it's increasingly clear that I, sweaty and frazzled, am no Isabel Spencer Brown. And let's face it: Teddy is definitely *not* my smooth, low-talking, elegant father, either, who could get everybody laughing and feeling just delighted to have been included. Leon's still trying valiantly to fill the role, teasing the older women a bit and trying to show the younger ones a good time, but anyone can see it's too much for one old man. He gets up and turns on Frank Sinatra and does his cool little ballroom dance routine with Krystal and then with Dana, and then he tries for Anginetta and Virginia again, but neither one of them will have anything to do with him.

Teddy and Mark stay by the grill, and when I go over to bring the basting brush, Mark grins and snakes one of his arms around me and leans into my face and says, "So, Mags tell you our little surprise?"

I draw back, thinking: baby. He *knows* about their little surprise?

He says, "The trip. Did she tell you I'm taking her to New Mexico with me on a business trip? First thing tomorrow morning." He is practically doing a wink-wink-nudge-nudge thing. "She's pretty happy about it, isn't she?"

"She is," I say. "She's thrilled."

"Yep, it's going to be the start of a big change for Maggie and me," he says, and I'm thinking, how nice, he's going to include her in his life. But then he says, "She'll meet the people I work with and then maybe she'll have a little more understanding about what I go through, how hard I have to work to provide for her, and she'll cut me some slack. Hey, Teddy? You know what I mean—some wifely slack? You don't have that problem anymore, buddy boy. You get all the wifely slack you want, and then some."

Teddy, pained, does a rather poor imitation of a laugh.

It's time for me to get back to the kitchen. Maggie comes walking across the lawn with Simon, saying to him in a loud voice, "I hear you can do a robot voice better than anybody else. Will you do it for Mark?" Poor Mags. I want to go over and hug her. Motherhood is not going to be an easy sell with this guy.

When I get back inside, Feather and Dana have discovered they were cheerleaders together, and they are hanging onto each other and doing some high kicks over by the table, laughing hysterically. Then they fall right over into the punch bowl, and Feather's arm is submerged up to the elbow. I can't watch.

"Ooh, it's just so lucky the punch is the same color as my dress," she says, and squeezes her wet scarf over the sangria.

I can't believe this.

Everybody starts saying, "Ewww, gross!" and I have to take the sangria and pour it down the drain, and then I can't think whether there's enough red wine to make any more. "Dana," I say, "could you look in the pantry and see if there's more wine?" But when I turn to look at her, I can see that she's way too drunk. Her eyes are unfocused, she's barefoot, and the strap of her halter top keeps falling off her shoulders.

She zigzags over to snuggle in the armchair with Seth and Teresa and Lainie. From the other room, we can all hear yet another argument breaking out. Anginetta is yelling, "Gay rights, my ass!" and I know she must be talking to Gracie.

I close my eyes and remember that breathing helps. But there's no time for that. Suddenly, the vegetables need to come out of the steamer; I need to toss the salad, melt the butter for the lobsters, slice the bread. Alex comes in and without a word starts shucking the corn. Kendall carries the baked potatoes to the table, and Maggie makes more sangria. Dana and Seth and Teresa and Lainie are all acting like the cool kids at high school, murmuring their remarks about everyone else and giggling, pointing at our shoes and our hairstyles, and remarking on what dorky things we're saying. I want to go smack them.

In fact, now that I think of it, I want to go smack the whole party, just take everyone outside and turn the hose on them until they say they're sorry and promise to dance nicely under the Japanese lanterns.

THE DINNER part is hard. People can't decide where to sit at the table. You can just see them calculating who's likely to be the worst table mate. They're practically like second-graders, trying to pick seats far away from certain people, trying to figure out who's likely to sit down in the chair next to them, and just how they would go about escaping should the wrong person come too close. The tension is almost palpable. Then, after everyone manages to sit down, I hear Anginetta ask Dana the deadly question: "So what in the world did you come back *here* for?"

"Because," she says in a calm voice. "I wanted to further torment my sister and find the meaning of life."

No one laughs, so I do.

"Lobster, anyone?" I say. "There's plenty for everyone, and let's see, there's also chicken and steamed veggies, for those of you who don't care for seafood . . . and for those of you *not* on the Atkins or South Beach diets, there's homemade bread . . ."

Everyone is silent. Only Leon laughs. He proposes a toast to me, for bringing everyone together this way. He says parties and life must go on, even though there are people we miss. He proposes a moment of silence, for those who can no longer be with us. The moment of silence, I notice, is not terribly different from what came both before and after it, except that afterward there's the sound of silverware clinking against plates as people get on with the business of eating.

Joe Wiznowski clears his throat and tries a new tack, conversation-wise. "Uh, thank you, Leon, for those remarks," he says, as though it pains him to talk at all. "Uh, lately, I realize I don't want to take my life for granted. I miss my wife, but I'm just glad for what I've got. I'm glad when the sun comes out, and I'm glad to see the moon and stars. Live and let live."

"Hear, hear," says Bob Arterton, and then this poetic vein of talk runs dry.

Virginia clears her throat at one point and says, "This is delicious, Lily. Or Dana. Whoever made it." There, I think: a nonhostile nod in Dana's direction.

"Lily did," says Dana without looking up.

More silence. Alex is sitting across from me. When I look up, he smiles and raises his eyebrows: *this is a weird party.* I telegraph back: *yes, take me away from here.*

Maggie, sitting with Simon in between her and Mark, says, "Simon, your mom told me you caught a firefly recently. Do you want to catch more?"

"No," he says. "I don't like it when they die in the cage."

She looks at Mark approvingly, as if to say, *See? That's another thing:* children can be very compassionate.

Feather and Dana whisper something to each other. Teddy stares into space, looking awkward. No one speaks. I wonder what would happen if I simply let go and slipped into delirium and couldn't stop laughing. I can feel the hysteria rising in my chest, but I clamp it down, make myself concentrate on each little bite. After a while, Leon gets up and puts on Miles Davis. "Dinner music," he says. "We must have dinner music." He winks at me.

People chew to the sound of trumpets.

Then, when it seems that the party has sunk so far down into despair that surely it can never be hauled back to life, far down at the end of the table, some new little piece of warfare breaks out. I can't make out what's being said, only that it's Gracie and Dana talking in low, furious voices, and then I hear Dana say, slurring her words, but still all too clear and all too loud: "Well, maybe I wouldn't *be* this way if you hadn't turned my mother into a lesbian."

All noise stops.

Gracie says something else, too low to hear. Then Dana drops her fork, which clatters on her plate, and demands, "Well, did you ever think of how she might even be alive today if it weren't for the fact that you were trying to steal her away from my father?"

Gracie leans across the table and says calmly, "Oh, come on, Dana. People don't steal people. You're old enough to know that by now."

Dana says, "But she wouldn't have been a lesbian if it wasn't for you! Everybody knows that."

"Wait," I hear myself say. "Dana, stop this. Our mother *wasn't* a lesbian."

"She was," says Dana. "Lily, stay out of this. You didn't know anything about what was going on. Gracie knows what I'm talking about."

"No," I say. "She wasn't a lesbian. She and Gracie were best friends. Women can be friends without . . ."

"Oh, Lily, give me a break," says Dana. "How could you not know?"

Anginetta leans over to me and says, "Dear, I never wanted to say anything, but I always thought those nude paintings she did really weren't quite, you know . . ."

"Those were art," Bob Arterton says.

"But still . . . you'd think she would have stuck to the landscapes," Virginia says. "She did such nice trees and oceans. In my opinion. It was such a shame when she let that go and did the other."

Leon says, "That doesn't have anything to do with it."

"Isabel was *eccentric*," Joe says, as if, "eccentric" were a third possible sexual orientation and should settle the question.

Everyone is looking at me. There's a roaring sound in my ears.

"She wasn't gay; she was married," I tell them weakly, though I know that that doesn't prove anything. Except, in this case, it really did. "Come on. All of you were friends with my parents. You saw this marriage close up. You know the way they were with each other." And in case they've forgotten, I remind them: my parents were always kissing, hugging, dancing around the kitchen. And then, every night, the way he took her upstairs. Are we to believe that was all milk and cookies and bedtime stories, and her real passion was with . . . *women?*

"Maybe she was bi," Bert offers. "I read that most people can be either one, given the right circumstances."

"I can't believe we're talking like this," I say. I look over at Dana, who has her head in her hands.

She makes a little noise in her throat, and then she says slowly, "She was going to leave Daddy, Lily. She was about to leave him and go to Italy to be with Gracie. And then they died."

My hairline freezes. I look at Gracie, who suddenly looks pale and very small, as if she's receding.

"Ohhh," Bob says after a moment. "Well, that does change things . . ."

Gracie carefully folds her napkin and puts it on her plate and stands up. "I'm going to be off now. Forgive me." She turns her gaze on my sister. "Dana, I would welcome a real, civilized conversation about this whenever you're ready. I don't think this is the time or the place."

We're all quiet as she gets up and goes into the house. The oxygen, which seemed to desert us some time ago, does not return to the porch. After a moment, I realize I should follow Gracie, I should make sure she's all right. When a guest leaves, you're supposed to walk her out, and so I find my feet somehow and walk. Before I pass Dana, I lean down and kiss her on the cheek. "It's okay," I say. "It's going to be okay. Don't worry. This is a misunderstanding." I run and catch up with Gracie at the front door as she's heading out.

"Gracie . . ."

"I'm sorry," she says. "I should have left earlier. I shouldn't even have come. I knew this was a mistake."

"I don't know what to say. I'm so sorry."

"Don't be sorry. Don't say anything, as a matter of fact. I just want to go home. I hate this fucking colony, you know that? Except for you and Teddy and Leon . . ."

"I'm sorry. I—"

"Stop saying you're sorry. This is how she feels. I knew that. Honey, we'll talk later. Okay?"

"Okay," I say numbly. "Good night."

She walks out and closes the door very quietly and deliberately. After she's gone, I realize I didn't get to ask the question I was meaning to ask, the one that goes, "Gracie, of course none of this is really *true,* is it?"

I GO UPSTAIRS to the bathroom to take two aspirin, but mostly just to have a moment alone. Could Dana be right? Of course not. Momma and Gracie were close friends. Nothing more. I stare at myself in the mirror and then sit down on the bathroom floor and wait to see if I'm going to be sick. I have no idea how long I'm away, but when I get back to the table, nearly everyone has left. There are plates and glasses and napkins and serving dishes all over. The chairs are all pushed together, as though there was some kind of emergency exodus, a bomb scare.

Maggie and Mark are the only ones there. She's trying to clear the table, and he's halfheartedly helping, but he keeps reminding her that their plane takes off at 7:00 a.m.

No one even had dessert, I say to them. "So, the guests: they just fled?"

"Fled," Maggie says. "Good word for it."

"Which we've got to do, too," Mark says.

"Go, go," I tell them. "It's okay. By the way, where are Simon and Dana and Teddy?"

"Simon's inside, and I think Dana and Teddy are down by the shore," she says and gives me a long look.

"So, Mags? Have you ever heard this before?" I say. "About my mom and Gracie?"

"I haven't."

"Do you think it's true?"

"Maggie, for pity's sake," Mark says. "We can't analyze this whole thing now. Lily, do you have any idea what time we have to get up to get to the airport on time?"

"Go, go," I say again, taking a moment to enjoy a wave of ha-tred for him.

Maggie says, "I'll call you, honey, from Santa Fe. Are you going to be all right?"

"I'm fine," I say.

When I go back inside, I'm startled to find Alex sitting in the armchair in the kitchen with Simon in his lap. They're reading *Goodnight Moon.*

I sit down on the arm of the chair next to him and think hard about breathing. I want to be in the great green room of the book, with a little old lady whispering hush. I'd like to be anywhere that's elsewhere—but just like this, with Alex and Simon next to me.

"Where's Kendall?" I say softly.

"Bathroom," says Alex, and without looking up, he takes my hand and squeezes it four times. And reads on.

19

$\mathcal{T}$he cleanup takes longer than you'd think. I keep having to stop and stare off into space, relive scenes from my childhood. That takes a lot of extra time.

Dana and Teddy don't come back in the house, and just after midnight, when I'm thinking of alerting the Coast Guard, he calls on the phone and says, "Dana's going to sleep at my apartment tonight. She's just a little bit traumatized."

She's a little traumatized? But I hear in his voice that Teddy is really talking about himself, and that her being there with him is making him feel useful again. So I say, "Okay. Is she all right? Can I talk to her?"

"I did some Reiki and some aromatherapy," he says, the way someone might say, *Oh, I gave her some black tea and a piece of toast and she kept it down fine.* "She's asleep now. So I think it's best not to disturb her."

"Yeah," I say.

We fall into what can only be called an awkward silence. I wait to see if his concern extends to how *I'm* doing. After all, wasn't I the one who: (a) did all the work for the party, (b) spent the evening trying to bring peace to all the different factions, and (c) got the biggest shock of all? Nobody led *me* away and gave me Reiki treatments and aromatherapy and tucked me into bed.

Now he's saying something about how he'll work with her further tomorrow, when she wakes up. *Work* with her? Is that what he's calling it? He's going to clear his appointment schedule, he says. In a very clinical voice, as though we are two colleagues consulting on a patient, he says, "Whether or not your mother and Gracie were having a lesbian affair, I think Dana's interpretation of the events has been at the core of what's been driving her away all these years. This liaison came at a bad time in her formative years."

And what about me? Sitting here trying to make sense of it all.

"Blah blah blah," I say. I can't help myself. I blurt out, "Let's just cut through the bullshit. What you're saying is that she's sleeping with you."

"She's not *sleeping with me* the way you mean it. She's just sleeping. Here."

"Does this truly seem like a good idea to you?" I ask him. "Have you thought this through?"

"Lily, what are you implying?"

"I just feel that you're maybe in a little over your head with her, that's all." I think back to the noogies and the way he looks at her. Something falls into place for me. "Okay, look, Teddy. I'm your good friend, you know that, but I see what's going on, and I just think that she's not really . . . ready for that kind of thing. Not to mention the fact that she *is* my sister."

"She is sleeping off a very traumatic day, is what I believe I said is happening here," he says coldly. "Give me a little credit, Lily. This isn't exactly the seduction scene from *Gone With the Wind*."

"Teddy," I say and take a deep breath. "Okay, speaking *not* simply as your good friend but as an advice columnist who hears about these situations all the damn time, may I point out that even people who are currently sleeping it off wake up, and that Dana is a very wonderful person but she's also very lost right now. And I have to wonder if she's capable of forming any kind of deep attachment, you know? And, besides which, I will say again, she's my sister."

He laughs dryly. "Okay, again, I'm functioning here as a therapist."

"Also, besides which, you're not her therapist," I say.

"It's *aromatherapy*," he says with a laugh. "It doesn't have any real power, remember?"

I don't see Dana for the next four days.

TWO DAYS after the party—two days during which only Leon has bothered to come and make sure I'm all right—I am outside doing warfare with the little green worms that are intent on devouring my rosebushes. It's late afternoon, and fighting worms is the only thing I seem suited for anymore. They are tangible opponents, at least. Simon, home from day camp, is marching his dinosaurs and his cowboy men into the beach plums, in search of aliens he can talk to, he tells me. Simon is an equal-opportunity story creator. He knows how to draw on all possible genres.

I have just removed a particularly fat, yucky lime green worm whose dream, I can tell, was to take over the entire world, and have looked up to fling him into outer space, when I find Gracie standing there in a long crinkle-cut black skirt and an embroidered tunic, looking pale and stricken.

"I need to talk to you," she says. I get to my feet, alarmed. She looks so frail suddenly, and ill.

"Are you all right?" I say. "Do you need me to get you something? Some water? An ambulance?" After I say it, I realize I shouldn't joke about ambulances. She might really need one.

"I just need you to listen to me," she says. "That's all I need in the whole world. I'm going to sit right here and tell you a few things, and then I'm going to go back home." Her tone of voice is like nothing I've ever heard out of her mouth, not even when her pipes burst and soaked all her poems and she'd forgotten to make backup copies, and she was so furious her head was nearly exploding. Not even when she came back from Italy, after Dana had left, and all life here had gone to hell. Or when I went over that second

Christmas when I was living all alone and asked her if it was spruce trees or fir trees that my mother had loved, and we sobbed together.

"You're angry with me," I say and suddenly feel like crying. The truth, I know now, is that I'm angry with her, and I hate that feeling worse than anything. Whatever she's about to tell me is going to make me sad. I feel like a little girl about to get a shot.

"No, no. Sit back down. I'm sorry." I sit, and she sits down next to me and says, "It's just that I'm feeling ferocious with myself because I woke up this morning and realized something I didn't know before."

"So you're now going to tell me about you and my mother," I say slowly. The outlines of things grow fuzzy.

"That's what I just realized—that you didn't *know* already. I guess I thought that because Dana knew that you did, too."

"But how would I have known? You didn't tell me."

"Isabel told Dana, so I assumed she'd told you, too, or that Dana had." She shakes her head. "This is what makes me so goddamn mad: family secrets! They end up hurting so many people." She looks over at me and drops her voice. "I would have told you myself, but I thought it was understood. It's been such a fact of my life for so long that I didn't—it didn't occur to me that you didn't know. I mean, we've talked about the gay thing, we've been open about that. But your mother—that's a whole different level of knowledge, isn't it? You poor baby."

Simon looks up from his dinosaurs in alarm, and I smile back at him, just to let him know that everything is fine. He's been nervous and whiny for the past two days, always asking me where Auntie Dana is and why she hasn't come back home.

"At the dinner party . . . ," I start to say.

"I know. And I thought you were just covering up, thinking the other guests didn't know. But . . . I feel awful about this. Are you all right?"

"Maybe I'm the one who needs an ambulance," I say in a low voice, hoping Simon doesn't hear. He's marching his animals along the edge of the reeds.

"You don't. You're fine. In fact, at some level, you really did know. Think about it. How could you not have?"

I try to think. Since the dinner party, of course, I've been thinking of little else—part of my mind has been suspecting that this could be true, reviewing its files, sorting through some old evidence. Just the way everyone at the party sat in silence, all the old colony people, as though they were surprised to hear about my not knowing, rather than surprised to hear the actual news. I want to lie down in the grass right now, stretch out, but I know that would make Gracie scared, so I don't. I stay upright and watch a sailboat skimming along the horizon, as if it's trying to trace the whole line of the world before dark.

". . . of course, when it's your *mother* we're talking about," Gracie is saying, "things take on a whole different meaning, I know that." I realize she's been talking for some time, trying to explain away how I could have missed this glaring, central truth of my life. Was I not present all those years? I'm thinking. I was a sensitive kid; I watched the grown-ups carefully for signs of everything—of love and romance, of intrigue—but all I saw when I looked at my mother and Gracie was a lovely, close friendship, and all I saw when I looked at my parents' marriage was, well, love mixed with pain. Ordinary love and ordinary pain. That's what I thought marriage was.

All those nights, all those dances, all those hugs and kisses . . . just for show. Because at the core of everything was Gracie next door, and my mother's studio in the duplex. *Don't come in. Don't bother us unless you've got to call the fire depahtment. We're workin'.*

Yeah, right.

"You and I are each other's family," Gracie is saying. "We've been through so much together, and we'll get through this, too.

You'll see, sweetie. This is just *life* stuff. It's not like anything has changed. And . . . well, the obvious fact is, that your mother is gone. In a big, fundamental way, this won't change anything at all."

I realize she's pleading with me.

I look over at her. She reaches over and pats my hand. "We're *family*," she says. "Nothing can change that. I love you like you're my own daughter. I *think* of you like a daughter. Remember when Simon was born, and I told you I'd be his grandmother? And I am. Look at us all here."

"How long . . . ?" I whisper.

"How long were we . . . together? Oh. Well, forever, really. Soon after you were born it started."

I close my eyes. The whole time. I guess I'd been thinking perhaps it was just simmering along and that nothing had happened until I went to college . . . that's why I missed the signs. But no. I missed the signs because they were so much in front of me that they seemed like ordinary life. I think about my father and feel a stab of pain.

Gracie is watching my face. "Your father knew about us," she says, "if that's what you're wondering. He accepted it. It was a part of who she was, and he loved her. I have to give him a lot of credit. He never tried to interfere, or to make her feel less than who she was . . ."

"Wait. What kind of man lets his wife have a passionate affair with a neighbor, male or female, and doesn't try to stop her?"

"Your father," she says softly, "was one of those incredibly generous, loving people, who can love without trying to control. Very rare. Very, very rare."

I feel my eyes brimming, thinking of him. That *is* who he was: generous and rare and expansive. But I also remember the heaviness of his steps on the stairs, the way he'd sit at the kitchen table with me and sigh when we did our work together late at night, looking off into space with his hooded eyes. Was that a deep sadness in him, thinking about Isabel, whom he knew he'd never have wholly to himself? I think he'd made a bargain he hated. That's the part Gracie never had to see—my father when he wasn't being *on*. The price he had to pay to keep his wife.

"I think it hurt him," I tell her. "He may have accepted it, but nobody can just sit back and let themselves not care when the person they're married to has someone else. That's not how people are made."

"Maybe some people are made that way. You just have to trust me that he was fine," she says. "He'd made his peace with it. Now I, on the other hand—well, I wasn't as generous as he was, I'm afraid. I had my times of acting badly. For whatever it's worth to you, I just want you to know that your mother was the love of my life. She was *it* for me."

The love of my life. I can't believe she's sinking to this kind of talk, as though we're in a soap opera. Is this how people always have to sound when they're talking about love that never quite measured up? I find a huge, fat worm underneath a leaf and with something awfully close to glee, I yank it off and fling it away.

"I always wanted more," Gracie says. "She had all the cards. All the cards. She had you and Dana and a husband . . . and me, waiting patiently next door. But it was all just stolen time. The crumbs. You know? No, maybe you don't know. You've never had an affair, I suspect. But that's what it's like. You're just always hanging onto little crumbs. Your mother got to dictate all the terms."

Stolen time . . . love of my life . . .

"Even so," I say. "There were lots of times when she was off with you and we couldn't get to her. I remember that part now."

"You see? You did know at some level, didn't you? You just didn't know you knew." She sighs, and I know she's back there, seeing my mother in that studio, reliving it all. It's all I can do to watch her face, see her remembering the thing that robbed my family of so much. "Well," she says. "Then I got the fellowship in Italy, and I wanted her to come. I wanted her so much, and I kept pushing her to come. We'd stay in a *pensione.* I'd write and she could paint. Your father was very busy with cases that year, and I knew he wouldn't really give her a hard time if she said this was what she wanted. All I wanted was that one year! One year out of—what?—the twenty that I'd been waiting. She said okay, but that she had to bring Dana with her, that she couldn't leave her with Avery. I said okay. Dana was a hard kid, and I always felt like your mother gave in to all her neediness and whininess and let her act too babyish. But what could I say? Isabel was psycho when it came to that child. And having Dana along was better than not having Isabel at all. And it was all set, practically about to happen, and then . . . well, they died."

"Dana was going?" I say. "Are you kidding me?"

"Yes. No, I'm not kidding. I'd just talked to her on the phone— they were coming back from that art show in Philadelphia—and she told me that Dana had finally agreed to come to Italy, too. That was the last piece in place. And so they were going to come a week or so later . . . but then that was it. They never even made it home. That truck . . ."

"That truck," I say. But what I am remembering is Dana's shock, how when I came back home, she seemed suddenly so young, and how I'd attributed it to her losing Momma, her best friend. She couldn't have articulated any of this back then. Maybe it was denial or maybe she was trying to shield me from knowing what had really happened. I want to go and call her up at Teddy's house, tell her I understand a little more now than I did before. But I can't move. So much time has gone by. So much damage done in the name of love. And I think I just have to wait until she's ready to hear this from me anyway.

I look over at the sailboat, which has finished sewing the seam of the horizon and is now tacking in toward the harbor. All I want is for Gracie to vaporize herself into the cool blue of the sky, to wait there until I can look her straight on again, until I can digest all these secrets.

She's my second mother, she's my family, but at this moment, if somebody said I never had to see her again, I would probably drop to the ground and kiss the earth.

Simon calls out to me then that there's a garter snake over in the weeds. Gracie and I scramble to our feet. He's all frantic and excited—I can't tell if he's fearful or if he wants me to make friends with it—but whichever it is, it seems an excellent time to tell Gracie good-bye, to take Simon into the house and close the door. I don't mind bringing a firefly inside, but I'll be damned if I'm going to let snakes come in the house.

20

*H*ere's something upsetting: no matter what time of the day or night I phone Teddy's house, Dana is unavailable. Either Teddy answers and says she can't talk now, or else the answering machine picks up.

I don't know what I'm going to say to her, anyway. Sometimes I think I want to tell her that I talked to Gracie and I now know the truth of the secret, and oh you poor baby, keeping this to yourself all these years, and please let's talk about it.

But other times I think that if she answers, I'll say, "What the *hell* are you doing, walking out on me that way and moving into my ex-husband's house?"

It's probably just as well that she doesn't answer. The truth is, as the days go on, my feelings are swinging away from feeling sorry for her and toward being incandescently furious.

On day three, I get an "Eeek!" letter from someone who says she's unable to move forward in life because her mother was a drama queen and was always in some kind of manufactured crisis and treated everybody in the family just rotten, and now the LW (that's what we in the advice business call the letter writer) is unable to finish college or sustain a loving relationship due to her mother's having been so manipulative. I go ballistic, thundering out a reply on the computer, my fingers flying over the keys. Later, when I see the reply in the newspaper, I realize I just might have gone overboard. I had written in all caps: GET A LIFE. THE STATUTE OF LIMITATIONS ON BLAMING YOUR MOM IS UP.

Casey tells me I've at last achieved true "edge."

I just want to cry.

ALEX CALLS ME at work one morning and asks if I'd like to have lunch with him at Claire's.

"Just the two of us?" I say.

"Unless you can think of anyone who wants to create a public scene for you. I know how you like those—the juicier the better," he says.

"You know, I am actually beginning to wonder if it's me, if I attract them or something."

"That's why I'm inviting you alone. It's an experiment. See if Lily can have a meal without bizarre things happening."

"No Kendall?" I say.

"God," he says. "No Kendall. *Especially* no Kendall."

I take a deep breath. "By that remark, am I to gather that you're not . . . you know, seeing her?" Might as well get this squared away *right now,* I think. I'm in a taking-care-of-business kind of mood.

He laughs a little. "Um, I rode with her in her car to your delightfully refreshing dinner party," he says. "But, no, I don't believe I've done anything that would constitute seeing her."

By the time I go to meet Alex, I am almost swooning from all the little crush molecules zooming around in my head. Walking along the sidewalk to Claire's, I realize this is the first time since the party that I've actually felt good. The sun is shining, there's a bright summer sky with puffy white clouds floating along in it, and—hey, so what that my mother was gay and was having a clandestine affair with the woman next door who's been practically my second mother for years now? And big deal if my sister seems to have moved in with my ex-husband, who is performing intensive aromatherapy on her. Life goes on.

ALEX LOOKS GREAT. That's the first wonderful thing that happens. His hair is all tousled-looking, flopping a little bit in his eyes, and he's smiling. He's got that boyish kind of quality about him, like somebody who's always about to make you laugh. While we're in line, he tells me about the band he was in and how they had a huge ongoing identity crisis. They never could figure out which kind of band they wanted to be and what look that would entail.

"Can you just see me as a heavy metal artist?" he says and points to his khaki pants and boat shoes. "I used to have to borrow my sister's eyeliner and red lipstick and paint long zigzags down my face."

"Is that when you dyed your hair green and orange?"

"No, I think that was our punk phase. That may have been worse. After that, I was like, hey, guys, let's go back to playing New Kids On The Block music!"

"No. Not New Kids On The Block!" I say.

"Well, not quite. I'm exaggerating. But I did write a song that sounded like Boyz II Men. But then we all broke up." He holds up a pretend microphone and intones, VH1-style, "Backstage, things were falling apart."

I like his teeth, white and even. I can see that I'm feeling better, coming out from underneath the funk I've been in.

When we get to our table, he leans over and says, "So, baby, how are *you*?"

Baby. If somebody described this scenario to me in a "Dear Lily" letter, I would tell that person that the relationship had just got moved up a notch. A promotion of sorts.

I start telling him about Dana never coming back home, but moving in with Teddy for the time being, and how maybe that's okay, but it's weird just the same.

"It's very weird," he says. "Yuck. Ugh, in fact." He shudders. "Are they . . . you know?"

"They claim not. Or rather, *he* says not. I haven't talked to her," I say. "So I don't think so, but who knows?"

I shrug, and then we sort of shift gears, and I tell him about the letters that came in this morning and how it feels to sit there with the whole box of them, knowing that I might be able to come up with just the right thing that could help somebody. My cookie philosophy of advice column–ing. And then about how lately Casey wants the replies to be smaller and more sarcastic, how I have to remember that I'm there for entertainment purposes only.

Someone on the wait staff calls out, "ALEX!" and brings over our food. Alex sorts out the plates, moving the bread and butter over, making room for everything.

Then he looks right at me and says, "I'm nervous."

I look blankly at his tostada as though the answer might be there. "Why?" I'm about to offer to trade food with him if he's thinking he might not like the tostada after all.

"Because," he says, "I'm about to tell you that I think you should quit that job at the paper and come and work with me at the radio station."

"You are?"

"Yeah. I don't think they treat you right."

I swallow. "You don't?"

"Your column is not just about entertainment; it's about everything that happens to people. Sure, there are the letters that people read just to get titillated, or to think they know everything better than the poor slobs who wrote them. But there are all those other letters that are really deep and questioning, and you give such deep responses back to them. Like there was one . . . oh, I don't know, a few months ago now, where the guy was really, really concerned about why he didn't have close friends like he saw other people having, and you just wrote this elegant, beautiful letter about friendship and patience and giving off the right signals, and I swear, I hung it up on my refrigerator. I read it every day."

I can't speak.

"And then the other night, at that party . . . with your sister and Gracie. Anybody could see that that wasn't going to get solved right then, or maybe it couldn't ever be solved, and I looked over at you, and you were just calmly going about tending to the wounded. You went after Gracie to help her, as she was needing to get out of there, but then on your way you stopped and leaned down and said something to Dana, just kissed her cheek. And when I thought about it later, I realized you were like that the whole evening, ministering to people with food and wine, as if it was your calling. Your ex-husband, those old people, your sister's friends. And I . . . I don't know. I just want that spirit on my radio station. And"—he takes a deep breath—"I don't for one minute think that Casey McMillen has any idea what to do with you."

"Oh, my," I say. I'm so moved I have to put down my pita bread.

"Plus, you have a copy of *Goodnight Moon,* which is one of my all-time favorite books." He says, "Do you have to go back to work right away?"

"I'm done. I answered the letters," I say.

He leans across the table toward me, gives me a little suggestive grin that makes me shiver. "I have my motorcycle here. Will you come for a ride? We could go to the station."

"The station?"

"The radio station. We'll record you doing some columns. Just for fun. To see."

And so we do. First, at his suggestion, we stop at the newspaper office and I run in and collect a bunch of letters to bring with me—just to practice reading aloud—and I tell Jackie I'm leaving for the day, and then we ride down Chapel Street with my hair blowing and tangling in the breeze and my heart banging away in my chest like it thinks it's found the way home.

Please, I want to say. *Please take away all the craziness. Let me feel normal again.*

But I don't know if I'm talking to myself or to Alex.

THE RADIO STATION is located in a little house off Chapel Street, and crammed full of people, all looking young and busy and full of fun. In the main studio, a guy is playing jazz CDs while a woman sits next to him, getting ready to read the news. Alex pokes his head in and says hi, and introduces me as Dear Lily, and everybody says hey and nice to meet you and oh, I love your column. Then he steers me into a side room and flicks on the lights. There's an engineering console in there with dials and switches and CD players all stacked up, but he motions me over to a round table with black padded chairs, all of which have huge, Tylenol tablet–shaped microphones hanging above them.

"Let's see," says Alex. "Now I'm seeing this as possibly a call-in show, so pick a column and pretend that someone has just asked you that question. And then . . . well, just talk. The way you would if you were having a conversation."

"But what would I say?"

"Anything that comes to mind. You can use your own experiences, you can ask the caller further questions, make sure they're asking the thing they really want to be asking about, not beating around the bush . . . whatever. Have fun with it." He grins and sits down by the console, and takes out the first letter and says he'll read it to me as if he's the caller. "You ready? Now if this isn't a good letter, we can try another . . ."

"No, no, go ahead. Let's see," I say.

The letter he pulls out is from a thirty-five-year-old woman who's been married for five years. Alex reads it very well, not making fun of her at all with his voice, but doing it straight. She and her husband are saving their money to buy a house and then they plan to start a family. They want three children, and they'd like to have a boy first, if possible. The problem is, she says, she's getting angrier and angrier when she sees all the people, teenagers and poor people, who just push out babies by the dozens, without any planning at all. "I'm sacrificing by waiting, and meanwhile I'm reading all the right books about child-rearing and I am saving my money until I feel I can be responsible for another life—and yet, all around me, people just go into parenthood without even giving it a second thought. People don't even care! Today, in Wendy's, I wanted to start screaming at a woman who had three rowdy kids she wasn't even watching. Why does she get to have these kids, and I have to wait and prepare? Lately I hate people like that, for not being careful and responsible. How can I get over this hatred?"

I close my eyes, listening, and then I know how to respond. Slowly, I say, "I could tell you simply that life isn't fair and often the wrong people seem to get all the goodies they want: the money, the babies, the private jets, the seats by the window at the restaurant. I could even tell you what a lot of specialists would tell you: that maybe you want to rethink buying an entire house and get busy making babies, if that's really your priority, because the house thing will fall into place in its own time, but your fertility probably won't wait.

"But, deeper in your question, I think I hear what's really bothering you. It's the fact that we can't dictate to fate the way we want our lives to be scripted. We think we can make all the plans and that will put us in control of our lives—that we can plot and make payments and save up money, and get what we want. But all that is just an illusion, and that is what I hear in your letter.

"I know who you are. I'm like this, too. You see yourself as doing everything by the rule book, and yet these others—who aren't as diligent or as practical or as smart as you, who forget to keep their payment books in order and maybe don't even take advantage of all the opportunities that you have—these people are out there living their lives, popping out all the babies, fixing supper, getting tired and cranky, taking up space in the restaurants, being noisy and unkempt and impolite, getting right in your way. And they don't deserve this good fortune—those roly-poly babies gurgling in their strollers, those toddlers learning to talk even though their parents are tired and not paying as close attention as they should. You know you *will* pay attention to your kids, and read them the right books and send them to the good schools and teach them love and tolerance . . . when you are ready to have them. In your plan, you will be the perfect mother, and your children will be perfect back. But in the meantime, how are you to stand your own feelings of hatred? That's the worst of all. You hate them, and it doesn't even matter. It just eats away at you. And how can you stand it?"

I look at Alex. Uh oh. I don't *know* how she is to stand it. Maybe she *can't* stand it. I think for a moment that I can't stand *her*. I hope she doesn't get any babies. She'll be one of those moms on the soccer field that you just want to start hitting—so perfect, so judgmental . . .

Alex is staring at me, and now he nods slightly, a *yes, go on* nod.

I swallow. "I think you have to start pretending you love them," I say, which surprises me a little. "It'll be hard at first. In fact, at first it will be all pretend, playacting. When you feel those awful, hateful feelings welling up, say instead, 'I love this woman. She is a part of life, and I am a part of life. She didn't get to dictate her life, and I don't get to dictate my life.' It sounds crazy to you, I'll bet, but you just try it. You'll see the change. It's a subversive thing to do. You'll start to really see her as another person who made her little plans, like you're making your little plans, and hers didn't come out like she wanted any more than yours have so far. Maybe yours will. You don't know yet. We're all fearful that everybody else gets the bigger piece of cake, and we get zip. While you're at it, love yourself for admitting it, and love that woman in Wendy's with the kids she's ignoring—and then work on loving the kids, too, and the worker behind the counter who's depressed and doesn't care what you want on your hamburger (she's going to put the pickles that you specifically said *not* to put on there), and the manager who's going to have to fire somebody today—love them, not because they deserve it or even because they need it, but just because once you love them, then you can love yourself."

I look over at Alex. He flicks a switch and says, "Wow."

I am almost trembling.

"Wow," he says again. "You nailed it. You really, really nailed it. That was fantastic!"

Come and hold me, I think. *Come over here and push this microphone away and lift me up and start kissing me.*

Instead, he gets up, but he doesn't come over to me. He starts turning dials and hitting buttons. I wait, holding my breath. He looks at me, and his eyes are like calm blue seas. He says quietly, "Lily, that was perfect. You have such empathy, such an instinct for this. And you can do it right on the spur of the moment. That's amazing."

He pulls a cartridge out of the player and writes something on it. Then he swings a microphone away, clicks another switch, crumples a piece of paper and puts it in the trash can. I get to my feet, wobbling a little.

"That was harder than I thought—both harder and easier. I feel as if the words just flowed out of me," I say in a whoosh of feeling. "Wow."

"That's the way it sounded," he says. "Very natural. You were meant for this. I mean it. I can't get over it. It was beautiful." He looks at me, runs his hands through his hair, and looks at me longer. "Oh, Lily," he says. The moment has come: we are about to start kissing.

Okay, I think. *Reach for me.* And when he doesn't—well, I reach for him. I almost can't help it. Mustering up all the spare courage I have floating around, I glide toward him and hug him. He just stands there, frozen into motionlessness. He's hardly even breathing.

Maybe, I think, panicking, he's just realized that there is no job here for me after all. Or maybe he sees a huge black widow spider that's about to drop on me from the ceiling and he's paralyzed into nonaction while he thinks of what to do. It's *that* kind of silence.

I tip my face up toward his in the universal kiss-me-you-fool position.

Taking just the tiniest step back away from me, he says, "Um, do you have time to go for coffee before you have to pick up Simon?"

In Starbucks, over iced double soy lattes, it becomes clear why we had to get out of the studio: he needs to deliver a death blow.

First, he wants to say he's sorry. He feels awful about this.

No, it's not the radio show. The radio show will work, will be fine. He's sure Dolores will approve it. They've been wanting more community involvement, local shows. This will play. Wait until she hears the demo tape.

Then . . .?

He purses his lips, looks down, looks pained, then looks at me directly, almost wincing as though he expects me to hit him with my purse or something. "I'm married," he says.

I notice the Starbucks speakers are playing a loud blues number by Ray Charles. "Oh," I say when I can talk again. "Well. That is big."

He leans across the table. Before we got too close, he had to tell me . . . didn't want to bring it up before . . . but now . . . a vibe . . . surely I feel it too? He knows this is a shock . . . really, he's sorry. It doesn't change anything, not really. But he had to say it. And do I understand?

I feel embarrassment squeezing my heart like a vise. He keeps talking.

"Well, actually, it's not a traditional sort of marriage. She lives in Washington, D.C., you see. Her father is a lobbyist with the tobacco industry—" He sees my face and wrinkles his nose. "I know. Tobacco, yuck. And she does organizing stuff. I guess you could say she's a lobbyist, too. An attorney. Kind of a high-powered type, you know. So . . . she's there, I'm here."

"You must be lonely for her." I can't look him in the eye.

He laughs, runs his index finger around the rim of his latte cup, and weighs his answer carefully. "Well, if I were honest about it, I'd have to say that I'm sometimes lonely, but not really for her." He looks up. "Oh, don't worry. I'm not going to start complaining about my marriage, or saying that my wife doesn't understand me or any of those tired old clichés. You know: 'We've grown apart.' 'She doesn't love me anymore.'" He takes a sip of his latte. "But—well, she doesn't."

"Really?"

"We don't really talk much lately. She stays in her life, and I stay in mine."

I clear my throat. "So what's going to happen?"

"With you and me?" he says, and it's crazy, but just the way he says *you and me* makes all my nerve endings ping. I am far gone on him, which is so, so too bad.

"No," I say with difficulty. "With the two of you."

"Oh. I don't know." He looks away. "It's confusing. It's just one of those impossible stagnant situations right now. Nobody has the energy to change anything."

"I know what that's like."

"No, you don't," he says. "You have the strength of ten of me and Anneliese. I can see that in everything about you. You make things happen, you change things around, and you keep moving. But she and I—I don't know. We just go along. Maybe it's that we throw ourselves in our work, and then the other life stuff doesn't get taken care of. We never figure anything out. But there you have it: the tragedy of Alex."

So her name is Anneliese. Hearing that, I picture her tall and beautiful, with ringletty black hair with tendrils curled around her face. She is slim and gorgeous, with no hair-color issues—but she's cold, a challenge a man would keep going after again and again, long after it's too hard. A lawyer for the tobacco lobby. Jesus. Probably makes piles of money, sends it to him by the armored carful. That's it: he's a kept man.

"Children?" I say.

"Pardon?"

I clear my throat. "Do the two of you have children?"

"Oh. No. No kids. She didn't want them. *Doesn't* want them."

Present tense, as if this is still a concern of his. "So," I say. He has no idea of the hundreds of calculations I've just performed in my brain.

"So," he repeats. He drums his fingers on the table between us and looks at me with regret. "I'm sorry," he says. "I didn't want to let things go too far, and I needed to tell you my, uh, my situation."

His situation. I have a moment of real clarity, thinking that I could just sail along in this crush for a very long time, and that Anneliese's name could start to make my teeth go on edge every time I heard it, and that I could really begin to go crazy when he repeated over time how he didn't have the energy to make changes in his life.

I could become Gracie, sitting on the sidelines, waiting for somebody to make a move.

"You know what?" I say. "And please don't take this the wrong way, but I think that I'm going to stay at the paper for the time being."

He nods vaguely.

"I think it'd be hard, working together. You know, if we're honest about things."

I know he won't try to talk me out of it, won't argue that he wants me to come to the station. Not even for the show, the idea of which I know he liked.

I stand up. It's actually time for me to go pick up Simon from day camp.

"Do you want a ride back?" he says. "On the bike?"

Starbucks is just down the street from Claire's, which is walking distance from the paper, where my car is parked. "I can walk," I tell him. "But thank you."

21

After I get my car, I go pick up Simon at day camp. I have a pounding headache and my hands are shaking, but there he is, smiling at me and playing trucks in the sandbox. He runs over and shows me a picture he has made of our family: four people standing in a row, big round heads, stick arms, and spirals of hair. "Ooh, tell me about it," I say to him, which the teacher has said is what you're supposed to say instead of, "What is this a picture of?" He sits down next to me and shows me who's who— he and I are standing together, with straight pencil lines where our mouths should be; and over in the other corner, Dana and Teddy are standing close together, looking just as pleased as punch, big red smiles taking up their whole faces.

"Why are Auntie Dana and Daddy smiling, but we look sad?" I ask him.

He studies the picture as if he's trying to remember. Then he says, "Oh. That's just 'cause somebody else took the red crayon before I drew us." He gives me an anxious look. I've made him feel bad. "When I get home, I'll give us big smiles with *my* crayons. Okay?"

"No, no, it's all right," I say. "I think we look fine. Very realistic, actually."

"What's 'realistic'?"

"Pretty. We look pretty."

"When *is* Auntie Dana coming back home?" he says, whining.

"I don't know."

"If you told her I drew her a picture, she'd come, I bet."

I feel tears sting behind my eyes. Really, I have to get a grip.

As soon as we walk into the house, the phone is ringing.

It's Alex. "You know," he says, "all that between us today . . . at Starbucks. I've been thinking, and I feel awful about how it all came out. But listen, Lily, I don't think it has to change anything. Just look at it as Full Disclosure or Truth in Advertising, you know? I think we could still work together. What do you think?"

I can't think of what to say.

"You were wonderful on that tape," he says. "Can't we go back to that part—where you were thinking you might take the job? Please?"

I feel pain and look down to see that I'm twisting the phone cord around and around my hand, cutting off the circulation. All I can think of is how much I'd wanted him to kiss me and how embarrassed I'd felt when he hadn't. I feel like an awkward teenager, is the truth of it. I say, "I don't know. I feel like I shouldn't make any quick decisions."

"Well," he says. "I respect that, but . . . I just think this is a better place for you. Career-wise. You and I both know Casey doesn't appreciate you. I listened to the tape again, and you were just so . . . so perfect. You really think on your feet, and that's rare."

"I don't know," I say again. I've got my eyes clenched shut so tight I'm seeing little stars. All I know is it would be agony for me, working with him every day and having to constantly relive how uncomfortable he looked when he backed away from me. All the way home I replayed the awful solicitous kindness in his tone at Starbucks. Obviously I must have seemed truly pathetic. In my head, I ticked off the reasons: (a) I'm divorced, which he probably sees as rejected; (b) I give stupid, weird parties with guests who are incapable even of civil dinner table conversation; (c) I claim to be an advice columnist, but I didn't even know my own mother was a lesbian; and (d) even my sister ends up leaving, choosing my ex-husband over me. And of course, the worst: I tried to make out with him in the studio just because he said I did a nice job on a demo tape.

I can feel him waiting for me to say something.

"Uh-oh," I say, because I can't think of anything else. "Something is boiling over on the stove. I've gotta go."

"Promise me you'll think about it," he says. "Just promise me that. You were great."

"Okay, I'll think about it," I say, and hang the phone up fast. Afterward, I sit there holding my head and thinking what a lame excuse that was. I say, "Oh, no, no, no" over and over until Simon comes over and pushes my hands away from my face and says, "Look, Mommy. Look at my picture. Now we're smiling."

THAT NIGHT Dana comes back.

It's late, and I'm outside on the porch, idly talking with Sloane while I deadhead the daisies in the flower box. Deadheading is such a terrific activity when you're madder than hell. Sloane has just come home from a club date, and he's telling me how his agent just upped and quit on the band, and now they don't have anything in the works.

"Can you imagine somebody being that shortsighted?" he asks. "Like, we're really going to make it, and then this guy decides he's going back to Nashville; he doesn't care about local bands anymore."

I'm making my sympathetic-but-encouraging noises when I look up and see Dana standing at the gate, watching us. I start. It's a little creepy, the way she's just standing there, motionless.

Sloane turns to see who I'm looking at, and then his eyes light up and he calls out, "Hey, Day-na! Dana girl! Get over here, you minx! Rimlinger quit on us! Can you believe it? Just like you said, the idiotic bastard. He's going to Nashville, and we're just left in the lurch!"

"Ohhh, Sloaney, that's awful," she says and comes traipsing

across the lawn, holding a bag of something. Probably her clothes. She's wearing a black tank top and sweatpants and her hair is sprouting out of the top of her head in a twist. She slides her eyes over at me almost shyly, gives me a little smile, then allows herself to be hugged by Sloane. "You guys'll get somebody else. You know you will," she says and kisses him on the cheek. He starts in giving her a blow-by-blow account of the quitting, and after a few minutes, I've had enough. I take my dead daisies and retreat into the house, shaking my head. How is it that she knows all this—even the name of Sloane's band's agent and how likely it was that he was going to quit? What the hell goes on around here while I'm gone, anyway?

After a while, I hear her come into the house and open the refrigerator door. I'm in the living room, picking up Simon's toys and heaving them forcefully across the room and into a wicker basket. In a moment, she's there at the doorway, munching on a peach and trying to look nonchalant.

"Hey," she says. "You still speaking to me?"

"Oh, don't give me that. You're the one who stopped speaking," I say. "And, *as usual,* you're also the one who just walked out without saying good-bye." I throw a stuffed animal into the basket. "*I'm* used to that kind of treatment from you, of course, but Simon, who happens to adore you, has been very upset."

She leans against the arch of the doorway, closes her eyes, and grimaces. "I'm sorry."

"Yeah, well, you explain it to him then. Tell him why you feel you have to get up from a dinner party and walk out the door and don't bother calling home until it pleases you again. *Four days later,* I believe it now is."

She sinks down in one of the ugly-ass beanbag chairs she's moved in here.

"So what exactly *are* you back here for?" I say. "Did you run out of clean laundry or something? Just tell me this, if you will: Have you officially moved in with Teddy, or are you just taking a little vacation over there? Should I forward your mail?" I look down at my hands, feeling something crunch. I've been holding a little matchbox car, and I see now that the whole time I've been talking I've been twisting the axle off it. The thing falls apart in my hand, and I hurl it in the basket.

"Wow," she says in a low voice. Then she looks at me. Her eyes are tired. "Are you finished yet?"

"Oh, I'm finished, all right. I am so finished."

"Good. Then I want to tell you that I'm sorry. I'm truly very sorry. Teddy told me that I hurt your feelings, and that I need to come back here and ask for your forgiveness very sincerely. That was a bad thing, just walking out like that and not telling you where I was going. And not calling, either. I'm sorry."

"Well, that's very perceptive of Teddy to notice. Too bad you didn't come up with that idea yourself. Then it might mean something."

She sits there frowning, looking like she didn't expect this and now she can't think of anything else to say.

"And for your information," I tell her, "not telling me where you were going was just part of it. How about not telling me that you were going to attack Gracie at the dinner table in front of everybody? And how about getting drunk at the party and making a complete idiot of me by starting that whole scene?"

"No one thinks you're an idiot. And I didn't attack Gracie. She said something about my behavior—I don't even remember now, because I had to get drunk just to make it *through* that hellish party—and I just went off. It was bad of me, but, Lily—like, who the hell is she to lecture me about how I'm drunk when *she* destroyed our family? Huh? And you tell me you're *best friends* with her and that she's like a *second mom* to you? I couldn't believe it when you told me that. Don't you get it? Gracie and Momma were going to run off together, and it was Gracie's idea."

"You know," I say, "that is just the kind of thing it would have been so *nice* if you had mentioned to me—oh, say, during any number of our talks when we didn't have sixteen people on our porch trying to enjoy dinner."

She actually throws back her head and laughs. "Trying to enjoy dinner? You think people were trying to enjoy their dinner? By that point in the party, most people were trying to think of reasons to keep from setting themselves on fire with the candlesticks."

We're silent. I feel laughter rumbling somewhere deep in my chest. "I know," I say at last. "It was pretty bad, wasn't it?"

"Bad? Bad? *Bad* doesn't begin to describe it. God. Is it any wonder I had to get away? I'm surprised *you* didn't have to go live someplace else for a while, too, after that fiasco! I mean, just the left-over *vibe* from that party kept waking me up in the middle of the night for days." She shudders. "I'm still not over it. I came home to count the survivors."

I start to laugh—high, hysterical laughter, but then right away it changes over to tears. I'm crying so hard I have to sit down on the arm of the couch and bury my head in my hands. "But why was it so bad? I tried so hard . . . I made all the right foods . . . they should have loved it, and all they did was yell at Leon . . . and they wouldn't be nice, or talk to each other . . ."

"I know, I know," she says and comes over and puts her arms around me. She smells like flowery soap. "You did it all up right, and they were horrible guests."

"You were horrible, too," I say, wiping my hand on my sleeve. "All of you!"

"You're right, I was. And I'm sorry." She settles back on her heels and strokes my arm. "And I should have told you about Momma and Gracie, Lily, but Momma made me promise I wouldn't."

"She made you *promise*? But why?" I feel I've been slapped.

"I don't know. Maybe she thought you'd disapprove of her. And then, when Momma and Daddy first died, I couldn't talk about it at

all because I thought . . ." She stops and starts again. ". . . well, because I thought that they died because of me."

"How could you have had anything to do with their dying?"

"No, you never knew this part." She takes a deep breath and
slides down on the rug. "The morning they died, they were in their
hotel after leaving the art show, and Momma called me up and said,
'All right, Dana. You've got to decide now what you're going to do.
Come and live with me and Gracie in Italy, or stay home with
Daddy.' And then she goes, 'But you should know that he doesn't
have the time to fool with you, and he doesn't want you to stay. So
what's it going to be?'" Dana stops and looks at me. Her cheeks
have two red circles on them. "That's exactly how she put it. I was
sixteen, and the last thing I wanted was to go live in a foreign country with Momma and Gracie and be known as 'the lesbians' daughter.' You know? What if I had to see them kissing each other? Or
worse? I wasn't ready for that. But it was so clear she wasn't going to
love me if I didn't do it, and that Daddy didn't want me to stay with
him. And then that morning, on the phone, I finally said I would
go, and . . . and I heard her tell him—and, oh, this part is awful. I
could hear him in the background, being told, and he made this
moaning noise, like he was crying or something—I swear it was like
an animal in pain—and I said to her, 'Oh, no, is he upset? Does he
want me to stay? I can't go and leave him like that,' and she just said,
'Dana, forget it. He'll be fine, it's best for everybody.' But then, Lily,
they got in the car to come home, and . . . then they died."

"Ohhh," I say. I close my eyes.

"Yeah. And so . . . well, I've always thought . . . if I hadn't, you
know—"

"Wait. Time out. You know, though, it *was* a truck that killed
them. They didn't die because you said you were going with her."

"Yeah. The truck did it," she says flatly. She sounds so young,
like she did back then.

"Listen, it was just such bad timing," I say. "It was horrible timing. But you didn't do it. You didn't make it happen."

"Yeah."

"Please, Dana. You don't—you really don't think this was in any way your fault? Tell me you didn't deep down, really think that." When she's silent for a long time, I remember how truly childish she seemed when I moved back home. I was struck by the fact that, at sixteen, she seemed way younger than she was, as though she didn't have any gumption to her at all. She was just passive and clingy, right up until the point when she started acting out. How could we have never talked about this?

I reach over and pat her shoulder, and she says in a low voice, "I thought he was so upset that he drove his car right into that truck and killed them both. That it was a murder-suicide."

"Oh, sweetie. I wish I had known. Honey, it's awful what you went through, but it absolutely wasn't anything to do with you. I have the accident report," I say. "The truck driver was drunk, and the truck crossed the median and crashed into them, head on. There's no way Daddy could have avoided it. Or caused it."

"I didn't know there was a report." She's crying now. "I always thought that he just didn't have anything to live for, and that if I'd said something else, he'd have had to stay alive. They wouldn't have died."

I take a deep breath.

"And I couldn't figure out how to live with myself. For months I'd keep waking up in the middle of the night, and you'd be there, sleeping so soundly, and I knew you were trying so hard to keep us both going, and making sure I went to school and that we had dinners to eat, and all I could think of was that if you knew . . . if you ever knew that I could have prevented it, then you would have hated me for it. I'd wake up in the night and worry about how I would tell you, what I would say if you ever found out."

"Oh, Dana. Even if . . . even if that had been the way it was, even if it had happened just the way you said, it still wouldn't have been *your* fault. *They* were the grown-ups. They were the ones with the secrets! You weren't in charge of them."

She's twisting the hem of her tank top in her fingers. "But, you see, I *knew* about those secrets. For years, Momma was always telling me about her and Gracie and how they loved each other. She said she and I were best friends, and that if I wanted to stay her friend I had to know everything about her." Her voice shakes a little. "But then, when you moved back home, it dawned on me that you didn't know. You had no idea, and I didn't know how to tell you. I couldn't even figure out if you needed to know."

I can't think of anything to say. I stretch out on the rug and watch her face, all contorted, just the way it used to be when she was little and would get upset. I feel as though we're back there again.

"So that's when I started getting blasted as much as possible. To forget about it." She pauses. "Not that it wasn't fun, with all those kids. I liked it. It was fun to be so shocking and bad most of the time."

"You *were* awfully shocking and bad."

She laughs a little. "Thank you. You know what Teddy told me?"

"Teddy?"

"Yeah. He said that I hate myself for all that, and that my task now is that I have to love that girl who was me back then. I have to love the druggie girl and the slutty girl and the Goth tambourine girl and the runaway. He told me that I didn't do those things to be bad, that I kept Momma's secrets because I was trying to keep my family together. He said to me, 'Where were the people who could have helped you? Why was it all up to a sixteen-year-old to solve her parents' marriage and to make everything right so her mother could have a secret affair?'"

"He's right."

"But Daddy was losing everybody, Lily. And I was the last one to abandon him. If you'd heard that noise he made, that cry . . ."

"That cry is an awful thing you've had to live with," I say. "But it still wasn't your fault."

"I know. I'm *trying* to get it. Teddy hypnotized me, and we went back there. He showed me."

"It wasn't your fault. None of it."

She smiles at me. "Thank you," she says.

I scoot over and hug her. It's amazing, this flood of love I feel for her. I wanted change in my life, and here she came, barreling in with all her old buried secrets and her tendency to change everything around to suit herself, buying furniture and painting the kitchen. Okay, so it's not the change I would have picked for myself had I been the designer of my life. I was thinking more along the lines of a nice man I could slowly introduce into my life. But apparently *that* dream is dead since Alex is married—so maybe I have to learn to accept that this may be the change in my life that I need to deal with. That's probably what I'd be telling myself if I were a letter writer. "Accept the change that's right in front of you; that's probably the lesson you're meant to learn."

But there's just one tiny little thing bothering me, I realize later as she and I brush our teeth and get ready for bed. "Dana," I say. "About Teddy . . ."

"Yesh?" she says. Her mouth is filled with toothpaste.

"There are just a few things you should know." I lean against the bathroom counter and watch myself in the mirror. How to put this? "He's very vulnerable and he gets attached really, really easily."

She smiles.

"Now I know that for *you*—well, you've slept with lots of guys and that's all *right*. I'm not saying there's anything wrong with that, you understand. But Teddy . . . well, he just hasn't done that so much. So you need to be careful about running to him when you have troubles and, you know, sleeping at his house, because he could so easily get the wrong idea."

There. I've said it.

She looks up at me with a perfectly innocent look. "Oh, Lily. It's fine. He didn't get the wrong idea."

Later, after she's asleep across the hall on the new sofa bed, and I'm tossing and turning on my new mattress, I think maybe I didn't ask the question I meant to ask. Which was: Did you sleep with my ex?

22

*T*he next week, Leon Caswell takes a fall and hits his head, which he claims was due to the curb in front of his house suddenly being four inches higher than his foot remembered it being, curbs being the diabolical, unreliable structures they are. But then, when he has another spill—this time in the bathroom in the middle of the night—he admits to Krystal that he's had quite a few dizzy spells lately. He gets diagnosed with transient ischemic attacks, which I learn means little strokes. And he's hospitalized for tests.

In the old days, this would have ignited a whole organizational Support Brigade in the colony, with people sorting out who would bring the meals, comfort his wife, and visit him in the hospital. The phone lines would have been burning up. But not anymore. In the deafening silence from the telephone, I look across the bay at the shuttered windows belonging to Anginetta and the Artertons and the Wiznowskis, and I can't believe no one even cares. But there you go. The colony is an altogether different place from the one I'd been imagining.

I drop by the hospital in the afternoons after work and bring Leon brownies, which are his favorite. He tells me they're talking CT scans, MRIs—all those alphabetical things. He does a little comedy routine, in which he makes his expression very serious and says, "So I had the DUI and the MRC, but then they also wanted the HIW, and so they hooked me up to the TR19 . . ." Okay, so it's not very funny. But how many stroke patients can come up with really good jokes? Finally they let him out, and he says it's because they're sick of him making all the other patients laugh and misbehave.

"Does he feel bad that no one else from the colony comes to visit?" I ask Krystal one day.

She shrugs. "He doesn't talk about it, but when the phone rings, I notice he perks right up, and gets himself all ready to have a conversation; and then when it's for me, or it's just a telemarketer, he gets kind of quiet for a while. Just stares out the window."

That does it. There have to be some changes made around here. When I get home, I call up Virginia Arterton and say to her, "Leon Caswell came and shoveled your walk every single day when Bob was sick in the hospital. And now he's had a stroke, and you've got to help him."

She sighs. "I don't know what to do for him."

"Bake a cake. Fry some chicken—no, don't fry chicken. That'd be bad for his arteries. Go play a game of cards with him. Call him on the phone. Come on, Virginia, you know exactly what to do." I hang up before I can hear her make a list of phony excuses.

MAGGIE COMES BACK from her trip to Santa Fe, and we go to Claire's for lunch to catch up. She has a sensational tan and lots of things to tell me, including the news that Problem Husband had sex with her exactly three times that week—a record!—and that each time, she managed to display her decoy birth-control devices in a convincing way. And she got to meet all his co-workers, including his secretary, Ashley, who is just the nicest person—and thank goodness, because if she weren't so sweet, Maggie would really have to be jealous of her. After all, as she and Ashley calculated one day by the pool, Mark spends probably twice his waking hours with Ashley rather than Maggie. But anyway, she goes on, her voice rising and falling in her excitement, she poked about ten additional holes into her diaphragm, egged on by the hotel maid, to whom she told the whole story one day when all the office people (including Ashley) had gone out to play golf.

"So, we'll see what happens," she says. I can see how much she wants this, even though I think she's crazy. Throughout this entire Ashley story, all my nerve endings have been going *ping ping ping,* but I don't say anything. Besides, what's done is done. It's now up to fate. "So how are you?" she says, taking a bite of her vegetarian lasagna.

"I don't know how I am," I tell her. It's kind of a bad day, actually. Casey has taken to lopping off the last paragraph of every letter I answer, as a way of forcing me to make the column snappier, and I've just come from an argument with him about that. I shift around in my seat and halfheartedly try to fill her in on everything: Dana's flight to Teddy's house, my conversation with Gracie, and then, of course, the huge talk with Dana when we sorted things out.

"But Dana's back with you now," Maggie says. "So what's wrong?"

I look out the window at the people walking along the sidewalk, none of them Alex. That's probably good. I don't know if I'm ready to face him yet, not in this restless mood I'm in. I'm not even sure I can explain to Maggie what I'm feeling. I don't even know myself.

"I know she's back, but everything's still the same, like the talk never happened. I mean, here we had that quote unquote *huge breakthrough,* if you want to call it that, and we both now understand what she went through as a kid and how that explains why she acted out as a teenager, and then why she had to dress all in black chains and go be a tambourine girl. But now that we've had that talk . . . well, she's just the same Dana, flitting around and acting like she owns my life or something. Flirting with Teddy all the time and making a big deal over how much she just *adores* Simon, jacking up the music way too loud and keeping me awake nights talking and talking . . . do you know what I mean? I feel like she's the real person in the house, and I'm just her pale, bland assistant or something."

"What did you think would change?" Maggie says softly.

"I thought . . . I guess I thought that maybe she'd be more responsible." *Responsible.* Is that the word? I twist my napkin around in my fingers. "But she isn't. She still acts as if life for her is just one big, giddy smorgasbord, all spread out for her to pick whatever she wants next. She's just like she used to be. Go be an event planner in Hawaii? Terrific! Grow vegetables and take care of babies in Vermont? Sign me up! Go back home to Branford and move back and forth between your sister's house and her ex-husband's house? Why not? She doesn't put a stake in anything. She just . . . takes whatever's out there and . . . oh, I don't know. It's like she's just always cruising for the next thing and the next."

Maggie's watching my face. "While *you* stay in the same old job that insists on devaluing your work, and you work hard to make sure Teddy's love life is all fine and dandy, and that Dana is all adjusted and happy and feeling right," Maggie says. "Not to mention your insistence that the whole colony should just hum along like it used to twenty years ago—and getting mad when it doesn't."

"Yeah," I say. I laugh a little bit. "Yeah, that's it. Why can't people behave like I want them to?" I rail up at the ceiling, in mock frustration. Then I take a sip of my water and settle back in my chair. Something else occurs to me. "But you know, Mags, when I went and did that demo tape with Alex, I got so excited about actually being able to answer somebody's *real* question in a *real* way, and hearing my voice say those things. It's so hard to answer on the spot, though—do you remember when we were kids and we'd play those trust games with the Scallopini? Just let go and fall backward and have faith that someone will catch you? That's what this is like. You just start talking into the microphone and you just have to trust that you're going to say something intelligent, because you don't have time to edit yourself. It was such a rush!"

She says, "So . . . what happened? They didn't have a job for you after all?"

"Well," I say. "Well."

She's looking at me expectantly.

I look around to make sure Alex isn't there, and then I lean forward and speak in a low voice. "*This* is the worst of it, really. I've fallen a little bit in love with Alex, and then I found out he's married, even though he doesn't live with his wife, and—well, he knows how I feel because we almost kissed. Or rather, *I* almost kissed *him* the day of the taping, and now I know he just thinks I'm pathetic. He feels sorry for me. And so, obviously, I can't take the job."

"Oh," she says and sits back. "My, this is serious."

"Married or not, he's still the person I think about. I've got to figure out how to stop. Dana, of course, would just take up with him and get her heart broken, and then have to move to Paris or something to get over him, and there she'd meet a musician and they'd hook up . . . and on and on and on . . ."

I'm running on like this when I realize Maggie is staring at me, trying not to laugh.

"What?" I say.

"I'm just so happy for you. You actually used the word *love,* you know that? I don't know why you're fighting so hard. It's so clear how this is going to turn out—clear to everybody but you."

"How's it going to turn out?"

"Um, how does the song go that we used to sing? Alex and Lily sitting in a tree, K-I-S-S-I-N-G . . ." I sing along with her: "First comes love, then comes marriage . . . But oh no, Lily, he's already M-A-R-R-I-E-D."

Okay, so it doesn't quite fit the line. She gets the idea. Only she doesn't care. "I think you need to trust, just like you did when you went on the air," she says, gathering up her purse and getting ready to go. "I'm quite positive that he doesn't see you as pathetic—and so what that you let him know you like him? I'll bet he was delighted.

If you ask me, you should take the job and see where things lead." She hesitates a moment and touches my shoulder. "You know, you could be a *little* more like Dana, and the world wouldn't end."

AUGUST COMES in with rain and thunderstorms. One stormy day, Alex comes to see me at the paper—for no apparent reason other than that he has some free time—and then he can't leave because it's storming so hard outside that he can't ride his motorcycle back. I am so glad to see him that my hands go all clammy. He sits in my office and tells me that he's talked to his boss and she really is very interested in talking to me about having the advice call-in show on the air, and have I thought more about it?

"I don't think we should alk-tay about it ere-hay," I say. "Casey may have the place ugged-bay."

He laughs. "Your answers in the newspaper are getting orter-shay and orter-shay," he says. "I loved the one today, from the guy who asked if there were any circumstances under which he would be allowed to read his girlfriend's mail. And you wrote: 'Her death.' Whoo! I got a chill reading that."

"Did you? That took me nearly twenty seconds of hard writing time, I want you to know."

He's smiling steadily at me. "I can't help but notice that you're wearing a hat again. Have you been fooling around in the hair dye again?"

"Dark roots," I say. "And now it's in bad condition."

"Let me see."

"No way."

"Come on. You know I'm in sympathy. Let me see."

"Absolutely not."

"You know," he says, "as your hair consultant, I think it's time I told you that I have a little bit more of an interest in your hair than I've copped to."

"Uh-oh. Is this another Full Disclosure, Truth in Advertising clause?"

"Yes, it is, as a matter of fact. My sister is one of the great hairdressers of all time, and her studio is just on George Street—and anytime you want to go see her and have her fix you up, just say the word. I've got her secret phone number."

"Really."

"Yes."

"And you've withheld this information from me this long?"

"I didn't want to brag about my connections. But now that I'm trying to woo you to my"—he looks around and whispers the words—"*radio station,* I am ready to pull out all the stops."

"Let's go," I say, standing up.

"What, now? It's storming out, and also I have to call her first."

"Ah, ah, ah! You're not backing out now, are you?"

"Just how is it that you can leave whenever you want? Don't they care where you go in this so-called journalism organization?"

"Hey, I've written my six words for tomorrow's three letters," I say. "Let's go. We'll take my car. Leave your bike here, and we'll come back for it. Come on, come on. Get up! Let's go. March."

I can't believe I'm acting this way with him. I suppose it's the only way to keep myself from falling at his feet.

HIS SISTER is named Cherie, and she's his twin sister, older than he is by seven minutes, she tells me. She has sandy brown hair like his, and the same blue eyes, but she dresses all funky—today in a patchwork skirt with big chunky coral-colored stones for jewelry— whereas he's sort of preppy looking. I like her immediately, just the way she gets so happy when she sees him. She has this great little salon, decorated with scarves and paintings instead of the usual hairstyle posters, and sure enough, she takes a look at me and says she knows just what I need. My hair needs retouching, and a deep conditioning treatment—and actually, now that she thinks of it, blond may not be the right color for me.

"Not blond?"

She squints at me, frames my face with her hands. "It's too harsh for your coloring. I think you need depth. I hate to say it, but you need your natural color back."

"Boring brown?"

"I know. You were tired of it. But it's really your true self." She thinks a moment. "I know! We'll add some nice rich auburn highlights to it."

"Okay," I say at last.

Alex smiles at me in the mirror and nods. "I told you she'd know what to do with you," he says.

He's sitting in the chair next to me, spinning in circles the way Simon would be doing if he were here. He stays there with me the whole time Cherie's working on me, teasing me a little when she has my hair all foiled up and sticking straight up in the air. He says I look like a satellite dish. I tell him I look like The Rooster, and then I have to explain that that's what we call Casey when he's not around.

"Hmm, I wonder what my staff calls me when I'm not there," he muses. "When you come to work at the station, you have to promise to get the insider info and then tell me."

"If I come to work at the station, hell will have frozen over, and there'll be no such things as nicknames for bosses anymore."

"Why aren't you going to work with him?" Cherie asks. "He'd be a nice boss, wouldn't he?"

"Well, I'm really a writer," I tell her. "And I'm just not sure I could do a radio show day in and day out. It seems much riskier to give advice live on the air than to write it down. You know?"

Alex laughs. "She's brilliant on the air. I think she just fears I'm a lothario who would corrupt her."

"A lothario? No one says *lothario* anymore," his sister says. "Anyway, that's not the way you are at all. Don't even flatter yourself."

He meets my eyes in the mirror and smiles.

"Now, now, don't you get into this," he says, teasing her. "Lily and I already know we have a little chemistry thing going that could easily lead to disaster. So don't try to push us together. It's hard enough as it is for us to resist each other."

I can't believe he's told her this, but she just laughs. "You're a smart one," she says to me, and then she sends him out to buy us milk shakes, saying that now that it's no longer raining, it's too hot to work without the prospect of ice cream drinks.

I'm afraid that once he leaves she's going to tell me she's guessed what a crush I have on him, and that I'll end up pumping her for information about his wife, trying to discern if he's likely ever to get a divorce, as well as get the whole lowdown from the twin sister's point of view, which has got to be oh so valuable. But she's cool. Instead she tells me all about a letter she's been tempted to write to me, asking for advice. She's getting married in three months, and her fiancé wants his nickname, Skip, on the invitations instead of his real name, which is actually Deuteronomy. She laughs and says he's never been called that, but her parents say if his given name is Deuteronomy, then that's what has to appear on the invitations.

"My father says, 'No daughter of mine is having it formally engraved that she's marrying a guy named Skip Storm,'" she says. "Like that's the important issue here." She shakes her head. "It's been battle after battle with them. First they tried to push me into having a big formal wedding like Alex had, and I said no. Then they wanted me to wear a white chiffon wedding dress, and I'm wearing a plain long deep blue skirt and a sun hat. After that, they wanted a big churchy thing with a priest, and I'm getting married in a field. So now Skip's name is where they're digging in their heels."

I sit there trying to imagine what kind of people would name a kid Deuteronomy Storm, and trying not to start hooting with laughter, when she leans down and whispers to me, "Just want to tell you this before Alex comes back because he doesn't like to talk about it. But I don't think his marriage is long for this world. I think last rites may be in order."

"Well," I say, keeping my face very neutral, which means not meeting her eyes in the mirror. "That's too bad. I feel sorry for him, but I'm not the kind of person who would ever root for somebody's marriage to end."

She looks at me and bursts out laughing. "Like hell you're not, girl! Who do you think you're talking to? I see you sitting here thinking it right now. He's cute, isn't he? My little baby brother."

"Baby brother? I thought you were his twin."

"Did I not mention the seven minutes by which I am older?" she says. "And I've made the most of those minutes, believe me."

"You know," I tell her, "I think the wedding invitation has *got* to say Skip. If you give in now with the Deuteronomy, you'll hate yourself."

"See? That's what I'm talking about," she says. "You're smart. I like that. You just have to take better care of your hair. Treat it like it's a patient and you want it to live. I want you to come in for deep-conditioning treatments every week for a while until we get it back on track."

"Well . . . ," I say.

"And," she whispers, "I'll keep you up to date on the demise of Alex's marriage."

ALEX SITS sideways in his car seat and studies me while I drive him back to the newspaper office to get his bike. The sun is now hot and the air is filled with humidity. I try not to mind being stared at. And besides, to ask him to please stop would only make him too happy. He's just in that kind of mood. I tell him I like his sister a lot.

"Yeah," he says "She's great. So, Brown. How's *your* sister?"

"Also great. She's back at home now. Doing fine."

"Back at home? Oh, yeah. She moved in with the ex. I remember. Wow! So she's back? But are they a couple?"

"No," I say. "They say no."

"Well, *I* think they're a couple."

"They're not. He was doing aromatherapy on her."

He starts laughing so hard I think he might fall out of the car. "She had to have live-in aromatherapy? Man, that must have been a tough case." He looks at me for a long, uncomfortable minute. "How is it that you're such a great advice columnist and yet one of the more gullible people on the planet?"

"I know, I know. It sounds weird. But I've been watching them since, and even though I know he likes her, I don't think anything is really going on. I mean, it would be weird if it were, right? Almost like incest."

"But oh so different in all the really important ways," he says. "The ways that get the state interested."

I laugh again.

"Listen," he says as we pull up to where his motorcycle is parked. He looks serious for once. "I just want to say one thing. I got a really strange vibe at your dinner party with those two, and I gotta say that what you've just told me hasn't made it exactly go away. So I just want to tell you that if you ever need a place to go—you and Simon—you can stay at my apartment."

"What? I would nev—"

"Shhh. Listen to me." He puts a finger on my lips. "You might. I don't have a beach to offer you, I'm afraid, but I do have tons of room now that Anneliese has decided to room with her dad. And, right this minute being a notable exception, I'm at work virtually all the time, so I wouldn't be in your way. Three bedrooms, a living room, a deck, the finest in bathroom towels and linens—and it's all furnished with massive old-lady furniture from the previous tenant who died but who I swear does not haunt the place. And I promise, cross my heart and hope to die, that I won't molest you while you sleep."

I start to say something, and he leans over and gives me a brush kind of kiss on the forehead, a grazing of lips on my skin, hardly even touching me. "That's to say I'm sorry for that horrible day at Starbucks, which I will apparently never live down, and also for today, when I embarrassed you by telling my sister we have a little thing going. Now one business question and then I will get out of your car and let you get on with your life: Are you even considering coming to work at the radio station? Should I talk to my boss?"

"No," I say. "Yes." I think harder. "Well, maybe. The truth is, I don't know."

He searches my face. "You may need to work on a more definitive answer," he says. "How is it that you can answer other people's questions so cogently, but you don't make a damn bit of sense when you talk about your own life?"

23

$\mathcal{I}$ pull into my driveway and sit in the car for a moment, admiring my new dazzling brown, shiny hair in the rearview mirror, and just for entertainment purposes, going over everything that Alex has both said and implied over the afternoon—when it suddenly comes to my attention that all is not right in Scallop Bay world. It's still midafternoon, way earlier than I usually get home, and I can't tell right away exactly what's amiss, but when you live in a place for your entire life, you know when things are the least bit *off*.

Something is not right.

I get out of the car, catlike, and stand there on the sidewalk, looking down at the half-dead red geraniums and the straggling daisies still in puddles from the morning's rain. I trace a crack in the cement with the toe of my sandal and listen. Then I hear it: a man's voice coming from inside my house. And it's not Teddy and it's not Sloane.

In fact, it has a Southern accent.

I push open the door, my hand on my cell phone as though it's a weapon, and I go in. I hear my sister saying from the kitchen, "Oh, *you*. You know you're just like some big ole gorilla when you want to be, baby. I'm gonna get us a couple slices of this pound cake right here and fix us up some Southern Comfort, and we'll go right back upstairs. You know, I've got everybody up here drinkin' these—" She sees me then and freezes with her hands in midair.

She's wearing a cowboy hat and black bikini underpants, and a man's denim shirt, unbuttoned. She starts laughing hard.

"What's so funny?" the guy says and turns around. He's big and red-faced and he's sitting at the counter island on a stool that looks as though it's going to sink from the sheer avoirdupois of him. He's not so much fat as he is humongous. It's like having a camel in the room or something. A very large, muscular, potbellied, jeans-wearing camel who's mindlessly, blankly chewing on something.

His face takes on one of those big, good-ole-boy grins, the kind that Northerners all know doesn't mean anything good. And then he gets up off the stool and gives me one of his hands, which is the approximate size of a baseball mitt and is damp and squishy. I have the urge to dry my hands on my pants after we shake.

"Ah'm Randy Slattery, from Texas," he says. "And you must be Lillian."

"Lily, actually," I say.

"Whoa, this is sort of embarrassin', ain't it? We weren't expectin' anybody. Button up, sugar, why don't you?"

This, embarrassing? I want to tell him. Why, I've been in this situation with her *lots* of times. This wouldn't even make the top ten of embarrassing walk-ins. At least *he's* dressed. That's a nice change from the early years.

"Don't worry about it," I tell him. "Dana, I'll have one of those Southern Comforts, too, if you don't mind."

"Sure," she says brightly, but she looks a little scared.

I look Randy over. He's dark-haired and vacant-eyed, a little on the dumb side, you can just tell, and friendly enough, but with something in his eyes that makes you know he could just go off if he feels like he's getting disrespected. I can't help but wonder if Dana has a plan here. How did he track her down?

I smile at him. "Wow! Long drive for you, from Texas. Did you just get in?"

"No, no. I got in yesterday. Dana's been takin' me all around, showin' me the sights. What's that lobster place we went to, hon?"

"Lenny and Joe's," she says, not looking at me. I fix her with my most penetrating stare. He got in *yesterday*? And just why hasn't she said anything? The last time I asked her about him, she said he'd decided she could keep the truck, and that they were better off apart, blah blah blah, and that everything was fine. Now she won't meet my eyes.

"So I got me a lobster roll, and come to find out they make it with butter—on a hot dog bun!" he says, as though this is the most amazing thing ever. "I always thought a lobster roll had to have mayonnaise and celery and onion all mashed up with it, like tuna fish salad or sumpin'. But no. They just butter 'em up like any ole lobster tail you'd order in a restaurant." He says it *rester-awnt*. "Say, Dana tells me you've got some lobster pots right out there in the water, yourself."

"Yep," I say. "Yes, sir, we do." I feel myself taking on my own version of a Southern drawl.

"Nice place you two own." His head very nearly scrapes the ceiling. He could never live here. He'd knock himself unconscious going up and down the stairs. "But I'll tell you what. Y'all don't seem to have any idea of what an *ocean* is supposed to be like," he says, laughing. "Y'all got to get you some *waves* if you want to attract the surfin' crowd. Why, you could really be sumpin' here if you just had a wave or two every now and then. Get you some tourists in here and get some revenue."

On the chance that this is Southern humor at work, I throw back my head and give a hearty impression of a laugh, and he does, too. Ah. So it was a joke.

"Randy just loves New England!" says Dana.

"Well, I'm a Texas man who couldn't ever live anywhere else, but I say you can't go wrong in a place where they put butter on lobster on a hot dog bun," he says. "I'm gonna suggest that to the folks back home." He looks at me. "Now what do you do, Lillian?"

"Lily's an advice columnist for a newspaper!" says Dana brightly.

Oh, my, he says, an *advice columnist*. Oh, my! Well, then. He guesses I have just about *all* the answers. Must be nice! But, hey, could he get some on-the-spot advice, ha-ha-ha, from one almost–family member to another? Gratis? He gets up and goes over and puts his arm around Dana and smiles down at her. Like maybe I can tell him what the appropriate penalty is for a bride who jumps up in the middle of the night and disappears on the man who loves her and is about to marry her, takin' his truck and half his CD collection, and all the Southern Comfort in the house. Huh? What should a guy do when that happens, huh, *Lillian*?

"Oh, Randy!" she says and kind of twirls out of his grasp and pokes him in the arm.

He pours us all a drink. "Think about it," he says to me with a big dumb grin. "You don't have to come up with sumpin' right away."

I FORGET at what point I start feeling kind of sorry for him. He sits there drinking and talking, and by the stories he tells, it becomes clear that here he is, just a guy who was kind of a loser and not doing so well in the world, and then his sister says to him that he can stay at her place, and oh, by the way, there's this gal staying there who's Willems's old girlfriend, and can you show her a good time? Be nice to her and make her feel special? (Subtext, I'm sure, is: Get her off our hands.) And so he does. He takes her to play pool and to parties and to the beach and to a couple of hotel rooms in San Antonio, and one thing leads to another—wink, wink—and pretty soon he's living in the back bedroom with this little gal at his sister's house, and sleeping with her in a double bed that's way too small for the two of them, so they get to know each other pretty well, ha-ha-ha, but things are good, she's fun to go out with, and all his friends think he's really lucky. And they go on like this and then suddenly his sister tells him it's time he got married to the girl—and well,

225

that's okay, too. You can't just keep sleeping with people without it comin' to somethin'. Everybody eventually gets married, don't they? And he loves her; she's cute, even though she's got that Yankee accent to her and she gets pissy sometimes. ("You know you do, sweetie pie. You get pissy like all get-out.") He buys a cherry red pickup truck and tells this little ole wife-to-be that she can drive it all she wants—and damned if she doesn't up and take it to Connecticut to see her sister, and then she never comes back.

So he's come for her.

She belongs in Texas now, he says. She's been up here cattin' around long enough, and he's sick and tired of bein' lonely and puttin' up with this. Plus, there's a weddin' to plan and she's supposed to be helpin' out Dreena Sue—the baby's gettin' big now, and there might be another on the way. He reaches over and taps her on her flat, bare stomach, and says, And we just might git us one started, too, right? When you git back. Nice to get a bun in the oven even before the weddin'. He looks at me. Y'all will come down and see us all. Be the maid of honor.

Dana winces and puts her hand where he's tapped her. I start thinking: How are we going to get him out of here—without Dana in the passenger seat?

He pours himself another large one, and she says, "Lily, I've got somethin' in my eye, darlin', can you come into the bathroom and help me get it out?" and she and I fly upstairs and close and lock ourselves in the bathroom, our conference room of old. She leans against the door and closes her eyes.

"What the *hell*?" I say.

"A little mismanagement, that's all. Not to worry. We've just got to figure out how to get him out of here."

"That's easy. Say, 'Here are your keys, buddy, sorry for your trouble, but I'm not going with you, and don't let the screen door hit you on your way out.'"

"No, I'm keepin' that truck."

"You're keeping the truck? What about his CDs?" I say sarcastically. "Can he take those with him on the Greyhound, or are we keeping everything the guy owns? Maybe we could get him out of his clothes and keep those, too, why don't we?"

"I like the CDs, but I'm willing to turn them over to him if he'll just get out and stay out," she says. "We can use them as leverage."

"Are you insane? This man has come here with the idea of getting *a,* you, and *b,* his truck—maybe not in that order—and we're giving him the consolation prize of six of his own CDs and sending him packing on the bus?"

"Dana!" he hollers from the kitchen. "Baby, I kinda wanted to git on the road before rush hour, and it's already gittin' past that."

I give her my one-raised-eyebrow look, but she pats my hand. "In a little while, he'll be drunk and he'll just fall over wherever he is and pass out, and we won't hear from him for the rest of the night. You'll see."

"He looks like somebody who can hold a *lot* of liquor. It could be quite a long time before he falls over."

"Don't worry. I know this guy."

"Also—not to put sort of a damper on things, but I don't really *want* a passed-out Neanderthal in my kitchen. Call me crazy."

"Well, what do *you* suggest?" she hisses.

"Gee, I might have suggested that you not invite him to *my* house without some advance warning. And then that you not have sex with him. What good did that do the cause?"

"Mellows him out. He's one of those guys who only speaks sex. He doesn't understand any other language of persuasion."

"I hardly think—"

"Listen," she says. "You don't know men. Okay? Try to keep that in mind. Your experience of men is not going to help you in this case. Teddy is a different ball game altogether."

"Hey, I'll have you know I've known more men than Teddy. Lots more."

She just laughs. "Shhh. I've gotta think."

"And what *about* Teddy?"

"What about him?"

"Does he know this Neanderthal is even here?"

"Hell, no. Nobody knew. If you'd come home when you were supposed to, even you wouldn't have known. I woulda had him out of here and had the place all cleaned up, with Randy on the Greyhound, and life woulda been fine."

From downstairs: "Daaaaay-na. It's five o'clock! We got to go, hon."

I shake my head.

"What?"

"The way you live your life. I can't believe this. You're whoring for a truck!"

"Oh, stop it. I'm not whoring for a truck. It's *my* truck."

"Is your name on the title?"

"Oh, who the fuck knows, Lily? Stop helping so much. I've gotta think." She paces to the window and back.

"I think the best bet would be to just give him his truck and say sayonara," I say.

"No. *No!* I'm not gonna do that. It's my truck."

"Is your name on the title?" I say again.

"Lily. He *gave* it to me."

"Your name is not on the title. Million bucks it's his truck."

"He. Gave. It. To. Me. What part of that don't you understand?"

"What part of it doesn't *he* understand, is the question. If I had to guess, I'd say the choices in his mind are: one, take you and the truck *with* violence or, two, take you and the truck peacefully. He strikes me as a very black-and-white thinker."

To my horror, this flips some switch in her brain, and she says, "Okay, then, we have to fight," and she purses her lips together and pushes her way out of the bathroom and downstairs. I trail along far behind her, my cell phone at the ready, and watch her go marching out onto the porch. He's out there, apparently sizing up the possibility of removing the porch swing. Perhaps he thinks it would make a nice hood ornament for the truck. Or else he's visualizing just the right little spot for it at his sister's house. I hear him say, "You ready to go, sweet stuff?"

That's when she goes into gear. I sit down on the kitchen stairs, out of range, and hear her take him on. First she cries, tells him how just being home has reminded her of all the tragedy of her life, with her parents dying when she was so young—and now he's betrayed her, too, cheating on her with that dog trainer, and, well, it just flipped her out completely, set her right back to that bad place she'd been in. She'd thought over the last couple of days that she'd be able to put the past aside and forgive him, but seeing him again has broken her heart all over again.

He says something about how the dog trainer has gone now, he's sorry—

No, she says. It's over.

"So you're saying you want me to just get in my truck and go back to Texas and not have anything to do with you? Is that it? You're not ever coming back?"

There's a long silence. I hear her sniffling. I lean forward, straining to hear this next part, which, when it comes, is spoken oh so softly. The night he cheated? Well, he couldn't have known, but that was the night she got the call. Yes, from me, her sister she hadn't talked to in years. I wouldn't have called, but . . . well, the boy . . . the four-year-old son . . . yes, him . . . well, that was the day he was diagnosed with leukemia.

Yes. Leukemia. And she looked and looked for Randy, to tell him. To be comforted by him—but where was he? Where? In Lurlene's back room at the dog place. Fucking Lurlene. In her hour of need. That's why she had to go the way she did. That's why she couldn't explain.

(More tears.) And so she's been back here helping out, driving back and forth from the hospital, where the boy is having his treatments—painful, horrible treatments—and he's so weak he just lies in the bed and doesn't complain. He looks like a little skeleton. A little brave ghost. The prognosis isn't so good, and, well, anybody can see that her sister is putting on a brave front, but it's so sad, really. Dana's the one holding things together right now. She has to. She's in that truck all the damn time so she can be there at the hospital when she's needed, and also to go and get things for me . . . there's no money for a second car, not right now, not with all the uncertainty.

I can't take it anymore. I've been sitting on the stairs, but now I go the rest of the way up to my room. The place is a mess: the bed is unmade, with the sheets all damply twisted up, and the comforter and the pillows every which way. Two glasses are on the bedside table, making wet rings on the wood. A man's watch and a pair of cowboy boots, approximately size fifty-seven, are on the floor. Next to them is the worst thing of all: a damp, wormlike condom is curled up on the carpet, obviously flung off in haste.

Recoiling, I go across the hall to my mother's old study and sit in the desk chair, quietly staring out the window at the empty street. I feel cold all over, that feeling like when you have a fever and your skin is hot to the touch but you're freezing just the same. I will my mind to stop thinking. After a while, I hear Dana come up the stairs and go into my bedroom. The closet door opens and closes, the toilet flushes, and then she comes down the hall and pokes her head into the study. She's dressed now, in jeans, and she's holding his boots in one hand.

"Hey, what are you doing in here? I just wanted to tell you that I'm takin' Randy to the bus station. I'll see you later. Don't mind the mess in the bedroom. I'll clean it up when I get home."

"Okay," I say without looking at her.

"Everything worked out fine. I did it! And guess wha-ut! I'm keeping the truck," she sings, doing a little victory shimmy, pumping her fist in the air. "Yesssss!"

"How nice for you," I say coldly.

She looks at me for another long moment—I can feel her eyes on the side of my head—and then she sighs heavily and says, "Look, it was for the best. What's wrong with you, anyway?" Then, after a moment more, she says, "Well, good-*bye,*" and slams the bedroom door before she goes downstairs.

24

*T*hat evening, Leon takes another fall. Krystal calls me from the hospital to say it's a more serious stroke this time, and she doesn't know how long they're keeping him. Since their ambulance ride, she says, he's been coming in and out of consciousness—so could I possibly go to her house, get her some shoes and a sweater and her toothbrush, and then come to the hospital? She left in a T-shirt dress and flip-flops, and it's cold there and she can tell they'll be there overnight. She can't bear to leave Leon; she's going to sleep in the armchair by his bed.

I say, "Of course." Leon and I have had each other's house keys for years. I look over at Simon, who's sitting on the floor watching me with his big brown eyes. I can't really take him with me to the hospital; he wouldn't be allowed in, and besides that, it's almost his bedtime.

"Where's Daddy and Auntie Dana tonight?" he asks me.

"I don't really know," I say. I'm aware that Simon and I had been halfway expecting Dana to come along all evening. We've been playing "trucks in danger"—a game he tells me she plays much better than I do. This is hard news for me: I'm not even the queen of my kid's games anymore.

"Why aren't I best at it?" I asked him. This is crazy: I know Simon loves me best, but still my heart twists with an old, familiar jealousy.

"Well," he said, and licked his lips nervously, just the way he had the other day when I asked him why Dana and Teddy were smiling in the picture he drew. I see that I'm making him worried about hurting my feelings. "She'll run around the whole house on her knees, but you only go a little ways," he said.

I pretended to chase him down and give him noogies. "Hey, you don't have to tell *me* twice," I said to him. "I'll run on my knees through the whole house if that's what it takes." I'd been clobbering my kneecaps on the hard wood floor, when, thank goodness, Simon goes upstairs to get his dinosaur.

I get up and call Teddy's house. He answers after about ten rings.

"Wow," I say. "I was just about to hang up. Do you know where Dana is?"

There's kind of a muffled noise, and then he says, "Yeah, she's here. What's up?"

I feel a little stab of fury. "What's *up* is that Leon's had another stroke, and I've got to take Krystal some things at the hospital. What's up over there?"

Another muffled sound, and then he says, "We'll come and keep Simon, if that's what you're asking. Just give us about ten minutes to wrap things up here."

"Oh, *absolutely,* take your time," I say. "It's not like a stroke is life or death or anything."

"Lily," he says. "You bringing Krystal things to the hospital isn't the life-or-death part. Leon's condition is the life-or-death part, and he's already being taken care of there. Am I right?"

"What *exactly* is going on, if I may ask?" I say, and I hate my tone of voice; in fact, I hate everything about this conversation.

"Aromatherapy," he says. "She had an upsetting afternoon."

KRYSTAL AND I sit together in the visitors' room off the intensive care unit, and she cries and I hold her. To cheer her up, I tell her stories of what Leon was like when I was a kid—how funny and brave he was, how he taught me to play the ukulele after my parents died because, he said, ukulele music is just about the most comforting, twangy kind of music there is, and it was all he figured he could teach me right then since I wasn't all that musically talented, he said. She and I eat the brownies I've brought in with me; store-bought ones, but who cares? We can barely chew and swallow anyway.

We sit there then in silence, and I think how it's a cruel joke the way they put fluorescent lights in these rooms where people are already despairing. Everybody in here looks green and saggy, as if the lights have sucked all the color out of our skin. There's an older couple across from us, leaning together and talking in low voices. Their daughter is gravely ill.

I've just started to say, "There should be dim lamps or candlelight, in here," when I look up and am amazed to see Gracie come in. I feel a flutter of gratitude to see her, before I remember that we seem to be unofficially avoiding each other. That day after our talk in the garden, I marched in the house and never—I realize guiltily—called her again. Whenever I thought of her, I decided that I was too busy with Dana and Simon and my hair, my job, my decision about my job, visiting Leon—all of it. But now she's here, and when she comes over and hugs Krystal and me, I realize just how much I have missed her, and I want to burst into tears.

When Krystal goes in to visit with Leon for her allotted twenty minutes, Gracie and I go down to the cafeteria for coffee. We talk about Leon's condition for a while, and then she reaches over and touches my hair. "Nice. I take it this wasn't from a kit."

"No. Professional help. Actually, Alex's sister did it. Remember I pointed out Alex to you at our lovely dinner party?" I hate to bring up the dinner party, but she doesn't seem to mind.

She takes a long sip of her coffee, loaded with cream and sugar, and says, "Ah, yes. I do remember there was a guy there you had your eye on. So, you're seeing him now?"

"Well, no," I say, and fill her in on the important points, minus my throwing myself at him, of course. I do tell her, though, about the possible job at the radio station and how thrilling and terrifying it was to try to do my column aloud instead of writing it. And then, when she's still watching my face as though she's waiting for more, I find myself telling her the startling fact that he offered to let me come and live at his house should things get difficult at my house. I expect her to be surprised, but instead she looks at me and says, "Ohhhh, you mean the Dana and Teddy thing?"

My mouth goes dry. "Yeah," I say, and my voice sounds far away.

She reaches across the orange Formica table and squeezes my hand. I wait for her to say something about how ridiculous it is to think of there really, in fact, *being* a "Dana and Teddy thing."

"It's hard, I'd imagine, but you look like you're holding up well," she says.

For a little while we chat about how awful it is that the colony people seem to have turned on Leon after so many years of their all being friends. Then I say, as lightly as I can, "Would you . . . you know . . . just tell me what *you* know about the Dana and Teddy thing?"

"Well," she says, looking a little concerned. "I don't think I know anything that everybody else doesn't know. Just that, you know, they're together all the time. I've seen them holding hands and kissing down by the beach sometimes. It doesn't seem like it's much of a secret." Then she sees my face and says, "Oh, Lily. You didn't know this? Oh, come here, my poor baby." She gets up and comes around to my side of the table and pulls me to her in a hug. "Shit. Why am I always the one telling you stuff you don't want to know? Huh? Don't tell me you're going to start avoiding me again."

THE NEXT DAY, Maggie and I have our usual Monday-afternoon lunch at Claire's. I am not exactly in the mood for lunch, I tell her on the phone, what with Leon being so sick and now this new thing with Dana and Teddy. When I got home from the hospital last night, Teddy was there alone, reading in the living room, while Simon slept upstairs. I had sort of thought we might talk about what was going on, but it was clear he was in no mood to talk. He got up quickly when I came in and said he had to get back. He wouldn't meet my eyes. So . . . *fine.* I'm not going to be the one to do all the heavy lifting, I tell Maggie on the phone. If there's something he wants to tell me, then he has to start the conversation. I'm not going to make it easy for him.

Maggie says, "Well, you have to have lunch with me. And promise me that when you're walking to Claire's, you'll notice how many babies you see on the way."

"What?"

"Count babies, okay?" Her voice is shrill and excited. "Promise!"

I see four babies on the way to Claire's, and I tell her this when I get next to her in line. She says, "Whew! I saw three babies, so together we saw an odd number. Good. I think that's very good. And seven is a good number anyway. Very lucky."

"And . . . *who* are you again?"

She laughs. "Today I am officially one day late, and so even though it's crazy, I'm looking for signs." She takes both my hands and shakes them with hers and squeezes her eyes shut. "Ooh, Lily, what if it really worked? What if I'm pregnant? Can you believe it?"

"Why don't we just get a pregnancy test and find out?" I say. "Don't they work when you're like five minutes late these days?"

She takes a breath so deep she practically has to go up on tiptoe. I stare at her. I've never seen her this way, not in all the eons we've been friends. Then she says, "Uh, I can't."

"Why not?"

"Scared."

"Ohhh, Mags. You're scared to know?"

"Yeah. So I'm looking for signs in the outside world. I made up some tests. If there's an odd number of babies out, then that's yes. If someone says—"

"No," I say to her. "No. We are not going to play games like that. Come on. We're going to the drugstore. You need to know for sure."

"I don't want to know!" she says, but she lets herself be dragged out. I steer her down the street, both of us laughing. She's still craning her neck for babies she can count, and I keep shaking my head and telling her I never knew she was this insane. When we get to the pharmacy, all the tests are locked up behind the counter, and there are four different kinds to choose from and no way of judging the different brands, and the lines are long, and on and on and on. Maggie's anxiety is contagious. She's fidgeting and twisting her hands around and around, and I have to ask her three times to *please* try to get a grip—she's making me absolutely frantic. She laughs at me. My hands are clammy, and I feel as though I'm on pins and needles. There are so many reasons this test *has* to be negative, and yet looking at her just breaks my heart, how bad she wants this.

I pay for the thing because she's incapable of counting out bills just now, and then we run back to Claire's, running just the way we would have done twenty-five years ago, tearing home from the store or across the beach to visit each other. Wow, I think, squeezing her hand, whatever the outcome, this is such a *moment* in our friendship. This, I'd like to tell Dana, is what you earn when you stay in one place, when you get to know someone as well as Maggie and I know each other. Her fear and excitement right now are my own.

Then, wouldn't you know it, there's a line for the ladies' room at Claire's. It's all I can do to keep from pushing these women aside and explaining to them why we have to go first. By now Maggie is so nervous her face is drained of all color. I remind her to keep breathing, and we stand there, holding hands, breathing deeply, counting breaths, until finally, finally it's her turn.

And then, after about nine years have passed in normal human time—after I've paced and looked out the window and eavesdropped on people's conversations and paced some more and outlined for myself all the comforting things I'll tell her when it turns out not to be positive—she comes out holding the little stick in her hand, her face all shiny with tears, and she says, "Look at this. Is this a line? It's a line, isn't it? Oh my God, it's a line!"

25

$\mathcal{D}$ana's cooking a hamburger when I get home. She's barefoot and wearing a halter dress, and the whole kitchen seems like one big about-to-be grease fire, with the oil popping everywhere. She's singing along to "White Rabbit" by Jefferson Airplane: "One pill makes you larger / And one pill makes you small . . ." Her former theme song.

I go in and put my bag down on the island and look at her with a sigh.

"Hi," she says. "What's *that* look mean?"

"Nothing. You should turn down the heat on that burner."

"I know how to cook a hamburger. This is the way I like to cook them: they get black on the outside and they're still raw on the inside."

"We can barely breathe in here for all the grease. The whole kitchen is going to have to be hosed down. And also, that's not a safe way to cook beef. It has to be cooked all the way through."

She sighs and turns down the heat, but the look on her face is that of someone appealing to a silent audience who will understand how oppressed she is. "How's work?"

"Fine." I look through the mail. "Maggie's pregnant."

"Oh! That's good, isn't it?"

"I guess. Yeah. Good news."

"What does old Marky Mark say about it?"

"I think she plans to tell him along about the time she needs to go to the delivery room. That's the latest plan, at least."

"Well. I'm sure he won't notice before then." She's busy scooping her burger onto a bun and then slathering it with globs of mayonnaise.

"So, if I may ask, why did you sleep at Teddy's last night?"

She looks at me and flushes just ever so slightly. "Uh . . . because I believe he's a *friend* of mine?" she says.

I look at her steadily. "I would really like to know what's going on."

"Nothing," she says. "He helps me. And I slept there because . . . ," she says very slowly, as if she's as curious as anyone to see what the end of the sentence will bring. ". . . Because I, ah . . . I was in no mood to come back here and get a big lecture from you about Randy. The lecture I feel I'm about to get right now, for instance."

"Oh," I say. "I'm supposed to just stand by quietly while you run a scam on somebody. Not say anything."

She rolls her eyes. "I didn't run a scam. That. Is. My. Truck. Mine. Dana Brown's. My truck. How many times do I have to tell you that?"

"You told him Simon has leukemia and that's why you need the truck. I call that a scam. It makes me ill."

"Well, it's just too bad you had to come bursting in on us about three hours earlier than you usually come home. I apologize that I didn't have my little tasteless, offensive discussion with him all wrapped up. I thought I had until the end of the business day."

"You know what? You'll say or do anything to get what you need. And the other thing, while we're at it: it's bad enough that you persist in leading Teddy on when I told you how vulnerable he is— even the colony people are starting to remark on it—but then, if that's not bad enough, I come in and find out that you've slept with Randy!"

"Old times' sake," she says and regards me coolly. "It's kind of a given that people are going to do that sort of thing, not that *you* would know." Then her eyes flash. "You know, when I was a kid this might have been an appropriate conversation. But I am an adult, and I can do whatever I fucking please. And that includes *leading Teddy on,* as you call it. He and I are both consenting adults, and this is insulting—"

"He's my ex-husband," I say.

She leans against the counter, eating a bite of her hamburger. Juices ooze down her arm. "You know what, sweetie cakes? He's not *your* anything. He's his own person. And I'm my own person, and if we want to hang out, who cares? Really. What's the big hairy deal? You think he might get hurt? He might not be able to stand his ground against the *big bad Dana?* Oooooh, poor Teddy!" She does a mock shiver.

I glare at her. "How is it that you and I always come back to this dysfunctional relationship we have? Why can't you go out and make your own life and leave mine alone? There are lots of other men in this world; why do you need to pick on the one I happened to have been married to? Is it to show me how easy it is for you? Is that it?"

"Maybe it has nothing to do with you at all," she says, and throws her half-eaten hamburger in the trash can. "Did you ever think of that?"

KRYSTAL CALLS ME the next day and tells me they've figured out a way to fix Leon: they've put a shunt in him so he can get more oxygen to his brain. At least, I think that's what she says. The good news is that he's home by the end of the week, and to make up for the colony women who will do nothing for him, I get to work making roasted chicken, escarole and beans, a spinach casserole, and blueberry pie, and take it all over to him. He sits on his deck, a blanket on his legs even though it's about ninety degrees, and he looks out at the Sound and explains the different cloud formations to Simon and me. Leon has been educating me about weather my whole life with the secret hope, I've always thought, that I would one day realize that meteorology is my true calling. Now, I think, he's decided he might have more luck with Simon. Simon, at least, is actually *looking* where Leon is pointing.

I feel happy just to be able to sit here with him again, I tell him. I don't say that it occurred to me, watching him there in the ICU, coming in and out of consciousness with his face turned the color of clay, that he really might die. That this could be it. It sounds odd, but Leon's death has always seemed something so far in the future that I didn't have to think about it—like Gracie's. They've both always been so lively and opinionated and *important* that I didn't really ever stop to notice how old they were getting or to consider how short the future might be. When my parents died, it was shocking and unexpected and devastating; but with Leon, I now realize that I am watching his slow demise, his fade-out.

He still looks a little bit gray, and his arms have bruises from the needles. Still, his eyes are as bright as they ever were. And we're here, sitting together in the late-afternoon sunshine, and maybe we have lots of time together. Or . . . well, maybe this is all we'll ever get.

Simon goes inside to play with the trucks he brought, and I lean over and say, "Leon, I have to ask you something. Do you think my father was unhappy because of my mother and Gracie?"

"What about them?" he says.

"Come on, Leon, I know the whole story now. You don't have to pretend with me."

He sighs and looks at me straight on and coughs a little. "Listen, your father was the finest man in the world. Anybody could be his friend, your father." He coughs again. I watch a vein near his temple tremble with each cough, and then I get up and get him a glass of water from the kitchen. When he recovers he says, "He was quiet, but he had a lot of love for your mother and you girls."

I know that, exhausted from coughing or not, he'll now launch into the story of how he and my father met when my parents restored the duplex and moved in; and then how my father helped Leon when the hurricane came and his seawall collapsed, and then how they took tango lessons together with their wives . . .

"It's okay," I say when he starts, but he keeps going. He needs to tell this. I listen patiently. This may be the last time I hear these old stories. These memories are like an ache deep in me that every now and then needs to be massaged with these words.

When he finishes, he looks over at me meaningfully. Krystal has come out onto the porch with a bottle of wine. Leon's voice is hoarse as he leans way over toward me and speaks quietly. "He knew all of it—the stuff—but it didn't matter for him. What mattered for him was love. He was a big-picture kind of guy. He knew what was important, and he didn't want to live without her. For him that was the most important."

"How did she get that lucky?" I say.

"How do any of us get that lucky?" he says and smiles at Krystal. "When it comes to love, you have to make your own luck."

We sit out there watching the light fade from the sky in beautiful purple streaks, listening to the katydids and the cicadas and bullfrogs. Krystal pours us three glasses of wine and brings out the chicken, and I feel my insides uncoiling themselves. Funny, I haven't realized how tightly I've been holding myself lately, but sitting there, with Simon playing trucks at the water's edge and singing himself a little song, and with Leon resting his head on Krystal's shoulder, I feel myself letting go. I look across the bay to my house, with its beautiful sloping lawn and dock and its lit-up windows. All the houses tonight, in fact, look so cozy and tucked in for the night.

When it comes to love, you make your own luck. I decide that this is one of those wise things that people in Leon and my father's generation know, and that I don't. I'm going to remember that, let it roll around in my mind. Maybe I'll use it in my column. I think how it would sound through the microphone: "When it comes to love, you make your own luck."

And then, from two houses down, I hear a woman screaming, "No, no, *no*—that's not how it was!" and then the sound of glass breaking.

It's Maggie. My heart takes a sudden free fall to my feet.

26

*T*hree days later, I see that pregnancy agrees with Maggie, unless you count one of its first side effects: the cut she got when Mark threw a vase into their sliding door and a piece of glass flew back at her and nicked her on the back of her left hand.

Which, she says, was totally not his fault. He was in shock. The vase just flew out of his hand in a totally involuntary way. Nevertheless, at my insistence, she was willing to move into our guest room that night—and she's stayed there for three days, even though she keeps assuring me that things are going to be fine and that I don't need to be so nervous.

"Really, it sounded way worse than it was," she told me when I went running over to her house after hearing her scream. Mark, after *involuntarily* letting go of the vase, was peeling down the street in his BMW convertible by the time I got there. That was just his "cooling-off" ride, Maggie said. She wasn't even crying. "Believe me, it's far better for everybody when he can just go out on the open road and do his thinking," she said.

"Are you on pregnancy-happy hormones or something?" I asked her. "Because I would be freaking out right now if I were you."

She laughed. "I do feel good—just a little tired is all. He can be kind of intense when he's surprised."

"Yeah," I said. "If that's him surprised, I'd hate to see him when he's all-out alarmed."

Anyway, over the next few days at my house, I see that she's really fine. Unbelievably fine. I'd be ballistic if a husband of mine threw a vase—or even a dirty look, for that matter—but Maggie seems placidly okay with everything. She says that Mark takes a long time to adjust to everything, and that this *was* big. She did lie to him, and that takes a little more time to get over. She goes to work in the morning and comes home in the evening with lots of books: books on the stages of pregnancy, diet, and nutrition; books with pictures of developing fetuses; exercise books; and one about baby names and what they mean.

I think, but do not say, that she might want to check out some books on single motherhood.

Then, on the fourth day, I come home to find her packing her suitcase.

"Guess what," she says. "I'm moving back home, and we're going to therapy."

I feel a little twinge of something—is it that I'll miss her or is this a real fear that Mark's going to keep hurling crockery?

I sit down on the bed and watch her put her veterinary uniform into the bag. "Are you sure this is what you want to do, Maggie? Maybe you should stay here while the two of you are in therapy, at least at first. You know . . . just to make sure . . ."

"Listen," she says. She sits down on the bed and looks at me. "I didn't want to tell you all this because I knew you'd freak out. But"—she takes a deep breath—"Mark and Ashley, his secretary, had been . . . you know . . . seeing each other on the side, and I found out about it on the trip. I could sense the vibe, you know. She's one of those really sweet-to-your-face types, very needy, and, well, *cute* obviously, and he just kind of . . . strayed."

It feels as if there's a hole in me that my stomach has disappeared through. I put my hand over my mouth and say, "Oh, Mags."

"No, no," she says. "Just hear me out. And so, when I told him I was pregnant, I also told him that I knew about Ashley and that we needed to make some hard decisions. I admitted that I'd lied to him about the birth control, but I said that he'd lied to me, too—"

"In a much bigger way," I interrupt.

"Well," she says, "the fact is, they're both lies, and they both have to be put right if we're going to make it. What I did—tricking him—was wrong, but now I know why I felt I *had* to trick him. He was not really with me, you know?" Her lip quivers a little bit but she shakes off my hand as I reach over to pat her. "His energy was elsewhere, and that was making me too needy and, well, we could have gone on that way for years. And then it would have been too late for a baby, or probably to fix our marriage at all. So . . ." She sighs and wipes at her eyes, and then puts her hands in her lap. "So! I'm moving back in, and we're seeing a marriage counselor, and we're going to rebuild."

"Be careful," I say. "Don't let him tell you that those lies were equivalent. He was cheating on you and lying every day! You just lied so you could get the child you've always wanted."

She smiles at me. "You're forgetting that you thought my lie was pretty horrible, too," she says. Then she stands up. "Lily, I know you think I should divorce him right now and be *strong* and raise my kid myself—"

"I never said—"

"No, but I see that you don't like Mark and you think I've made a bad decision in staying with him. But I love him and I'd be miserable without him."

I'm about to say that she wouldn't be miserable—oh, maybe at first, but then she'd be better off. He would just continue to disrespect her and cheat on her. And now there'll be a baby to shield from all this as well. I'd help her. We'd deal with this together. . . .

"Everybody is not like you," she says. "That's the bottom line. We can't all do what you think we should do. We just can't. We're not perfect and strong. You know? I *need* him, flaws and all."

27

On Wednesday, the day before school is supposed to start, I take Simon with me to work. I can't find Teddy, or Dana, either, for that matter, and so even though I don't want to drag Simon around—I also am supposed to go see Cherie after work, to get a much-needed protein conditioning for my hair—I don't quite know what else to do. It won't be so bad, I tell myself; I won't stay at work long. After all, The Rooster now chops my carefully thought-out columns until, to me, they seem to lack all heart—so why should I spend hours writing and rewriting them, in the hopes that just once he'll run them as I intended them? Lately, our arguments about this are growing tiresome and pointless. I'll say, passing him in the hall, "Don't cut today's column, especially letter two." And he shoots back, "Ha-ha. Don't write it to *need* cutting."

Periodically, I think of picking up the phone and calling Alex and saying, "Let me meet your boss. I'm ready," but something always stops me. Sometimes, I'll admit, it's the memory of the almost-kiss (which has become legendary in my mind), but often it's just the fear that I won't succeed on the air. It almost makes it worse that Alex thought I performed so well the first time I tried; what if that was a fluke, and I really can't do it again? What if I get in front of the microphone and stammer or, worse, give somebody awful advice? Or what if the caller is someone like Maggie, and I advise her to leave her son-of-a-bitch cheating husband, and she answers back on the radio, "Not everybody is like you. We can't all do what you think we should do"? What then?

No. Better to stay at the paper, fighting with Casey and praying that I can somehow help people in one easy, simplistic paragraph. And, hey, it's a job. Most people in America don't like their jobs, and mine is a particularly cushy one. I shouldn't complain.

Simon and I have barely gotten settled in—he's in the corner drawing a picture, he tells me, for each letter of the alphabet, "just in case kindergartens make you do that," he tells me grimly—when The Rooster comes crashing into my office looking as though he just might explode from glee.

"We have an actual journalistic 'Dear Lily' emergency today, if you can believe such a thing exists," he says in a more excited voice than I have ever heard out of him. "This is your chance to redeem yourself, to ingratiate yourself, to make yourself the favorite person in the world of the publisher. And of course, in my world." He sees Simon over in the corner and looks startled. "Who's this?"

"This is my child, Simon. Simon, this is Casey."

Casey barely nods in Simon's direction. "Okay, now listen," he says excitedly, rocking up and down on his toes. "Lance's sister, Evangeline, is getting married on Cape Cod next month. A nice September wedding on the beach, the merging of two of your major financial families—the sun and moon will rise and set differently on this wedding day just to please the entourage, the whole nine yards, lots of celebrities, business tycoons, God himself will probably be in attendance, yada yada yada. Are you getting my drift?"

"Yeah, Kendall told me she was getting married to a rich guy."

"Oh, this is waaay more than just some rich guy. *This*, I'll have you know, is the dude she's been engaged to practically since the two of them were in diapers. No shit." He glances over at Simon. "Oops, sorry. It's, like, been a foregone conclusion that this big stellar moment was coming for, like, two decades now. This is *big*. Bigger than big. And now the Big Day is upon us, the invites are issued to one thousand of the families' closest friends, the papers are signed, and the bride is about to be signed, sealed, and delivered . . . and what do you think? She's decided, Lance says, that she *might not want to.* Get it? She's tired, she says, of thinking about him." He does this cute little mincing thing when he represents the bride's point of view. Charming. "Now, she doesn't hate him or anything. Lest you get the wrong idea here, let me assure you that he has not turned into a baddie, hasn't cheated on her, doesn't do illegal drugs, didn't even get an alarming haircut or stop brushing his teeth. She's just wigged out on the idea of getting married."

"Hmm," I say. "Imagine."

"And Lance says—here's where you come in, Lily—that she told him she wanted to know what *you* would say." He rocks back on his heels and looks very roosterishly pleased with himself. Cock of the walk and all that. "Your column has *arrived.* This rich chick is going to listen to what you say before she gets married to this dude she's been with since she was a drooling little baby."

"Well, great," I say. "Wow."

"It's *more* than wow. You hold the keys to the kingdom."

"So where's the letter she wrote?"

"I have it . . . right *here!*" He pulls it out with a flourish and hands it over to me. It's written out on fancy-schmancy stationery, the kind with, believe it or not, a family crest at the top. Evangeline, whom I've heard Lance call Van, has loopy, pedigreed handwriting, big and flowing, with unnecessary loops and swirls to it. I don't do handwriting analysis, but even I can see this is a woman who belongs to the society circuit and has been told what to do and how to do it for as long as she's breathed oxygen.

"Okay," I say. "Thanks. I'll answer it right away." I put it on the desk.

"You betcha you will!" he says. "This is really something. A chance to influence real people! Important people! Who woulda thought there could be a genuine column emergency, huh? You know, *this* is why the column is named 'Eeek!' This is what we were aiming for."

Simon gets up and comes over and leans against me, watching Casey closely.

"So what do you think, little dude? Isn't this exciting for your mom?"

Simon looks at me, and I smile at him reassuringly.

"So . . . ," says Casey. "Can I get you anything? Coffee? Water? A babysitter?"

"Nope. Just go away so I can get started."

"Can you really do this with the boy in here? Because for this I can send Kendall up . . ."

"Nope. We're fine," I say.

"Well. Okay then. Call me if you need anything. And, Lily, for once, you can write as long as you want."

He stands there for a few more moments, rocking on his heels and clasping and unclasping his hands, and then he goes over and looks at Simon's drawings, gives him the thumbs-up sign, and disappears.

"Mommy," says Simon, "is that guy weird?"

"He's just a little excited right now," I say. "He's okay."

"I want to go back home."

"In a while we'll go home. I just have to knock out an answer to this lady first. Why don't you go draw more pictures? What letter are you up to?"

"I'm up to *D*," he says. "I'm making a dinosaur." He oozes himself over to his drawings and settles down again with a big sigh.

I pick up Evangeline's letter and start to read. Some sad letters have crossed my desk in the year or so I've been doing this column, but for sheer despair, this one may be the most pitiful of all of them. I read it through twice. Then I feel like going to the telephone and telling Van that she should put on her tennis shoes right now, grab her car keys, and hightail it out of there.

She's miserable, she says in the letter. Everything has always been decided for her, and now she's about to sign away the rest of her life, to be married to Ellsworth Penn III. And he's okay, she guesses, but he's got a lot of opinions about how the world works that she doesn't really agree with. He believes God gave him and his family all that money because they're better than other people. Also— she says this is probably a small thing, and she shouldn't complain— Ells insists that she's not going to work after they get married. Right now she runs a little nonprofit horseback-riding camp, but he says she has to stop because he wants them to move to the Hamptons, where he'll do his business deals and she'll be busy throwing big parties and hanging out with the wives of the other movers and shakers. But, no offense, she writes, she doesn't *like* those people Ells hangs out with. And she detests having even to go to those parties, much less give them. She's shy. Ells and her family all know this about her, but they say it's time she grew up. "I really do love Ells, but lately he is being so insensitive and saying that my little horse camp doesn't matter because it doesn't bring in any money. I would never say his work doesn't matter!" she writes. "Meanwhile, my mother is making all the decisions about how the wedding must look, and every time I make a suggestion, somebody tells me I'm wrong. Like I wanted horse-themed centerpieces. NO! they said. My sister told me I'm the luckiest person in the whole world and just to get married because it will make everybody in both families happy. Is it possible to be the luckiest person in the whole world and still not want what you have? Maybe I'm just a baby, and these are just prewedding jitters."

But it's the end that really chills me. "PLEASE HELP," she writes. "I wake up crying and think, what if I was meant for something else altogether? What if my life has no meaning for me?"

I pace around the room for a while, play a game of Clue with Simon, do a couple of stretches and some jumping jacks. I try to tone my feelings down some. It is possible that I have a low opinion of marriage just now. Maybe Van shouldn't run away. Maybe she should just order her own horse-themed centerpieces and start screaming at anyone who objects.

Then I go sit at my desk and start typing. I start slowly. I say that when it comes to getting married, we have to remember that it's a union of two people, not of the whole world of our parents and their parents and all of their money. Not really. It's she and Ellsworth who have to face each other at the end of each day, and at the end of their lifetime. Then I tell her that if she's not ready, if she has doubts, then she has to honor those doubts. She has to stand up for herself and not be bullied into doing what's expected of her. You see, I write, we all get this chance in life to be the people we can respect, and we shouldn't give that away. And by the way, I say, can we really call it "love" if he insists that she stop doing the things that make her happy so that she can have more time to do the things that make *him* happy instead?

Break it off for a short time, I write. Tell people you need more time. And then look inside yourself. Go on a pilgrimage. Talk to wise women in your life. Be kind to others. Help the homeless. Feed the poor. Go inward, and you'll know the answer.

I take a deep breath when I've finished. Simon has been practically chewing on me through most of the time I've been typing, and I've got to get him out of here. He's got the whining thing going so hard I'm afraid his whole body may implode from it.

I turn in the column and kiss Simon, and we fly out the door to the New Haven Green, where we run around, pick some dandelions, and eat the peanut butter and jelly sandwiches that I brought. Then we feed some pigeons our crusts and head back to the office.

WHEN WE come back Casey is sitting in my office sizzling. He's actually giving off heat, like a big nuclear reactor sputtering away in the corner. He paces around, slamming his fist into the piece of paper he's carrying, which is evidently my answer to Evangeline. He's going on and on almost incoherently about family dynasties and the importance of money staying in families and about my job being on the line.

"How is it that you somehow managed *not* to know the right answer?" he says. "How did you miss that? What is the matter with you?"

"I gave the only right answer I know."

"Well, think up another right answer, because this one isn't going to fly. And let me give you a little hint about the answer, a peek at the back of the book, as it were: it should end up saying 'marry the guy.'"

"She shouldn't marry him! Did you read her letter? Did you see how trapped she feels?"

"I did. I understand. But to paraphrase somebody intelligent, the rich aren't like you and me. When we feel trapped, we have no choice but to break off engagements. They can go and buy a third world island for themselves and forget about it."

"Casey, that's horrible."

"It's true, though. This wedding has to go through."

"Why?"

"Because Lance told me it did, that's why." He laughs his hyena-style laugh.

Even Simon looks alarmed. He says, "Mommy, let's go."

"Well," I say. For good measure, I slam my desk drawer. "I can't do it. Write it yourself. But be sure to sign your own name to it."

"No. You have to do it. Look, why am I always having so much trouble with you over stuff like this? Just write the answer that everybody wants you to. Why is that such a big deal? The man is a very nice man. He'll make her happy." His voice softens. I see that he's pleading, as if he's a little boy who wants a Nintendo and I'm the mom with the checkbook. "She just has the jitters, and there is no right or wrong answer here. Just write the answer that'll make your publisher happy. It's simply not a moral dilemma. Just say, 'Yes, you're being a baby. Suck it up. Everybody freaks out about their wedding. You'll have good days and bad days. Marry him.' Make it flowery, like you really give a shit. Boom. Outta there."

Simon says, "Mommy, I'm bored. Can we go?"

"Play with your dinosaurs for a few minutes longer, honey," I tell him. "Casey, I can't do it."

"I have to go pee," Simon says.

"I'll take you in a minute. Please go play for a few more seconds. Casey, I don't know what to say. What you're asking of me is immoral."

"There's nothing immoral about this. Look at it this way: Her family loves her. They adore this girl. And they wouldn't want her to marry him if it was the wrong thing. They know this is *right* for her. Just trust them and do it," he says.

"I can't."

"Trust me, you can," he says. "I want this column in my office in fifteen minutes, or Lance is coming in here to explain to you why we're not running the 'Eeek!' column anymore. Simon, you come with me. Kendall's downstairs and she wants to play tic-tac-toe with you."

"No!" I say.

Casey looks at me.

"Simon's staying here with me," I tell him.

"Fifteen minutes, and I'm not joking," he says. He goes out and closes the door behind him.

So I sit down and write a sniveling little letter. Let's face it: Evangeline Hamilton is no doubt going to marry Ellsworth Penn III, no matter what I say. By the time she's this far along, she's not going to be able to get out of it because some advice columnist says she should.

"Everybody feels this way," I write. "You'll have good days and bad days. Remember that your love for your fiancé has gotten you this far. Think of the life ahead of you with hope and pleasure. Think of ways that you can express your soul in your life whether married or single. You'll be fine. Remember to breathe, and throw your bouquet high."

CHERIE'S SALON is like an oasis. She fixes glasses of iced tea for herself and for me, and brings out action figures and plastic dinosaurs from the back room for Simon to play with, and then she massages the conditioners into my scalp. She tells me that her parents have practically decided she's a lunatic because she wants Skip's name on the invitation. "But," she says, "I just kept thinking of what you said, and I've stuck to my guns. I'm not marrying a guy named Deuteronomy. I'm marrying a guy named Skip."

Did I say that? I tell her that weddings this summer have meant nothing but trouble. There must be some astrological convergence going on that's making them impossible for families to work through. And then I explain the deal with Evangeline and her family. Cherie grows silent when I tell her that my boss made me change my answer.

"I kind of had to," I say, closing my eyes and feeling her hands working the conditioner through my hair and scalp. "It's just the way the boss wanted it, and I can't stay there and fight all day."

She massages the conditioner a little harder into my hair.

We're quiet. Bonnie Raitt is singing about a woman who's been in love too long. After a while, Cherie sighs and says, "Sometimes people just need someone to give them the courage to do what they know they ought to."

I don't know if she's talking about Evangeline or about me. I close my eyes, try to concentrate on the fact that my straw hair is going to turn to corn silk, and that my life is going to calm down, and that Evangeline Hamilton will thrive no matter if she's married or not, with or without my help.

"Like with me," Cherie continues. "I mean, I already knew

what to do, but you just gave me the focus. You pointed out that it was *my* wedding. I had courage, but I'd fought so long that I'd forgotten that I had any. You know?"

"But that was an easy one," I murmur. "You and I were sitting right here together. I could *see* you and know who you really are. With this other letter . . . well, my boss *said* . . ." I laugh a little, to show that I wish it didn't have to be this way, but it is. *Bosses, you know.*

"Well," she says at last. "I don't have a boss, so I shouldn't talk. You did what you had to do. I don't mean to sound superior or anything. I probably would have done the same thing. You have to keep your job, after all."

We're quiet again. Norah Jones sings about walking the long way home. Simon is on the floor at my feet, bouncing his dinosaurs along. One of the T. rexes says to a stegosaurus, "*I am the boss,* and I will tell you what to say!"

Cherie leans down and says close to my ear, "I shouldn't tell you this, but I think you've cast a spell or something on my brother. He was over here last night, and when he saw your name in my appointment book, he said he was going to try to drop by to see you. And watch: he'll make it look like a coincidence, of course."

"Really?" I say.

"And I think—well, he should tell you this next part himself, but I can't ever keep my mouth closed, and you know how men are. They can go forever without telling you the main thing you need to know. But his *wife,* I believe, has filed the papers."

"Filed the papers?"

"The divorce papers."

"Oh."

"Don't let him know that you know."

"Oh, don't worry," I say.

She puts me under the hair dryer, where I have time to bake in my guilt over the letter to Evangeline Hamilton. Actually, I go back

257

and forth. Yes, my answer might save her. No, it really doesn't matter so why should I get myself in trouble at work? I fidget around under the dryer; this thing is so *hot*. Why am I an advice columnist if I'm too scared to say what I really think? I don't deserve this job. I *have* to go back and change my answer! I should do it this minute, in fact, before the conditioner gets done! No, no, no . . .

You see how it goes with me. I twitch around in the chair, restless. I need to pace, but you can't pace with a hair dryer. Simon climbs onto my lap and, finding it inhospitably fidgety, climbs off again.

It's three o'clock. After this interminable conditioning process is over, I'll go back to the paper and tell Casey we have to change the answer. Simon will be nuts, and Casey will go crazy, but that's the way it has to be. My reputation . . .

No. No. No. Who cares about this? I'll just stick with the answer that Casey made me write . . .

And then I look up and Alex is there, smiling at me, activating dimples.

"Wow," he says. "Fancy meeting *you* here. I just dropped by to see if my sister wanted to go out to dinner with me later."

"Alex!" I say, and push the big bulb of the hair dryer off my head. Instantly I feel cooler. "I've done such a terrible thing!"

So that's how it happens that at eight-thirty that night—after Alex and Cherie and Simon and I have gone out to dinner, after we've played Frisbee on the Green with Simon, after we've walked endlessly around New Haven, talking and debating, and after we've dropped Cherie off at Skip's apartment near the beach in West Haven—Alex and I drive aimlessly through the city. Simon, who chased seagulls on the beach until he was exhausted, falls asleep in the backseat. Tomorrow is his first day of kindergarten, so it's good he's gone to sleep, even if it is in the car instead of in his own bed. In my gloomy mood, I see this as his last real day of freedom from society's expectations. He's going to need all the rest he can get.

Alex is saying, "People listen to you because you're honest. That's what you offer. Otherwise, you might as well just be Ann Landers reruns."

Then he says, "Casey is an idiot if he doesn't appreciate that kind of integrity. But then—well, we've seen that he *is,* in fact, an idiot. Restricting you to short answers, not letting you answer the kinds of questions you want . . . I don't know. For me, the answer would be clear. I think you know what you have to do."

"You're right, of course," I say. I stop at a red light, and he reaches over and takes my hand, curls his fingers in mine. "I think my original answer is still in the computer. I'll just go there and put that one in."

I look out the window. Two teenagers dressed in Goth are smoking cigarettes on the corner. An older couple, both gray-haired and wearing khaki shorts, are swinging a bookstore bag between them, and a young woman dressed up in a sparkly blue evening dress is hurrying somewhere with her head down. Evening in the city. Stores are just closing. The air is so heavy and humid, it feels like the inside of a dog's mouth, I think as the light turns green.

"Are you going to call Casey and tell him what you're doing?" Alex says. The wind from the car blows away some of his words.

"And have him stop me? I don't think so." I shiver.

"Wow," he says when I stop at the next red light. He looks over at me, and his eyes are shining in the glow of the streetlights. "Wow! A guerrilla attack by the advice columnist! Whoo-hoo!"

"Yeah," I say. "I'll just run up to the production room and have the night editor there substitute my old answer for the new one." I feel flushed and a little dazed.

"And that person will do it?"

"Oh, yeah. I'll just say there was a mistake in the copy that I just remembered I didn't fix. Oh, yeah. It won't be a problem at all."

"I'm impressed."

"Yeah. It'll work." I stare out the window. "I'll feel much better about everything. I couldn't live with myself if I didn't do this."

"Well, I didn't think you could," he says. "But I figured you'd just have to have it out with Casey again . . ."

"Nope," I say. "We're beyond that now. This is just me, acting on my own." I do a theatrical squaring of my shoulders and point westward. "We're going to *The Edge!*"

"How appropriate," he says. "This is so exciting. There's a part of me that wishes we were going to have to do something really dramatic here, like scale the wall of the building and then sneak in a window."

"I know," I say and laugh.

"Lily, I've gotta say, I'm so proud of you for this."

When we get to the paper, he waits in the car with Simon, who's still sleeping, and I go inside. It all goes as planned. George, the head copy editor, waves me in, and when I tell him I just have to change something in the column, he frowns for just a minute and then says, "Not the length of the column, though, right? I have the ads all placed on the page already."

"No, no, not the length," I say. "Just a quick substitution."

"You came all the way back here just to correct a mistake?" he says when I come back from inserting the new copy. "My hat is off to you. You're a real pro. Not many people would care that much."

THEN I DRIVE Alex home. This is the first time I've ever seen where he lives, in a two-story duplex on Elm Street in the Westville section of town, a street dappled with maple trees underneath streetlights. It's so lit up it looks almost like daylight here.

"Take a look around," he says. "This may someday need to be your refuge. The deal still stands, you know."

I lean out of the window and look. His house has a big front porch on both the first and second floors, long, shuttered windows that are all dark now, and a tiny strip of grass in front with some formless rhododendron bushes. From the glare of the streetlight, I can see that he has a big porch swing—much like the one I have.

"Nice," I say.

He doesn't get out of the car right away, just sits there smiling, his arm resting on the back of my seat.

"Well, this has been real," he says. "You've got some brass ones, that's for sure."

I laugh and say, "Well, we'll see . . ." and when I turn my head back toward him, he reaches for me and tilts my head up to his and kisses me. Then he looks into my eyes and pulls me to him, and we start kissing in earnest. I can feel actual neural synapses melting in my brain.

We've been kissing for a while when he whispers, "You know, if only . . ." and nods toward the backseat, where Simon is sleeping.

I smile. It's true. If Simon weren't here, if I were alone . . . but then I think maybe I'm glad there's a reason to leave. I am so not ready for what this will lead to. One major upheaval a day is all I can really manage. And even that's a stretch sometimes.

I'm still smiling and trembling when I get on the highway to go home.

28

As soon as I pull into the driveway, Teddy comes charging out of the front door, looking even more frazzled than usual. His hair is frizzed from the humidity, his glasses are askew, and his shirt is untucked. He stands there on the step while I park the car, running his hands through his hair and looking wild-eyed. Really, he looks so ridiculous, so . . . *Teddyish,* that I almost want to laugh.

"Where have you been?" he says.

I smile at him. "How about saying 'hi' first? As in, 'Hi, Lily. How are you? Isn't it a lovely evening?' "

I haven't talked to him for a long time, long enough, I realize, to actually miss him a little. I can't wait to tell him about Evangeline's letter.

"Where have you been?" he says again in his high-pitched, hysterical way, and then, in typical Teddy fashion, he doesn't even give me a chance to answer. "I've been out of my mind worrying about you. Where were you? Did you forget that Simon has his first day of school tomorrow? Why weren't you home putting him to bed at a decent hour?"

"Shhh. He's fine. He's sleeping," I say. "Look at him, how darling he is. How about a little help? You can carry him inside, and I'll bring his stuff."

"What stuff?"

"His backpack with his toys. He was at work with me today."

"Don't even try to tell me you've been at work all this time. Where were you?"

"I'm not trying to tell you I was at work, although, actually, I was until just very recently," I whisper, laughing. "What I'm trying to do is bring Simon in and put him to bed without waking him up." I lean into the car and undo Simon's seat belt, and motion to Teddy to scoop him up.

We go upstairs together, and I turn down the bed while Teddy eases him into it. Simon makes a *mmmmphhh* noise as I take off his sandals and put him under the covers, turn on the fan in his room, and then snap off the light.

"Come on," I say, heading down the hall to the stairs. "Let's go have a glass of wine on the porch. Boy, do I have a story to tell you! I'm probably going to be fired tomorrow, but you know something? I don't care. Get Dana, and let's go sit outside. I feel like I haven't been home forev—"

I stop and look back at him. He's just standing there in the hall with a stricken look on his face, his hands balling themselves up into little fists and then coming apart again. I feel my smile fade.

I put my hand over my mouth. "Oh, no. Has something bad happened?" I say. "Is it Leon? Dana? What's happened?"

"Come into the bathroom," he says. "I want to show you something."

I don't know what to expect—his look suggests it might be blood and guts, if not an actual corpse on the floor—but I follow him to the bathroom off my bedroom, already feeling my heart sinking in dread. There, on the sink, is a pregnancy test, just like the one Maggie and I bought the other day. I feel confused. This isn't the *same* pregnancy test, surely? What does it mean? I look up into Teddy's face.

"It's Dana," he says, his face white. "She's pregnant."

"Dana? You're kidding," I say. My voice sounds far away, even to me. The test strip, I now see, has a clearly defined line. A swarm of bees seems to start up in my head.

He's watching my face. "It's mine," he says in a hoarse whisper, looking guiltier than I think I've ever seen him look. Then he says, "I felt I had to come tell you. First."

"Wait." I can't seem to get this. "You . . . and Dana are . . .?"

"Yes." He looks down.

Another thought struggles its way to the surface of my mind. "Is she, you know, planning to keep it?" I say.

He nods.

We're silent. The floor seems to get closer and then farther away. Teddy's face is swimming in front of me. I wonder briefly if I'm going to faint. "So where is she?" I say. I clear my throat. "Where *is* Dana?" My voice seems to be coming from the far end of a tunnel.

"I don't really know where she is *now.* I think she's out with friends. Seth Tomlinson and that crowd." He sighs, runs his hands through his curls again. "She's kind of scared of you, you know. She didn't want to be here when you heard." He looks at me and shrugs, and suddenly everything comes into focus again, and I have the urge to slap him—just reach over and slap his guilty, horrified little face for lying to me, and then slap him again for standing there looking so fucking scared and passive, so deer-in-the-headlights frozen. I've been lied to. That's the thought that swims up to the surface of my consciousness. He *lied* about what they were doing. I've been his friend and I've protected him, and he said he was helping her. And how stupid was I, to believe even for one second that they weren't sleeping together? *Hello?* Dana sleeps with everyone she can. I knew that. Hell, *he* should have known that.

In the bright bathroom light, he looks gray and drawn and guilty as hell. A vein is pulsing in his jaw, and the lines in his face have become long, deep grooves from either side of his nose down to his mouth. It's over for him. There's no more protecting him, trying to look out for him. He's done it now, fallen for my flaky sister's helpless act, given in to her.

Poor, poor Teddy, I think, you poor idiotic bastard. You have no idea what you've just done to your life. I've tried to help you through so much, but even I can't save you from this one.

CASEY MCMILLEN gets up much earlier than you'd think. By 7:00 a.m., he's gotten his newspaper and started reading it, and has even made it to the inside page where the "Eeek!" column resides. I know this because, by 7:03, he's called and fired me.

The phone conversation we have is very one-sided. Lots of sputtering, lots of expletives, a great deal of yelling. I have to hold the phone far away from my head so that my eardrum can stay intact—which is fine, since I can't get a word in edgewise anyway. He's shocked and appalled at such fucking deviousness . . . there are no fucking words . . . he can't believe it . . . the fucking audacity! To send him a fucking *decoy column* and then go there in the fucking middle of the goddamn night and say the fucking opposite of what we'd agreed upon . . . incredible fucking insubordination . . . can't find the brain cells necessary to comprehend this, this *fraud*. I'm to come in later today and clean out my fucking desk, take down my fucking pictures, get my fucking philodendron, and get *out*. And he's keeping the fucking Rolodex! I shouldn't even *think* of keeping that.

I can't help it. I say that I don't even want my Rolodex. What good is a Rolodex to an advice columnist? I tell him good riddance to all of it, and when I hang up, I'm singing, "Take This Job and Shove It." Frankly, I haven't had all that much sleep. I'd lain awake going back and forth between thinking about Dana and Teddy and thinking about what was going to happen at work. Now, at a little after seven, I'm feeling almost grateful to know how at least one of those scenarios is going to play out.

Also, as I put the phone down, I realize that I'm perhaps a little bit—oh, untethered. *Wild,* perhaps. Free for the first time in my whole life, is what it feels like; it's as if a big bomb has just landed and blown my whole life apart, and now there are huge, airy caverns that are mine for the filling. There's devastation, that's for sure, but for now the room seems to have so much more air in it than I remember. Frankly, I can't believe how *huge* the world seems right now, how lit up. I shake my head. I feel like a coal miner being brought up into the light.

I make myself a cup of strong coffee and then go upstairs and wake up Simon.

"It's the first day of school!" I sing to him, opening his curtains and letting in the sunlight. A Sunfish skims across the Sound. It still looks like a summer day out there, not a school day—and Simon still looks like a preschooler, not a kindergartener. But there you have it. The world is moving on. I still look like an advice columnist for a newspaper, too, and somebody who was once living a calm, orderly, uptight existence. And now I'm neither of those things. And yet I'm still me. How extraordinary this is!

I snuggle with Simon for as long as he'll allow it. I have this gut feeling that it's all about him and me now; we're the only ones I have to look out for. Then I look at the clock and, my goodness, we've got to get moving. His first day of school *ever,* and we're already running late. We both zoom around the room, laughing, racing to pick out his clothes and gather up his new backpack, his brand-spanking-new Spider Man sneakers, his markers and crayons. Then we hurry downstairs and I fix his favorite breakfast—oatmeal with blueberries—and we're about to go stand outside and wait for the school bus, when I get a great idea, the greatest idea *ever.*

I stoop down to his level and hold onto his arms. "What if I drive you to school today? That way I can go in with you and say hello to your teacher. Won't that be fun?" I tell him. He looks doubtful. He'd looked forward to the ride on the school bus; he'd even rehearsed it. Evidently, though, he can see that I'm a little insane this morning because he doesn't argue. I run upstairs and comb out my hair, brush my teeth, put on some lipstick and blusher, and—oh, yeah, at the last minute I remember to put on my best underwear and change out of my T-shirt and into a pair of jeans and a white blouse—and off we go.

Miss Simone, his teacher, is exceptionally nice, so nice that she's willing to abandon her personal fashion sense and wear a Winnie the Pooh smock that makes her look like she's an overgrown kindergartener herself. I inspect the classroom and ooh and aah at the bulletin boards and the round blue rug the children will sit on for Circle Time, and admire the weather board and the fish tank and the cage that will hold a hamster when the class gets one. Miss Simone has black fluffy hair and a singsongy voice for speaking to children, and when she smiles, her eyes get so squinty you wonder if she can see out of them.

When at last it's Circle Time and Miss Simone looks as though she might like to handle the class single-handedly from now on out, I blow kisses to Simon and his twenty-two fellow students, and then I run to my car. I drive straight to Alex's house.

My heart is beating so fast when I ring his doorbell that I think I might pass out. But it's not from fear; that's what I realize as I'm waiting for him. I hear his footsteps coming down the stairs, and I straighten my smile. I'm not one bit afraid of what's about to happen. I'm just anxious to get on with my life, like I'm in overdrive or something. I feel braver, in fact, than I have ever felt before. *When it comes to love, you have to make your own luck.*

And sure enough, when he opens the door, holding a mug of coffee, I just step inside and take the mug out of his hands very carefully and place it on the floor. My hands are shaking just the tiniest little bit. And then I straighten up and turn to him, smiling, and reach up on tiptoes to be kissed. The last thing I see before I close my eyes is his amazed expression.

I HAVEN'T had sex for four thousand years or so, but my body is pretty sure it remembers what to do. My mind is not as certain. Even back when I was still having sex, it wasn't like this—never with somebody I was falling in love with. I am so manic, so out of control that it's all I can do not to start barking and running around the room with my underwear in my mouth. I feel as though part of my mind is hovering somewhere up by the ceiling watching the rest of me have sex, and I try to remember how to slow myself down. I take deep breaths, concentrate on Alex's warm, soft skin, his lips, his eyes, let myself feel the sensations of being touched.

Afterward, we lie there for a long time with my head resting on his chest, and gradually my heart stops flinging itself against my ribs like some kind of caged animal that wants out of this body. I can't believe how wonderful he smells, or how cozy his bed is—like a nest with its soft cotton sheets and cascade of pillows—or how comforting it is just to hear his deep breathing. I need sleep, but I can't close my eyes. Every time I try to let myself rest, they fly back open as though they are spring-loaded.

"So," he says after a long while, "did you get really bludgeoned by Casey? Was it so bad that you needed some love therapy?"

"You knew?"

"Well, Lily, it's not hard to guess." He laughs a little bit. "I've never seen you like this. I figured something bad had happened."

I swallow. "Nah. It wasn't bad at all. Just a lot of sputtering, overheated, roosterish outrage. You kidding? I was expecting it, after what I did." I sit up in bed and act out an imitation of Casey screaming curse words into the phone, which makes Alex laugh. "A colony has revolted, and King Casey will not tolerate such insubordination. 'You will pick up your things and get out. And don't you *dare* take that Rolodex!' The *fucking* Rolodex, as I believe he called it. Who knew that was the technical term?"

"Ah, the Rolodex?" he says, cracking up. "I guess that's so you won't call up people to offer them freelance advice now that you're not on staff anymore."

"I suppose. Who knows what he thinks I might do?" I settle back down on his pillows.

"So you're all right? Really?" He turns over and looks at me closely. His eyes are so tender and concerned I have to look away.

"Oh, I'm totally fine," I say. "I'm actually *relieved,* if you want to know the truth. It was unconscionable of him to think he could dictate what a letter should say."

"That's good," he says and hugs me. We lie there a moment more, then he says, "Say, you wanna get a bite to eat? I'm not positive what's in that scary kitchen of mine, but I'm pretty sure I can offer up some Cheez Doodles and perhaps, if we're really lucky, some not-very-stale potato chips."

It turns out he also has five eggs and some cheddar cheese, so he sets to making us an omelet while I make us some toast. Then I wander around the kitchen, which is not scary, just old-fashioned. It has Depression-era cabinets and fixtures, a stained porcelain sink, and a cracked red linoleum floor that's worn away to nothing in spots. You can see the old wood of the original floor underneath. One long window with a tattered yellowish shade looks out onto his backyard, where there's a tire swing hanging from a maple tree and a tiny garden patch growing vegetables. From here, I can see there are four other rectangular backyards bumping up against his, all divided by fences and filled with trees and grass and plastic lawn furniture.

He sees me looking. "Not much like Branford and the beach," he says.

"A city backyard," I say lightly.

"So . . . tell the truth now. No regrets at all? Really? It's hard to be fired, even for a good cause."

"Nope. No regrets."

I'm feeling drained and shaky. I must be hungry. I'll feel fine again when we eat. He puts the omelet on the table with the salt and pepper shakers, and gets us plates from an overhead cabinet. "I only have these cracked and chipped old-lady dishes," he says to me over his shoulder. "Anneliese and I packed up all our plates before we moved here—before, that is, *I* moved here and she made the sudden decision to live with Daddy-o in D.C. And then, when it became clear she wasn't joining me, I couldn't see the point of unpacking all that crap and playing house by myself. So I just use what's here."

I realize my head stopped really hearing him after the word *Anneliese.* I'll have to get used to that, the fact of her. That he's actually married. Here I am, standing in his kitchen naked under a T-shirt of his, and he just goes and mentions her name as though it's the most natural thing in the world that he has a wife. It is important, I think, not to flinch. Not to show any emotion. I clamp down on any stray feelings that might show up on my face.

He gets forks and knives and spoons out, and then pours us cups of reheated coffee and motions for me to sit. He sits down next to me and clears his throat.

"Okay," he says. "I mention her name as a way of gracefully segueing into the fact that she filed the papers last week." He pours some cream into his mug. "So it looks like I'm going to join the ranks of divorced humans. I thought you should know. If you're going to, you know, be getting into my bed from time to time." He smiles at me.

"Okay." I take a deep breath and wonder if I have the strength to say this whole sentence. "Well, if we're telling stuff, then I should tell you that I found out last night from Teddy that Dana is pregnant and that he's the father."

"Holy shit." He puts down his fork and looks at me for a very long time, searching my face. Outside, a siren wails in the distance—a city noise. When it dies down, he says quietly, "I think I'd better call the radio station and tell them I'm not coming in until the afternoon. Do you want to go back to bed?"

WE SPEND the next few hours in bed. I don't really want to talk about Teddy and Dana, I tell him. She's insane. She leads people on, she doesn't stick to any one thing. She'll be leaving Teddy soon, probably even before the baby is born. Hell, by the time I get home, I'll probably find out she's broken up with him already. I laugh, too shrilly. That's just the way she is: she tries on lives. And now she's come here, noticed that my life is pretty good, and decided to make the same one for herself. She's even picked out the same father for her kid. Can you beat that?

Then I laugh again. "For somebody who doesn't want to talk about something, I've said way too much. I'm just going to forget about it now. End of subject."

He strokes my arm. "You must have felt so blown away," he says. "I mean, think of it—you got fired from your job and got this news about your sister, all in one twelve-hour period."

"Well," I say, "eight hours, really."

He gives a low whistle. "You've got post-traumatic stress disorder. We have to take care of you."

Eeeeasy, don't cry. Don't let yourself fall into feeling bad. Remember that you're really strong, remember how life is going to fall into place now. When it comes to loving—how does that go again? You make your own luck. I am here, making my own luck.

"No, it's fine, really. It's got to be some kind of cosmic collision taking place, just loosening all these fake little bonds that were holding me. I feel so free and so strong right now. I've got to tell you, I feel *wonderful*. Really."

"Well," he says, "that's amazing, I guess."

When we make love again, it's different—not so many of the fever gremlins jumping in and directing things. Less of me is floating up near the ceiling, and more of me is right there in the bed with him. Still, though, I know I have to hold back. I don't want to let everything out, all that pain that's lying in wait deep down in my stomach. It could spill over, and I could scald him.

When it's time for me to go, he walks me to the door and then pulls me to him. "Okay, Wonder Woman, let me just tell you one thing. I know you're the strongest woman alive, but this is still a crazy time in your life. Promise me that if you get to feeling all wacky and can't stay in that house with those free-loving bacchanalian parents-to-be, you'll come here."

"Oh, no. I'm staying there," I tell him. "It's my house. No matter what else happens, it is my house."

29

Okay, so it *is* my house, but it's the damnedest thing: I get in my car and I find I don't actually want to go to it. Not just yet. I drive around town listening to furious revenge songs on the radio. It's amazing how many of them there are; I flip around, and on nearly every station I can find somebody screaming about somebody else just about to get some justice rained down on their heads.

Then, when it's nearly time for school to let out, I park in the circular driveway in front of the building and take my place in the foyer with all the other parents doing pickups. The school smells just like it did when I went here—and what *is* that odor anyway? It's got to be a mixture of mimeograph ink, old textbooks, floor cleaner, and, of course, the pervasive odor of the cafeteria's always-simmering vegetable soup. And chalk. Funny how this never changes, how you could be blindfolded in the desert thousands of miles away, and you'd recognize the smell of your elementary school hallway.

There's a pink plastic barrette in the shape of a bunny on the floor. I lean down and pick it up. Another thing that never changes. Why, I remember walking down this hall when I was in kindergarten—the doors were so much bigger back then—walking from the school bus with Maggie. She always wore just these kinds of barrettes in her smooth pageboy hair, and I was so envious of how they always matched her outfits. Sometimes, if she was wearing a dress that *didn't* have corresponding barrettes, she explained to me, she would have to wear white ones. But mostly that didn't happen. There were so many colors, and Maggie's mother kept a whole basket of barrettes on the counter in the bathroom. They selected the correct pair each morning, right before her mother curled Maggie's hair just slightly underneath, a perfectly smooth roll.

My mother didn't believe barrettes were necessary, especially these colored animal-shaped plastic ones with the little clasp on the back. She liked girls to wear ponytails—neat, clean, off the face, she said.

But oh, how I wanted some for myself. I *ached* for barrettes. And then one day on the bus, Maggie opened her book bag, smiled shyly, and handed me her white pair. Without a word, she helped me loosen my ponytail just enough so that I could clasp a barrette onto either side of my head. From then on, we had a system: she'd call me in the morning to see what color I had on, and each day she would smuggle a matching pair of barrettes out of her house without her mother knowing it, and then I would give them back to her on the homeward bus. I think that was when I knew Maggie was going to be my best friend for life.

"Excuse me, are you all right?" a mom standing next to me asks. Her face is filled with concern. I realize that I'm holding this pink bunny barrette and tears are running down my cheeks. I start to tell her I'm fine, but suddenly I'm sobbing so hard I can't speak.

What has just hit me is that Maggie and Dana are having babies at the same time, that someday it will be *their* little children, not mine, walking together down this hallway, navigating their way through the mysterious rules that adults adhere to. It might even be two little girls, sharing a barrette just like this one.

Dana, who has never committed to a thing, has just swooped down and carried off something else that belonged to me. And I am blinded by the pain of it all.

Dana avoids me for days. Apparently she's moved in with Teddy, which is fine by me. The less I have to do with her right now, the stronger I feel. I am dreading my first encounter with her. And then one day I come home from the grocery store, and she's standing in my kitchen making a smoothie—and a big mess. Strawberries, blueberries, yogurt, and honey are spilled all over the counter, while she has the blender on full blast, attempting to grind up ice cubes.

When I come in, she looks up, startled, and then I see her carefully rearrange her features into something of a smile.

"Turn it to medium before you burn out the motor," I tell her, and go outside to get more grocery bags from the car. My hands are so clammy the handles of the plastic bags stick to my palms. But I take a deep breath and go back inside.

She's drinking her concoction. "You want some of this? It's supposed to be healthy."

"No."

"It's really gooooood," she singsongs.

"No. Thank you."

She takes a long, steady drink and then says in a flat voice, "Teddy doesn't have a blender, so I had to come here."

"Take the blender back with you if you want it. I don't care."

"Ohhhkay." She takes a deep breath. "Before you say anything, I just want to clear the air a little bit. Teddy says we need to talk, so I want to tell you that no matter what you're thinking, this baby is not an accident. I want the baby." Her chin is thrust out and her eyes have that opaque look to them that I remember from when she was a kid.

"Well, then, good for you. You must be very happy," I say coldly. I put the butter and milk away in the refrigerator. The inside is so cool and gleaming that it is a good place to hide for a moment, compose my thoughts. But then I remember that I don't have to hide. I am in control here. I am fine, strong and fine.

She slurps down the rest of her drink and puts the glass on the counter. After a moment, she says, "Teddy said you lost your job. Bummer."

"Yep."

"If it's any consolation, I didn't like the way they were handling your column anyway. I think you have something better coming to you from the universe." When I don't answer, she lets out a big exhalation and says, "Okay, Lily. Let's talk. I know that I didn't do things the right way here. I know you're pissed as hell at me, and I'd probably be pissed, too, if I were you. But things are going to be okay, and you just need to trust me, because I just know it."

"How do you know things are going to be okay?" I say, turning to face her. "Because this is what you decided you wanted in the last week or so? So, therefore, this is it for you?"

"Yes, because that's the first step to happiness—just deciding to be happy. And that's what I'm going to be. I'm very good with babies, and I've always wanted one of my own, and now I'm going to have one."

"Dana, I can't talk to you about this. This makes me so mad I'm having trouble breathing. Take the blender and go back to Teddy's. For God's sake. Take the strawberries and the blueberries, too. And the honey. Take it all."

"Why are you so mad? It's a baby, for God's sake."

"It is a baby with my *ex-husband*. Doesn't that feel in any way *wrong* to you? That we both have babies by the same man? Isn't that so sleazy that it makes you want to throw up?"

"If you want to know the truth, I don't think it has to be that big a deal," she says. "I mean, I know it seems weird at first, but then, when you *really* think about it, it's actually kind of perfect. You and Teddy are divorced but you still get along, *and* you were even trying to fix him up with other women. So I think it's a good thing that it's me, because if he hooked up with somebody else, that person might not love Simon like I do, or she might not want to be friends with you—and then you'd be the one who lost out. This way, at least, we all get to keep going on like we're doing. We're just making our little family group bigger. You know?"

I stare at her. "Are you insane? That's it. You're a complete lunatic. This—what you've done—is wrong on so many levels it boggles the mind."

"What levels?"

"No. Don't draw me into this. I'm not going to debate this with you."

She runs her fingers through the strawberry juice on the counter and then licks them. I can't watch. I turn away and put the canned goods on the pantry shelf. My hands are shaking. When I have finished, I go outside on the porch and start deadheading flowers again. My favorite outdoor pastime these days: pulling the heads off flowers and flinging them in the dirt.

After a moment, she follows me out there. "Even if you're right, and me hooking up with your ex-husband *is* the sleaziest thing that anybody ever did to anybody else, you're eventually going to have to get over it. You know you are. We're family. And whether you want to admit it or not, that makes a huge difference."

"Family? *You* are going to play the family card here? You who just *love* family right up until you decide to walk out and go live a whole different life with a bunch of other people? Then family doesn't mean a thing to you."

She sits down on the swing. "I'm not going to leave."

I bark out a laugh and shake my head. How lovely. How ironic. Just when I'd cheerfully wave good-bye to her forever, she's put down roots. Great.

She pushes off with her foot and swings, an earnest look on her face. "This is what I need to grow up. I know I didn't do it the *normal* way, but I did it just the same. Hey, it's *me*—what do you expect?" She does a little self-deprecating laugh and waggles her fingers in the air around her head. "I'm a flake, okay? How am I going to turn around and start being so-called *normal* now? Nobody would believe it's me! Can't you still love me?"

I fling a dead geranium stem to the ground. "You don't love Teddy. That's the bottom line."

She says, "Oh, get a grip. You wouldn't believe me no matter what I said. I don't happen to have much information on what love really *is*, you know? I can't sit here and prove it to your satisfaction that I am in love with Teddy. He's a good guy. I know that I want a baby, and I want to stay here, and he makes me feel safe, and he's real and he's nice to me. He doesn't sleep with the dog trainer . . ." She trails off with a little laugh.

"That's not love," I say. "That's 'I'll just take something from column A and now something from column B.' That's *using* some-body. It's just more of the same of what you've always done."

"Well, but so what? What can we do about it now? Teddy's happy, and I'm happy. So what's the big deal if anybody got used?" She shrugs, puts her palms in the air. "It's life. And I'm making *more* life, right here in my little belly." She pulls up her shirt and gazes fondly at her flat stomach, rubs little circles around her belly button. "Do you think I'm already getting a little bigger?"

I throw a huge wad of dead petunias to the ground.

Then she says, "You *know*, maybe this isn't the right time to bring this up, but we're going to have to figure out what to do about the living arrangements. Teddy's apartment kind of sucks."

I don't say anything. I don't trust myself to speak right then.

She looks at me levelly. "I think we can make this work. We just have to be open. Like, for a while, I think . . . the baby and Simon *could* share a room. Or maybe we should kick Sloane out and use his place."

I hear the far-off hoofbeats coming ever closer. When I speak, it's with such a dangerous icy edge that she should be very afraid. She should cower under the house, hearing this voice. "You and I,"

I say, "are not going to share a house, a husband, and two children. Not ever. Not over my dead body. I don't care how *open* you think we can be."

"Forget it, forget it. Let's not decide it now," she says. "I was just thinking out loud anyway. I'm sorry. Don't hate me for getting all excited."

30

$\mathcal{S}$imon loves kindergarten. Miss Simone is nice, although, he tells me, she talks to kids in a weird way, like they're still babies. She has a high, squeaky voice, and she's always saying, "Now, *child*ren . . ." And she wears those cartoon shirts all the time. He doesn't think a person should always wear cartoon shirts.

"Does she think we wouldn't like her in a normal shirt?" he says to me. "That's so sad. We'd like her in anything."

He is well on his way to being either an advice columnist or a therapist, I think. He will probably have Miss Simone psychoanalyzed by the end of the year, and will be treating her by second grade.

Kindergarten has it all over preschool when it comes to activities: not only do they have the daily discussions at Circle Time, but they also have show-and-tell and a weather calendar. And soon, Simon says proudly, it will be his week to tell what the weather is each day. Now every morning before school, he and I go outside on the porch and decide which little felt picture should be put up on the calendar: the sun, the cloud, or the raindrop. It's like a rehearsal for the real thing when it comes.

"There are rules about it," he tells me one day as I'm driving him to school. I try not to get depressed about the fact that kindergarten turns out to be as rule-heavy as the rest of life, or that my child is obsessing about his weather week days in advance. "You can put two pictures on the calendar square for the day, but you can't put three. You can do sun and clouds, or you can do rain and clouds. But if it's sunny and cloudy in the morning, but then it starts to rain, that's too bad." He looks out the car window at the threatening sky. "I hope that doesn't happen on my week."

The next week, one night when I'm putting him to bed, he says he has a new problem. Here we go, I think. I've been waiting for him to ask me what's going on around here, why we don't all hang out the way we used to. If Dana and Teddy come over now, it's usually together—safety in numbers, you know—and then they just visit with Simon and take off before they have to spend much time with me. Surely Simon has noticed that. And for all I know, he's overheard that there's a baby coming.

"I have a question about life," he says after we finish the stories and the songs.

"Okay, what about it?"

He's lying on his pillow, with the light from the hallway shining on his face.

"Well, I have two girls who like me at school." He frowns.

"You do? What are their names?"

"Becca S. and Maya T. And they both always want me to come into the dress-up corner at playtime and be the husband." He furrows his brow even more. "But how can I be the husband to two girls?"

"But do you really have to be anyone's husband? I would think you could just be friends."

"Oh, no, they want husbands."

We lie there and think about this. He seems so burdened. I say, "I have an idea. Maybe you don't have to go to the dress-up corner every day. I bet you'd like to play in some other part of the room some days. So maybe you could just ease yourself out of the picture, and they could find other husbands." *Or maybe they could find satisfying careers that don't involve boys.* "You think so?"

"Okay," he says slowly. "But what about lunch?"

"Lunch?"

"Yes. They want me to save them seats next to me in the lunch-room, but the teacher doesn't let you save more than one seat. So one girl is always mad at me."

"Hmm," I say. "This *is* very complicated. Let's see . . . oh, I know. Why don't you go and sit with some other kids and not save any seat at all? Then the girls would get the idea and start leaving you alone. That's called letting them down gently."

"Mom," he says, looking at me as if I'm crazy, "how am I going to keep girlfriends if I don't save them some seats?"

THE NEXT DAY, Dolores Hunter, the radio station owner, calls and asks me if I can come down to talk about a possible job. Alex has warned me this might happen. Usually, he explained, Dolores doesn't have a hand in the hiring and firing but, as she tells me on the phone, this is such a big departure for the station—a live advice show! real people and their problems!—that she feels she should "touch base" with me to "make sure we're on the same page."

I tell Maggie that I have trouble with the kind of people who say phrases like "touch base" and "on the same page" and probably will flunk the job interview. But Maggie laughs and says I'm just nervous and I should dress nice and be polite and agree to whatever Dolores Hunter wants me to do. "Then she'll go back to wherever it is she comes from, and you won't have to deal with her saying annoying phrases to you anymore," Maggie assures me.

During the interview, Dolores Hunter is just as businesslike and chilly as I remember from when I met her at Claire's, the day Dana invited her and Alex to our porch party. She straightens all the papers on her desk so they are at precise ninety-degree angles, purses her lips, and drops the bomb.

"I think," she says heavily, "that I'm going to need to ask you to do another audition tape in front of me. This is just too important for me not to see you think on your feet, in person. So I'll make up some pretend questions, and you answer them."

My heart takes a dive to my toes, and all the moisture dries up in my mouth, but even so, the tape goes well. Luckily for me, Dolores can't even imagine the twisted questions real people ask. She pretends to be someone with an alcoholic mother, and nods, pleased, when I come up with all the rational, calm things anyone would say, and end with suggesting that the caller contact Al-Anon. Then she acts out two other simplistic letters and scenarios, and again, it's as though the words just float down into my head the precise split second before I need them. It flows.

When it's over, she smiles her metallic smile, taps her pen against her clipboard, and tells me the show will be called "Ask Lily" and it will run every evening between seven and ten, five nights a week. She wants to know what I made at *The Edge*, and then she offers me two hundred a month more than that. Now for the first few weeks . . .

I'm still back two sentences ago. "Wait a minute. Evenings?" I say. My pulse is loud in my ears. "Really? You want this program to be on at *night*?"

"Well, yes. I don't think most people can very well call for advice from work," she says, her smile fading. "Night is when our callers need you. That's not a problem, is it?"

"No. No, it's fine." It has to be.

She says that for the first few weeks, until the show catches on, they will have an engineer ready to play music during the lulls between callers. Also, Alex will work the switchboards at the beginning, until things get rolling. Calls will be screened for content, and I'll get a brief description of the nature of each call just before I pick it up.

She smiles and gathers up her folders. Could we record some promos now and then start next week?

DRIVING HOME, I tally up all the ways my life has just changed. For one thing—and this is the worst—I won't be home for the bed-time routine with Simon. True, we'll now have the afternoons after school to be together and play, but I'm going to miss the stories and songs and snuggling with him before he goes to sleep. That's going to have to fall to Teddy and Dana, I realize grimly. And that means that they'll now be at the house every damn night. The wheels in my mind start turning: if the show starts at seven, I'll need to be there by six-thirty, which means that we'll have to eat by five-thirty, et cetera, et cetera. No doubt this means group dinners for us, and then some kind of interaction with Dana and Teddy when I return home after ten—all of it. The whole nine yards. One big happy family.

I consider for a moment turning around and driving back to the station and telling Dolores Hunter that I'm so sorry, but I can't take the job after all. But what will I do instead? I can't stay unemployed, and I certainly don't want to take an office job somewhere and be gone from nine to five.

No, I have to do this. And it will work out fine.

When I get home, I sit in the driveway for a moment, listening to the engine ticking under the hood. I used to love coming home, the feeling of going from outside to in, coming through the front door and looking down the open hallway through the kitchen and out at the Sound's many moods, whether it was sparkling in the sun-light or being pelted by rain. I loved the way the floorboards squeaked under my footsteps; the certain way the light fell across the kitchen counters; seeing the flowers in the vase, the scrubbed sink, the gleaming, uncluttered surfaces of things.

But now it's all different. The kitchen walls are a loud, orange-red instead of the lovely, delicate wallpaper that had been there throughout my childhood. There are crumbs and canisters, unopened mail and magazines lying everywhere. In the living room, the couches have been moved around, and beanbag chairs put in their places. My mother's artwork is gone, given away to Sloane, and in its place are bright monochromes in black metal frames. Hideous. And, worse, I gave my permission to all of it every step along the way.

THERE'S A message from Leon on the answering machine, saying that he needs to see me, so, glad to get out of there, I grab some homemade blueberry muffins and take the shortcut across the beach. It's still early afternoon, cool for September, with a bright Crayola blue sky. Summer has finally loosened its mad, hot, white grip on us.

The first shock is that Leon is sitting in a wheelchair outside on his deck. Can this really be the same man who was dancing at my house just a few weeks ago? He looks shockingly old, gray and drawn, as though there's a murky film coating his once-sharp features. He is actually fading away, I think, like a Polaroid picture developing in reverse.

"My goodness. What in the world are they doing to you?" I say. "Did you call me because you want me to stage a rescue raid and run away with you to Mexico or something?"

He laughs, a hard barking cough of a laugh. "It's sitting in this damn wheelchair all day that's doing it to me," he says. "They don't want me to walk around anymore. Much less dance. I have to look into wheelchair dancing."

He reaches for a glass of water on the table, but can't quite reach it. I hand it to him.

"Anyway, I didn't call you over here so you could bitch at me about my health," he says. "I called you over here for a very important reason, and I want to make sure Krystal can't hear me."

"No, I won't go out with you," I say. "You're married, and that's that."

This would normally make him almost purple with pleasure, a joke like that, but now he doesn't even smile; he just motions me over and makes me bend close to his ear. "She doesn't like it when I talk about when I'm gone," he says. "Can you believe that? She's a nurse and yet she can't deal with death."

"I don't want to talk about when you're gone, either," I say.

"Well, you have to. Somebody has to. I have something to give you. You're the only one I can count on." He coughs for a while, and then he straightens himself up. "When I go, I'm leaving an envelope just for you. All sealed up. Now don't get excited. It's not money. It's a separate little will. My social will."

"Your *social* will? What the heck is a social will?"

"Yeah. There's the legal, official one, of course—but then I drew up this little will that's just between you and me. A social will means that I tell how I want the memorial service to go and all that. It's all my bossy instructions. Krystal knows about it, but she hates when I talk about it." He looks around. "I'm not going to tell you what's in it, but I want you to promise me you'll do what it says."

"Of course," I say. "I promise. Now how are you—"

"No, really promise."

"Well, sure . . . I mean, if it's legal, I'll do whatever. What are you asking me to do anyway?"

"You'll see. Promise me now."

"Wait. Do I have to pick up a rattlesnake or go back to Teddy or anything like that?"

He laughs. "That'd be something, wouldn't it? But you wouldn't go back to Teddy. He's not the right guy for you. I never thought he had enough stuffing to him. Nice guy, but no oomph."

I sigh. "Yeah, well, he found a little bit of oomph somewhere and got my sister pregnant. And now we're all going to be the outrage of the colony, just you watch. You and Krystal can say good-bye to your days of being the major scandal, let me assure you. Dana and Teddy are taking over for you."

He shakes his head. "She's a firebrand, that Dana. Always was."

"Yeah. I thought I had it bad when she was gone and I was worrying about her. Now I see that the reality of having her around is so much worse."

He snorts a laugh. "Be careful what you wish for, huh?" he says. Then he laughs for real. "So, Krystal and I aren't going to be the latest scandal anymore. Hmm. I'm not sure how I feel about that. After all, how many men my age get to be known as a sex rascal in their own community?"

"A sex rascal. I like that."

"You know," he says, lowering his voice. I see his eyes brighten just a tad, and he motions me over closer. "You *know*, it's true that the colony doesn't like anything more than good sex gossip, but the truth is they've all had some, ah, *interesting situations* themselves through the years—and not just your ma and Gracie, either, which nobody ever knew for sure was really going on. I could tell you a thing or two that would curl your hair."

I pull my chair even closer. "Oh, please. I insist."

He grins, and for a moment his face is transformed to what it used to be. Spreading gossip, I think: a healing pastime.

"Well, for one thing, Anginetta's grandson recently got busted for dealing drugs out of his father's house in Maryland, and now the Feds have seized Bert's house. That's why he's back living with his mother now. You thought it was just family loyalty, I bet. Heh-heh. But no. No loyalty there. Just a lot of crow to eat. And Anginetta herself: I don't have anything on her, but everybody knew that her husband, the late great Dominic Franzoni, for years frequented prostitutes in the city. There was a rumor going on for a while that he actually had a son by one of them, and had to pay child support until the kid was grown. And let's see—the Artertons. Oh, yeah, Bob Arterton did a little funny stuff with his taxes a few years ago and had to go live in the pokey for a year or so. They told everybody he was traveling on business, but I don't think he did much traveling.

Just to the federal penitentiary is all. And so while he was gone, Virginia got back at him by propositioning anyone she could think of, including *moi* and your dear, sainted father."

"No! Get *out*. When did everything start seeming like Jerry Springer's America?"

He laughs. "It was always this way. And I'm not telling you all the rest. Suffice it to say that the human race isn't as lovely as some would have us believe. Everybody's got a little skeleton dancing around in a closet somewhere. So, believe me, this with Dana and Teddy will blow over in no time. In five years, if they stay together, people will forget it wasn't always that way." He looks at me. "Anyway, I'm not worried about them. What do they matter, frankly? It's you I'm thinking about. You gotta let go, kid."

"Yeah, yeah."

His eyes are serious. "No, you do. Think of Gracie sitting there all those years waiting for your mother to get free, and then she never did, bless her heart. Don't let your life get caught up with other people's fates."

"I'm not," I say, bristling.

"You're waiting for something," he interrupts. "Just like Gracie was. It might not be something you know just yet, but I see all the signs there with you. You're turning out to be just like her, patiently sitting by while life happens all around you."

"I don't know what you're talking about."

"It's later than you think. Time to figure out what you want and go get it. Don't spend time fretting over your sister getting pregnant by Mr. No Oomph. Waste of time."

I look across the bay at my house, standing in the early afternoon sunlight. Not long ago, I considered myself as having been brought up there in the most normal family in America. I shake my head. "Did you notice what Dana has done with the place? She painted the kitchen walls *red*."

"So *what*?" he says and pretends to swat me. "Do I have to get up out of my wheelchair and smack you? You think the color of the walls matter? God, I *oughta* smack you. Someone ought to. Get *out of there* and get going on your life! What's with you people anyway? Wait until you read my social will. God, I wish I wasn't going to be dead when you read it."

"You *could* give it to me now," I say.

He looks like he's considering this, but then he says, "No. No. It's for when I die. Krystal will give it to you. It's all sealed up."

"But we are talking years and years from now, right?" I say.

"Yeah. Right. I wish," he says and gives me such a soft-focused, loving look that I get a sinking sensation, as though something has just breathed ice-cold air on the back of my neck.

31

$\mathcal{B}$y the end of the next week—after my first four days doing the radio show—I realize that I'm accustomed to that icy cold feeling, the sense that the roller coaster I'm on has just plunged two hundred feet straight down.

I may even be addicted to the exhilaration of answering people's questions on the air. I thought I'd miss the boxes of letters, people's handwritten pleas for help, but this is so much more thrilling. When I'm actually there in front of the microphone, I'm fine—calm, rational, and collected. But as soon as I stop and notice what a daring thing this is to be doing—well, then the adrenaline rush is almost overpowering.

I hardly recognize my life anymore. For one thing, Alex and I have fallen into a harmless little sex-and-breakfast habit now that we're working together every night. It's wonderful. It started on Tuesday, when he invited me over to analyze the previous evening's show and talk about the callers and how we might attract even more of them—and well, one thing led to another.

It's adrenaline, I know, that's given me the courage to hurry to his house every morning after I drop Simon off at school. If it weren't for the pounding excitement of sex, I think, followed by the comfort of being held in bed and laughing with Alex, I'd be much more of a hysterical jellified wreck than I already am.

And yet . . . and yet . . . if I'm honest with myself, there are moments even there, in what I call his Alex nest, when I suddenly stand back and wonder what I'm doing. It's so strange: I'll be kissing him or talking to him, and then it's as if a switch has been turned on and I am flooded with uneasiness. This is not my life! Who is this man, *really*, and is he important to me, or am I just covering up some deep sense of loneliness by sleeping with him?

On Friday morning, though, I'm not thinking of that. I've aced my first four days of radio shows—twelve hours on the air, answering the questions so nimbly it's as though the answers are being typed into my head as I'm speaking them. I'm already unbuttoning and unzipping as I walk through his living room. By the time I crawl into his bed with him, I am ready for love. This morning I feel so connected to him, not uneasy at all, as we fall together, rolling over and over in the covers. Afterward, we drift into the kitchen and exchange coffee-flavored kisses while the banana pancake batter sizzles in butter.

Today we can't hang around long after breakfast. He has a staff meeting at the station, and I have a dentist appointment, after which I plan to go to the grocery store. When we kiss good-bye at our cars, he says to me, like he always does, "Remember. If things get crazy at your house, don't hesitate to come back."

"I won't," I say, and we blow each other kisses. I have no intention of taking him up on this, of course, but it's sweet that he still mentions it. Sometimes when I'm there, he'll show me some quirk about the house—the precise way you need to hit the refrigerator door with the heel of your hand when the fan gets stuck and starts to screech, for instance—and when I laugh, he says, "Pay attention. This is stuff you may need to know someday."

The day perks along just fine: I don't have any cavities, and the dentist praises me for my excellent gums. There aren't any lines at the store, so I get out of there in record time, and amazingly, there's hardly any traffic. The weather is perfect. And—hurray!—I've almost made it to the weekend, which I intend to spend reclaiming and scrubbing my house. Doing my Saturday-morning cleaning ritual, clearing out a week of having Dana and Teddy presiding over the evening hours.

Honestly, having them watch Simon hasn't been as awful as I imagined. Each night, although I've cooked dinner for the four of us, Simon and I have managed to eat together, just us, before they arrive to stay with him. Best of all has been the fact that when I return home in the evening, they're not both hanging around, waiting to talk, pretending that things are just the same as they ever were between us. Usually Teddy has already gone back to his house, and Dana is upstairs, sleeping in the guest room. I haven't had to deal with them as much as I feared.

If it weren't for the fact that my heart is racing all the time, things would be just about perfect. But, I think as I pull up to the house, maybe this is just the New Me: slightly off-kilter, motor running full blast, but basically okay.

This must be what change feels like, I think.

THE FIRST SHOCK comes when I unlock the front door. There's Maggie's voice from the kitchen, along with Dana's laughter. I hear Maggie saying, "You see that? I think it's a stretch mark, isn't it? No, right here. The first stretch mark *already*. Come on, you can tell me."

I go into the kitchen, surprised to see them together. They were never good friends; Dana was historically the annoying, and sometimes dangerous, younger sister whom Maggie and I had to take refuge from. But now here they are. When I walk in, Maggie's got her shirt hiked up, and she's pointing to something on her stomach, and Dana is laughing and saying, "I don't think you can officially have a stretch mark when you're not even showing yet. You haven't, you know, *stretched*."

Maggie looks up and smiles at me apologetically. "Hi! This is a meeting of the Early Pregnancy Complaint Committee," she says. "We're the Scallop Bay colony chapter."

"Oh, that's nice," I say and smile back at her. I'm actually happy to see her, even if it is startling to find her here with Dana. "I haven't seen you in so long! How are you doing? Are things good with you and Mark?"

"Much, much better," she says and starts to say something, but then Dana interrupts.

"Nope," she says, "this is definitely not a stretch mark." She straightens up from staring at Maggie's belly and looks in my direction without meeting my eyes.

"Thank you. What the hell is it, do you think? Come look, Lily," Maggie says.

I come over and look at it. Dana stiffens and moves over a mere inch or two so I can get closer. Maggie is telegraphing me with her eyes: *Please don't worry, I'm just trying to help her by being nice, I really love you best.* I give her a reassuring look: *It's fine.*

"My diagnosis: random red mark," I say. "Nothing bad." I give her a hug. "Wow, Mags, this is so great. You don't have to work today?" I'm about to say we could go get some lunch and catch up, but I see Dana slide her eyes over to Maggie, and Maggie says, "Well, I have a lot of days off coming that I have to take by the end of the year, and then Dana called me, so we decided that we were going to get together and discuss how often we pee and stuff like that." She laughs. "Maybe grab a bite to eat. Do you want to come?"

"You can come only if you remember how often you peed in your first trimester with Simon," says Dana.

I hear the annoyance in her voice. "Actually, I'm going to get Simon soon, and I want to hang out with him," I say. Then I remember the rest of the groceries. "Yikes, I have ice cream melting in the car." I go back outside and take my time gathering up the bags, balancing them in my arms so I don't have to make more than one trip. My nice clean teeth, I notice, are gritted.

When I get back in the kitchen, Maggie is smiling and leaning on one elbow while Dana is telling her how she has to eat something at four o'clock or she goes berserk. Maggie nods and says it's even harder when you work in an office where people don't know you're expecting. Then she and Dana get into the problem of telling people: when and how. Then back to how many times they get up in the night to pee, and how their backs hurt already, so how will they possibly make it the whole nine months?

I put away the food and every now and then try to contribute something—and perhaps it's my imagination, but every time I try to say something non-pregnancy related, Dana grabs hold of the conversation and hauls it right back. After a few minutes, she says she's starving and why don't they leave to go eat. Also, there's some baby furniture she'd love for Maggie to look at with her downtown.

"Baby furniture?" I say. "You haven't even had your first OB appointment yet."

This is the wrong thing to say. Dana's face darkens and she silently goes over and gets her purse and puts on her shoes. "Let's go," she says to Maggie.

Maggie, ever the diplomat, gets her purse and starts telling me how much she likes my radio show, and Dana has to chime in with how she hasn't once gotten to hear it because she's waaaay too busy with Simon each evening to catch it. "Even when I finally get through all his little rituals and get him to sleep, Teddy and I are just too tired to listen to the radio," she says to Maggie. "It's hard work, being pregnant *and* watching a child. But—well, I'm up for it."

There's a silence, during which I wonder if it would be too upsetting if I took this gallon of ice cream and, say, hurled it through the sliding glass door. My pulse is beating in my ears. Then Dana says, "Whoops. Gotta go pee—fourth time just this morning, if you can believe it!" and dashes off.

Maggie and I look at each other in the whoosh of silence Dana's left behind. I feel something in my pocket, and reach in to find the pink plastic bunny barrette. I hand it to Maggie. "Remember when you used to bring me your barrettes from home when my mother wouldn't buy me any?" I say softly. I know Dana's listening to us from the bathroom, or at least trying to.

"Wow," Maggie says, turning it over in her hand. "I didn't know they still even made these things."

"Well, if your baby's a girl, you've got her first barrette," I tell her. "Consider this your first of many baby gifts."

Without warning, Dana's back, fastening her pants as she hurries in, straining to see what we're talking about. She peers over Maggie's shoulder, still not looking at me. "A barrette! Oh, cool. Wouldn't it be something, Mags, if we both had girls?"

I wish this didn't make me want to kick the trash can, but after they leave, that's exactly what I do. I kick it as hard as I can, which is very satisfying, even when it falls over and wet, gloppy garbage spills all over the floor. Then, while I'm on my hands and knees picking up eggshells and old lettuce leaves, I give myself a good talking-to. This is nothing new, what's happened here. I, myself, had considered that Maggie and Dana might bond over their pregnancies.

"Get a grip, will you?" I say to myself out loud.

LATER, I pick up Simon from school. He comes out of his classroom in a huff and won't talk until we get in the car. I buckle him into the backseat and look at his sad, frowning face in the rearview mirror.

"Are you okay, pumpkin? What's the matter?"

"The weather didn't have any clouds."

"True—it turned nice and sunny all day."

"You said there would be clouds, and I put clouds on the calendar."

"Oh, well," I say, pulling out of my parking spot and managing to keep from being rear-ended by a woman who's charging ahead and not watching. I beep my horn at her. "I guess nobody ever really knows what the weather's going to be like until it happens. Welcome to the hard life of a meteorologist. That's what Leon used to do for a living, you know."

He stares out the window of the car. "Do you have to go to work again tonight?"

"Yes, but it's Friday. Tomorrow is a home day and so is Sunday, so we can just have fun."

"But I don't *want* you to go. You're always gone at night."

My heart does a little lurch, hearing the edge in his voice. He must be tired after his whole week being a big boy in kindergarten. "I know, sweetie," I say, "but we have this afternoon to have a good time. What would you like to do?"

In a pouty voice, he says he wants to go to the ice cream place, the one that has a waterwheel and some goats and rabbits. But when we get there, he sees somebody from school—a big scary fourth-grader—and he's too shy to get out of the car. We wait for the kid to leave, but that just doesn't seem to be happening. Finally I have to bring Simon an ice cream cone to the car, and then he gets upset with himself when it drips on the upholstery. To my surprise, he cries when I tell him it doesn't matter.

"It matters! You know it matters! People can't just drop ice cream everywhere!" he yells. "You can't have sticky old ice cream everywhere! That's what Auntie Dana would do—she never wipes anything up when it spills. She just says it's okay."

I get out of the car and calmly go get some napkins and come back and start scrubbing the drips of vanilla ice cream. He keeps whimpering and kicking the back of the driver's seat with his sneaker.

"It's clean now, it's all clean," I say soothingly, but when I go to wipe off his arm, he pulls away and glares at me. "What's the matter?" I say. "Tell me what's the matter."

He doesn't say anything.

"Did something happen at school you want to tell me about?"

Silence.

"Do you want to get out and go look at the goats? I think the fourth-grader is leaving in a minute. Look, he's throwing away his trash."

"*No*, I don't want to look at the goats! And I don't want a baby at our house!" he bursts out.

I must look stunned, because he says, "Don't you know anything? Don't you know that when you're gone, they decide things, and now they've decided to get a baby to live with us? They didn't even ask you, did they?"

I look over at the goats, little furry things in the distance, leading their simple goat lives. "I knew about the baby . . . ," I start slowly.

"Did you say okay?" he asks me, furiously.

"It's not . . . well, it's not something I could say okay to . . . it's not up to me . . ."

"Well, *I* said no! I told Daddy I don't *like* it, and he said it was okay to be mad, but I'd get used to it and that I would always be his first baby. AND I AM NOT A BABY AND I DON'T WANT A BABY!"

People are beginning to look over at our car. Even one of the goats in the pen seems to be concerned. Simon is crying hard now. I've been sitting in the backseat with him, but now I get out and tell him that we'll go home and talk about everything. I'll explain to him what's happening, I say. Damn it, I should have told him before, not just assumed that Dana would keep quiet until I felt the time was right. It's just that it was so early. Why does she have to do this stuff?

"Come on, honey. We'll go home, and I'll tell you everything. It'll be all right."

"It won't ever be all right!" he says, and then he starts sobbing. I sit back down, take him out of his seat belt, and bring him onto my lap. He slumps up against me and I sing him songs while he cries and cries and cries.

NOT SURPRISINGLY, I'm shakier than usual when I get to work that night. Simon has clung to me in the driveway, begging me not to go—to the point where I almost considered either bringing him with me or calling in sick. What *will* happen, I wonder, if I ever can't come in? Do they have a backup plan? Dolores Hunter forgot to mention that, and I haven't thought to ask Alex, either.

Finally, with Simon wailing for me to stay, Teddy comes outside and picks him up very gently and carries him back inside—but the last view I have of my child is his tear-streaked face and outstretched arms as I pull out of the driveway. I call home as soon as I get in, and Teddy says everything is fine. Simon is upstairs with Dana, taking a bath. And yes, he's stopped crying.

"You guys shouldn't have told him," I say. "This was something we should have talked about together."

"Yeah, I know. But Dana just blurted it out because she's so excited. Either way, it'll all work out. He'll get used to the idea."

Who are you? I want to say to him. But it's time to go on the air. Luckily, the callers' questions jog me out of my funk. It's good to see that this job takes over the part of my brain that might otherwise be worrying and fretting all night. People seem to be asking interesting, but not terribly difficult, questions tonight, and I'm taking plenty of deep breaths.

From the control booth, Alex, wearing headphones for the telephone, smiles and holds up a sign for the next caller. It says, BOYFRIEND NOT PAYING ATTENTION. CINDY FROM HAMDEN. I listen carefully while a woman details all the romantic crimes that have been perpetrated on her. I advise her to tell her boyfriend how she feels. Then Alex writes: STAY-AT-HOME WIFE BORED WITH LIFE. BRAD FROM WOODBRIDGE, and I'm off, explaining to a well-meaning but clueless husband the difficulties of child-tending.

FAMILY MEMBER QUESTIONING LIFE CHOICES. ISABEL FROM BRANFORD, Alex's sign reads. I feel the vein in my temple pulse slightly.

"Isabel, you're on the air," I say.

"Hi, I'm a twenty-eight-year-old woman who's just moved back here after many years," begins the caller in a false, singsongy, almost taunting voice. I wish to God I had waved off this call, gone to a musical interlude instead. It's Dana. She's disguised her voice and is using our mother's name instead of her own. I look up at Alex and lick my dry lips. There is no way he knew my mother's name was Isabel.

"Anyway," Dana/Isabel is saying, "here's the thing: I kinda sorta fell in love with my sister's ex-husband, *whom she does not love . . .* and now that he and I are so happy and are going to have a baby . . ."

I look up at Alex, desperately. He shakes his head and closes his eyes. We're just going to have to barrel through.

The question turns out to be: How can you convince family members you're doing the right thing when they're mad at you?

"You can't convince anybody of anything," I say. "It's your actions that bring about changes in people. If you act honorably and honestly, then possibly you can repair the damage you've done to your family relationships."

Suddenly she giggles. "Hey, Lily, guess who—" she starts, but it's too late. Alex has cued the music, and we're out of there.

WHEN I GET home, she's standing at the kitchen sink drinking the last of a Coke. "Hey," she says. She's wearing a T-shirt and underpants. "Nice show tonight." Then she laughs. "So at what point did you know it was me?"

"Listen, that is not cool, calling me like that. And worse, what you did at the end . . ."

"He cut me off! That bastard didn't let me say who I was. I thought that would be so funny for the listeners, if they heard that part. It would humanize you, you know."

"I don't need humanizing. I need you not to call there anymore."

She puts her glass down hard and sighs. "What was it you said? Oh." She mimics me: " 'If you act honestly and'—what else?—'oh, honorably, then possibly you can repair the damage." She laughs. "Fat chance of that working, though, right? That is so not happening. You'd rather hold a grudge, no matter what I do."

I don't know why, but I start patiently trying to explain all the ways that what she's doing *isn't* acting honorably. Telling Simon about the baby before we talked about it and decided how to proceed, making dates with my best friend and trying to exclude me—

I know she'll object. And sure enough, she starts loudly claiming that it's *nice* of her to try to be friends with Maggie; she's trying to be a part of the community she now lives in. And as for telling Simon—she thought he'd be excited. Kids love babies! It's just more of me trying to control everything. Why do I always have to take everything the wrong way? Even calling the radio station tonight: it wasn't malicious. She did it for *fun*. She thought I'd be amused by it.

There are footsteps, and then from the top of the stairs I hear Teddy's voice: "Guys, you might want to keep it down. You're being too loud."

I look at her. "Um. He's not . . . you're not having him sleep here, I trust."

"Oh, *what* is the big deal with everything with you? Yes, he's spending the night here! So what? It's not like it's a secret that we have sex. So is this now *another* thing I was supposed to ask your permission for? I can't take this."

And then she charges past me and marches upstairs. I hear them talking in low, intense voices at the top of the stairs, and then the bedroom door closes and that's that.

I stand there for a moment looking around the messy kitchen:

the Coke bottle still out, a ring of spilled soda on the countertop, the dinner dishes still not washed. I inhale deeply. A little trail of sweat snakes down my back. And then my eye falls on something over by the glass door: a large brown paper bag with a hardware store logo on the side. I go over and look inside. There are two large gallons of paint and some rollers and brushes. The label on the paint says the color is Deep Marine Blue.

At first I'm confused, but then it all comes back to me. That night—the night we did my hair, Dana and Maggie and I—Dana said she wanted to paint the living room so it would look just like an aquarium. Wouldn't that be great, she said, to have a room that made you feel like you were underwater? So cool and refreshing.

And now, apparently, the time has come. Had I ever said that was a good idea? Did I ever act as though I could *bear* to live in a house with an aquarium-looking living room?

Quietly I slip out the sliding door. I don't know where I'm going. I just need some air. The next thing I know, I'm walking across the wet grass to Gracie's house, where there's one welcoming light glowing from her kitchen. When she opens the door, I fall into her arms, enveloped by the giant sleeves of her green kimono. She smells like talcum powder and wine and comfort as she leads me inside.

32

We sit in her kitchen, drinking wine, and I cry harder than I've ever cried in my life. Harder than I cried when my parents died, or when Dana left, or when I knew that I didn't love Teddy enough to stay married and watch him make both of us unhappy. It's as though I've hit a bottomless well of tears and I'm unable to shut off the flow.

She just listens while I tell her all of it: about not only the pregnancy (which she already knew about, of course), but the untenable living arrangement, Dana's overexcited behavior, my new job, Simon's reaction, Maggie, Alex and the adrenaline addiction of making love to him—everything. Even the sorrow of not really knowing my mother, of being the only one not in on the family secret.

Gracie hands me tissues, rubs my back, pours more wine, gets me a cold cloth for my head—and then, when I'm winding down, she says, "Can I show you something?"

"Sure," I say, thinking she's going to produce something that is going to lead me back to sanity. My heart sinks when instead she hands me a picture of my mother when she first moved here. My mother, young and slim and blond, with such a look on her face it makes me almost draw back. She looks full of the devil, as though she's realized she needs something different from what she's just signed on for with my father, and she's going to get it, no matter what.

"Thank you," I say, and push the picture away. "She's not exactly the role model I'm aspiring to right now."

She laughs. "You know, over the years I have thought that if a truck hadn't come and killed your mother, I would have had to do it myself," she says. "I say this to you with all respect, since I know this is your mother we're talking about. You probably wish she wasn't killed the first time, much less thought about it happening a second time."

"Don't worry, I think I understand," I say.

"Well," she says. She looks down at the photograph, and the look of love and longing on her face is so naked that I have to look away. "She could be difficult, that was for sure, although she didn't see herself that way. She was—she was like somebody who just knows she's on earth for all the right reasons, for love and for poetry and for dancing and music."

"She was certainly a good cook," I say dully, and we both laugh at how faint that praise seems. But, really, it's all I can come up with. "Listen, she went into her studio and shut the door and didn't want me around. I don't see her as having the most perfect set of priorities."

Gracie laughs. "No. I suppose motherhood wasn't her thing." Then she sighs, still staring at the picture, and I know she's seeing something there that I can't possibly see. Her voice is dazed. "Being *reliable* wasn't her thing, either. She never once did what she said she'd do. Something would always come up. Every time we were going to be together—oops, sorry, can't do it after all."

I do not want to hear this, and can't for the life of me think of how it is relevant to my situation next door, but I'm too tired to do anything but sit and listen. She tells me about all the times she sat at home looking out her window at our house next door—all lit up and ringing with music and children's voices, the smells of cooking wafting out onto the lawn—and how all she could do was wait.

"It's so pathetic, but sometimes I'd sit at the window in the dark so nobody could see me, and I'd watch what was going on, trying to piece together what was happening over there," she says.

"What are you talking about? In my memory, you were right there with us."

"Well, not always," she says. "There were times I'd actually grow something resembling a spine, and I'd decide I was going to lead my own life, not just be a hanger-on in your mother's life. And that's when I'd miss her the most: just seeing little glimpses of your family life in the windows." She turns suddenly and looks at me. "So I'd always go back."

She's looking at the photograph again, and her eyes are blurry. "And then one day your mother came over to my house and told me that she was pregnant. She said it in the most casual way you can imagine, as if it was something I should have seen coming, maybe even congratulate her about," she says. "Believe me, I had no idea, silly me, that she and your father were still intimate, much less that they were trying to expand the family. That's how naïve I was back then." She laughs and shakes her head. "I thought that when you loved somebody that you couldn't also love somebody else at the same time." She takes a big sip of her wine. I'm aware suddenly of how old she looks. "So I was pretty much devastated. It was just one more reminder that while I was at home writing my little poems in the evening and preparing my little lessons, she was involved in a whole rich life, with sex and laughter and children and whatever else she wanted. Plenty of money, a man who loved her enough to let her have her outside playtime, a chance to do her art, the respect of the community, two beautiful children—and me to be her life-time secret soul mate."

She sets down the glass and looks at me steadily. "I don't think it would have occurred to anyone to say to me, 'Gracie, you're wasting your time loving this woman. Get out and find yourself somebody else, somebody who will give back to you what you deserve.' But that's what I needed to hear, and that's what I'm saying to you: Get out and find somebody else."

"But you don't understand. I don't love Teddy," I say. "That's not my situation."

"You don't love Teddy per se," she says. "But there's something about this situation that you love. Maybe it's that you love it that Teddy needs you and depends on you. Maybe you love it that you get to sacrifice your life to make sure other people live the right way. I don't know. I've been trying to figure you out for a while now. But what I do know is that when I look at you, I see somebody who's wasting away from the same waiting disease I had. And so I say to you: Get out. Take a break. Go on a vacation. Let people handle their own lives for a while. Get the hell out."

"Funny, that's kind of what Leon said," I say slowly.

"Yeah, he would say that. He's seen a lot, that Leon."

We sit quietly for a while. "You're right," I say after a while. "I can't go back and live in my house with Dana and Teddy. I'm so filled with hate and rage right now, it kind of scares me."

"That's a pretty good sign that you can't go back."

"Why do I have to be the one who leaves? Why can't *they* be the ones who have to go?"

"I don't know," she says softly. "That's just the way it is."

I'm thinking aloud. "All right. I can't very well go to Maggie's house," I say slowly. "She's all crazy working out things with Mark. And I can't come here, because you have bookshelves where other people have stoves . . . and . . . maybe I should go to a hotel." I think a minute. "How long do I have to stay gone, do you think? Forever? Should I rent an apartment?"

"Maybe that's what it's going to come to, but I don't think you have to go out and sign a lease right away. Who knows how long you have to stay gone? You just go and then you figure it out. You'll find yourself knowing. Things change. That's the good part."

I look down at the photograph of my mother on the table. "*She* wouldn't have been agonizing like this," I say. And then I'm crying again. "I just . . . I just . . . wish I could have been what she wanted. I wish she had liked me."

Gracie says, "She loved you very much. Here, let me show you something else." She gets up and rummages through a box.

"Ack! Not another picture. Puhleeze."

"Just one more." This one is of my mother and me sitting on the beach, right in the spot, I realize, where I dug all those holes. She's holding me and smiling at me. Not at the camera, at me. I must be about three. I have plump sunburned arms, and my hair is up in two carefully formed pigtails sticking out from the sides of my head. My mother's touching my nose with her index finger and laughing, and the way she's looking at me is just about enough to knock me sideways. She is actually gazing at me with an expression that looks like love. This could be a poster for motherhood, even.

"So she was also a hell of an actress when the camera was pointed at her," I say.

"No. Don't be that way. She loved you a lot. She really, really did. You know what her motherhood problem was? I think she was afraid of all those feelings of need and dependency. She didn't like attachment. Kind of like Dana, come to think of it. They both just jump into things and then think them through later."

"You know what? I really do have to get out of this place," I say. "Look at that beach. I've been looking at that little stretch of dirt my whole life." I stand up. "I have to go." The adrenaline starts coursing through me again. "I'm going to Alex's house."

"You are? Tomorrow?"

"No, now." I look at her clock. It's one thirty in the morning. I don't want to spend the night at home. Mostly I don't want to have to wake up in the morning and have to playact my way through a whole little domestic scene—breakfast around the table, just the four of us. And I really don't want to see Simon's confused look when Teddy is clearly Dana's partner and not Mommy's. "You know something?" I say. "I'm going to go pack up the car and get Simon and just leave."

She looks a little concerned. "Oh, my lord. What have I done?" she says.

"Nothing." I kiss her on the nose. "Can I use your phone? I want to tell Alex I'm coming."

"What if he's sleeping? What if he says no?"

"He's not, and he won't," I say. I've never been more sure of anything in my life.

33

I never knew how exciting it is to pack and leave in the night, to stuff duffel bags with your clothing as though you were your own worst nightmare: a cat burglar making off with your possessions in the dark. I tiptoe around, working quickly and quietly. I get all my clothes together—jeans and slacks and shirts and shoes—and then flit into Simon's room and put his toys in a big garbage bag and fill his Barney suitcase with enough clothes to last him for a few days. In the bathroom, I open the cosmetics drawer and empty the entire box of creams and lotions into my old backpack. Who knows how long we'll be gone? If it's longer than a few days, I can always come back and get more.

The important thing is, we're getting out of here. My heart is jumping around like it's the last day of school or something.

I load up the car, closing the door very, very softly, and then go upstairs and scoop up Simon—pillows, blankets, stuffed animals and all—and make my way down with him to the car. He wakes up, startled, as we get to the front door and he looks around.

"Shhh," I say. "I'll tell you what we're doing when we get in the car. We're going on an adventure."

He rubs his eyes and shivers happily. "Really? An adventure?"

"We have to whisper," I say. "It's a secret adventure."

I get him all settled in the car, look around to make sure I have everything, running through a checklist in my mind: my clothes, Simon's clothes, pillows, blankets, toiletries, toys, shoes, jackets, purse, alarm clock . . .

I smile at Simon in the rearview mirror. "You ready?"

He nods, eyes bright.

"Oh!" I say. "A couple more things." I run back inside and grab the garlic press. Then the hand blender, the olive oil decanter, and the cheese slicer. I've noticed that Alex's kitchen lacks a few of the essential amenities.

As a last thought, I scrawl a little note to Dana and Teddy, saying we've gone to Alex's. I'll be in touch when I'm ready.

IT'S AWESOME being there. Alex helps us bring in our bags, and then the three of us eat English muffins and honey in the kitchen: nobody is in the mood for sleep after the excitement of our arrival. I may never sleep again. The blackness outside has made the windows like mirrors, and I can't get over how calm and right it looks: Alex and me with Simon, eating a middle-of-the-night snack and talking. Simon looks around the apartment, and Alex shows him how everything works, and points out all the neat little touches, like the little button on the floor of the dining room, which was once used to summon the servants during dinner.

"Wowie zowie, we stayed up all night long!" says Simon, his eyes shining. It's true; it's nearly 4:00 a.m. by the time I get his bed made up and manage to settle him back into it. I put Boo Bear and Sausage Duck and the rest of the menagerie all around him.

"You like it here?" I whisper, and he nods. "That's good. Now get some sleep, and stay in bed as late as you want to. No kindergarten tomorrow, and I don't have to go to work."

"Mommy," he says, "I was just wondering. Why are we here?"

"An adventure, remember?" I say. "We're going to take a little vacation."

"Where are you going to sleep?"

I point to the double bed three feet away from his single one. "Right there. You'll be able to see me when you wake up."

"Do Daddy and Auntie Dana know where we are?"

"Sure they do. I left them a note."

"Are they going to come and try to make us come back?" he asks.

"No. Now shhh. It's late. Let's get some sleep."

THE NEXT DAY we sleep late, and when we wake up, Alex puts on what he calls some "welcome to Alex's life" music—John Prine and Norah Jones. I unpack everything and put our clothes in drawers, and put the kitchen stuff out on the counter. Alex laughs when he sees the garlic press.

"Good thing you brought this along," he teases me. "I meant to tell you mine is out for repair and they don't know *when* it's going to be fixed."

He gives us Apartment Lessons. You have to wiggle the handle on the toilet twice after you flush or it runs forever. The shelf in the linen closet is loose and sometimes, if you grab things off it too fast, the whole shelf falls down on you. The wallpaper is peeling a little bit in Simon's and my room, and if you're interested, you can sit there and take a tour back through the centuries by peeking under each layer, all the way back to the time of Queen Victoria and possibly the dinosaurs. He winks and tells me that, after I called, he even did a special cleaning of the bathroom because he knows that women see dirt in bathrooms that no man can see.

"This," he says, "is, I'm afraid, as good as it gets in here. If you see soap scum or filth, then I'm sorry. I just don't have the chromosomes to do any better."

"No, it looks pretty good," I say. "Scintillating, actually."

"Scintillating," he says and runs his hands through his hair. "I like that."

Then he takes Simon to the backyard and pushes him on the special tire swing, and introduces him to two kids next door, Brandon and Sean. Later, the three of us go to the playground at East Rock Park, and I watch another woman watching us push Simon on the swings. She must think we're just a regular mother and father, out taking our boy to play.

Saturday drifts by, and then Sunday goes much the same way. We read the paper, cook dinner together, watch a video with Simon on the couch. Whenever I meet Alex's eyes, he smiles at me. I can feel all my insides untwisting themselves and then retwisting themselves in whole new ways.

On Sunday night, after Simon is tucked into bed in what he calls "my new room," Alex brings out two glasses of wine, and turns the music down low, and he and I stretch out on the living room floor and talk. We have to be on the floor, the old-lady couches are too scratchy and tend to sag in the middle. After you've sat in them for even two minutes, I tell him, it's as though your chest and thighs are fused together.

He laughs. "I haven't spent much time on them since I moved in. This has been more like a hotel room than a home." He hesitates a moment and then asks, "So how are you feeling? Are you okay with everything? Is your garlic press feeling at home here, do you think?" He smiles, and I reach over and brush his hair away from his eyes, and then we're kissing. He moves over on top of me and cradles my head in the cup of his hands.

"I'm not sure we can do a whole lot here, with Simon in the next room," I whisper. "Kids have a sixth sense about these things, you know. He'll be in here with us in no time."

To my surprise, he suddenly rolls off me and onto his back, as though I've admonished him. "I'm sorry. I should have thought."

"No, no. It's fine. I mean, I *want* to. I just know how awkward it could be." I let my fingers walk over to his chest and stroke him.

He's quiet for a moment, and then he says, "By the way, I arranged with Steve at work to handle the board and the phones tomorrow night for you."

"You're not going to be there?" I feel a pang of disappointment.

"Well," he says, giving me a long look. "I thought I maybe should be here, putting Simon to bed. But now I realize I should have asked you first. You might have made other plans. And he might not want me to watch him."

"Oh," I say. "Wow. I feel ridiculous. I hadn't even planned that far. I didn't even think . . ."

"I mean, if you'd rather take him back to your house, and have Dana and Teddy watch him, I understand."

He's looking as though I've hurt his feelings. I reach over and take hold of his hands. "No! No, I'm glad you called Steve. I don't know what's gotten into me, not even thinking of what would happen tomorrow night. But, no, you're right. I think Simon would much rather be here with you than with Dana and Teddy right now."

"Well," he says, "I think I'm going to turn in early."

"Yeah."

He gets to his feet. "So . . . another thing. Since I'm not going to be at work tomorrow night, then I've really got to go in during the morning. Check on things. Get the paperwork done."

"Oh. Sure. Of course." I know he's telling me no sex and pancakes. I pick up our hardly touched glasses of wine, and we go into the kitchen. Things feel so awkward I can't stand it. I feel like turning to him and saying we have to clear everything up right now. But it wouldn't help.

"You'll be fine here, though, right? Got everything you need?" he says, not looking at me.

"Oh, sure."

The phone rings just then, and before I can think, I reach over and pick it up. It might be Teddy, I think, who's worried sick and has looked up Alex's number in the book and can't stand not knowing for one more second how we're doing.

"Hello?" I say.

There's a long silence, and then a woman's voice says, "Oh! Is . . . *Alex* there, by chance?"

"Sure. One moment." Embarrassed, I hand him the phone.

He grimaces and says, "Hello?" And then, with a guilty look: "Oh, hi. Wait. Okay, okay. Just stop for a minute. Let me get on the other extension." He hands me the receiver. "Would you mind hanging this up for me?" He mouths the word *Anneliese* just before going off to his bedroom and closing the door.

I wait for him for awhile, listening to the muffled sound of his voice in the next room, punctuated by long silences. When his conversation goes on for half an hour, I take my miserable self off to bed and lie there listening to the noises of the city at night: dogs barking, cars braking, even the distant roar of traffic from the main roads. After a long time, I hear his bedroom door creak open and then the bathroom door closing. I squeeze my eyes shut and put my pillow around my head. That night I dream I'm lost and scared in a deep dark hole, and at last someone is coming to rescue me. But then, in the dim confusion of the dream, I realize the rescuer turns out to need rescuing, too. Both of us just go sliding on down.

34

$\mathcal{M}$onday morning, I drive Simon to kindergarten and then go back to the apartment by myself. It feels weird to be there without Alex. All this big foreign furniture, the stuffy couches, the vague, wavery photographs on the walls. The only tiny piece of Alex in here is his desk. I stare at it, hungry to start going through it to learn more about him. I want to know what he writes in all those looseleaf notebooks, how he arranges his pencils and pens in the drawers. I want to turn on his computer and read all his e-mail and his documents. But I don't. This is so odd, the third day of living in a man's house, eating together, sharing a bathroom, coordinating showers and bedtimes—and not really knowing him. I've never been a stranger in anyone's house, I realize. I can't imagine that I'll ever really be comfortable here.

It's so horrible being at the beginning of things, the way we're not used to each other's moods and silences. Cringing, I think of all those strained moments between us, the over-apologizing, the feeling of walking on eggshells. This is too soon in our relationship for us to be sharing a place, I realize. That's what's wrong. This was never supposed to happen.

You don't have to be comfortable here. This is just a transition while you figure out what to do and where you belong. This, Lily, is what we call change.

I manage to walk away from the desk, leaving it untouched, but then I find myself in his bedroom. I open his closet door and stand there looking at all his shirts and jeans and pants, staring into the closet as though the way he hangs his things up might tell me what I need to know. On the floor is a jumble of shoes, and I sit down and look at them without touching them. The whole time, I'm halfway listening for his key in the lock, hoping that I'll have enough warning of his arrival that I can spring back over to my own room. It would be awful if he came in and caught me here gazing at his possessions, my hands clasped behind my back so that I won't give in to the pitiful temptation to caress them.

This morning at breakfast he'd cleared his throat and apologized about the phone call last night. Here we go, I thought, with awkward apologies again.

But I did my part. I said, "Oh, no, no. I felt bad that I answered, and that she was possibly upset that . . . well, that someone else might be here, you know."

"Oh, yeah. Well, that's going to happen, I suppose. You can't not answer the phone. What if someone needs you?" He took the last sip of his coffee. "I guess I now understand why people have those caller ID thingies. I always thought people who had them lacked a sense of adventure about picking up the phone."

Simon looked over at him, hearing that word. "We're on an adventure," he said solemnly. "That's why my mommy and I are here."

Alex laughed and tousled Simon's hair as he took his cup to the sink. "That's right, my buddy Simon. We're all on a great adventure here."

AFTER SCHOOL is out and we've driven back from Branford, Simon and I go off to explore the neighborhood and play at the park. I tell him that after supper I have to go to work, and that Alex will read him stories and put him to bed. I'm expecting that he'll make a fuss, but he doesn't. He just looks concerned for a moment, gazing off into the distance, but then I can see him shift gears, those little wheels turning in his head. After a moment, he says, "When are we going back home?"

"I don't know," I say. "Do you want to go back home?"

He hesitates just a moment, and then he says, "No. We're on an adventure."

On the way home we stop at a mom-and-pop market on the corner, and I pick up dinner: a tray of store-made lasagna and some lettuce for salad. The Italian man behind the counter gives Simon a lollipop and winks at me, as if we're in cahoots somehow. I smile back at him, and he asks me how long I've lived in the neighborhood.

"Well . . ." I'm about to explain that I don't really live here when Simon pipes up: "Two whole days. We came for adventure," and the man laughs.

We walk back along the sidewalk toward Alex's house and Simon says, "Do you think that Auntie Dana has had her baby yet?"

"Oh, no. That won't be for a long time."

"She says I have to share my room with the baby."

"How do *you* feel about that?" My breath is high up in my chest.

"Babies make a lot of noise."

"Yeah, they do. You don't really have to share your room with the baby, you know."

"Will we still be here when the baby is born?"

I look at him. "I don't think so. Why? Do you want to be?"

"Do *you* want to be?"

"No, no," I tease him and lean over to tickle him. "Do *you* want to be?"

He laughs and squirms away from me, and we chase each other around in circles on somebody's patch of grass next to a large two-story house with a wraparound porch. "No, no, no! Do YOU want to be?"

"The great thing," I tell him when we finally stop and have collapsed right there on the grass, "is that we don't have to figure that out just yet. We can do whatever we want."

ON TUESDAY morning, I come out from walking Simon to his classroom and nearly run smack into Teddy. I didn't even see him at first. But there he is, lurking in the shadows of the hall, looking drawn and worried. He is unshaven, with his curly hair sticking up in little right angles. When I reach him, he steps in front of me.

"What are you doing here?" I say, surprised.

"Obviously I came to talk to you," he says. He looks awful. I don't think he's slept in days. There are huge bags under his eyes. "Can we go somewhere and talk?"

"All right," I say warily. "What about the diner? You look like you could use a caffeine fix."

We drive there in separate cars. Naturally I get there first; Teddy drives the same way he does most things, with a complete certainty that something bad might befall him, so he needs to go very slowly so he can prevent it. By the time he comes in, I already have a table by the window, and I've ordered us coffee.

He slides into the booth and immediately picks up a napkin and starts shredding it. "How's Simon doing?"

"He's fine."

"So you're at Alex's. He's that guy I met at the party, Dana said."

"Yeah."

He clears his throat, frowns, looks down at his pieces of napkin, and pushes them away. "So. He must be a nice guy, huh? Have you known him a long time?"

"Longer than you've known Dana, I suppose. Although with, uh, less intensity." It's cold in the diner. I fold my arms and watch him. I've known Teddy long enough to know this agitated look means that I'm about to get a cry for help from him.

"Are you always going to be this mad, or do you see this going away anytime soon?" he says finally.

"I have no idea." I take a sip of coffee. The waitress glides up, and we give our order. Teddy wants poached eggs, well done, and a side of tomatoes. I say I want two eggs over easy with a side of wheat toast. The waitress's bracelets jangle as she writes everything down.

"You shouldn't eat eggs over easy," Teddy says, "because you never can be sure they really cook them thoroughly."

The waitress looks at me. "Over easy is fine," I say to her, rolling my eyes. Then I turn to Teddy. "You know, this is one of those long-standing arguments that we don't have to have anymore. It's just one of the benefits of not being married to each other."

"But I care about you."

"But it's not up to you how I eat my eggs."

"Okay. You're right. You're absolutely right. I'm sorry." The waitress smiles at him and goes away. He looks uncomfortable, starts turning his wristwatch around and around, and then he lets out a huge sigh. "Listen, this isn't easy, but I have to tell you some stuff."

He has that same look on his face that he used to have after one of his dates I'd set him up on, like he's wondering how to make me really understand why this latest woman didn't work out. So this is it, I think, what I've been expecting. Enough time has gone by now, and he can't take it. He's now going to start listing his complaints about Dana—all those picky little things he finds wrong with women, plus now the big one: *And then she gets pregnant and claims the baby is mine. What will I do, Lily? You've got to help me get out of this . . .*

He shakes his head. A piece of spittle is caught in the crease of his lip. "God, this shouldn't be so hard. Okay. I'm just going to say it." He laughs a little, lays his hands flat on the table, palms down. "All right. It all sounds like a stupid cliché, but I've got to tell you: I have fallen so hard for your sister. I have never in my life known I could feel this way about anybody."

I stare at him.

"She's—well, she's amazing," he says. "God, Lily, she's *you*. She's you without all the . . . the togetherness, you know?" He exhales loudly and runs his hands through his crazy hair. "Without being so put together. She's you but weak and cuddly and vulnerable and confused. And I love that. Oh, she's screwed up as hell. Even I know that. God, the things she comes out with. The way she's painted that goddamn cottage. I can only imagine how you feel when you look at it there, what she's done to the place . . . it's criminal what she's done to that cottage." He laughs.

My mouth is hanging open. I clamp it shut.

He looks at me. "But she just got to me anyway. Who knows why? I just fell in love with her. That's all I wanted to say. I thought you should hear it from me. It's the weirdest, goddamnedest thing that's ever happened to me."

"Then you're happy about the baby?" I say when I can locate the power of speech.

"Oh! The baby. Well. Everyone knows that shouldn't have happened this way." He shrugs, very Teddylike. "Why couldn't I just do things the proper way, I ask myself. Why not—if I find I'm in love with a woman—why not marry her, get to know her well, and *then* have the baby, after we've figured everything out? That's my way. Taking a long time, as you know. But that just didn't happen. This baby came roaring into my life, just the way Dana did." He sighs. "But it wants to be born, this baby. It's coming, ready or not."

"Yes," I say. "Apparently so."

The waitress brings our plates over and asks, "Anything else?" When we both shake our heads at her, she rips off the check and puts it down on the table, in the wet ring left by a water glass. I see that the ink from her ballpoint pen leaves a little mark on the table. At another table, somebody is playing the little jukebox: "Love Me Tender" by Elvis. Outside the window, cars are crawling past on Main Street.

Teddy doesn't touch his eggs; he just looks at me. His hands, I see, are shaking slightly. "Anyway, here's what I've just learned. News flash," he says. "Love doesn't always come in the package you think it's going to come in. I never would have dreamed it was going to be your *sister*, for God's sake. That's just trashy, is what that is. Sleazy, even. So that's why I want to thank you. I owe you such a debt—"

"Me? I had nothing to do with her."

"Yeah, you—for not going back to me that night when I said we were two misfits. Remember that? You were right. We weren't misfits. Well, hell, maybe I'm still a misfit, but somebody loves me now, and that's good enough for me. You know what else I figured out?"

I am just the slightest bit weary of all these proclamations, but I'm a little mesmerized, too, at this new Teddy.

"I'm always so scared of everything, like even your getting those eggs uncooked. I'm going to stop doing that kind of thing. I realize that everything is eventually going to go to hell; it's all going to disappear. My body is going to get old and die. Long Island Sound is probably going to get so smelly and polluted that fish grow hind legs and start walking on land—and so what? So *what*? Dana's not my type, Lily. She doesn't stick with anything. We know that. She just goes off to whatever is next, whatever is bright and shiny. But you know something?" His eyes are so bright I think they might have tears in them. "I don't *care*. The thing about people like her is, they're just these bright lights. That's who she is: a bright light. And who knows? This may last for the next eighty years, or it might end after eighty days. Hell, I might be raising this kid all by myself while Dana goes off to new worlds. But who cares? That's life. It's worth it."

"Teddy, what has happened to you? Are you on drugs?"

He laughs his hyena laugh. "No. I think this is love," he says. He hasn't touched his food, and he reaches over and takes my two hands in his. My fork clatters to the plate. "Listen, Lily. Listen to this. I hope to God this Alex guy is worthy of you. You're excellent, you know that? Just too put together for a wretched type like me. You're the kind of person who can do anything. Dana and I can't do half of what you do. But I'm just so sorry if we've hurt you, if along the way you got wounded because of us. That would be the very worst thing."

I actually feel my eyes welling up a little. I can't think of what this feeling is, but then I know. Well, I *think* I know. I'm relieved. Maybe this is what relief feels like, after all these years with him. He's doesn't need me. He's not going to turn to me and try to make me help him get out of this. I don't even have to worry about him.

"Teddy," I say slowly, "this is it. This is the day of our divorce. Our decree came through more than two years ago, and yet this is the day I finally feel divorced from you." I don't add that I think he's clinically insane.

35

When I get back to Alex's house, I find out that Leon Caswell is dead.

He died while we were at the diner. The message is on Alex's answering machine. It's from Dana, saying that Krystal called looking for me. Leon had had another episode and had been rushed to the hospital unconscious—and when he arrived there, they pronounced him dead.

"So," Dana says in the message, "sorry to bother you in your new life, but I thought you'd want to know. Call Krystal at the emergency room." And she gives me the number.

I sit back on the bed, stunned. A million things are going through my mind, not the least of which is that I should have told Krystal I was leaving home, should have given her Alex's number. But when you leave in a snit, in the middle of the night, you don't call as many people as you might otherwise.

I get in the car and drive to Yale–New Haven Hospital, and find Krystal at last in a back room of the emergency unit. She looks young and pale but very brave. This is her element, I remember: she's a nurse. They are just about to take Leon's body out of the room, but she persuades them to wait for another few minutes. "Could you hold on for a moment? Lily was practically Leon's daughter," she says. Then she turns to me. "Do you want to sit with him and me for a moment?" she says, as if I'd just shown up on their deck to find the two of them drinking a beer together.

I *don't* want to, actually. I don't think I can bear to see Leon's face without Leon inhabiting it, but I can tell she needs me to do this. So we go in and sit in the chairs by his bedside, and she and I hold hands, dry-eyed, while we watch him. All the machines hover around his bedside as though they feel the same grief we do, now that their services aren't needed and they've been disconnected. I make myself look at his face; it's gray and calm and empty. I've never been with someone who's dead before. I never really thought, when I saw him the other day, that this was going to happen so soon. After all, he talked so much, he was so clear and sharp—how could somebody that present in life now be dead?

Krystal's staring off into space. She looks like she's been crying for so many hours she has nothing left in her. "Remember the last time we were here? You told me all the things he did for you when you were young," she says. "I wish I had known him then."

"Well," I say, "you had him at the end—at the culmination of all his Leon-ness. You may have gotten the best possible Leon there was."

I don't want to ask her what she's going to do next. It seems impossible to think of her remaining at his house, remaining in the colony. But it doesn't seem like a conversation that should take place before the body is quite cold. I look over at him. It's beginning to get to me, sitting next to his body, and I tell her I think we should say good-bye to him and leave. I'll help her with whatever arrangements there are—phone calls, anything she needs.

"Oh!" she says, and reaches into her bag. "The envelope. He wanted me to be sure to give you this."

I take it out of her hands. "Shall I read it now, do you think?" I ask her and she nods. So I open it up and read two sentences and immediately start laughing. "Come on, Krystal. Let's go find a comfortable place to sit while we hear from Leon."

It seems weird, leaving his body in favor of a piece of paper. But the truth is, this paper has more of him living in it than the shell of his body does. I blow him a farewell kiss and we go downstairs.

WE FIND a little table in the hospital atrium, by the fountain. People are milling around everywhere, so we pull our chairs close together.

"Lily," I read aloud. "I'm speaking to you from the Eternal Peace and Quiet, and if you think it's fun being here, think again. I can tell you right now that even up here in the afterlife, even if there are angels and harps and God Himself stopping by to wish me a good morning, I would rather be sitting next to you while you read this. I hope to hell you are someplace comfortable, because I've got a few requests to make. First, kiss Krystal for me and give her a big hug. I know she's just handed you this envelope, and she's probably a little bit sad. I'd kiss her myself if I could."

I look up at her, and we blow each other kisses. "Go on," she says.

"I've been giving a lot of thought to how I want to be sent off to the afterlife. Never mind a funeral in a church. I want a memorial service, and I want it to be the biggest party this colony has ever had. I made this letter out to you because I think you're the only one who can make it all happen. My only regret is that I'm too dead to see it. However, if there is an afterlife—and if I'm not too pooped out from being sick these last few months—you can bet I'll be looking down and watching to make sure you follow all my instructions. And boy, if you don't, when you get here—in sixty years or so—I'm really going to let you have it."

The next page lists his requirements for his service:

1. It's to be held on the beach, rain or shine, cold or hot, on the first Saturday evening after I die. (A lot of people work on weekdays, and I don't want to exclude anyone.)
2. No complaining is to be tolerated. There will be no griping or whining of any sort at this wingding. Even if it's raining or freezing, everybody has to buck up.

3. Frank Sinatra music is a must. There must be dancing like in the old days. Everybody who knows how must try a tango. Yes, I know the sand makes it difficult. Suck it up. You want to complain about it, when I'm dead here? You know how much I'd like to be there doing the tango with you? So just pipe down.

4. I'd like all the colony people to come, even though they were pains in the ass when Krystal and I got married. (And yes, now that I'm dead, I can use whatever language I want, so don't roll your eyes.)

5. I want someone (Sloane?) to be the sergeant-at-arms to keep people in line and to enforce the no-complaining rule. If people complain, or if they say bad things about each other, or argue, there will be fines levied. The fine is a hundred kisses to the person you've most wounded—and there have been a lot of wounds in this colony, so pucker up.

6. All topics of conversation are allowed, and even insisted upon. Nothing is off-limits except insults. You think death is fun? You think I *want* eternal peace and quiet? Just be glad you can be there with each other, and be glad somebody's taking the trouble to point out how much time you've already wasted with these petty squabbles.

7. I'd like my ashes to be flung out into the Sound, with everybody flinging just a little bit.

8. I want people to join hands and sing two songs: the first is "We Are the World," because I've always liked that song, and it just doesn't get enough radio play these days. Oh, and then, while you're still there, a chorus of "It Had to Be You," because whether you know it or not, you're all stuck with each other for reasons none of us knows. (Words are enclosed.)

9. I'd like you to make a bonfire on the beach (don't forget to get a permit; we don't need the police here), and once you're around the fire—this is the tricky part—I'd like you all to apologize. That's right. Don't even *try* to skip this part. The following

people need to apologize for crimes I've observed over the years, and if anyone knows of any other crimes that I perhaps didn't see, they should apologize for those as well. You don't have to specify the crime you committed, but do not make me come down there! You have to apologize, and it has to be public and heartfelt and real.

10. SCHEDULE OF APOLOGIES: Lily must apologize to Dana. Dana must apologize to Lily. Both Lily and Dana must apologize to Gracie. Gracie must apologize to the memory of Avery Brown, and to Dana and Lily. Teddy must apologize to Lily and to Simon. All of the colony kids must apologize to their parents, and then all the parents must apologize to their kids. Grandchildren need not apologize to their grandparents, except for Bert's son who sold drugs in Bert's house. Anginetta must apologize to everyone, and everyone must apologize to her. Mark needs to tell Maggie he's very, very sorry. And from heaven, believe me, I'll make sure all the deceased ones are apologizing right then to the rest of you. They have a lot to answer for, too, believe me.

11. And then I want you to dance all night, eat the lobsters and shrimp and prime rib that I am buying for you and having delivered. On second thought, better do the eating first and the apologizing afterward. And then you can go and live the rest of your lives any old mean way you want to. Only I hope you've learned something—that each of you is precious. I have loved you every one. Wish I was there. Love, Leon.

That night, I can't help it: I talk about Leon on the radio show, telling the radio audience all about him—how he took care of me when my parents died and how he kept trying, always, to get me to be a braver person, impossible though that was. I mention that he was always available for killing horrible bugs, even in the middle of the night, and that when I was distraught, he taught me how to play the ukulele, because he knew music could be a solace. I tell them about his marriage to Krystal, his wife's nurse, and how people always thought he'd disgraced his dead wife's memory, but that he insisted he'd enhanced her memory because he loved marriage so much he had to get married again. I almost start to cry as I'm describing how he could do the best imitation of Jimmy Durante ever seen outside of Las Vegas, and that recently I threw a dinner party and he was the only guest who let himself try to have a good time.

Then I tell about the social will he made up to be read when he died, and I even read it on the air, leaving out the names of all the guilty parties, of course.

Throughout the evening, people call up with comments. This seems to hit a nerve with the general population. One woman says he was a great guy to go to the trouble of trying to bring people together even after he was dead. Another caller, a man, says it sounds good on paper, but that he doesn't think people can be bossed around into doing the right thing.

"If his friends don't want to do it, I don't see how a piece of paper is going to make them," the guy says. "But good luck."

"I'm not exactly sure it's going to work, either," I say into the microphone, knowing that nobody in the colony will be listening. "But if anybody could make it work, Leon could. We'll have to see."

When I go back to Alex's apartment, he meets me at the door and draws me inside. Then he leans me up against the wall and covers my face with hundreds of silent little kisses, all along my lips and cheeks and hair and jaw. "I know we can't make love or anything with Simon here," he says at last, "but I just wanted you to know that that was so beautiful and spontaneous, what you said on the radio. And I love you." He kisses me some more.

"Listen," I say when all these little kisses have turned me to jelly. "Maybe it's time we see if the lock on your bedroom door really works."

36

$\mathcal{B}$y the time the memorial service takes place the following Saturday, I'm a jumble of nerves and doubt. Who am I kidding, thinking this is going to work? More important, who was *Leon* kidding? The colony people are not docile little children, ready to fall for this. And I should know: I had to call them all to invite them, and just from their incredulous reactions when I told them what was expected, I can tell that the no-complaining rule alone is going to be broken in the first five minutes. And will they pay the fine of kisses? Oh, please.

Saturday morning I wake up feeling jumpy, nervous, and sad. I call up Krystal, and she says she's been feeling the same way.

"If we cancel, though, he'll come down from heaven and beat us up," I say, and she laughs.

Before we hang up, she says, "I just hope everybody sees in this how much Leon loved them. But I'm just so afraid they're going to take all his instructions the wrong way."

"They take everything the wrong way," I tell her. "Oops—is that a complaint? Has the no-complaining ordinance gone into effect yet?"

"Not yet," she says. "I think you can complain right up until the thing starts, at four. Which is exactly what I intend to do."

I sigh. "Well, I think you and I just have to let it unfold the way he wanted and not be too attached to the outcome," I tell her. "It's his show, not ours."

JUST BEFORE FOUR, Alex, Simon, and I walk down to the beach. The sky is the color of slate, with puffy clouds that seem to be piling up toward the west, and even though it's not fall yet, it's the kind of day that seems to be advertising summer's demise. When I look back at my house, I can see fallen leaves bunched up near the flower beds, and the slant of light is already different across the porch. I also can't help but notice that the hose has been left out, and that from here, at least, it looks as though all my daisies and geraniums are dead in their flower boxes. Things sure have gone to hell fast.

To my surprise, when we get to the beach, only Krystal is already there, plus a bunch of natty little uniformed waiters setting up tables and blankets on the sand. They have big coolers and boxes and evidently an oven of sorts that they've made in the sand. It's a clambake, I realize. Leon always talked about wanting a clambake.

I try to make conversation with one of the waiters, but he's almost robotic in his reply. Krystal, who's wearing a floaty-looking gypsy skirt and a black shirt, nervously whispers to me that these waiters don't seem to talk at all. "I think that might have been part of their instructions," she whispers. "Leon didn't want us to have outsiders to talk to. He wanted us to talk to each other."

Simon goes running off down the beach happily, windmilling his arms and leaping over to the edge of the water and then jumping back. I call him to come and take off his shoes. Krystal and Alex and I sit on a blanket and watch the clouds racing across the sky. No one else comes.

One of the waiters brings us over glasses of wine in long-stemmed goblets.

"What time is it?" I say to Alex.

"Four thirty."

"See? They're not coming," Krystal says. "Is this unbelievable? They've been so mean, and now . . ."

I feel the same. Worse, I think, because I'll have to announce this on the radio on Monday. "Folks, no one showed." I can't believe that even Dana and Teddy aren't here.

"Oh, wait. Look," Alex says, standing up, "they're coming all together. They're just fashionably late." Sure enough, I turn and see Anginetta, in a black parka, walking over the little embankment, leaning on Bert's arm, followed soon by his three kids, who are kicking up sand and throwing stones at the reeds like the hoodlums they are. The Artertons come soon after, Virginia frowning and leaning on Bob. And Mr. Wiznowski looks pained, as if he's arriving for the emotional equivalent of a root canal.

Dana comes next, walking along between Maggie and Mark and wearing some kind of hippie-looking kimono with all kinds of embroidery and little mirrors and beads sewn on it. Her hair is down and spread across her shoulders. Maggie waves and comes over to embrace me, and Mark, wearing a business suit and dress shoes, of all things, heads over to where the waiters are getting prepared. He feels comfortable among the robots, I guess.

After a while, Teddy comes along, holding onto Gracie's arm. Simon runs to meet them, and Teddy leans down and gives him a big hug. Dana goes flitting over to them and picks up Simon and twirls him around. I can see him asking her something, and she smiles and shakes her head and points to her belly. Sloane, the sergeant-at-arms, shows up next, looking grim. I see that Simon has attached himself to Dana's side. She looks over at me and gives a funny little wave and makes a "isn't this the craziest thing ever" face. I look away.

Everybody seems startled as hell to see the waiters and the good china and the crystal all being set up on the beach. The staff has come to life now, scurrying around handing out glasses of wine and passing around trays of hors d'oeuvres—little scallops wrapped in bacon and stuffed mushrooms for the adults, triangles of grilled cheese for the kids. One of the waiters starts a bonfire and turns on a boom box playing Frank Sinatra music. We all stand around, huddled against the wind, talking in low, puzzled voices. Anginetta has sand in her shoes and almost starts grumbling about that, but then Joe Wiznowski leans down to her ear and points to Sloane, evidently reminding her of the decree, and she stops talking and looks up, embarrassed.

I hear Virginia saying to someone in a defensive tone of voice, "I never realized he was all that ill. Who gets so sick and dies in a matter of a few weeks? We just saw him."

I go over and tell her, "I did call you . . ." but she turns away. I know she must feel guilty.

Bob Arterton is shaking his head and saying, "A helluva thing, drinking wine on the beach. It doesn't seem legal, does it? And look at all those clouds. We're going to have rainwater wine, yesirree."

The kids—including the bad one, Bert's son Kyle—get into a rowdy game that involves running in circles and screaming, kicking up sand over near where the waiters are working on unearthing the clambake. I expect one of the automatons will turn and tell them to knock it off, but no one does. Finally, Bert groans and hands his mother his wineglass and goes over to speak to them. Kyle shouts something insulting to his father, and everyone looks at Sloane, whose job it is to assess penalties for this sort of thing. He dutifully picks himself up and goes over to talk to Kyle in a low, ominous voice, delivering the sentence of one hundred kisses.

I hold my breath.

Kyle says, "No way!"

He's shown a piece of paper, no doubt a copy of Leon's decree. There's much arguing and pointing over there. I'm trying to talk to Krystal and Maggie, but I can't stop watching out of the corner of my eye.

"You have to do it," Sloane says loudly. "One hundred kisses for your father. Come on, it won't kill you."

Bert stands there, waiting. The party—if you can call it that—comes to a hush.

Anginetta says, "Oh, this is the most ridiculous thing I've ever heard of. Leon Caswell was out of his mind."

Sloane looks at her. "Mrs. Franzoni, you're next . . ." and everybody laughs.

"I'm not kissing anybody. They can kiss my hind end, if they want," she says.

A little scuffle breaks out between the kids just then, and Sloane steps in and takes Kyle by the arm and walks him over to Bert. For a moment, father and son just glower at each other. I can't bear to watch but can't look away, either. We all wait, holding our breath, to see if Kyle will kiss his father. Time seems to drag on, and then Kyle stomps away, up over the hill and toward his grandmother's house. Anginetta says, "Good God in heaven! Look what Leon brings out in people! What kind of asinine thing *is* this anyhow?" and follows close behind him.

I can't bring myself to look at Krystal, so I look down at my glass of wine and feel my eyes fill with tears. This party is never going to work.

SOON, the waiters—I've decided they're like the Oompa Loompas in *Charlie and the Chocolate Factory*—start herding us over to eat. They hand out real china plates, fine silverware, and glasses with curvy stems, and for a while we all sit in a circle on the sand, picking apart lobsters, helping the children with their lobster crackers and picks. The old people get folding chairs, but the rest of us sprawl everywhere, concentrating on our food, watched over by these perfectly neutral waiters, who do little but step in to help, to fetch new napkins and more drawn butter, without being asked. It's like *my* party, I think, when no one could think of anything to say. Even with Leon giving explicit directions, still nobody will talk.

Alex is sitting next to me on the sand, staring down at his plate. I wonder if he wishes he hadn't come. I can't imagine what he must think of us. I'm too miserable to look at him.

Just then Dana comes and plops herself down on the other side of me. Simon is on my lap and I'm reaching around him, trying to liberate the claws of his lobster and hand-feed him the meat.

She says to me, "I have to apologize to you."

"I know, and I to you." I can feel her intensity. I feel that if I look in her eyes, I'll be tacitly approving of everything she's ever done. "Let's do it later. Unless you want to just say a quick 'I'm sorry' and be done with it."

"No. I want to apologize beyond what Leon meant. I want a full-bore apology."

I look up at her. "Let's not. Just leave it at a nonspecific 'I'm sorry,' shall we?"

"No," she says, and sticks her chin up. She's got that intense Dana expression on her face, like when she's about to do something you're going to regret. I think, *Oh boy, here we go.*

She puts her mouth close to my ear. "It's always going to be weird between you and me, isn't it? You're not going to get used to me and Teddy being together. I see that now. You won't even look at me."

I try to rip the front claws off the lobster without using a nut-cracker. I feel like prying it apart using only my bare hands. I start to say something, but then can't bring myself to talk. I can feel her eyes boring into the side of my head. Just *stop,* I think. *Stop talking. Stop staring at me.*

"Will you please look at me, Lily? Could you do that? Do you hate me so much that you won't even look? I'm trying to tell you how I feel."

I'm aware of the silence all around us. People turn in our direction, but of course she doesn't notice that kind of thing.

"Keep it down," I whisper. "In fact, could we have this conversation another time?"

"Leon *said* this was the time to talk about everything."

"He meant everybody else," I say. "He didn't mean us."

"No, I think he *really* meant us, and anyway, I'm tired of secrets. I am so tired of secrets that I just want to scream," she says. Before I can stop her, she gets to her feet. "Hey, while y'all are eating your lobsters, I have to tell you a secret about me. This is in honor of Leon, okay? I've done something really bad to my sister, and I didn't even know how bad it was. I mean, I've done a lot of bad to her in our lives together—running away when she was taking such good care of me was awful, but that was years ago, when I was just a kid." She puts her hand on my shoulder, as if she wants to hold me in place. I can't bring myself to look up at everyone.

"But now I've come back," she goes on, "and I've maybe done a worse thing. I've gotten involved with—well, the truth of it is, I fell in love with Teddy. Who, as you all know, she's not married to anymore, so I thought it would be okay." She laughs. "That's how dumb *I* am! I thought when you get divorced from somebody, you're . . . you know, like done caring about them. But I found out that was wrong." I feel her do a little curtsy. "Sometimes I think I don't get all the memos everybody else gets."

I hear a little bit of laughter from the group, and I feel Gracie moving toward me, scooting closer to the circle. I just sit there, rooted to the spot. Everyone is looking at Dana with interest in their faces. I stare at my hands. "Will you please sit down?" I whisper.

But she's relaxed now and into this. She could talk for the rest of the night. She laughs again. "I'm probably not telling y'all anything you don't already know. You've probably been talking about us," she says. "Oh, I remember the way y'all colony people are—you know everything about people almost before the people themselves know." There's another little tittering of laughter. "But—okay, here's the tough part to say. Teddy and I are gonna have a baby. Y'all knew that, too, didn't you? And that hurt Lily a lot, and she went away, 'cause maybe we didn't do everything the really careful way. And I'm just so sorry about that. I saw it as a good thing, embracing life, but sometimes I think I give myself a pass on a lot of things, calling it 'embracing life,' when it's really just doing what I want." She stops, takes in a breath. The sky, I realize, has suddenly slipped into dusk, and our faces are lit only by the fire. Everybody's looking at Dana. She runs her toe in the sand for a moment and then she says suddenly, loudly, "Leon was a big old crazy man, and he'd do any-thing for any of us, but . . . you know something?" Her tone changes, becomes outraged. "You know what? This whole thing is kind of bullshit, in a way. This apology thing. Somebody should go get Kyle and Anginetta and tell them to come back here and that they don't have to apologize or kiss anybody they don't want to kiss. They should be part of us even if they *don't* want to do what Leon said. We should be together tonight."

Somebody—I think it's Bob Arterton—says, "That's right," and there's a slight commotion as one of the other Franzoni grand-children—I realize I don't even know his name—gets up and goes off to fetch them.

Everybody looks back at Dana. "Anyhow, that's what I wanted to say. I'm just sorry, is all. But I'm here to stay. I'm back home."

She sits down. I hear a lot of murmuring. Gracie leans over and hugs her, and at first I think, don't hug *her*! Look at what she's doing to me.

Virginia says, from across the circle, "Jesus Christ, do we have to air everybody's dirty laundry? Can't we just try to get along?" Alex reaches over and takes my hand, and then I realize Maggie is there, too. My support team.

Dana leans into me. "If you came back," she says softly, "maybe we could paint the dining room cream again, and put up Momma's paintings if you wanted . . ."

"No, we couldn't," I say. My eyes are smarting from the smoke.

I hide my face in Alex's chest, to get away from the glare of the fire and all the little sparks that seem to be chasing me. I would just like to disappear inside his shirt to get away from all of them.

"This isn't what Leon had in mind," I whisper to him.

"But you know what? It's working," he whispers back. "I don't know why, but it is."

"It's crazy. I want to get out of here."

IN THE END, we don't do even half of what Leon ordered us to. Anginetta and Kyle come back, but they never do apologize *or* kiss anybody. When Anginetta hears what she missed—Dana's little revelation and speech—she says, "Oh, for heaven's sake. Did we really need to know all of *that?*" and Virginia says, "Exactly my point."

No one bothers to tango, much less even dance. And when it comes time to sing the songs, nobody remembers the words, and we can't read the lyrics in the dark. "I always thought that 'We Are the World' song was too sappy anyway," Bob Arterton says, and Joe Wiznowski says he never heard of it. And as for "It Had to Be You"—well, it just ain't going to happen. The fire is dying down, and we're all standing around thinking of how to get away, but staying just the same.

"Maybe Leon didn't realize that none of us is the way we used to be," Gracie says. "Standing around on a beach isn't going to change any hearts."

"Yeah," Anginetta says. She turns and looks at Gracie. "So, do you play bridge? Virginia and I have been getting together with some ladies downtown on Thursday nights. Do you want to come?"

Gracie shrugs, smiling. I can see she's pleased.

Maggie and Dana are comparing bellies, and Mark and Teddy stand there with them, laughing at something. Mark, here on the beach in his business suit, still looks stiff and hard to talk to, but despite that, Teddy seems to be happy talking to him. I see Mark smile, and I remember that Maggie has told me he goes with her to therapy every week and that they're making some progress. She said they've now covered all their problems in fourth grade and will soon be able to tackle their middle-school issues. When I looked surprised, she laughed. "I'm kidding, Lily. I'm kidding!"

Now Sloane comes over and puts his arm around me. "The whole party has gone to hell, because I'm such a rotten sergeant-at-arms." He looks at me. "That was some speech Dana made. I had no idea. Are you all right?"

"Yeah. I'm fine."

"Where are you living now? I've been trying to find you."

"Oh . . . I moved out. Temporarily, I think."

He smiles. "I've gotta do that, too. In fact, don't be mad, but I have to tell you that I'm skipping out on my lease."

"Wait. Did we have a lease?"

"I thought we did. But if you say we didn't, that's great. So do you remember me telling you about our agent dumping us? Well, long story short, best thing that coulda happened. We got somebody new, and he got us a contract—and we're going to Nashville."

"Nashville? You're kidding."

"Nope." He's grinning. "My mom's gone ballistic, of course, but that's okay. She'll get used to it. I'm taking my longtime girlfriend with me, too."

"*You* have a longtime girlfriend? Since when?"

"One month," he says. "She's been with me a whole thirty days."

I grin at him. "So when are you leaving?"

"I'm catching the train on Wednesday night."

"Wednesday night? Wow, you don't give much notice, do you?" I realize suddenly that I'm freezing. Alex is on the other side of the fire, talking to Kyle. His face is glowing in the yellow light of the flame, and suddenly I remember that he told me last night that he loved me, and now—maybe it's the wine or maybe just that I see I've survived this party, but I want to go over and hear him say it again.

"Well," I say to Sloane, but I'm distracted by watching Alex laugh. His hands are shoved down in his pockets, and he's leaning forward, listening, *really* listening to Kyle. I can't believe how grateful I suddenly feel that he came with me today. I force myself to turn back to Sloane. "We'll miss you lots," I say.

"You know," he says and leans forward, "you should seriously think about living in that unit, you know. I mean, it needs a bunch of stuff—paint and furniture—but all your mom's paintings are hanging up there, and let's face it, they're better than that crap Dana has hung up in the other part of the house."

"Maybe," I say. I feel like I'm in a daze. "Maybe so. It might be hard, though."

"Hard?" he says, as though he's never heard of the word. "Lily, *hard* is moving to Nashville and trying to write songs under pressure when you have a full-time girlfriend. And she's a handful, believe me."

I laugh. "You'll do fine."

"So will you," he says. His eyes are bright. "But, Lily, really. Don't give up your house."

Everybody's standing up by now, and the waiters have whisked all the plates away and are loading things into huge boxes. Then Krystal yells, "Oh my God, everyone. We forgot the most important thing!" We all look at her, her face illuminated by the last glowing coals of the fire. "We forgot to throw Leon into the Sound. I mean, throw his *ashes* into the Sound." She stops for a second. "He wanted me to say it that way first, so you would laugh."

We all do laugh a little bit, amid the groans.

She walks around and hands out little green plastic containers of ashes and smiles at all of us. I look down into my container and see what looks in the dimness like any ordinary gray dust. It's hard to believe this is what is left of Leon's body—that break-dancing,

Jimmy Durante–imitating body. This is not really Leon, I say to myself.

As a group, we take off our shoes and walk down to the edge of the water, struggling in the wet sand in our cold, bare feet. Krystal and Teddy have flashlights that they shine up into the sky. It takes some doing to get us all organized, but finally we're clustered just right.

"Okay, at the count of three . . ." Krystal says. And when she gets to three, we all fling our ashes skyward. Little particles of Leon go showering into the beam of the lights in a perfect arc—and then, as if on cue, a huge gust of wind kicks up, and before we can move, the ashes fly back at us, as if they are not yet willing to let go.

It's an odd, stunning moment. Nobody knows what to say, or how to behave. We're all slightly damp from the night air, so we get coated with ashes. Should we scrape them together and try again to send them out to sea? We're all a little speechless.

And then Joe Wiznowski says, "Leon is trying to break dance his way into not going into the sea," and that makes us laugh. Only Krystal starts to cry just then, and like one big organic group, people surround her, patting her, soothing her. I hear somebody offer her a place to stay if she doesn't want to be there alone in that house tonight. Someone else says, "What will you do, honey? Are you staying here for good with us?"

And then it starts to rain. At first it comes in drops so huge they hurt when they plonk on us, and then, after an impressive crack of thunder, it comes down in sheets. We scream and scatter in the dark, all running around in circles, picking up blankets and shoes and stray children, and then make a run for home. I take hold of Simon's hand and we run up the hill, getting stuck in the sand and having to haul ourselves out of it again and again, while the torrents of rain hit us in the face.

Everyone is screaming and laughing, calling to each other through the buckets of water. My shoe comes off, and I stop to pick it up, but then—I don't know why—I just stand there, watching them all, all my people, with their hair and clothes plastered down, hobbling together up the hill drenched and ruined and yet holding onto each other for dear life, all laughing and yelling at once. Simon tugs on me and says, "Come on!" But I can't move. It comes to me then, like a sharp pain in my side, the realization of all that I have lost, through time and carelessness and waiting for perfection: my mother and father, a whole decade of knowing my sister, and now Leon. I lost my idyllic fantasies about the colony grown-ups, and, hell, I never *did* figure out how to make the cottage really my own home. Is that a chance that's forever gone, too? And besides all those things, I lost the cream-colored walls, my parents' bed, and—oh, let's say about five million chances to stand up for myself.

Up ahead, I see Dana hurtling herself through the sheets of water, pulling Gracie along with her, and I know I cannot stand to lose any more. Not one more thing.

I suddenly wonder if Alex would ever come and live with me here, in my mother's old studio. Not now, maybe, but when the time is right—when we can be together without feeling we have to apologize to each other fifty times a day. Could I ask him to do that?

I will try. Tonight I will say the words.

Anginetta is making an unearthly sound from behind me. I see that she's laughing. So this is how Anginetta sounds when she laughs. I'd almost forgotten. Her mouth is open and turned toward the sky. "This is Leon's storm!" she yells to me. "Remember how he loved this? If you can catch the raindrops, it'll bring you good luck!"

About the Author

SANDI KAHN SHELTON is the author of *What Comes After Crazy* and a feature writer for the New Haven *Register*. A former "Wit's End" columnist for *Working Mother* magazine, she is a frequent contributor to several magazines, including *Woman's Day, Family Circle, Redbook,* and *Salon*. The author of three previous books on parenting, she is a mother of three and lives in Guilford, Connecticut, with her journalist husband.